Joanna Bourne has alwa...
She's drawn to Revolutio...
Regency England because, as sh...
and sacrifice, daring deeds, clashing ideas and really cool
clothing.' She's lived in seven different countries, including England and France, the settings of the Spymaster series.

Joanna now lives on a mountaintop in the Appalachians with her family, a peculiar cat and an old brown country dog. Visit her online at www.joannabourne.com, and connect with her via Twitter @jobourne, www.facebook.com/joanna.bourne.5, or www.jobourne.blogspot.co.uk.

Irresistible reasons to indulge in a Joanna Bourne historical romance:

'Joanna Bourne is a master of romance and suspense' Teresa Medeiros, *New York Times* bestselling author

'Bourne is an undeniably powerful new voice in historical romance' *All About Romance*

'Destined to be a classic in the romance genre' *Dear Author*

'Exceptional characters, brilliant plotting, a poignant love story' *Library Journal*

'Unusual, resourceful, and humorous heroines' Diana Gabaldon, *New York Times* bestselling author

'Distinct, fresh, and engaging' Madeline Hunter, *New York Times* bestselling author

'Addictively re...

By Joanna Bourne

Spymaster Series

The Forbidden Rose
The Spymaster's Lady
My Lord And Spymaster
The Black Hawk
Rogue Spy

The Spymaster's Lady

Joanna Bourne

headline
ETERNAL

Published by arrangement with Berkley,
a member of Penguin Group (USA), LLC,
A Penguin Random House Company

First published in Great Britain in 2014
by HEADLINE ETERNAL
An imprint of HEADLINE PUBLISHING GROUP

1

Cataloguing in Publication Data is available from the British Library

ISBN 978 1 4722 2245 9

Offset in Times Lt Std by Avon DataSet Ltd, Bidford-on-Avon, Warwickshire

Printed and bound by CPI Group (UK) Ltd, Croydon, CR0 4YY

Papers used by Headline are from well-managed forests and other responsible sources.

HEADLINE PUBLISHING GROUP
An Hachette UK Company
338 Euston Road
London NW1 3BH

www.headlineeternal.com
www.headline.co.uk
www.hachette.co.uk

For Leo

Acknowledgments

I want to thank my literary agent, Pam Hopkins, and my editor, Wendy McCurdy, for their faith in Annique's story.

I'm grateful to the Beau Monde Chapter of the RWA for their tireless effort in promoting historical accuracy in Regency-period books. Their resource materials have been enormously helpful. Thanks also to my crit partners, Mary Ann Clark and Sofie Couch. You have been endlessly patient and encouraging.

I want to express my profound appreciation for the fellowship and support I have found at the Compuserve Books and Writers Forum. I thank Allenne Edwards, Barbara Rogan, Beth Shope, Betty Babas, Carol Krenz, Cat Dubie, Darlene Marshall, Diana Gabaldon, Donna Rubino, Janet McConnaughey, John S. Kruszka, Joyce Moye, K.C. Dyer, Karen Watson, Karl Hagen, Kim Laird, Kris Reekie, Linda Grimes, Margaret Campbell, Mark Mussari, Marsha Skrypuch, Martin McArthur, Pamela Patchet, Steve Lopata, Susan Adrian Barth, Varda Amir-Orrel, Vicki Pettersson, and many others.

One

SHE WAS WILLING TO DIE, OF COURSE, BUT SHE had not planned to do it so soon, or in such a prolonged and uncomfortable fashion, or at the hands of her own countrymen.

She slumped against the wall, which was of cut stone and immensely solid, as prison walls often are. "I do not have the plans. I never had them."

"I am not a patient man. Where are the plans?"

"I do not have—"

The openhanded slap whipped out of the darkness. For one instant she slipped over the edge of consciousness. Then she was back again, in the dark and in pain, with Leblanc.

"Just so." He touched her cheek where he had hit her and turned her toward him. He did it gently. He had much practice in hurting women. "We continue. This time you will be more helpful."

"Please. I am trying."

"You will tell me where you have hidden the plans, Annique."

"They are a mad dream, these Albion plans. A chimera. I never saw them." Even as she said it, the Albion plans were clear in her mind. She had held the many pages in her hands, the dog-eared edges, maps covered with smudges and fingerprints, the lists in small, neat writing. *I will not think of this. If I remember, it will show on my face.*

"Vauban gave you the plans in Bruges. What did he tell you to do with them?"

He told me to take them to England. "Why would he give me plans? I am not a valise to go carrying papers about the countryside."

His fist closed on her throat. Pain exploded. Pain that stopped her breath. She dug her fingers into the wall and held on. With such a useful stone wall to hold on to, she would not fall down.

Leblanc released her. "Let us begin again, at Bruges. You were there. You admit that."

"I was there. Yes. I reported to Vauban. I was a pair of eyes watching the British. Nothing more. I have told you and told you." The fingers on her chin tightened. A new pain.

"Vauban left Bruges empty-handed. He went back to Paris without the plans. He must have given them to you. Vauban trusted you."

He trusted me with treason. She wouldn't think that. Wouldn't remember.

Her voice had gone hoarse a long time ago. "The papers never came to us. Never." She tried to swallow, but her throat was too dry. "You hold my life in your hands, sir. If I had the Albion plans, I would lay them at your feet to buy it back."

Leblanc swore softly, cursing her. Cursing Vauban, who was far away and safe. "The old man didn't hide them. He was too carefully watched. What happened to them?"

"Look to your own associates. Or maybe the British took them. I never saw them. I swear it."

Leblanc nudged her chin upwards. "You swear? Little Cub, I have watched you lie and lie with that angel face since you were a child. Do not attempt to lie to me."

"I would not dare. I have served you well. Do you think I'm such a fool I've stopped being afraid of you?" She let tears brim into her eyes. It was a most useful skill and one she had practiced assiduously.

"Almost, one might believe you."

He plays with me. She squeezed her lids and let tears slide in cold tracks down her cheeks.

"Almost." He slowly scratched a line upon her cheek with his thumbnail, following a tear. "But, alas, not quite. You will be more honest before morning, I think."

"I am honest to you now."

"Perhaps. We will discuss this at length when my guests have departed. Did you know? Fouché comes to my little soiree tonight. A great honor. He comes to me from meetings with Bonaparte. He comes directly to me, to speak of what the First Consul has said. I am becoming the great man in Paris these days."

What would I say if I were innocent? "Take me to Fouché. He will believe me."

"You will see Fouché when I am satisfied your pretty little mouth is speaking the truth. Until then . . ." He reached to the nape of her neck to loosen her dress, pulling the first tie free. "You will make yourself agreeable, eh? I have heard you can be most amusing."

"I will . . . try to please you." *I will survive this. I can survive whatever he does to me.*

"You will try very, very hard before I am finished with you."

"Please." He wanted to see fear. She would grovel at once, as was politic. "Please. I will do what you want, but not here. Not in a dirty cell with men watching. I hear them breathing. Do not make me do this in front of them."

"It is only the English dogs. I kennel some spies here till I dispose of them." His fingers hooked the rough material of her dress at the bodice and pulled it down, uncovering her. "Perhaps I like them to watch."

She breathed in the air he had used, hot and moist, smelling of wintergreen. His hand crawled inside the bodice of her dress to take hold of her breast. His fingers were smooth and dry, like dead sticks, and he hurt her again and again.

She would not be sick upon Leblanc in his evening clothes. This was no time for her stomach to decide to be sincere.

She pressed against the wall at her back and tried to become nothing. She was darkness. Emptiness. She did not exist at all. It did not work, of course, but it was a goal to fix the mind upon.

At last, he stopped. "I will enjoy using you."

She did not try to speak. There was no earthly use in doing so.

He hurt her one final time, pinching her mouth between thumb and forefinger, breaking the skin of her dry lips and leaving a taste of blood.

"You have not amused me yet." He released her abruptly. She heard the scrape and click as he lifted his lantern from the table. "But you will."

The door clanged shut behind him. His footsteps faded in the corridor, going toward the stairs and upward.

"PIG." She whispered it to the closed door, though that was an insult to pigs, who were, in general, amiable.

She could hear the other prisoners, the English spies, making small sounds on the other side of the cell, but it was dark, and they could no longer see her. She scrubbed her mouth with the back of her hand and swallowed the sick bile in her throat. It was amazingly filthy being touched by

Leblanc. It was like being crawled upon by slugs. She did not think she would become even slightly accustomed to it in the days she had left.

She pulled her dress into decency and let herself fold onto the dirt floor, feeling miserable. This was the end then. The choice that had tormented her for so long—what should be done with the Albion plans that had been entrusted to her—was made. All her logic and reasoning, all her searchings of the heart, had come to nothing. Leblanc had won. She would withstand his persuasions for only a day or two. Then he would wrest the Albion plans from her memory and commit God knew what greedy betrayals with them.

Her old mentor Vauban would be disappointed in her when he heard. He waited in his small stone house in Normandy for her to send word. He had left the decision to her, what should be done with the plans, but he had not intended that she give them to Leblanc. She had failed him. She had failed everyone.

She took a deep breath and let it out slowly. It was strange to know her remaining breaths were numbered in some tens of thousands. Forty thousand? Fifty? Perhaps when she was in unbearable pain later on tonight, she would start counting.

She pulled her shoes off, one and then the other. She had been in prisons twice before in her life, both times completely harrowing. At least she had been above ground then, and she had been able to see. Maman had been with her, that first time. Now Maman was dead in a stupid accident that should not have killed a dog. *Maman, Maman, how I miss you.* There was no one in this world to help her.

In the darkness, one feels very alone. She had never become used to this.

The English spy spoke, deep and slow, out of the dark. "I would stand and greet you politely." Chain clinked. "But I'm forced to be rude."

It was a measure of how lonely she was that the voice of an enemy English came like a warm handclasp. "There is much of that in my life lately. Rudeness."

"It seems you have annoyed Leblanc." He spoke the rich French of the South, without the least trace of a foreign accent.

"You also, it would seem."

"He doesn't plan to let any of us leave here alive."

"That is most likely." She rolled off her stockings, tucked them into her sleeve so she would not lose them, and slipped the shoes back on. One cannot go barefoot. Even in the anteroom to hell, one must be practical.

"Shall we prove him wrong, you and I?"

He did not sound resigned to death, which was admirable in its way, though not very realistic. It was an altogether English way of seeing things.

In the face of such bravery, she could not sit upon the floor and wail. French honor demanded a Frenchwoman meet death as courageously as any English. French honor always seemed to be demanding things of her. Bravery, of a sort, was a coin she was used to counterfeiting. Besides, the plan she was weaving might work. She might overcome Leblanc and escape the chateau and deal with these Albion plans that were the cause of so much trouble to her. And assuredly pigs might grow wings and fly around steeples all over town.

The English was waiting for an answer. She pulled herself to her feet. "I would be delighted to disappoint Leblanc in any way. Do you know where we are? I was not able to tell when I was brought here, but I hope very much this is the chateau in Garches."

"A strange thing to hope, but yes, this is Garches, the house of the Secret Police."

"Good, then. I know this place."

"That will prove useful. After we deal with these chains," he clinked metallically, "and that locked door. We can help each other."

He made many assumptions. "There is always the possibility."

"We can be allies." The spy chose his words carefully, hoping to charm her so she would be a tool for him. He slipped velvet upon his voice. Underneath, though, she heard an uncompromising sternness and great anger. There was nothing she did not know about such hard, calculating men.

Leblanc took much upon himself to capture British agents in this way. It was an old custom of both French and British secret services that they were not bloodthirsty with one another's agents. This was one of many rules Leblanc broke nowadays.

She worked her way along the wall, picking at the rocks, stealing the gravel that had come loose in the cracks and putting it into her stocking to make her little cosh. It was a weapon easy to use when one could not see. One of her great favorites.

There was a whisper of movement. A younger voice, very weak, spoke. "Somebody's here."

Her English spy answered, "Just a girl Leblanc brought in. Nothing to worry about."

". . . more questions?"

"Not yet. It's late at night. We have hours before they come for us. Hours."

"Good. I'll be ready . . . when the chance comes."

"It'll be soon now, Adrian. We'll get free. Wait."

The mindless optimism of the English. Who could comprehend it? Had not her own mother told her they were all mad?

It was a tidy small prison Leblanc kept. So few loose stones. It took a while before the cosh was heavy enough. She tied the end of the stocking and tucked it into the pocket hidden beneath her skirt. Then she continued to explore the walls, finding nothing at all interesting. There is not so much to discover about rooms that are used as prisons. This one had been a wine cellar before the Revolution.

It still smelled of old wood and good wine as well as less wholesome things. Halfway around the cell she came to where the Englishmen were chained, so she stopped to let her hands have a look at them as well.

The one who lay upon the ground was young, younger than she was. Seventeen? Eighteen? He had the body of an acrobat, one of those slight, tightly constructed people. He had been wounded. She could smell the gunpowder on his clothes and the wound going bad. She would wager money there was metal still inside him. When she ran her fingers across his face, his lips were dry and cracked, and he was burning hot. High fever.

They had chained him to the wall with an excellent chain, but a large, old-fashioned padlock. That would have to be picked if they were to escape. She searched his boots and the seams of his clothing, just in case Leblanc's men had missed some small, useful object. There was nothing at all, naturally, but one must always check.

"Nice . . ." he murmured when she ran her hands over him. "Later, sweetheart. Too tired . . ." Not so young a boy then. He spoke in English. There might be an innocent reason for an English to be in France, in these days when their countries were not exactly at war, but somehow she was sure Leblanc spoke truly. This was a spy. "So tired." Then he said clearly, "Tell Lazarus I won't do that anymore. Never. Tell him."

"We shall speak of it," she said softly, "later," which was a promise hard to fulfill, since she did not expect to have so very many laters. Though perhaps a few more than this boy.

He struggled to sit up. "Queen's Knight Three. I have to go. They're waiting for me to deliver the Red Knight." He was speaking what he should not, almost certainly, and he would injure himself, thrashing about. She pushed him gently back down.

Strong arms intervened. "Quiet. That's all done." The other man held the boy, muffling his words.

He need not have worried. She was no longer interested in such secrets. In truth, she would as soon not learn them.

"Tell the others."

"I will. Everyone got away safe. Rest now."

The boy had knocked over the water jug, struggling. Her hands found it, rolled on its side, empty. It was perfectly dry inside. The thought of water stabbed sour pinpricks in her mouth. She was so thirsty.

Nothing is worse than thirst. Not hunger. Not even pain. Maybe it was as well there was no water to tempt her. Perhaps she would have become an animal and stolen from these men, who suffered more than she did. It was better not to know how low she could have fallen. "When was the last time they gave you water?"

"Two days ago."

"You have not much longer to wait, then. Leblanc will keep me alive for a while, in the hopes I may be useful to him. And to play with." *In the end, he will kill me. Even when I give him the Albion plans—every word, every map, every list—he will still kill me. I know what he did in Bruges. He cannot let me live.*

"His habits are known."

He was large, the English spy of the deep voice and iron sternness. She sensed a huge presence even before she touched him. Her hands brought her more details. The big man had folded his coat under the boy, accepting another measure of discomfort to keep his friend off the cold floor. It was a very British courage, that small act. She felt his fierce, protective concentration surrounding the boy, as if force of will alone were enough to hold life in him. It would be a brave man indeed who dared to die when this man had forbidden it.

She reached tentatively and discovered soft linen and long, sinewy courses of muscle down his chest and then, where his shirt lay open at the neck, a disconcerting resilience of masculine skin. She would have pulled away, but his hand came to cover hers, pressing it down over his heart.

She felt the beat under her palm, startling and alive. Such power and strength.

He said, "I know what Leblanc does to women. I'm sorry you've fallen into his hands. Believe that."

"Me, I am also extremely sorry." This one was determined to be nice to her, was he not? She took her hand back. She would free him, if she could, and then they would see exactly how delightful he was. "These locks," she jiggled his manacle, "are very clumsy. One twiddle, and I could get them off. You do not have a small length of wire about you, do you?"

She could hear the smile in his voice. "What do you think?"

"I do not expect it to be so simple. Life is not, in my experience."

"Mine also. Did Leblanc hurt you?"

"Not so much."

He touched her throat where she was sore and bruised. "No woman should fall into Leblanc's hands. We'll get out of here. There's some way out. We'll find it." He gripped her shoulder, heavy and reassuring.

She should get up and search the cell. But somehow she found herself just sitting next to him, resting. Her breath trickled out of her. Some of the fear that had companioned her for weeks drained away, too. How long had it been since anyone had offered her comfort? How strange to find it here, in this fearful place, at the hands of an enemy.

After what seemed a long time, she roused herself. "There is another problem. Your friend cannot walk from here, even if I get him free of the chain."

"He'll make it. Better men than Leblanc have tried to kill him." Not everyone would have heard the anguish beneath the surface of that voice, but she did. They both knew this Adrian was dying. In a dozen hours, in at most another day, his wound and thirst and the damp chill of the stones would finish him off.

The boy spoke up in a thin thread of polished Gascon French. "It is . . . one small bullet hole. A nothing." He was very weak, very gallant. "It's the . . . infernal boredom . . . I can't stand."

"If we only had a deck of cards," the big man said.

"I'll bring some . . . next time."

They would have made good Frenchmen, these two. It was a pity Leblanc would soon take her from this cell. One could find worse companions for the long journey into the dark. At least the two of them would be together when they died. She would be wholly alone.

But it was better not to speculate upon how Leblanc would break her to his will and kill her, which could only lead to melancholy. It was time to slide from beneath the touch of this English spy and be busy again. She could not sit forever, hoping courage would seep out of his skin and into her.

She stood, and immediately felt cold. It was as if she had left a warm and accustomed shelter when she left the man's side. That was most silly. This was no shelter, and he did not like her much despite the soft voice he used. What lay between them was an untrusting vigilance one might have carved slices of.

Perhaps he knew who she was. Or perhaps he was one of those earnest men who go about spying in total seriousness. He would die for his country in a straightforward English fashion in this musty place and hate her because she was French. To see the world so simply was undoubtedly an English trait.

So be it. As it happened, she was not an amicable friend of big English spies. A French trait, doubtless.

She shrugged, which he would not see, and began working her way around the rest of the cell, inspecting the floor and every inch of the wall as high as she could reach. "In your time here, has Henri Bréval visited the cell?"

"He came twice with Leblanc, once alone, asking questions."

"He has the key? He himself? That is good then."

"You think so?"

"I have some hopes of Henri." There was not a rusted nail, not a shard of glass. There was nothing useful anywhere. She must place her hope in Henri's stupidity, which was nearly limitless. "If Fouché is indeed upstairs drinking wine and playing cards, Leblanc will not leave his side. One does not neglect the head of the Secret Police to disport oneself with a woman. But Henri, who takes note of him? He may seize the moment. He wishes to use me, you understand, and he has had no chance yet."

"I see." They were most noncommittal words.

Was it possible he believed she would welcome Henri? What dreadful taste he thought she had. "Leblanc does not let many people know about this room. It is very secret what he does here."

"So Henri may come sneaking down alone. You plan to take him." He said it calmly, as if it were not remarkable that she should attack a man like Henri Bréval. She was almost certain he knew what she was.

"I can't help you," the chain that bound him rattled, "unless you get him close."

"Henri is not so stupid. Not quite. But I have a small plan."

"Then all I can do is wish you well."

He seemed a man with an excellent grasp of essentials. He would be useful to her if she could get his chains off. That she would accomplish once those pigs became like the proverb and grew wings and went flying.

Exploring the cell further, she stubbed her toe upon a table, empty of even a spoon. There were also chairs, which presented more opportunity. She was working at the pegs that held a chair together when she heard footsteps.

"We have a visitor," the big English said.

"I hear." One man descended the steps into the cellar. Henri. It must be Henri. She set the chair upright, out of her way, and drew her cosh into her hand and turned toward the sound of footsteps. A shudder ran along her spine, but it was only the cold of the room. It was not fear. She could not afford to be afraid. "It is one man. Alone."

"Leblanc or Henri, do you think?"

"It is Henri. He walks more heavily. Now you will shut up quietly and not distract me." She prayed it was Henri. Not Leblanc. She had no chance against Leblanc.

The Englishman was perfectly still, but he charged the air with a hungry, controlled rage. It was as if she had a wolf chained to that wall behind her. His presence tugged and tugged at her attention when it was desperately important to keep her mind on Henri.

Henri. She licked her lips and grimly concentrated on Henri, an unpleasant subject, but one of great immediacy. There were twenty steps on the small curved staircase that led from kitchen to cellar. She counted the last of them, footstep by footstep. Then he was in the corridor that led to the cell.

Henri had always thought her reputation inflated. When he had brought her the long way to Paris to turn her over to Leblanc, she had played the spineless fool for him, begging humbly for food and water, stumbling, making him feel powerful. She was so diminished in her darkness he thought her completely harmless. He had become contemptuous.

Let him come just a little close, and he would discover how harmless she was. Most surely he would.

She knew the honey to trap him. She would portray for him the Silly Young Harlot. It was an old favorite role of hers. She had acted it a hundred times.

She licked her lips and let them pout, open and loose. What else? She pulled strands of hair down around her face. Her dress was already torn at the neckline. She found the spot and ripped the tear wider. Good. He would see only that bare skin. She could hold a dozen coshes and he would never notice.

Quickly. Quickly. He was coming closer. She took another deep breath and let the role close around her like a familiar garment. She became the Harlot. Yielding, easy to daunt, out of her depth in this game of intrigue and lies. Henri liked victims. She would set the most perfect victim before him and hope he took the bait.

Hid beneath layer upon layer of soft and foolish Harlot, she waited. Her fist, holding the cosh, never wavered. She would not allow herself to be afraid. It was another role she had crafted; the Brave Spy. She had played this one so long it fit like her skin.

Probably, at the center of her being, under all the pretense, the real Annique was a quivering mouse. She would not go prying in there and find out.

THE grilled window in the door glowed ghostly pale, then brightened as a lantern came closer. Grey could see again. The details of his cell emerged. Rough blocks of stone, a table, two chairs. And the girl.

She faced the door, stiff and silent and totally intent upon the man out in the corridor. Not a move out of her. Not the twitch of a fingernail. Her eyes, set in deep smudges of exhaustion, were half-closed and unfocused. She didn't once glance in his direction.

He watched her draw a deep breath, never taking her attention from that small barred window in the door. Her lips shaped words silently, praying or talking to herself. Maybe cursing. Again, she combed her fingers through her hair in staccato, purposeful, elegant flicks that left wild elflocks hanging across her face.

She was totally feminine in every movement, indefinably French. With her coloring—black hair, pale skin, eyes of that dark indigo blue—she had to be pure Celt. She'd be from the west of France. Brittany, maybe. Annique was a Breton name. She carried the magic of the Celt in her, used it to weave that fascination the great courtesans created. Even as he watched, she licked her lips again and wriggled deliberately, sensually. A man couldn't look away.

She'd torn her own dress. The curve of her breast showed white against the dark fabric—a whore, bringing out her wares. She was a whore, a liar, and a killer . . . and his life depended on her. "Good luck," he whispered.

She didn't turn. She gave one quick, dismissive shake of her head. "Be still. You are not part of this."

That was the final twist of the knife. He was helpless. He measured out his twenty inches of chain, picturing just how far a fast kick could reach. But Henri wasn't going to wander that close. She'd have to subdue Henri Bréval on her own, without even a toothpick to fight with.

There were red marks on her skin where Leblanc had been tormenting her and the tracks of tears on her cheeks. She couldn't have looked more harmless. That was another lie, of course.

He knew this woman. He'd recognized her the moment Leblanc pushed her stumbling into this cell. Feature by feature, that face was etched in his memory. He'd seen her the day he found his men, ambushed, twisted and bloody, dead in a cornfield near Bruges. If he'd had any doubt, the mention of the Albion plans would have convinced him. The Albion plans had been used to lure them to Bruges.

He'd been tracking this spy across Europe for the last six months. What bloody irony to meet her here.

He'd have his revenge. Leblanc was an artist in human degradation. Pretty Annique wouldn't die easily or cleanly or with any of that beauty intact. His men would be avenged.

If he got out of here . . . No, *when* he got out of here, Annique would come with him. He'd take her to England. He'd find out every damn thing she knew about what happened at Bruges. He'd get the Albion plans from her. Then he'd take his own vengeance.

She'd be supremely useful to British intelligence. Besides, he wouldn't leave a rabid hyena to Leblanc.

The peephole went bright as Henri held the lantern up. His heavy, florid face pressed to the grill. "Leblanc is furious with you."

"Please." The girl wilted visibly, leaning on the table for support, a sweet, succulent curve of entrapped femininity. "Oh, please." The drab blue of her dress and the crude cut of the garment marked her as a servant and accessible. Somehow her disheveled hair, falling forward over her face, had become sensuality itself. "This is all a mistake. A mistake. I swear . . ."

Henri laced fingers through the bars. "You'll talk to him in the end, Annique. You'll beg to talk. You know what he'll do to you."

There was a sniffle. "Leblanc . . . He does not believe me. He will hurt me terribly. Tell him I know nothing more. Please, Henri. Tell him." Her voice had changed completely. She sounded younger, subtly less refined, and very frightened. It was a masterful performance.

"He'll hurt you no matter what I tell him." Henri gloated.

The girl's face sank into her upturned palm. Her hair spilled in dark rivers through her fingers. "I cannot bear it. He will use me . . . like a grunting animal. I am not meant to be used by peasants."

Clever. Clever. He saw what she was doing. Henri's voice marked him as Parisian, a man of the city streets. Leblanc, for all his surface polish, was the son of a pig farmer. And Henri worked for Leblanc.

Henri's spite snaked out into the cell. "You were always Vauban's pet—Vauban and his elite cadre. Vauban and his important missions. You were too good for the rest of us. But tonight the so-special Annique that nobody could touch becomes a blind puppet for Leblanc to play with. If you'd been kind to me before, maybe I'd help you now."

"Leblanc has become Fouché's favorite. With the head

of the Secret Police behind him, he can do anything. You cannot help me. You would not dare defy him." She rubbed her eyes with the back of her hand. "I will do whatever he wishes. I have no choice."

"I'll have you when he's through with you."

She went on speaking. She might not have heard Henri. "He will make me oil my body and do the Gypsy dances I learned when I was a child. I will dance in the firelight for him with nothing but a thin bit of silken cloth upon me. Red silk. He . . . he prefers red. He has told me."

Grey wrapped the chain around his hand, gripping tight, seized by the image of a slim body writhing naked, silhouetted in the golden glow of fire. He wasn't the only one. Henri gripped the crossed bars of the grill and pressed his face close, salivating.

Annique, eyes downcast, swayed as if she were already undulating in the sensual dance she described. "I will draw the crimson silk from my body and caress him with it. The silk will be warm and damp with the heat of the dance. With my heat." Her left hand stroked down her body, intimately.

Grey ached from a dozen beatings, thirst was a torment every second, and he knew exactly what she was doing. He still went hard as a rock. He was helpless to stop it. God, but she was good.

Huskily, dreamily, she continued. "He will lie upon his bed and call me to him. At first, only to touch. Then to put my mouth upon him, wherever he directs. I have been trained to be skillful with my mouth. I will have no choice, you see, but to do as he demands of me."

Henri clanked and fumbled with the lock. In a great hurry, was Henri. If the Frenchman was half as aroused by Annique's little act as Grey was, it was a wonder he could get the door open at all.

The door banged back against the stone wall. "You must not come in here, Henri," she said softly, not moving, "or touch me in any way without the permission of Leblanc."

"Damn Leblanc." Henri slapped the lantern down and cornered her against the table. His fist twisted into her skirt and pulled it up. He grabbed the white shift beneath.

"You should not . . . You must not . . ." She struggled, pushing futilely at his hands with no more strength than a tiny, captured bird.

"No." He threw himself at Henri. And jerked short on his iron leash. The circle of pain at his wrist brought him back to reality. He couldn't get to her. He couldn't fight Henri for her. There wasn't a bloody thing he could do but watch.

"Do not . . ." Her flailing arm hit the lantern. It tilted and skidded off the table and clattered to the floor and extinguished. Darkness was instant and absolute.

"Stupid bitch," Henri snarled. "You . . ."

There was a small squashed thud. Henri yelped in pain. More thuds—one, two, three. The table scraped sideways. Something large and soft fell.

No movement. He heard Annique breathing hard, the smallness of it and the contralto gasps uniquely hers.

Planned. She'd planned it all. He crouched, tense as stretched cord, and acknowledged how well he'd been fooled. She'd planned this from start to finish. She'd manipulated both of them with that damned act of hers.

There was a long silence, broken by intriguing rustling sounds and Annique grunting from time to time. Her footsteps, when she walked toward him, were sure and unhesitating. She came in a straight line across the cell as if it were not dark as a tomb.

"What did you do to Henri?" The issue, he thought, had never really been in doubt.

"I hit him upon the head with a sock full of rocks." She seemed to think it over while she sat down beside him. "At least I am almost sure I hit his head once. I hit him many places. Anyway, he is quiet."

"Dead?"

"He is breathing. But one can never tell with head

wounds. I may have yet another complicated explanation to make to God when I show up at his doorstep, which, considering all things, may be at any moment. I hope I have not killed him, quite, though he undoubtedly deserves it. I will leave that to someone else to do, another day. There are many people who would enjoy killing him. Several dozen I can call to mind at once."

She baffled him. There was ruthlessness there, but it was a kind of blithe toughness, clean as a fresh wind. He didn't catch a whiff of the evil that killed men in cold blood, from ambush. He had to keep reminding himself what she was. "You did more than knock him over the head. What was the rest of it, afterwards?"

"You desire the whole report?" She sounded amused. "But you are a spymaster, I think, Englishman. No one else asks such questions so calmly, as if by right. Very well, I shall report to you the whole report—that I have tied Henri up and helped myself to his money. There was an interesting packet of papers in a pocket he may have thought was secret. You may have them if you like. Me, I am no longer in the business of collecting secret papers."

Her hands patted over him lightly. "I have also found a so-handy stickpin, and if you will lift your pretty iron cuff here. Yes. Just so. Now hold still. I am not a fishwife that I can filet this silly lock while you wriggle about. You will make me regret that I am being noble and saving your life if you do not behave sensibly."

"I am at your disposal." He offered his chained wrist. At the same time he reached out and touched her hair, ready to grab her if she tried to leave without freeing him.

She put herself right in his power—a man twice her size, twice her strength, and an enemy. She had to know what her writhing and whispering did to a man. Revenge and anger and lust churned in his body like molten iron. The wonder was it didn't burn through his skin and set this soft hair on fire.

"Ah. We proceed," she said in the darkness. "This lock is not so complicated as it pretends to be. We are discussing matters."

She edged closer and shifted the manacle to a different angle, brushing against his thigh. With every accidental contact, his groin tightened and throbbed. All he could think of was her soft voice saying, "I will oil my body and dance in the firelight." He was no Henri. He wasn't going to touch her. But how did he get a picture like that out of his head?

"And . . . it is done." The lock fell open.

She made it seem easy. It wasn't. He rubbed his wrist. "I thank you."

He stood and stretched to his full height, welcoming the pain of muscles uncramping. Free. Savage exultation flooded him. He was free. He bunched and unbunched his fists, glorying in the surge of power that swept him. He felt like he could take these stones apart with his bare hands. It was dark as the pit of hell and they were twenty feet under a stronghold of the French Secret Police. But the door hung open. He'd get them out of here—Adrian and this remarkable, treacherous woman—or die trying. If they didn't escape, it would be better for all of them to die in the attempt.

While that woman worked on Adrian's manacle, he groped his way across the cell to Henri, who was, as she had said, breathing. The Frenchman was tied, hand and foot, with his stockings and gagged with his own cravat. A thorough woman. Checking the bonds was an academic exercise. There was indeed a secret pocket in the jacket. He helped himself to the papers, then tugged Henri's pants down to his ankles, leaving him half naked.

"What do you busy yourself with?" She'd heard him shifting Henri about. "I find myself inquisitive this evening."

"I'm giving Henri something to discuss with Leblanc when they next meet." It might buy them ten minutes while Henri explained his plans for the girl. "I may eventually regret leaving him alive."

"If we are very lucky, you will have an eventually in which to do so." There was a final, small, decisive click. "That is your Adrian's lock open. He cannot walk from here, you know."

"I'll carry him. Do you have a plan for getting out of the chateau with an unconscious man and no weapons and half the Secret Police of France upstairs?"

"But certainly. We will not discuss it here, though. Bring your friend and come, please, if you are fond of living."

He put an arm under Adrian's good shoulder and hauled him upright. The boy couldn't stand without help, but he could walk when held up. He was conversing with unseen people in a variety of languages.

"Don't die on me now, Hawker," he said. "Don't you dare die on me."

"ME, I SHOULD NOT BE PLAYING NURSEMAID TO a couple of English." The woman shifted to take more of Adrian's weight. "We go left here, English, if you are set upon coming to this place."

"It's the closest church?"

"It is indeed. There is the Church of St. Cloud midway down the hill, of course, which is a more proper church—in daylight you could see the steeple—but the chapel in the orphanage is by far closer, if you do not mind that it is ruined, which I suppose is a matter wholly indifferent to you. It was burned in the Terror. They are all gone now, the nuns and the orphans, to God alone knows where."

"If it's the closest church, there'll be a message." If he were lucky, his friend Doyle would be waiting for him.

"The English spies in Italy had a similar arrangement. I am all comprehension."

Night stretched unbroken on every side, lightless, but decent and clean after that cell. He took a deep breath. The possibilities seemed endless, under this sky, breathing this pure, empty chill. They'd come this far. He'd get them all to safety. He'd find a way.

"I do not know why I am helping you. It is an example of disinterested benevolence, this." He could imagine the resigned shrug. Already he knew her that well. "And therefore doubtless unwise. Ah, we have removed ourselves from the road slightly. We shall edge back. Yes. Thusly. Take care."

They supported Adrian between them while Annique tapped the path ahead with the broomstick she'd picked up in the chateau garden. She'd saved his life again and again tonight. It was Annique who'd counted out the steps of a complicated route through the maze of the chateau cellars. She'd known the secret of the door hidden in the back of a storage closet. In utter blackness, with assurance a cat would envy, she'd threaded a way past the unseen hazards of the gardens. She found water caught under leaves in a deep stone basin. As long as he lived he'd remember that water. He'd remember Annique cupping water in her hand and holding it to Adrian's lips before she took a drink herself.

He could never have lifted Adrian over that last wall alone. It had been an endless, agonizing ordeal, accomplished in uncanny silence, while fifty yards away guests came and went on the front steps of the chateau and music of unearthly purity hung in the air like crystal.

Now she led them forward and whispered encouragement and direction and caustic complaint. "The ruts are deep because wagons turn to go into the back gate of the chateau." "The wall on the right is abundant with sharp stones. Avoid it." "Ah. That is a low branch. You will come to it in a moment." He could see her walking into hell saying, "On the right, take note of the chained demon. Take care to walk around him." His respect for her, and his wariness, grew with every step. He'd take every care, capturing her.

She said, “It is not far, the gate to the orphanage.”

On the other side of the River Seine, a line of pinprick lights marked the city of Paris. A few streets away, a single bright window hung in the night. Other than that, it was black as the belly of a cow. “How the devil can you tell?”

She laughed in the darkness. She was another one glad to be out of that cellar. “I walked this road many times when there was daylight for me. My memory is most excellent.” Joy lilted in her voice, like singing. It was strange to hear her sound so young, like a brave child, instead of the coiled serpent he knew her to be. “This tree we stand beneath,” she banged the stick against bark, “which naturally you have not been introduced to and cannot see anyway, is a beautiful cherry which was old already when I first came here. I have climbed it and stolen many cherries in my time. The whole corner smells of the fruit that fell a few weeks ago. The road you seek, the driveway to the Sisters of the Orphans, is opposite. There.” She touched his shoulder lightly, showing where she meant.

Her night vision was extraordinary. “I can’t see a thing.”

“Stop trying to see, English. Listen instead. The night is telling stories all around you. The Rue Bérenger lies ahead . . . oh . . . fifty paces perhaps. The baker on the corner is even now making bread. One can smell that. Rue Bérenger runs east toward the bridge, to Paris, where men of your profession likely have friends. Or go uphill to the west, and you will come after a time to England, where you have even more friends, beyond doubt. The little wind in our face—feel it—is blowing from the northeast, from the Bois de Boulogne.”

He closed his eyes and tried to sense the currents of the night as she did. She was right. It was easier listening and feeling the wind on his skin, not straining to see. “You’re good at this. You’ve done your share of sneaking around in the dark.”

“More than I would like, certainly.”

"Did you learn all that working for Vauban? You were one of his people, weren't you?"

"You ask many questions. Have I told you that? Now pay attention and I will teach you secrets. When you face the wind you will always know where you are. It is the direction of the river scent." He heard her swallow. "The smell of the water."

And with that, he'd found the bait to lure her in. Her voice gave her away. The catch basin in the garden held barely enough to wet their mouths. She was thirsty. Hurting with it.

He chose his words carefully. "I'll be glad to get to the chapel. I hope there's water." He felt her attention quiver. Good.

"It is most likely."

He picked a few more insidious words. "There should be a well. Do you think we'll find a bucket or something to draw the water up?"

"You will doubtless discover. It is not far, as I said." Her voice had thickened and he heard her swallow again. "I shall leave you to your so-secret rendezvous. Me, I have business elsewhere. I am not anxious to enlarge my acquaintance with the English spy community of Paris." But her voice said she was thinking about water.

"Probably nobody's there. I can't manage Adrian alone. And you can show me that well."

"Do not nag at me, monsieur." He heard her stick grind the dirt of the road. "It is not an attractive trait."

"He needs your help. What is it, a hundred steps?"

She snorted, a delicate, French snort of exasperation. "I do not know how it is the English have the reputation for being stoic, for you are not in the least." She gathered Adrian closer to her. "Come then. We will find your water that obsesses you so. Most certainly we will stop loitering here in the roadway, chatting, for anyone and his cat to remark upon. This is the gate."

The broomstick clicked angrily along the iron railings as they went through.

"I go as far as the steps of the main house. Not beyond that," she said. "Not one inch. Not if you have a dozen young spies upon your hands, all wounded horribly. It is thoroughly illogical that you should ask it of me." Their feet crunched on gravel and the way led steeply downhill. "I have had little to do with the English before this. I see now that was wise, though there are doubtless many sorts of Englishmen who are more reasonable than you. Perhaps I will reserve judgment."

He could detect no trace of a human presence ahead. But then, he wouldn't. Not if it was Will Doyle waiting there.

A few steps forward and she stopped. "I do not like this." And right she was. She had excellent instincts. "No. I will not go farther. Take the boy . . ."

Adrian, even half-conscious, must have been listening. He played his part then. He moaned and sagged against her.

She staggered and held him up. "Your friend has fainted again. We must . . ."

At his side, close enough to touch, Doyle said, "It's about time you showed up." A burly presence coalesced from the night. "I was getting ready to storm the place."

Doyle. Thank God. Two tons of worry rolled off his shoulders. "Adrian's hurt."

The instant she heard Doyle's voice, the girl pushed free of Adrian and backed away into the woods. She stilled, out of reach.

"Give him to me." Doyle was a big man. He picked Adrian up bodily and carried him. "I heard he went and got himself shot. We've been wondering how bad it was. I stole a coach just in case. It's down the drive."

"Good." He turned his head to one side and the other, listening, locating the girl. There. The whisper of her breath betrayed her. *Feel safe in the darkness, Annique. You just do that.* "I need water for my guide," he called after Doyle.

He could swear Doyle read his mind. "There's a couple flasks in the coach, nice and cold. I'll fetch it down. Good clean water." They were the right words, offhanded and calm.

He felt a tremor in Annique's waiting silence. *Keep thinking about water, Annique. Keep thinking about how thirsty you are.* "I'll get that flask for you, mademoiselle, with my thanks. That's the very least I owe you."

She hesitated, an almost inaudible rustle of indecision. She must be desperate for water.

If he grabbed for her and missed, he wouldn't get a second chance. She was too fast in the dark, too comfortable slipping around with that stick of hers. He'd have to tempt her close. "Wait," he said softly. "I'll bring water."

The smell of fresh paint led him to the coach and a spiderweb of faint lines leaking from a dark lantern. When he slid the tin sheathing aside, a wedge of light sprang up across the weed-grown courtyard.

Doyle settled Adrian in the coach. "Where'd you catch it, lad? Shoulder? No. More along of the chest. Just the one bullet?"

Adrian said hoarsely, "One's enough . . . don't you think? Waistcoat's a total loss."

The coach rocked as Doyle spread a blanket over the boy. "Dunnoh how I'm gonna face yer tailor, knowing that. Here, put some water in you before you faint on us."

"Set it where I can reach it. Let's get out of here."

"An' who died and left you in charge, lad? You tell me that sometime." Doyle swung down from the coach. "He'll do. How many after you?"

"The whole nest of hornets. I'll pay off my guide and we can go. Where's that water?" He swung the lantern around. Yes. Oh, yes. Now he had her. She hung back well beyond the reach of his light, making herself a shadow among shadows, wise and wary. But it was already too late for her to be wary.

Doyle met his eyes. "Of course. Have it down in just a tick, sir." Doyle climbed the rungs to the top of the coach, hand over hand, with the curious, slow, lumbering grace of a great brown bear. "I got food, too. Big basket here. Bread, cheese, sausages. Some wine."

Out in the darkness, Annique would be listening. She'd be hungry. Leblanc would have seen to that. "Some bread. But water first. Give me something easy to carry. The water bottle. That one."

Doyle passed down a water bottle and half a long loaf of bread, still fragrant from the baking. That was all the bait he needed. He had her. It was just sliding the trap closed.

"Mademoiselle?"

She'd backed farther into the dark. Careful. Nervous. When he walked closer, he could see she had her eyes shut against the lantern light to preserve that remarkable night vision of hers. But then, he already knew how clever she was.

She leaned heavily on that old broom handle she'd collected. Her clothes were filthy with dirt and cobwebs, her skin bone-white with fatigue. Alone, exhausted and on foot—how far did she think she'd get before Leblanc ran her down? He was doing her a favor, really, gathering her in. Whatever he did to her it couldn't be worse than what Leblanc had in mind.

He set the lantern down carefully on the gravel, freeing up his hand.

Water sloshed in the bottle. With any luck, that would be enough to nail her to the spot. He strolled toward her, bottle swinging loose between his fingers, the loaf tucked casually under his arm. Simple tricks work best. It was like catching a filly in a field. You go slow and steady and act like you're thinking about something else.

"Do you want cheese, too? I can have him bring some down." He spoke as if Doyle were still on top of the carriage. He wasn't. Without looking, he could have charted Doyle's course, circling in silence, cutting off the woman's escape. They'd worked together ten years. He knew where Doyle would position himself. He'd be a dozen feet behind the target and to the right of the pathway. "Bread and water doesn't begin to pay the debt I owe you."

"I do not collect debts from English spies." She shuffled uneasily. "A debt ties you to people."

"Water's not much of a debt. A little cool water." He tossed the word like a looped noose. Let her think about thirst, not about him closing in. He was nearly there.

He could almost hear her instincts screaming for her to run. The intent, listening tilt of her head said it all. How long had Leblanc kept her without water? She must be desperate to take this risk.

One last step, and he clamped an unbreakable grip on her arm. She was his.

She tried to jerk away. "I do not like people touching me, monsieur."

"This is the best way. You don't have a chance against Leblanc. At least with me—"

Pain exploded in his elbow. The broom handle spun, smooth as glass, and cracked across his kneecap. White, cold, unbelievable agony knifed up his leg. He fell. Slammed down onto his shoulder. The girl flicked free, like a fish out of a badly cast net. There was nothing in the dark but scattering gravel.

"Bloody. Damn. Hell!" Blind with pain, he staggered up and limped after her. Idiot. He was an idiot. He'd seen what she'd done to Henri. He knew what she was.

That was almost the end of it. She was unbelievably fast in the dark. He heard her stick clacking into trees, finding a path. She was getting away.

But Doyle was the wiliest of old campaigners. He'd put himself where he could see the girl outlined against the glow of the lantern. He didn't show at all in the dark shrubbery. She barreled straight into Doyle's massive arms, and he scooped her right in.

Almost scooped her in.

"Son of a buggering . . ." He arrived to find Doyle clutching his belly, sputtering colorful Breton dialect. ". . . gangrenous sea cow." The girl was loose and scrambling to her feet. She was damned good if she could land a blow on Doyle.

Oh yes. It was going to be a pleasure bringing Mademoiselle Annique in.

He dodged that blasted lethal stick of hers, stepped in, and twisted it out of her hands. That had her disarmed. Then he had to deal with the surprising, elegant little fight she put up. She was strong for a woman, all lean muscles and neat, sturdy bones, but she had no weight on her. The top of her head didn't come even to his chin. She never had a chance.

It took less than three minutes. When it was over, he pulled her arms behind her, not hurting her more than he had to, but not letting her hurt him either. She panted, her sides heaving in and out, and every muscle in her trembled in shock. It had been a hard night for Miss Annique. Then it was step by step back to the coach, dragging her, letting her fight enough to tire herself out. She wouldn't have much strength left.

He felt a sense of fierce, primitive possession. His. She was his.

Rubbing his belly and grumbling, Doyle ambled up. "Fast as bedickens, ain't you, me girl? Bring her over here to the light." Doyle took a handful of hair and tilted her head back. She was still fighting, her eyes closed in furious concentration as she tried to kick somebody.

"God's little parakeets. Annique Villiers." Doyle gave a low whistle. "You collect the damnedest things, Grey. What the hell are you doing with the Fox Cub?"

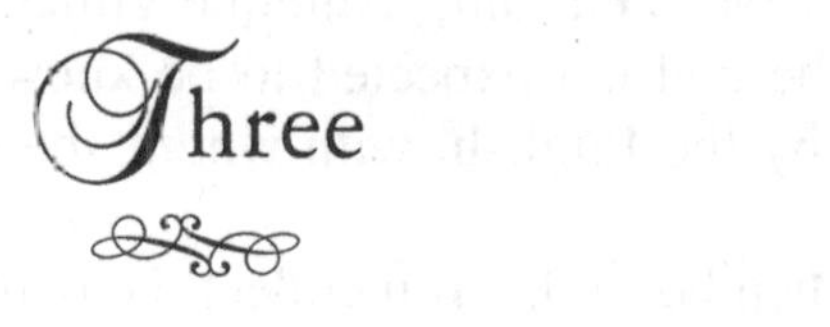

Three

Sometimes, Annique thought, one pays dearly for a tiny mistake. She should not have been tempted by the water.

It had been a short, inglorious fight. She had no chance against this English spy she had stupidly freed from Leblanc. They were both blind in this night, and she had practiced, endlessly, fighting without sight. But it gave her no advantage. She summoned up all the dirty tricks she had ever learned and pulled them out, one by one. The big man knew them all. He was much better at this business of fighting than she was.

It ended quickly. He flattened her hard against him and wrapped her up like a troublesome little parcel, and she could not escape. His muscles were iron and polished wood, invulnerable, endlessly strong. She could feel savage satisfaction coursing through his body. He was positively gleeful to trap her like this. She became very afraid of him.

An hour ago, she had set her hand against his heart and wanted nothing more than to stay beside him. She would now do exactly that. The universe had been treating her with great sarcasm lately.

She was dragged forward. The coachman—the English spy pretending to be a coachman—took her hair and looked at her face and said, "Annique Villiers."

She had not expected to be known. Not this far north. Not by the English, with whom she had had so few dealings.

Then he said, "You collect the damnedest things, Grey." The shock of that removed her breath.

Grey. The English spy was Grey? She was most definitely fighting above her station. By the good God, no wonder they had gathered her up in this way. She had stumbled into the disorderly tail end of some major British operation. For no other reason would Grey himself be in France.

It was the most astoundingly bad luck. The man called Grey was Head of the entire British Section, directly under the legendary Galba himself. Grey had no need to be wandering in Paris waylaying female spies. He was a man of many agents all across Europe and numberless important activities, all of them more complex and vital than provoking and tormenting her in this way. Grey should be—she tried angrily to decide what was appropriate—he should be plotting Napoleon's downfall in an office at the Whitehall or in some other suitable place. It was altogether dangerous and stupid for him to be lurking about in France, where he was in great jeopardy and anyone at all might lock him into cellars at any time.

Grey was indisputably in France. Held pinioned in his arms, she felt weariness and thirst and the long weeks of running alone in the dark and this senior English spy defeat her all together. Her heart failed within her, and she lost whatever effectiveness she had ever possessed as a fighter. "Please do not do this to me."

"Easy does it. Up with you." Grey dragged her into the

coach as if she were a trophy he had won by great cleverness. As she was. "No more fighting. I really wouldn't try it."

"Please. I will betray nothing of you. Not a whisper." Her words were muffled against the cushions where he pinned her. He was made of perfectly solid muscle and extremely heavy.

"No, I don't think you will," he said.

He was content that she should thrash and kick beneath him until she wore herself out and became somewhat easier to manage. She saw at once what he intended, but it took her a long time to become wise and accept the inevitable and lay her forehead down on the cushions and give up, to be simply gasping and limp like a fish upon a bank.

She was in great trouble. She had not been trapped in this way because the English wished to collect minor and unimportant agents. It was Leblanc's stupid words concerning the Albion plans that interested them. Every spy in Europe was looking for those plans. Leblanc might so easily have held his tongue. There was no good luck for her lately.

She considered what a man like Grey might do to discover the whereabouts of the Albion plans when he took a French agent away from Paris to somewhere solitary and she was alone with him. She could imagine how he might extract the information he wanted and then silence a French spy who knew many awkward secrets. She knelt in the iron grip of his hands, covered with sweat from fighting, but inside she was as cold as January.

"Finished?" Grey asked.

She could only nod.

"I'm glad you two finally settled that." Adrian was upon the other seat. His voice was feeble but perfectly full of laughter. "You keep banging into me."

"It's settled," Grey said, "except she's going to bite me if I let go."

Her terror diminished with those words, for the attitude

of Grey was not that of a man about to do murder, and the boy Adrian was entirely lighthearted, which only a monster would be if she were to die in the environs of Paris at the hands of these English.

"I should have left you to rot with Leblanc," she said. "I wish I had."

"It's a little late to wish that, mademoiselle," Grey said.

"I beg to differ. It is never too late. I will probably wish it for the rest of my life. What is your intention to do with me?"

"I'm not going to hurt you, Annique."

Yes, he would. Did he imagine she was stupid? "I have saved your life. This is no fit repayment, what you do to me."

"You're right. It isn't." Then there was some silence in which he did not at all amplify his response.

There is a transition to be made in the mind. To admit one is beaten. She admitted defeat most privately to herself and felt weakness and despair flow throughout her muscles. Grey, who held her pinned most effectively, would feel it also. He relaxed his hold somewhat. She muttered, "It was said by Socrates that no evil can befall the good, either in life or after death. I am not so sure of this as I once was. What do you want from me?"

"Your company. For a time." There was deep satisfaction in his voice.

"How long will you keep me?"

"Until I let you go."

"Oh, but you are witty, monsieur. Forgive me if I do not laugh. I am not in good humor tonight." She let her cheek lie against the seat, against the cool leather, unutterably exhausted and beaten. Fox Cub they called her, her friends and her enemies in the little world of spying. No fox's trick would free her this time. Nonetheless, she tried one last time to pretend to be stupider than she was. "You waste your time with me. I am the small agent, the quiet mouse in the wall, the messenger. I hold no secrets of interest to the English."

And thus she pretended to know not a thimbleful about Albion plans or the invasion of England or what had happened all those months ago in Bruges, or much else either. She did not expect to fool him.

"Is that so?" He did not sound very interested.

"Most certainly. You have heard Leblanc say otherwise, but he is a fool." When he said nothing, she clarified, "He speaks of the Albion plans, of which I know not the least morsel. Leblanc makes the old quarrel, you understand. He has hated Vauban since the days of the Revolution, when they were both young and ambitious agents, and my mother also. She is dead now, which frustrates him utterly, so he invents plots that never were. He destroys the daughter because he cannot have the mother. It is small-minded of him."

"You, of course, are innocent."

"It pleases you to be ironic. It is not that I am innocent. I am only innocent of these particular matters. That is the truth, English."

"Your truth has more layers than an onion. We'll see what happens when we will peel off a few of those layers."

She did not like the sound of that.

The English did not believe her. He would hold on to her like grim death, no matter what convincing lies she told. Soon, the questioning would begin.

She was tired beyond measure of these stupid and intransigent plans, which kept trying to cause her death and had no resting place anywhere. They were the most sharp of two-edged swords, those plans: deadly to the land of England if they remained hidden, perilous to France if given to the English. It was foolish beyond measure that Napoleon should have ordered them made and she was entirely disgusted with the whole business.

The driver hitched the horses, backing them with a

shuffle of hooves, harnessing them with jingling reins. That was no trivial job for one man, alone, in the dark of night. But Grey would not descend to help him. He stayed where he was, holding her arm behind her back in that clever way that did not hurt and did not allow her to move. It was like being constrained by a stone statue or some other object impervious to argument.

He said, "Let's put an end to this. Are you tired of crouching on the floor, Mademoiselle Villiers?"

"Extremely, Monsieur Grey."

"Then I suggest we make an agreement. You will promise to sit quietly and stop kicking me. I will let you sit up and give you something to eat and drink. Do you agree?"

So. They would begin thus. She recognized the first of many little compromises he would force upon her. Each "yes" made the next one easier until, as he hoped, it would seem wholly natural to do exactly as he told her in all things.

"Leblanc uses such methods," she said. "You would make me accept this kidnapping in return for a few ounces of water. It is profoundly discouraging how similar spies are everywhere."

"Very philosophic. Do I have your agreement?"

"I make you no agreements. It is indifferent to me whether I sit on the seat or lie tied on the floor, unless the carriage is infested with fleas, which is of course a possibility. The question of water will resolve itself, I think, in another day."

The driver could be heard, walking a circuit of the coach, kicking stones away from the wheels. The carriage rocked as he climbed up to the box. They lurched forward, up the hill, past the ditch that marked the old gate, jouncing on ruts in the Rue des Orphelines, clattering on the cobbles of the Rue Bérenger. They turned right. West. Toward England.

Toward Soulier, who was posted to London, serving the Secret Police and France. Soulier, who would give her sanctuary from Leblanc. With Soulier's protection, she might even live long enough to deal with the Albion plans. These men were taking her ever so swiftly in the direction she wished to go. Of a certainty, there was an evil, humorous angel in charge of her own particular heavens.

"I wonder whether I should call your bluff." Grey's hands tightened. "Shall we—"

From the other side of the carriage, Adrian spoke, "For the gods' sake, Grey, leave the girl be."

"It's not your teeth she's trying to kick in."

"I was not aiming for your teeth, monsieur," she said.

"No, you weren't, were you?"

"So entertaining." Adrian's voice was a satiric croak. "Why don't we torture her later . . . when she's stronger. So much more fun."

"Hell." Grey hoisted her to the seat. She was free to turn away from him and huddle in a corner.

"Harmony is restored." The boy Adrian adjusted himself on the seat with creakings of leather and the swish of cloth.

"Easy for you to talk. You're not the one she's planning to emasculate," Grey said sourly.

"That's the entertainment . . . I was talking about."

"You should save your chivalry. You don't know her. This is a beautiful little snake."

"But I do know her, by reputation, at least. The Fox Cub and I are old rivals . . . from the days in Italy. We snakes have to . . . stick together."

She knew then who this Adrian must be, though he had used a different name in Italy. Such stories were told of him. Certainly she had fallen among deadly company this night.

Grey did not leave her to digest this new information in silence. He leaned across and brushed her hair back, settling it around her ear, uncovering her face, nudging her chin up. The outside lanterns would reveal her completely. She kept her eyes shut.

Adrian must have been looking her over, too. "She's afraid of you, if that's what you wanted. It comes and it goes. She's afraid now."

"I want her afraid. I want her too afraid to give me any trouble. Annique, just how afraid of me are you?"

"Immensely, monsieur. As much as you could wish." Her voice broke. *Dieu.* Was there any way on earth she had not betrayed herself in these last minutes? "Entirely terrified, in fact."

"What do you think?" Grey asked Adrian. "Real or just playacting?"

"Real enough. I saw many frightened women in my interesting youth. You're very easy to be scared of. Believe me, I know."

"Maybe she'll behave herself. In deference to your delicate sensibilities, however, I'll beat and starve her later." He let her go.

This was infinitely comforting. She had known several men who tortured people, and not one of them had the least trace of humor.

She turned to the corner and put her hands up as if she were rubbing her eyes for the headache. She had been so very, very stupid to be caught like this. How Vauban would scold when he heard. He had trained her better than this. She had been so stupid. It was no doubt possible to be more shamed than she felt right at this moment, but she could not imagine how. Her hands shook where she held them tightly against her eyes.

"I'm not that easy to manipulate, mademoiselle," Grey said. "You'll find I have a singular lack of pity. And don't even think of fighting me. Take this."

"This" was a flask, half full. The water was stale and tasted of metal, but it was lovely as the finest wine on her tongue. Despite her boasting, he could have demanded many things from her in exchange for this water he tossed to her so casually. He must know that.

He dropped a loaf of bread into her lap. It was the same one he had used to trap her with, dusty from landing on the ground.

She brushed off the sand and tore a piece of the good bread and ate it slowly, alternating bites of bread with pulls of water. After a time, she no longer wanted to cry. It was magic, this bread and water, and it gave her heart again. Escape seemed possible once more. Now, perhaps.

Deliberately, she leaned back on the cushions, eyes still closed, her body slack and weary. The carriage lamps outside burned with a thick, oily smell. In that flicker of light, they were certainly watching her with all attention. The least tensing of a muscle would give her away.

She filled her voice with discouragement, of which she had any amount handy. "I think you win. See—I take your food, and I no longer fight you." She lifted the bread as if it were heavy and took another bite and chewed and swallowed. They would not expect her to escape while she was in the middle of chewing. "It is no huge triumph to defeat me. I have not eaten for several days. You are not so clever, Monsieur Grey."

Adrian snickered from his place on the opposite seat. Grey said nothing at all. The carriage rocked and jolted. They made some speed through the silent countryside, heading uphill, away from Paris. This road—she knew it well—wound through a region of compact stone villages and fields and grand houses surrounded by huge gardens. She could smell the late-blooming roses of the gardens and the country grasses. Occasionally there was the smell of apples. Everywhere the smoke of hearth fires filled the air, burning to keep the night chill out of the little stone houses.

It was the perfect place to run, the perfect time.

She had reached an accommodation with darkness months ago. She knew a thousand tricks of moving without sight that these men had never dreamed of. The night was her friendly kingdom, ready to hide her. None of them could outrun her in the dark.

She swallowed the bite of bread and pretended to take another. Now. This was the moment. It is not good to plan such things too much. The opponent feels it.

She twisted sideways in the seat and kicked Grey with all her strength. This time, for variety's sake, she kicked him in the belly.

Four

"THANK THE GODS." ADRIAN COLLAPSED ACROSS the bed, fully dressed. His coat stank of wine. That was to explain him staggering with every step.

"You're bleeding again."

"Nobody saw."

"Hell. That's just fine, then, if nobody saw." Grey slung Adrian's feet up and began pulling the boots off. "Damned fool."

"They'll be looking for somebody with a bullet hole in him. Not some . . . idiot carrying a bottle."

"Carrying a bottle and singing off key, strolling right through the middle of the innyard."

"Nobody sees you when you . . . don't hide. Pure genius."

It might have been, but it had used up the last of Adrian's strength. "Next time, do what you're told." When Grey unbuttoned the striped waistcoat, the front of Adrian's shirt was soaked red. More blood lost. And they still had to get the bullet out of him.

". . . and I wasn't off-key. I have a particularly fine baritone."

"So does an ass. Don't sit up." Roussel, the innkeeper, already had Doyle's red valise ready on the dresser. Lockpicks and a collection of subtle weapons were lined up in the barbering kit, disguised as complex grooming aids. There was a choice of scissors. "I'll cut that coat off."

"More wardrobe sacrificed to the needs of the Service." Adrian's lips quirked. "Take it. Take it. We're sick of one another's company. I've been wearing it—what's it been—three days?

"Four, since you got shot."

"Ah. I lost a day."

"That day was no loss. I was there."

They spoke French. Even alone, even in this inn that belonged body and soul to the British Service, they never broke into English. It was one of the thousand habits that kept them alive. Voices change when they change to a new language. Grey's own voice was refined and smooth in the drawling Toulouse French he affected. In English, his normal tone was a grating deep growl, heavy with the underlay of his native West Country accent.

He rolled his sleeves back and selected a pair of scissors. "There are sharp points on these. Hold still."

"Behold me, motionless as a clam." Adrian let his head fall back onto the pillow. "We shouldn't have brought her here. We could have dumped her in any of those villages."

"I need her. You, I can dump in a Normandy village and say good riddance." He cut through wool and the heavy silk of the waistcoat and the linen of the shirt. "Lift your arm. Yes. That's got it."

"You've brought a French agent to a British Service shelter house. This is Roussel's bailiwick. He's going to want to slit her throat."

"Roussel doesn't get everything he wants." The bandage

beneath was heavy with fresh blood, stiff and brown at the edges. Five, six snips, and he cut it away.

Adrian curled up to peer at his chest. "Looks like a hell of a mess from here. How is it?"

"Not bad." Under a plaque of gummy dried blood, the wound was draining thin, straw-colored liquid. Was that normal? He kept his opinion off his face. "Better than I expected."

The Hawker, unfortunately, could read any man living. He leaned back and opened and closed his hand a few times and looked away. From the open window came the faint sound of men talking at the tables outside. "Any chance for a doctor?"

"Roussel doesn't trust the local man. We'll manage on our own."

"How intrepid of us."

The fever was down, fought to a temporary truce by the Hawker's leathery toughness. That couldn't last much longer. This sneaky, brilliant boy was going to die because Grey couldn't risk getting a French doctor to him. Because they'd been too slow running down an alley in Paris four days ago. Because he'd sent Hawker into France in the first place.

He was going to kill the boy tomorrow, digging that bullet out. Damn and damn and damn.

Roussel's daughter had brought up water. Grey poured some in the basin. It was hot, almost too hot to touch. "We'll clean up. We'll eat well and sleep soft tonight. Tomorrow we put more distance between us and Paris, then stop and pull the slug out." He made himself study the jagged pucker of red skin. "You'll have a beautiful scar."

"It will add to my manifold charms. Who digs into me—you or Doyle?"

"We talked it over. My hands are better with small work."

"You flipped a coin. I know." Adrian sketched a grin.

"We could wait till England. I know a man in Chelsea who has a fine, artistic way with a bullet."

"Coward."

"Fervently. Tomorrow then. If you're set on this, I suggest you choose someplace private. I will whine in an unmanly fashion."

"I'll keep that in mind."

There were towels stacked beside the basin. Grey tried to remember what they did in the medical tents, after battle. There'd been wounds soaking under hot cloths. That worked with horses, too. He'd try it. He wet linen in the steaming water and wrung it out gingerly. "This is hot."

"Ach!" The boy jerked. "Hot. Yes. Right you are." He took a slow, tight breath between clenched teeth. "Oh, that's toasty hot. Listen . . . Carruthers has my last report. That's safe. Tell Giles to take what he wants from my room at Meeks Street. George gets the watch in my dresser drawer. I promised it to him if I didn't make it back from some jaunt."

"You're making it back from this one." Grey lifted the cloth and looked at the wound.

"Orders. You know how I am about obeying orders. Are you going to keep gawking at the bullet hole? Grotesque, if you want my opinion." Adrian fixed his eyes on the crack that ran across the plaster ceiling. "Grey, if the fever comes back . . . Don't let me talk."

The Hawker had more than his fair share of secrets. "I won't."

"Thanks." He took a deep breath. "Oh. Money. There's a pile of it at Hoare's Bank under the name Adrian Hawker. And some deeds." He winced as the cloth lifted. "Find Black John. I'm godfather, if you can believe it, to his oldest son. The money goes to the boy." Another deep breath. "I think I owe the tailor. Pay it off for me, will you."

"You sound like Socrates over a mug of hemlock." He squeezed the cloth in hot water again and laid it back on the wound.

"Who's . . . ach . . . Who's Socrates?"

"A dead Greek. Annique admires him."

"Wasted on him, if he's dead. That is a woman born to be appreciated by some man who's warm and alive." Adrian's thin, dark face was a dozen shades paler than it should have been, but he managed an unconvincing leer. "Me, probably. She doesn't care for you at all, *mon vieux*."

"She's not supposed to like me. She's supposed to be afraid of me and stop trying to escape. She can like you." Grey worked awhile in silence, swabbing blood off the rest of the boy's chest. "I'm going to sit you up. Don't help. Let me do the work."

"Right."

The boy felt light, and brittle as glass, when Grey lifted him. He stuffed pillows to prop him up. "Rest a minute."

He tipped the dirty water out the window, down into the pawlike ivy that climbed the stone walls. It was a warm night. On the terrace below, men lingered late around the tables. They were local farmers mostly, but a few were travelers carrying the accents of Paris or Normandy. A pair of men playing cards chatted softly in the patois of the Brittany coast. Candles flickered on the tables, illuminating a peasant cap, a fashionable chapeau, and a shock of fair hair. One of Roussel's plump, dark-haired daughters sidled between the men, collecting glasses. Beyond the innyard gate, the shadowed fields were full of the trill of crickets.

They'd be safe tonight, in this tiny village, in this obscure inn, which was a waystation of the British spy network in France. Tomorrow was going to be hell.

The bed creaked. "You're handling her wrong," Adrian said. "She's battering herself to bits against you. It's sickening."

"Tell me something I don't know. It's like wrestling a starved cat."

But he lied. It was wrestling lightning wrapped in silk.

Annique Villiers wouldn't admit she was beaten. Desperately, madly, she kept throwing herself against him, trying to get out of the coach. Again and again, he'd trapped a kicking, writhing, squirming body beneath him. Every time he pinned her, she'd sigh and lie back and accept another defeat. The sharp angles melted. The pulsing energy went quiescent in his hands. It was like the soft, sweet letting go of a woman after climax. She was everything beautiful and insidious. Addictive as opium.

Hell of a way for a senior officer to feel about a treacherous French bitch. "I'm trying not to hurt her. It's not easy. She's fast as a little cobra." He put the dressing in place and set Adrian's hand to cover it. "Press hard." He tied up the last corner of bandage. "I doubt she's looking forward to the discussions I have planned. I know what's she's done."

Will Doyle pushed into the room, balancing a tray. "What *has* she done?" He had a roll of clothing bundled under his arm, a swirl of burgundy and white, moss green and slate blue. He edged the door shut with his foot. "Besides run rings around us in Italy and Austria the last couple years?"

"You're supposed to be watching her."

"I put a pair of Roussel's boys at the door and window. Annique Villiers ain't going to run when there's thirty people milling around downstairs. She's not an idiot. Robert, there's something wrong with her."

"I don't have to hear this from you, too."

"She wouldn't even turn around and talk to me. Not a word." Doyle slid the tray to the table and dropped clothes in a heap on top of the dresser. "I saw her at work in Vienna. She chatters like a magpie. Something's wrong when she shuts up."

"I've hurt her then." *All those tiny bones, strung together with catgut. So fragile.*

"Or Leblanc did. He had her longer than we did."

He didn't want to think about her being hurt. It was too

easy to feel sympathy. Too easy to forget what she was. "I'll take a look at her when I put her to bed."

"That's an intriguing notion," Adrian said. "Wasted on you, I expect."

"And ain't you feeling better." Doyle lifted the napkin tented over a flowered blue and white bowl and sniffed appreciatively. "Roussel's stew. Leeks and chervil, smells like." He tipped a spoon into the bowl and handed it to Adrian with a brusque, "Eat."

"To hear is to obey. Toss me some of that bread while you're at it."

Doyle tucked the loaf against his forearm and sawed a slice with quick, practiced strokes. "I been downstairs making excuses to Roussel—who wants your blood, by the way, Robert, for bringing her here. I pretended to know what's going on. You going to explain?"

"One lives in hope," Adrian said piously.

Doyle said, "You start discussing that stew with yer belly. The Head of Section don't explain himself to the likes of—"

A sharp crash broke the peace. Outside and nearby. Doyle froze. Adrian's eyes snapped to the window.

My gun's in my bag, on top, loaded. There's another in Hawker's. Doyle carries his on him. The stairs are defensible. They'd—

Masculine laughter rumbled over the sound of a woman's rueful giggle. Chairs scraped on the stone. A dozen low-voiced conversations resumed. It was some kitchen mishap. Not Leblanc's men. Not yet.

Grey took his hand off the valise. "I've been out of action too long."

Adrian slid a dark, thin-bladed knife back under the covers.

"We're all on edge," Doyle said, "not least from having that damned dangerous woman locked up in the next room. Are we going to get rid of her any time in the foreseeable future?"

"He's going to drag her all the way to Meeks Street. I'd lay money on it. Any brandy on that tray?"

"For you, wine." Doyle uncorked the jug with his teeth. "I gave her that indecent nightgown, Robert. She weren't best pleased."

"I'm not trying to please her."

Doyle slopped wine into a glass, then added water till the deep red went pale. "I don't like what you're planning for that girl."

"I'm listening."

"First off, I don't like dressing Annique Villiers in some whore's castoffs." Doyle nodded to the bright dresses heaped on the table. "That's what Roussel had in the storeroom—the leavings of some ladybird who flew off without paying. It'll fit her, but it's brothel wear."

"She's worn less in the service of France." He picked up a dress. The complex, enigmatic blue was the color of her eyes. Thin, soft cotton clung to his fingers. Brothel wear. "Very nice. Paris work."

"Not the garb to blend into a Normandy village, is it? She won't get far if she gets loose." Adrian took the glass. "There's a bench in hell reserved for men who water good wine."

Doyle poked around the tray and helped himself to a flaky square of pastry. "You can read print through some of those dresses. It's going to be distracting."

"She could wear sackcloth and be distracting." When he put Annique in this, she'd look like what she was—an expensive courtesan, a woman born to entice men. She sold those sweet little breasts like apples in the market. "I watched her take Henri Bréval down with a cosh she slid behind her skirt. These won't hide a toothpick."

"You're making a mistake, Robert. She's one of us. One of the best. She's been in the Game since she was a child. You don't take one of the great players and treat her like a doxy. You put her in that nightgown or one of these flimsy dresses and you're going to start thinking she's a whore."

"She's not. For one thing," Adrian chased vegetables around the bottom of the bowl, "she can kill you with the odd bit she finds lying around the house."

"She's probably stropping something down to a sharp edge right now." Doyle scratched the scar on his cheek. It was a clever fake. When he wore it a long time, it itched. "She's not really safe, left alone for any length of time. I do wish that girl worked for us."

"No, you don't." Grey crossed the room, hunkered down at the hearth, and set a thin log of beechwood on the fire. They'd need more wood in here. Adrian would feel the chill if his fever came back. The flames teased him with images, flickering and writhing. In tongues of fire, a dozen Anniques danced Gypsy dances, gleaming with sweat, sleek with scented oil. "She was at Bruges."

He could feel the change in the room.

"Bruges," Doyle said.

"I was in the market square, in the café by the tower, waiting to be met. On the other side of the square was a half-grown Gypsy boy, juggling. He had four or five knives in the air, laughing. Enjoying himself the whole time."

"Annique," Doyle said.

"Annique."

"I've heard she makes a reasonably convincing boy."

"I didn't know she was a woman till I saw her at Leblanc's."

He'd nursed a cup of coffee, there in the square at Bruges, letting himself soak in some of that joy and brightness, letting it seep through the tense watch he was keeping. He'd remembered, later, that he'd been glad to see that boy. "He made a game of it, throwing 'em, hitting small, exact targets. Collected a fair capful of coins before he wandered off."

"She's good with knives. Not up to the Hawker's standard, but good."

"Nobody's up to my standards," Adrian said.

There were pinecones in the box on the hearth. Grey lay a few on the fire and shifted logs with his fingers, coaxing a draft in. "An hour later Fletch came to tell me they'd been ambushed, and the gold was gone. McGill, Wainwright, and Tenn's brother were dead."

Adrian put his bowl on the table. "I served with Wainwright in Paris."

"Tenn's brother was one of mine," Doyle said. "That was his second mission. Stephen Tennant. I took it hard when I heard." He hooked his thumb into the boy's bowl, tilted it, and looked in. "You going to finish this?"

"No."

"Drink the wine, then." Doyle stacked plate and bowl with big, tough hands. "It was supposed to be an easy exchange. The Albion plans for the gold."

The Albion plans were the tactical details for Napoleon's invasion of England: the exhaustive accounting of troops, supplies, ships, routes, timetables; the date of the invasion; the landing points and the routes inland; the alternate dates for bad weather.

With the plans, the English could turn back the invasion. Or they could ambush the incoming French fleet and blow it from the water. The plans were a priceless mine of intelligence about France: the strength of every ship, the soldiers of every company, the production of every factory. They could turn the balance of power.

Thirty-six complete copies had been made. One copy, rumor said, had gone missing. When the offer came, he should have smelled treachery. The asking price was a handful of gold. Nothing. He'd have paid a hundred times that.

He'd jumped at the chance to buy the plans and led his men into a trap and let them die. His mistake. His responsibility. "She was in Bruges. I've been looking for that Gypsy for six months."

Doyle said, "You think she did it? Because it was knife work?"

"They died from single, exact hits to the neck. Expert throws, made from ambush. The French meant to kill us, right from the beginning."

Doyle was already shaking his head. "It's not her. The girl was trained by Vauban, for God's sake. That was a bloody, clumsy business at Bruges. Vauban wouldn't have touched it with a barge pole."

"Bloody, not clumsy," Grey said. "Three neat, identical wounds. How many people throw like that? And she was there."

"It's not her. Hawker?"

"It's not her style." Adrian took a sip of watered wine and grimaced. "We get reputations in the Game—you, me, Doyle, all of us. Annique Villiers is playful and wise and stealthy. Slip in, slip out, and you never know she's been there. If she killed anybody, I never heard about it."

"That just means she's good enough not to get caught." Grey poked the fire a last time and stood up. "Leblanc says Vauban had the Albion plans."

Adrian snorted. "Leblanc's an idiot."

"A truth widely known." Doyle fingered the stubble on his chin. "But Vauban, meddling with treason? That incorruptible old revolutionary? I don't believe it. Easy to accuse him now he's dead, but—"

"Vauban's dead?" Adrian moved incautiously and winced and put his hand up to the bandage.

"You hadn't heard? The news is slow making the rounds. He died in his sleep. Ah . . . I guess it was six weeks ago. He was the last of the old guard. We won't see his like again." Doyle dropped the napkin on the tray. "I can tell you this, though—Vauban would chop off his own ballocks before he'd sell French secrets. That girl's been with him since she was a pup. She's made of the same steel he was."

Annique was in it up to her pretty eyebrows. Grey could

see that, even if Doyle and Adrian didn't. He'd know for sure once he got her behind the bars at Meeks Street. He'd find out where she stashed the Albion plans. Give him a few weeks, and he'd know the color of her bedroom walls when she was seven. "You need me anymore? Adrian?"

"I'll manage. You're wrong about her, you know."

"I'll find out, won't I? I'll go eat and wash, then get her settled in." He had control of his voice, but the latch clanked savagely in his hand as he opened the door.

Damned if he'd fight her again. Or maybe this time she'd play the whore and offer to part those sweet thighs for him. If she offered, maybe he'd just take her. They could wrap themselves around each other and tussle that way for a change. He'd use her and roll aside and forget her. There'd be no magic to the woman when she was slick and sweaty underneath him. She'd be just another warm, willing body.

That was a damned unprofessional way to think about a prisoner. "And maybe I'll just chain her to the bed." He didn't glance back.

Doyle said, "Robert . . ."

Adrian said quietly. "Let him go. It's between them, now."

Five

"IT'S DARK IN HERE." GREY'S VOICE WAS A RASP of sandpaper and velvet. He spoke in the familiar form, as one speaks to the most intimate of friends or to children or animals or servants. Or prostitutes.

"Light candles if you wish. It makes no difference to me." She spoke in the formal mode of speaking, which is how one talks to foreign spies who have kidnapped you.

"I thought Doyle told you to get into the nightgown."

"He did, most certainly. I will let you know if ever I begin taking orders from Monsieur Doyle." She faced the window, the nightgown twisted between her hands, and did not turn toward him. The night ahead would be one of immeasurable difficulty.

Wind came to her off the fields, smelling of cows and the earth and apples. She felt a longing, sharp as a physical pain, to see the fields and the stars above them. It never left her in all these months, that ache.

The shirt she wore billowed loose, then flattened possessively over her breasts and her hips, then blew loose again.

Grey's shirt. She had some wide knowledge of men. There were those who would find her alluring, so incongruously within a man's shirt, with her feet bare on the floor and her hair *farouche* and uncombed about her face. In the so-obvious silk rag she held in her fingers, she would look the whore. Wearing a man's shirt, she appeared the wise and subtle courtesan. There were no right choices for her tonight.

She heard him lock the door behind him.

"You've decked yourself out in my shirt. Well, well, well." He was never without that undercurrent of incomprehensible anger when he spoke to her. "Maybe I should have expected that. The nightgown is blatant. Nobody could accuse you of being blatant."

"Have you not tormented me enough for the sin of being French and a spy? This is the middle of France, Monsieur Grey. I am not your lawful prey. Let me go. It is the only sensible answer for any of us."

"After you give me the Albion plans. We'll pay, you know, if that sort of thing matters to you. Extravagantly."

Oh, but Leblanc had much to answer for. It was the final straw among great heaps of straw that his words should set this English upon her, demanding the Albion plans.

How much she would like to say, "You desire the Albion plans? But yes, I have them tucked here in my garter, you see? Take them away and stop Monsieur Napoleon from making this stupid invasion of your island, which will kill many thousand French soldiers and countless English and will not succeed at all."

It was not that simple. It had never been that simple.

She lied, immediately and convincingly. "I do not have these plans. Never, not once, have I laid eyes upon them."

"You lie well. I suppose I'm not the first man to tell you that."

She hit the windowsill with her fist. "No and no! I am sick of this folly. Leblanc spits poison like a toad and you believe him for reasons wholly incomprehensible. You kidnap me into Normandy for nothing. You endanger me and yourself with this mad insistence to—"

"Turn around and look at me. I'm damned tired of talking to your back."

"You, I do not find attractive or interesting. In fact, I wish you would go away altogether."

Adamant hands gripped her and turned her, without pain, but very, very firmly. She kept her head lowered, concealing her face from him in the dark.

"You're thinking about fighting me. Don't. Believe me, little fox, you wouldn't like what I'd do to you. Don't make me show you how thoroughly you're trapped."

"Trapped? But yes, I admit it freely. I am easy to snare these days. A dolt like Henri can do it."

"I haven't found it particularly easy. I'm changing the rules of this game we play."

"I do not play games against Grey of the British Service. I would not dare."

"You're playing one now."

Where the many nerves ran in the joining at her shoulder, his fingers explored, drawing idle, poignant circles, which entirely paralyzed her. Then he slid, smooth and slow, down her arm. How powerless it made her feel to learn his hands could secure themselves around her upper arm like large bracelets. At her elbow he found a great sensitivity.

Fighting points. He caressed the fighting points, lingering till she shivered with it. She had never thought of this obvious truth. At the weak places where one strikes an opponent, the nerves run exposed and vulnerable and receptive. Receptive to any touch. He knew that. It was disheartening to encounter so much admirable expertise in an opponent.

She squeezed her eyes closed and wished for the hundredth time she could see his expression and guess what he was going to do to her. Nothing so simple as to hurt her.

The rumble of his voice vibrated across her skin. "That shirt's more erotic than I would have believed possible. To see my shirt wrapped around you and know there's nothing . . . but you . . . underneath it." He plucked at the fabric, considering it with his fingertips. "You take the prerogatives of a longtime lover when you help yourself to my clothes. I should be disarmed. Clever Annique."

"I am not so clever," she muttered, being sincere.

His hand traveled to rest over her heart. "You have exactly the right number of buttons undone. I congratulate you. One less, and you'd be playing the timid virgin." He slipped two fingers into the shirt, tugged briefly, and left the top button loosed behind him. "Virgin isn't a convincing role for you."

He could say such things to a woman he was going to take to his bed. She could not reason with him when he was like this. She could do nothing but stand and listen to him and tremble everywhere.

He stroked downward and found the next button. "Too many unfastened, and there's no challenge to it." He slid it open. "Men enjoy challenges."

The beat of her heart shook her whole body. Did he know she was growing excited for him, at that place between her legs where he would want to pleasure himself? It was most probable he did.

He set another button free. He would have her naked soon. Her plan of reasoning with him did not seem to be working.

"A man itches to peel you, veil by veil, laying your secrets bare, opening you up to reveal mysteries."

Her body was not mysterious in that place he so poetically discussed, merely hot and anxious. She squeezed herself together, which did not help, but indeed made things worse. She could not stop herself doing it either, again and again, so matters grew progressively more complicated for her. "Me, I have no mysteries. You delude yourself."

"It would be so easy to lure the honey out of you. All I have to do is this . . ." His fingers grazed her breast, through the shirt. ". . . and two sweet little berries come nudging up against the cloth, begging to be tasted. Like that. Yes. That's honest enough. It might be the only kind of honesty you have in you."

"Do not be superior. You know nothing about me."

"I know you like your work. Not every woman would. You give us exactly what we want, don't you, pretty Annique? Leblanc. Henri. Me. You become every man's private fantasy. What he dreams of, alone at midnight. You're doing it now. Before I realize what I want, you're offering it to me. I never knew a woman could do that. A man touches you in peril of his soul."

"You may keep your soul. I do not want it."

"I don't give a damn what you want, Annique Villiers. You're good, though. That sound you make in your throat, that buzzing like a hive of contented bees. That's perfect. I felt it through my whole body when you did that."

His muscles were dense with tension, shaking. That was his anger, which she had not yet earned, and his hunger for her, which would have been obvious to an idiot. How she was to ride these twin beasts to her advantage she could not at all imagine.

"You like to set the puppets dancing, don't you? Tweak a string here. Tweak a string there. Be soft and vulnerable and . . . responsive. I don't think there's a man on earth who could resist you."

Without warning, he twisted his fist into the shirt and pulled tight. She was jerked and dragged forward, up onto her toes. She gasped and grabbed to hold on to him. "Don't try this again." He shook her, once, briskly. "Not with me."

"I do not—"

"No more games. Go shuck yourself out of this damned teasing shirt. Put on the silk I sent in or slither into bed naked. I don't care which."

"I will not wear that indecent thing. I am not—" She stopped herself and swallowed and made herself say, "I am not some woman of the streets to be bought for the price of a hot meal. I do not—"

"For God's sake, don't be so bloody dramatic." She was set upon her feet. His grip loosened slowly and released. "And damn your nonexistent modesty. From now on you wear clothes you can't hide weapons in. That's all. Get in bed and sleep."

"I will sleep as the mouse sleeps beside the cat. Do not lie to me, English. I have no patience with it."

"I don't have a hell of a lot of patience myself right now. So unless you're offering me a poke at this . . ." The deep vee of her shirt flipped open. Cool air rushed in. ". . . experienced, devious little body, get into that nightgown and get to bed."

"Monsieur, do not do this to me."

"Not a damn thing's going to happen to you if you behave. You follow orders, and you'll be treated well. Fight me one more time, and I swear I'll tie you to the bedpost. Accept it."

Accept it, he said. But he lied to her and to himself, too, if he thought he would lay her down in that soft bed and not take her.

He was no monster. He would not force her. But he wanted her fiercely, and he thought she was of light morals, and willing. Tonight, in the long quiet hours, he would put his hands upon her and confuse her until she made the answers he wished, softly, in the intimacy of the covers. In the end he might make her want what he did to her. She was not strong and sensible when it came to this man.

That was yet another reason she must escape.

When all other weapons are gone, one must depend upon cunning and lies and terrible schemes. Vauban had taught her that. Maman had taught her. René and Françoise and wise, cynical old Soulier had taught her that—all her old friends in the spying Game. She had known this since she was a child. Sometimes one must do things one does not exactly like.

She could not commit despicable acts as Annique. She must be someone of greater resolution. There were roles within her . . . She took a steadying breath and chose. She would be the Worldly Courtesan. Had she not played this role often in Vienna?

She crossed her arms over her breasts and bowed her head and let the role of the Courtesan settle across her spirit. It wrapped round her like a thick, protective cloak. The Worldly Courtesan was years older than Annique, knowing and cynical. She did not give a fig whatsoever about an enemy English. The Courtesan would not worry about wearing that obscene scrap of cloth . . . or whatever else it might become necessary to do.

She raised her chin. The Courtesan was not dismayed because a man desired her. It gave her power.

She shrugged. "You have won this futile small victory of yours." Being the Courtesan, she could push past Grey, impatient and contemptuous, and saunter across the room. It was three long steps from the window to the table; she had counted after dinner. She turned her back on him and tossed the slippery silk of the nightgown across the table, next to the candlestick. She touched that one last time. Her bones and muscles would remember where it was when all was in disorder. The scene was set. Everything was prepared.

"Go away. I will dress in this vulgar garment. But I will not strip naked in front of you." Her voice was cool and patrician, heavy with ennui. The Courtesan's voice. She set two fingers on the tabletop to keep her body oriented exactly as she wanted it. "Whatever you think, I am not a woman of light amusements with strangers."

"It's too dark to see much. Do it now, before I strip you down and toss you into bed myself."

"How alluring you make it sound." The Courtesan she

had molded around her mind could say that. "With the women of England you are a great success with such methods, no?" Playing the Courtesan, she could reach nonchalantly for the hem of the shirt, as if she undressed every night in some man's company. "If you will not leave, at least turn your back."

"To preserve your modesty?"

"It is not such a large favor to ask. I am less accustomed to humiliation than you seem to think." The shell of her role cracked, and a quaver of her shame and fear showed through. She could not have done better if she'd practiced a week.

"That much I can do."

She heard the rustle of his movement. Now she must undress. It was hard, playing the whore, the first of several difficult acts. She lifted the shirt up over her head and revealed her nakedness. Perhaps the room was dark enough that he would see nothing. Perhaps he had turned his back as he said. If not, she must hope he would be distracted, as men always were by her body, and not notice exactly what she was doing.

Now. No more delay. Now.

One. Two. Three. She tossed the shirt onto the table. Under cover of that, she picked up the heavy brass candlestick. She flipped it to be a club. Spun toward Grey. Lunged toward the sound of his breathing and swung.

Missed.

She staggered, off balance. Where was he? She tried to hear him. Where?

A whisper of air. Pain exploded in her wrist. She dropped her weapon. He'd kicked her wrist. Hit the bone of it. The candlestick rolled clattering on the floor.

"Sapristi!" Such pain. This was disaster. She had made a miscalculation of great magnitude. She backed away quickly, unarmed and naked before him, shaking her hand out to get feeling back within it. "You are fast, monsieur."

"Fast enough."

Another step back. Here was the table. Thank *le bon Dieu.* She scurried for the other side, plucking across the wood till she touched silk. The nightgown. "You did not look away. That was deceitful."

"Let's talk about deceit, shall we?"

"That is a problem between us, I agree."

Feverishly, she grappled with the nightgown, one-handed and clumsy. It was vital she get this on. She got it right side up and pulled it around her and pushed one arm into the sleeve, then the other. Here was the cord. Good. Very good. Fumbling, she tied it.

He made his way around the table, edging her ahead of him by slow, deliberate footfalls. She was not stupid enough to think she could escape. It was no surprise to feel his hands close on her, gentle and insistent, as if he held a sack of rebellious eggs. He was being careful with her. His hunger for her vibrated between them like discordant music. His touch was perfectly impersonal. She was totally unnerved by this.

He said, "You've decided then. I tie you up. It's simpler this way."

"Undoubtedly." Her voice was ragged in her ears. "But I would much rather you did not."

"At last. You've said something I believe." He backed her toward the bed, step by step. Not roughly. Gradually. A little pressure was all he needed. "Prudent of you to put on the nightgown, even if it's too late. Were you planning to kill me with that candlestick?"

"I would not kill you on purpose, but I am clumsy these days and might have misjudged. Is there anything at all I can say to keep you from doing this to me?" She was trembling badly.

"Nothing I can think of, right off."

"What if I promise not to try to escape again, not at all, till we reach England?"

"No." He was most chillingly ordinary and calm. "I have extra bandages I don't need for Adrian. I'll use those. They're nice and soft." How provident of him. Perhaps he took prisoners frequently. How would she know what the British did? "It won't be too uncomfortable. You may even get some sleep."

"I am harmless, really. You should reconsider."

"You don't have to be afraid," he said. "I don't hurt women. Not even women like you."

More of his incomprehensible insults. As if he did not have his dozens of women agents working for his Service. It was illogical that he should despise her.

The mattress bumped against her thigh. He twisted the hold upon her shoulder shrewdly, and she lost her balance and fell downward onto the bed. Coverlets flapped and clung as she scrambled away from him through the treacherous softness, to the wall. That was as far as she could flee. Her back pressed to the cold plaster. Silk slicked against her skin. She drew herself together and set her face to her knees. The Fox Cub was cornered at last.

All her clever roles had deserted her. No one was left to deal with this situation but Annique. And Annique was afraid. Afraid.

She listened to him cross the room. The leather valise creaked. Small sounds told her he searched within it. Then his steps returned toward her.

"Grey . . . monsieur . . . I will promise not to attack you again. I will swear it by whatever you like."

The bed sagged as he sat next to her. "You could offer me a couple French secrets. Maybe the ones you were discussing with Leblanc."

"The Albion plans." She made herself say it lightly. "Leblanc obsesses himself with them lately."

"I'm obsessed with them myself. We're going to talk about the Albion plans for a good long time, you and I."

She was cold inside. Cold and sick. "But this is foolish.

I am a small player in the Game. I do not make the grand political intrigues. You will be disappointed if you expect important secrets from me."

"You won't disappoint me." There were many nuances in his voice.

The bed jiggled as he worked with something in his hands. That would be the linen bandages he spoke of—the ones he would tie her with. He was preparing them. Soon she would be helpless and all chance of escape gone.

"I do not wish to be tied up," she whispered.

"I don't think you can convince me. You could try, though. Offer me just a small secret, and we'll see."

Not secrets. Something else. She had known, deep in her heart, that it would come to this.

One last plan. There is always a last plan one has hoped not to use. She gathered the silken nightdress about her and crawled toward him, to his side, till she was close. Till she could almost feel the heat from his body. She made herself kneel on the bed, her knees apart. She had seen prostitutes do this in the whorehouse her mother kept for a time in Paris. Doubtless Monsieur Grey had visited many whorehouses and would recognize what she offered.

She heard him draw in a deep, uneven breath. The bed dipped as he shifted his weight. His finger closed on her arm, but he only brought her right wrist upward. "Did I hurt you?"

"No." Smoothly, she eased her hand away from him. "It is nothing."

"That's another reason I don't want to fight you. I'll end up hurting you again. I don't want to hurt you."

"I do not want you to hurt me either. Or tie me up."

He gave a grunt. She felt him turn away. And still his breath was unsteady.

The Courtesan had no fear of any man living. No fear of touching and being touched. Ageless knowledge had the Courtesan.

It was time to begin. She found the long, smooth cord

and pulled the knot free. It was thin, twisted silk, very strong. Her night-robe slid open, like wind unfolding. He would feel the silk fall upon his skin. Even in the darkness, he would see her body as light and shadow. She felt herself blush.

She whispered, "It has its own appeal, you understand—to be tied. But it is limiting. I would rather be . . . inventive." It might have been the Courtesan who reached out to caress him, full of knowledge. It might have been Annique, being curious.

The skin of his neck was dry and warm, rough in texture. To touch him did not feel like stroking an animal or her own skin. His cheek was a landscape of bristles with the muscles of his jaw bunched tight beneath. His mouth, unexpectedly, was silk. It opened under her fingertips, and she felt the touch of his tongue. She did not know what to do when a man tasted her fingers. It brought a shamed little clench of heat between her legs. If she'd allowed herself, she would have been scared silly.

He said, "What do you want?"

"I will not speak secrets. But I will please you, if you give me one final chance."

"How very tempting. Why?"

"Perhaps I am tired of fighting. It grows discouraging."

"That's not it. Tell me why."

So stern. He must trust her enough to let her close. In the silence, she could hear the crickets from the fields and the murmur of voices in the courtyard below.

"I desire you." Truth. She would tell him truth. How ironic. "I desired you when I first touched you, in Leblanc's small dungeon. In the coach, when we fought . . ." She drew words from the deepest privacy of her mind. "It is a great intimacy to fight with a man as I have fought you."

"I'll grant you that. It's intimate."

"We fought. But you did not hurt me. You were entirely exasperated with me and you held me down, very heavy on top of me. I imagined . . . how it would be in bed with you." Each word was a humiliation, stripping her mind as naked as her body. But this would fascinate a man like Grey. This would distract him. "I am . . . at need, inside me."

"Awkward for you."

"I do not wish to feel this way. We are enemies." He could not begin to imagine the awkwardness it was for her. Even now, when she should be wholly involved in useful schemes and lies, a warm trickle of wanting coursed through her. If things had been different . . . She put the thought away.

Her fingers, hidden in the folds of her nightdress, worked away at the cord of the nightgown. She slid it, inch by inch, out of the long casing that held it. "We need not be enemies, in the dark, where no one sees. What happens in this room . . . it is as if it has not happened at all."

"An intriguing thought."

"You may tie me up afterwards if you wish. You have made no promises." Amazing to hear that teasing in her voice. She crept an inch closer to him.

"I can tie you up right now. I don't trust you worth a damn."

"You are wise not to trust me. But sometimes I am not an agent of France. Sometimes, I am only Annique."

His weight shifted again. She heard a metallic click as his ring touched the table beside the bed. He was setting something there. He had turned away from her.

She wound the silk cord quickly, three times, around her left hand. When she leaned toward him, she touched his back. She lay her forehead upon the hard prominence of his shoulder blade. "Here in the dark . . . I can be anything you want." The ache between her legs, which was the ache of wanting him to be exactly in that place, throbbed.

She kissed through the thin linen of his shirt. His muscles twitched under her lips. He had formidable control, Grey, as a man in his position must, but he was not indifferent. He was stretched taut in every tendon, ferocious with wanting her, vulnerable as a strong man is to his own passions. She moved to the bare skin of his neck and tasted that.

"You take a lot for granted," he growled.

She laughed, a deep, throaty sound, copied exactly from Maman. "I will do nothing you do not desire."

She wrapped the silk line around her right palm. Once, twice. Again. In her lap, two feet of slack stretched between her fists. She pressed close to him. She must be very close to do what she intended.

Oh, but it was hard for her. Touching him unnerved her beyond bearing. Her naked breasts brushed warm cloth, heated by the muscles beneath. The shock of it struck through her like twin lightnings. She could not remember to breathe. She was wholly the stunned rabbit.

He rumbled deep in his chest, like a mountain, grumbling before an earthquake.

Somehow, the Courtesan within her knew what was to be done next. There was the back of his neck to be kissed, again and again, working her way upward along leathery muscles. The sudden taste and texture of his hair against her mouth made her quiver, it was so surprising.

He would feel that shiver through her. It would make her seem more harmless. If only her mind did not skip and skitter so. She opened and closed her hands, where they held the wrapped cord.

She rose up, kneeling, and took his ear into her mouth to lick it and swirl it with her tongue, finding it bitter and salty and oddly shaped. She bit down gently. She had wanted to do this to a man for some time, to see what it was like.

Almost time . . . almost . . . The silk cord was damp in her hands. *I will not hurt you,* she promised silently. *I will take immense care.*

"I was wrong. You can be blatant." Grey's touch came to her thigh. He would push her away in a moment, or pull her to him. She was not sure which. But she knew he could stand no more. "What happened to that finesse of yours?"

Now. It had to be now. *I do not want to do this. I do not want to do this at all.*

She whispered, "I am all finesse."

One so-slight pull on the silken cord between her hands. She crossed her arms and made a loop of it and leaned forward. She kissed him softly, just under the ear. With the kiss, she flipped the cord over his head and circled his neck. She snapped it closed and jerked hard, cutting off his air.

Six

HIS LUNGS CONVULSED. A DEMON WEIGHT CLAMPED HIS back, locked at his throat, choked him, pulled him down. He grappled at it with numb hands. He couldn't . . .

He threw himself back and forth, trying to beat off the enemy that held him. Black alternated with red flashes. He twisted. Punched out with his last strength. He didn't feel the impact when he hit.

Too late. The thought spiraled with him, down into nothingness. This was what it felt like to die.

Suddenly the intolerable pressure on his throat was gone. He sucked air. Agony swept through his chest. The world washed blood red as he kicked and pushed free. He rolled away fast, ran into a wall, and wedged his back against it. Gasping, he waited for the next attack.

It was dark when he opened his eyes. Night. That was why he didn't hear guns and horses. The battle was over. He'd been left behind, wounded, for the human vultures that scavenged the death fields. Where were his men? They wouldn't have left him. They'd lost then. Disorderly retreat. A rout.

Beside him, someone was choking. Maybe dying.

There was softness under him. Not dirt. He bunched up a handful. It was . . . cloth. The disorientation was so great it made him dizzy. Then he knew. He was in bed, not on the battlefield. In France, at Roussel's inn.

Fighting Annique Villiers.

The death rattle beside him was Annique. He remembered now. He'd hit her. Hit her with fists that could kill a grown man. *What have I done?*

It was too dark to see, but he could hear her. He found the curve of a hip and ran his hands up and down her body. She was naked and she shook like she was breaking apart. *Hell. Oh, hell.*

He needed light. He staggered up and blundered across the room. In the hearth, the embers were alive under the ashes. He kicked, flat-footed, at the logs till orange showed through. The candle was on the mantelpiece. He held it to the ember, snarling with impatience, for the long second it took the wick to catch fire.

She was on the mattress, bent double, clutching her stomach.

He slapped the candle onto the spike of a holder. She was pale as the sheet, gasping for air. When he took hold of her, her skin was cold and clammy. He flipped the whole defensive ball of her onto her back. Eyes wide and blank and blind as a doll's slid past him with no recognition. It scared the hell out of him.

Where did I hit you?

There was no blood on her face, no mark on her throat. Thank God for that. He'd hit her only once—he was almost sure of it. Only once. If he'd battered into those fragile little bones on her face, she'd have shattered like glass.

She was wrapped around her belly, so that must be where he'd hurt her. Her rib cage. Had he broken her ribs? He felt down her sides, probing fast, line by line. He'd feel a break in her ribs, wouldn't he? She had thin, delicate bones with no flesh on them. He'd feel a break.

He pulled her into his lap. It took only little force to pull her arms away, a little more to unroll her enough to see what was what.

Little breasts. Pale skin. Just below her heart, surrounded by old bruises, was a red mark the size of his fist. He'd slammed her dead center in the solar plexus. No wonder she couldn't breathe.

"Lie still. You've had the wind knocked out of you. That's all." *Dear God, I hope that's all.* Her diaphragm was hard as a board. She was fighting her own lungs. "Easy now. There's plenty of air."

"C . . . c . . . aa . . ."

Nothing broken on the arch of her rib cage. Nothing he could feel. "Your chest's clamped down where I hit you. You'll be fine in a minute." He pressed in with the heel of his hand, pushing those locked muscles, telling them they better damn well get back to work. "It's already getting better."

She scooped a breath in. Coughed. Every muscle spasmed.

"I've got you. Easy now." He kept up a flow of meaningless words, massaging the rock-hard diaphragm while she arched back, dragging at air with her whole body. "Everything's fine. Steady. Steady, girl." He sounded like he was talking to one of his brother's high-strung mares. But it was working. She hauled in a sharp gasp and held it. Let it go. "That's better. That's right." Her hand clenched tight around his. He could feel her hanging on to the certainty in his voice.

Her head fell back against him. She pulled in long, jerky sobs. Let them out. Breathing. It sounded like she'd keep at it.

"You're going to be fine." Unless he'd cracked one of those ribs. Unless he'd hurt her inside where it didn't show. He pressed deep, hand by hand, across her belly, and she didn't wince any place in particular. That had to be a good sign.

He stroked from her breasts downward, again and again, over that abused diaphragm, down the flat plane between her hips. Her muscles were tight bunches, distinct and hard under his palm. She lay in his arms with her eyes closed, twitching hard about every third breath. Her breasts quivered when her breath rasped in and out. The nipples were lighter pink than he would have expected. That'd be because her skin was so white.

He kept stroking her belly, feeling her loosen and relax, muscle by muscle. She had satin skin with not an ounce of fat under it. The hair between her legs was ebony black and curly. Luxuriant as a little sable. Looked soft there.

"No! Let me go." She jerked away, flung herself to the far side of the bed, turned her back to him, and tucked herself tight as a hedgehog.

That was good. She wouldn't twist up into a pretzel if she had a broken rib. "You've got your breath back."

She faced the wall, taking deep breaths. "I guess we're no longer being friendly in the dark where it doesn't count," he said.

No answer.

Rags of the flame-colored nightgown wrapped around her, like she lay in the middle of a shredded exotic orchid. Her hair was inky black, stark on her white skin. She hadn't had an easy time of it lately. He could count her ribs. The shadow of old bruises marked her everywhere, a whole collection, in all stages of healing. Under the damage was a truly lovely body. Not lush, but perfectly shaped. If they'd made naked china figurines at that factory at Dresden, they'd have looked like her. Trust the French to find something this beautiful and make a spy of her.

The garrote she'd used snaked over the edge of the bed, absurdly red. That made it part of her nightgown and something he'd ordered into the room. Stupid of him.

It was twisted silk, unbreakable. An elegant and lethal weapon. If she'd wanted him dead, he'd be dead.

"One of us," Doyle had called her. "One of the best." Grey had her naked and battered and so weak she didn't even brush her hair back off her face. Utterly defeated. All he'd had to do was catch her starving and exhausted and on the run from every police agent in France. And knock her half-conscious. And outweigh her by seven stone and be a trained killer. Simple, really.

She'd attacked him with forty inches of goddamned nightgown cord.

Congratulations, Robert. Another French spy routed. Splendid job. Damn, but he hated fighting women.

The quilts had scattered to the floor in their little altercation. He picked one up and pulled it across her. With that, she finally acknowledged his existence. She pulled the quilt close, up to her chin, and curled into it. "Did I hurt you?"

Whatever he'd expected, it wasn't this. "Did you *what*?"

"With the garrote. Did I hurt you? I was afraid I would kill you. It is very dangerous to attack someone with the garrote. But I had no choice, so I ventured."

That was some mad logic for you. He sat on the bed and slipped his hand under the quilt, taking hold of her shoulder. She didn't react. She might not have noticed. "You ventured, did you?"

"When the candlestick did not work. It was my last reserve, the garrote. I was almost certain I would not kill you, but there is always a large element of chance."

That calm, considering voice was one of her lies. He didn't need to see her face to know that. In her skin he could feel the fine-grained trembling that said fear, exhaustion, numbness. Shock. He'd seen this in men after battle, in prisoners under questioning. Push a man hard enough, and he becomes detached, almost uncaring. Annique had come to that place.

"The element of chance," he prompted softly.

"I have no experience with the garrote, except one afternoon using it upon René, in Françoise's kitchen, when he taught me. He most certainly did not fight me so horribly as you do. I suppose it was because of the good china."

"The china would be a problem."

"Françoise would not have been pleased if we had broken her dishes." She pulled one hand out from under the quilt and scrubbed it across her face. "René thought I should become somewhat dangerous because I was so small. He taught me many deadly tricks, but they were never as useful as he expected." She let out a long sigh. "I should not have attempted the garrote. I knew that, but I did not listen to myself saying so. And it was useless anyway. I was clumsy and have done nothing but enrage and hurt you."

She hadn't been clumsy with the garrote. She'd lost control because she wasn't willing to kill him. "You didn't hurt me."

"Most likely I did, and you are being composed and manly about it. Though it is obvious I did not break your neck, which was my great fear." The quilt wriggled as she uncurled. "I will tell you I am not sorry in the least, even if I hurt you gravely, because you should not make off with me this way. It is wholly despicable to entrap women and kidnap them with you across France and force them to wear indecent nightclothes only because you do not trust them."

"We're in a despicable profession."

"I am reminded of this from time to time." She shrugged and shifted away. "You need not hold on to me. I am entirely subdued, I assure you."

"Docile as a lamb." He kept his hand on the intricate scaffolding of her collarbone. Tension radiated from where his palm rested. It intrigued him, that tension. Her body was telling him secrets.

"You are the skeptic. It is your profession, of course. Still, it is sad you cannot trust such great simplicity as I offer."

Simple? There was no end to the labyrinth inside Annique Villiers. He'd work his way through, given time. Already, he had one of her lies unraveled. He was almost sure . . .

He drew a finger along her shoulder and felt the shimmer of startled awareness. Nervousness danced under her skin. It was like stroking one of his brother's new colts, a young one that hadn't felt a man's touch yet.

Not jaded, not hardened. Not practiced and knowledgeable. How had he managed to convince himself this was a woman used to being handled by men? Adrian said she wasn't a whore, and Adrian was never wrong about women.

How many men, Annique? Not many, I'll bet. Did your masters keep you unawakened so you could play the boy more convincingly? Their mistake. It left her vulnerable. Achingly, ignorantly vulnerable. He'd use that against her, sooner or later. "What the devil am I going to do with you, Annique?"

"Let me go?"

"No. Not that."

"I did not think you would agree, though it would be wisest for both of us if I arose from this bed and went quietly into the night. You have no need to keep me."

"What happened at Bruges?" He felt her skin answer. She knew. "That's why I keep you. You might try trusting me. Better me than Leblanc."

"I am hoping to escape you both." She sighed. "Even now, there is a chance."

"It's possible. You're skilled." In his network of spies, he could count on his fingers the agents who matched Annique's caliber. A spy like this was worth a cavalry division. "That's one more reason I'm not letting you go."

"I have known several men of your type. None of them was amenable to reason." She sounded more and more resigned. "We come to an impasse, you and I. What will you do with me?"

"Damned if I know. Take you to England and decide there, probably. By then we'll understand each other better."

"I meant, what will you do with me tonight? I am eating life in very small bites these days, monsieur."

There were men who'd push the interrogation now—badger her, keep her groggy and talking and see what she'd give away. She was so exhausted she could barely think. Keep hammering away at her, and she'd start making mistakes. Scare her enough, mix it with a little sympathy, and she might break. He'd seen it a hundred times.

Except tactics like that wouldn't work with Annique Villiers, even if he could make himself do it.

"I won't do anything with you tonight. I won't tie you up, at any rate." He ran one last brisk caress across the tangled black mane. It was the first step in seduction, getting her used to being touched. Besides, he wanted to. "Do you think you can hold off killing me till after breakfast?"

"I must rest before I try again. It is very exhausting, fighting with you."

He laid a second quilt on top of the one she was wrapped in. It was just as well she didn't roll over and look at him. His arousal was obvious as hell. Maybe he'd let Doyle guard her tomorrow—imperturbable, thoroughly married William Doyle. "You might as well go to sleep. Unless Vauban and the others taught you some way to kill me with a feather pillow."

"They did." She snuggled into the warmth like a nesting animal, giving a deep, feminine chuckle. She found that amusing, did she?

The last quilt had found refuge under the bed. He fished it out and spread it across the rush-bottomed chair. When he propped his feet up on the windowsill, he pulled the ends around him. It would get cool later on.

Annique's chest rose and fell gently, slow and even. That either meant she was asleep, or she was getting ready to attack him again. He'd wait and see.

Seven

ANNIQUE WOKE LAZILY. SHE WAS WARM AND THE bed was soft. That was a great comfort to the many sore places on her body. She smelled bread baking.

She realized she was naked.

She snapped alert, knowing in an instant exactly where she was. It was not the first time she had awoken surrounded by enemies. She made not the least movement, allowed no change in her breathing. The quilt had slipped down her body at some time in the night. Now it slanted across her buttocks, not hiding them at all. Grey could see any of her he wished to. It made her feel odd inside, knowing that.

He was not in bed. It was not such a large bed one could lose an entire person in it. When she listened, she heard him breathing, off to the left.

How long had Grey looked upon her while she slept? Did he desire her? She did not want to hear that question in her mind, but it was most assuredly there.

She had always been a woman of measured detachment

toward men. Now she lay in bed hoping a spymaster of the British would look upon her nakedness and be aroused. It was, perhaps, a form of madness. In any case, she did not want it.

"I can tell you're awake." His voice came, closer than she'd expected. "You might as well get up and stop pretending."

"I am hoping you are a ghastly dream and will go away if I stay asleep long enough."

"I can't be a nightmare. It's morning, and I'm still here."

She sat up, pulling the quilt across her breasts. Her forehead she put down upon her knees to hide her face. She was entirely miserable about this whole situation. Leblanc might find her at any moment. She was plagued with an inconvenient passion for this English. She had no clothes. Soon she must face Grey, with open eyes, in the daylight. It was all most discouraging. "I am used to nightmares that are still there in the morning."

"Do you have any idea how silly it looks when a woman of your skills sulks like a five-year-old?"

"I do not sulk. Why do you not go away so I can get dressed." Perhaps Grey would wander somewhere else for a while or even fall off the face of the earth altogether if she were exceptionally fortunate.

"I'm not leaving you alone. I don't have time to hunt you down this morning. I don't want to fight with you either." He sounded impatient. "Look at me. I'm tired of talking to your spine and a handful of bedspread. I don't evaporate just because you ignore me."

She didn't move while he crossed the room toward her.

"I don't . . . For God's sake, will you look at me when I talk to you?"

It was time. When he was close, she lifted her head and faced him squarely and opened her eyes.

Darkness. As always. It had been darkness for five

months. She no longer expected anything else when she opened her eyes, unless she was roused suddenly from sleep and did not remember where she was.

He stopped abruptly. He was a man who did not make noise while he was thinking. Either he talked or he was silent. She waited. After a time, she felt a wind across her face. They tried that sometimes, waving their hands at her to see if she would blink.

"You're blind."

"I am not *blind.*" Always, it made her angry, these people who thought they knew everything. "I cannot see. That is all."

"Dear God." He took her chin tightly and tilted her face from side to side, though she could have told him nothing showed. "I can't believe this. How? When?"

For some reason she told him the truth. "Last May. It was not even a battle. Just a village and a . . . a game for a patrol riding through from one place to another. They destroyed that little place for no other reason than that they were armed men and bored and they could. I took a saber cut on the head."

She should not have spoken of it. Memory assaulted her—the last images she would see with her eyes. A bright tablecloth trampled by horses. The long, dark hair of a woman, flying loose as she tried to run. A man crumpled on the ground. Death after death. Even women and children. A village of innocents with no chance to fight back, dying for nothing at all.

Her eyes closed convulsively, and she pulled free from him and turned away, dragging her quilt with her. She took the pictures of death and folded them away small, as if she were packing winter clothes into a press and closing the lid tightly down. Mostly she did not think of that last day at all, except in bad dreams.

He said, "There's no mark."

"It is not the eyes themselves." She took a deep breath.

She hated speaking of this. "The doctor at the university in Marseilles—he was a very important man with unpleasant breath—said it is the head wound from the saber. Something presses upon the optic nerve, a knot of blood or a splinter of bone. With a great many Latin terms, he says this, you understand, since he is charging my mother a great deal of money for each long word."

She made a good broad gesture to take his attention away while she wiped her face with the other hand. A conjurer's trick. "If that something should go wandering about in this skull of mine, the so-important doctor says, I will see once more. But then I will most probably die at once. Or possibly not, which is the other choice. He does not commit himself. Instead he advises me not to get hit on the head again, which is advice anyone could have given without poking at me for an hour first. Me, I think he does not know very much." There. She had the tears wiped off. Perhaps he had not noticed.

"You've been like this for five months." She was not sure what was in his voice. It was not pity.

"I am not like this or like that. I am me, and I have been like me for much longer than five months. My eyes are not me."

He snorted in her face and took hold of her again to go searching through her hair for the thin, smooth scar above her temple. He drew the line of it with his fingertips. "Here, was it?"

"As I told you." She was furious with him that he examined her this way and she could not escape. To be naked before him was nothing to the exposure she felt when she uncovered this secret. She wished, oh most completely to the bottom of her heart, she wished she had escaped before she was forced to reveal this to Grey.

"It's healed cleanly," he said.

"Most pleasingly. I am told one cannot see the scar now that my hair has grown out again."

"You were with your mother when she died, weren't you? How did you get from Marseilles to Paris, blind?"

"It is no concern of—" His hands tightened on her. She decided not to try his temper further this morning. "I walked."

"You . . . walked? You didn't just walk. Not blind. Not alone."

"Maman has . . ." Pain clenched at her throat. Maman was dead. "Maman had . . . many friends. It was a network all her own from the years even before the Revolution. They helped me." So many people had helped her. Maman's network. Friends of Vauban. Friends of old Soulier, who had been Maman's lover and who was most senior in the Secret Police. Friends of her colleagues René and Françoise. Men who had known her father. Friends she had made herself over the years. She had come so far because of a legion of ordinary people she could call upon for a favor worth a life.

The British did not know how remarkable her memory was. Her mind held more than the Albion plans and her many, many secrets. Five thousand names and directions were safe in her head—names that meant sanctuary and aid in any corner of France. She would call upon some of them when she shook herself loose of Monsieur Grey. "I was passed from hand to hand for the whole way, until I was betrayed, and Henri came to take me to Leblanc."

He said nothing, just explored this scar of hers, which could be of no great interest since it was not in any way unusual. When that was finished, he thrust deep into her hair and held her head so she could not turn away. God only knew what he thought he would see. It was not the first time he had observed her, after all.

It disturbed her intensely to be touched by this man. She did not want to desire him. This hunger was something that had befallen her, like an illness. He was as unsuitable for a lover as a penguin or the shadow of a large tree. A hulking, grim stranger who was an enemy and in the profession of spying, which was a type she did not admire. She could not have chosen more stupidly.

His fingers combed through her hair to the end before he let it fall. It was strange to feel him do that, an intimacy no one attempted before. There had been a number of things she had done with this man and no other. More than she liked. She had not the smallest idea what was in his mind.

"You've mastered it well. Being blind." There was a note in his voice . . . Vauban had spoken to her in that way when she had done something that impressed him. For Vauban, she would have walked through fire to hear him speak to her so. Perhaps there were men who would do that for Grey.

"I am almost used to it, except that it is inconvenient and may get me killed soon."

"You're good at hiding it. I never guessed. Not once."

"It has been night, when I have been with you. Or I pretended to sleep, as I did in the coach."

There was more of this thoughtful pause. "This makes you easier to manage, doesn't it?"

She said, politely, "Henri was of your opinion, monsieur."

Incredibly, he laughed. He was truly the most heartless man she had ever encountered. She would not be coated with a treacle of sympathy by this one. "I won't make Henri's mistakes. I intend to take very good care of you, Annique."

For a Head of Section, he was also remarkably stupid. "Can you not see how this changes everything? Leblanc will have every soldier in France looking for a blind woman. I am the most dangerous luggage for you to cart around."

"Then we won't let anyone know you're blind."

Still he did not see. How could he be such a fool? "It is me Leblanc seeks. It is my mouth Leblanc must stop at all costs. I know such secrets about him . . . Let me go, monsieur, and he will follow me, not you."

This inn could not be so far from Vauban's small village. If Grey would only help her to go there. Vauban was old and tired now, his mind confused and wandering since the last attack. He could give her no orders for what must be done with the Albion plans. That lay upon her shoulders now. But she could sit beside Vauban's fire one last time and hold his hand and talk with him about little things that he still remembered. In Vauban's house she would find trusted friends to take her to the coast. From there, she would go to England and find safety with Soulier and make her decisions and, perhaps, become a traitor to France.

If Grey could be made to see reason . . . "Leblanc will not pursue uninteresting British spies only for the pleasure of committing slaughter upon them. In the Game, we do not kill one another in this bloodthirsty manner that would leave us all dead. Without me, you are safe."

Grey walked across the room. Not pacing. This one would always have a destination in mind when he set one foot in front of the other. When he came back he was carrying something. She could tell when people were carrying things. They walked differently. She had trained herself to notice this.

"The dress should fit. It's blue. And for God's sake, stop calling me monsieur. It's getting ridiculous, you trying to kill me and calling me Monsieur Grey in the next sentence." He dropped a bundle of clothing into her lap.

"I will speak to you exactly as I wish. You are telling me 'no.' "

"To letting you go? Don't be ridiculous. Of course I'm not letting you go. What in the name of sweet reason have you done to your feet?"

"My feet are also not your concern."

His hands came and pulled her feet from hiding.

She had a vivid and delicious image of kicking him. She did not do so, however, for she found him most wholly intimidating. Besides, if she provoked him and they fought, he might end up on the bed, on top of her. If that happened, she might be infinitely unwise.

"You're going to get blood poisoning if you keep on like this." His voice sounded odd. "Your shoes don't fit."

"They are not, strictly speaking, my shoes. And no, they do not fit terribly well, but going barefoot would make me conspicuous. You make a great fuss about a few blisters. I have traveled for weeks and weeks with worse than this."

"There are three pairs of shoes in that pile. One of them must be better. If not, I'll find some others." He held her, and he was not as careful as he usually was. His fingers dug into her. "Don't try to escape, walking on those feet, Annique."

"Ah, that is a most sound advice. I shall flap my wings and fly." It always amazed her how few spies had any sense of humor. Grey did not seem susceptible to amusement at the moment.

He released her so suddenly she bounced against the mattress. "Get dressed. You have ten minutes."

He slammed the door behind him when he left. It seemed Grey was a man who most definitely needed his breakfast before he became at all possible to deal with. Maman had said that was the case with some men. She would remember that in the future.

GREY SLIPPED ANNIQUE INTO A CHAIR ACROSS from Adrian, guiding her with a light, invisible touch she hardly needed. She was expert at the deception. If Leblanc's men came asking after a blind woman, no one would think of the dark-haired lass who'd had breakfast so openly on the terrace in front of the inn, carefree in the early morning sun.

She sat, eyes demurely lowered. Her fingers skimmed the edge of the table till she found the napkin. She shook it out across her lap.

He saw the exact moment Adrian looked into Annique's beautiful blank eyes. Saw the snap of assessment. Shock. Instant comprehension. "She can't see."

"Keep her inconspicuous," Grey ordered.

"My pleasure. Oh my, I do like a surprise, first thing in the morning." The boy was in pain, but alert. He'd do for a while.

"You're on display." He said the obvious, so Annique would know. "Twenty minutes, and I'll get you out of here. Hold out that long. Eat." That was for both of them.

Across the courtyard, Will Doyle was playing coachman, pacing the off-side horse, a big piebald mare, in a wide circle around the innyard, watching its gait. He made a first-rate coachman. He also made an excellent German count, merchant banker, Cockney pimp, and vicar of the Church of England.

Doyle rounded one last time and brought the mare to a stop. "Nobody's sniffing around yet."

"They'll think we've gone to ground in Paris. Gives us a head start." But men on horseback could always outrun them.

"We amble along, slow and innocent, and we'll do."

With luck. Lots and lots of luck. "I want that bullet out as soon as we can. Look for a likely spot past St. Richier. You have everything we need?"

"Whole surgeon's kit. I stole it from a naval surgeon in Neuilly. This here's his horse, too." He patted the mare's flank. "Wish I'd thought to kidnap that sawbones."

"So do I. I don't suppose you've ever dug a bullet out of anybody in that long, varied career of yours?" He turned his back to the inn. Adrian could read lips. "I'm going to kill him. I don't know dammitall about pulling bullets out of people. Sure you don't want to try your hand?"

"He'll do better if it's you digs into him. He trusts you. That helps." Doyle knelt and ran his hands up and down the horse's leg, being a coachman. "He ain't going to die of a bullet or two. Born to hang, our Hawker. How'd it go with the girl?"

"She's not what I expected." He realized he'd turned to watch her. He hadn't noticed himself doing it.

They were a fine matched pair, Hawker and Annique, sitting next to each other at the cozy table on the broad terrace under the trees. Coin-sized patches of sun streamed down through the trees and danced across them. They were the same age, with the same spare, compact grace of body. Black hair, glossy in the sunlight, tumbled forward across faces that were eerily alike—not in feature; there was no real resemblance—but in expression. The same faint air of wicked mirth clung to them, as if they were imps on temporary reprieve from one of the minor hells. They ate, leaning together, intent on a flow of low-voiced conversation.

"He likes her." Doyle was watching, too. "Hope she don't try to scamper out on his watch. Shape he's in, he'd have to hurt her to stop her."

"We're safe as long as it's daylight. Will, she's stone blind."

Doyle's face didn't change—he wouldn't blink at the announcement that Annique was empress of the Chinese—but some signal of surprise leaked through. The mare shuffled nervously. Doyle made an odd whistling sound between his teeth, and the animal quieted.

"Crikey. Blind?"

"She took a saber cut to the skull, five months ago. There's a scar hid up in her hair, if you go feeling for it."

"Cats in hip boots." Doyle fetched a little ivory pick out of his waistcoat pocket and began a ruminative exploration of his back teeth. "Why don't I know this? I heard she was in Marseilles with the mother. Never heard a whisper about the Cub being out of commission. Not from any of my sources. Not a syllable."

"She's good at hiding it. She must've spent months practicing." How long had it taken her to learn to fight in the dark?

"That's why we got her so easy. Blind and on the dodge."

". . . and hungry and hurt and exhausted. It only took three of us to haul her in." She picked up the coffee cup, eyes demurely lowered, smiling. He'd been wrong about the blue dress. It didn't make her look like a whore. It made her look young and chic and carefree as a spring butterfly. "You ever hit a woman?"

Doyle eyed him. "Missed doing that somehow. Fun, would you say?"

"Not much. Makes you feel shabby as hell afterwards."

"Accident, I imagine."

"I was stupid. That doesn't make it an accident." He was the officer in charge. She was his prisoner, and he'd hurt her. There were no excuses. "I punched her solar plexus so hard she stopped breathing for a while. I don't think I did any permanent damage, but keep an eye on her."

"I keep an eye on everything." Doyle squatted and curled the mare's hoof up against his thigh, matter-of-fact as any blacksmith. After a brief inspection, Doyle searched one-handed in his jacket pocket and fetched out a blunt probe. He scraped along the edge of the hoof, taking his time with it. A perfectionist, William Doyle. It'd saved their bacon a few times. "You going to talk about it?"

"I let her get a line around my neck." He slid a finger inside his cravat and pulled it aside to show the red line. It still hurt to swallow.

"Now how the devil did she . . . ?"

"That damned nightgown. The cord tying it."

"The cord. Oh, hell. I should have spotted that. She made a garrote. Clever as a flock of jackdaws, that girl."

"You could say I achieved my objective. She's stopped fighting. Do you know how much you have to hurt that woman before she gives up?"

Doyle released the hoof. "I've known you a good long while, Robert. What's it been?"

"Ten years, maybe."

"All of that." He moved on to the next hoof and picked it up. "Sometimes it shows, you coming in from the army instead of up through the ranks in the Service. If you'd spent even a year as a field agent, you'd know how dangerous our pretty little Annique is. You'd forget she's got breasts and do what you had to. Then you'd eat a hearty breakfast the next morning."

"I did eat breakfast." He sounded testy even to his own ears.

"But now you're brooding about it. Being a gentleman. Get yerself killed, doing that." Doyle grunted and stepped back. "You stopped being a gentleman the day you joined the Service."

"Fine. Next time, you kick her in the belly, and I'll hand out advice." Across the courtyard, Annique chuckled at something Adrian said, a sound like water gurgling, sweet and easy, out of a china pitcher. Ordinary. Intimate. Relaxed.

It irritated the hell out of him. "Leblanc's men could ride into this courtyard any minute. She sits there giggling."

Doyle followed his gaze. "That, my friend, is sheer, unmitigated guts. She's running for her life. There's not a rock in Europe that girl can hide under."

"Leblanc's going to kill her. Nothing to do with the Albion plans. He's covering some private secret, something particularly damning. Any ideas?"

Doyle shook his head. "With Leblanc it could be anything. He's an evil bastard."

"What's Fouché doing?"

"Right about now, he's probably wondering why one of his agents hasn't reported in." Doyle gave his imitation of a man contemplating fetlocks. Nobody knew more about the workings of French intelligence. "She could go to him—to Fouché. He won't let Leblanc kill her, unless she's been dabbling in treason with the Albion plans, which I take leave to doubt. But she's useless to him, blind. That brothel the Secret Police keeps, the one in the Faubourg Saint-Germain. He'll put her to work in that, with his other girls."

The thought made a foul taste in Grey's mouth. "Decadent place. Does she know?"

"Bound to. He's been trying to use her as a whore since she turned fifteen. The mother's dead. Her old master, Vauban, is dead. Soulier would help her—he's senior enough, God knows, and she's been his pet since she was knee high—but he's sitting on our doorstep in London.

Everybody who could protect the Cub is dead or out of France. Fouché's going to pimp her."

"That's cold-blooded, even for the French."

"No malice in it. He's old school, Fouché is. Don't much like a female agent working anywhere but on her back." Doyle stooped to check the buckles on the girth straps. "There's men who'd enjoy bedding a blind girl."

"Hell."

"We all know the risks, being in the Game." Doyle dusted his hands, nothing in particular on his face. "But it's worse for women."

It could be a lot worse for women. He hated sending his female agents out into the field.

The innyard gates stood open to the road. High cirrus streamers and a gray haze shimmered on the horizon to the west. That was tomorrow's weather, and the next day. It'd be raining when they ran the final gauntlet down to the coast. Leblanc's men would be waiting for them. "She was running for England when she left Marseilles. I'm sure of it. It's the only place she's safe from Leblanc."

"Makes sense. Leblanc on one side, Fouché on the other. No refuge in France. She was headed for Soulier, in London, for help."

"And she runs into us instead. She's ours." *Mine.*

"We got ourselves one little French agent." Doyle smiled. "I'll bet she's just packed with secrets. She'll deal with us. She's got no choice at all."

"She'll realize it, after a while." He'd take her to Meeks Street, to his headquarters. She'd be safe there, and he'd have all the time in the world to delve into that clever, complicated mind. She'd tell him everything he wanted to know. He was good at what he did. "She's already getting used to the idea. Making accommodation."

"Is she now? Then I don't have to worry about choking me lungs out on some spare bit o' string she picks up, do I?"

"If you don't turn your back on her."

Doyle turned his frown to the horse. "I'll be careful. Blind. Stone the crows."

At the rustic table, between coffee cup and a basket of rolls, Adrian lounged on his elbows, looking like he'd had a hard night of it, drinking. Annique kept her eyes downcast, looking slightly abstracted. She had a way of sweeping her fingers out before her when she reached for things, a slow, graceful gesture without hesitation or clumsiness. Adrian didn't look wounded. Annique didn't look blind.

"Grand, ain't they?" Doyle gave no sign he was looking at them, but, of course, he was. He worked his way along the reins, slipping them back and forth in the terrets, laying them grain side up, checking for wear. "Professionals. It's a pure pleasure watching 'em work. Wish we could recruit her. I could use that girl, even blind as a bat."

The wind had kicked up a bit, tugging tree shadows back and forth across the terrace. Annique smiled down into her coffee like it was a treat Adrian had invented just for her. That smile was like a stroke down his groin. Madness. He wanted to stomp across the courtyard and drag the girl upstairs and show her why she shouldn't go smiling like that in public.

He made himself stop watching her. "Tell me about Annique Villiers. There's no folder on her in London for some reason."

"Odd. Well, they don't use her against the British. What do you want to know? She's Pierre Lalumière's natural daughter, for one thing."

"Lalumière? The one who wrote *The Ten Questions*?"

"And *Natural Justice and the Law*, and *Essays on Equality*, and the rest." Doyle gave that a chance to sink in.

Pierre Lalumière. He'd read every word that man had ever written. At Harrow, they'd sat up late in the common room, arguing passionately about those books. He'd come away half a revolutionary, reading Lalumière.

"The mother used a couple names. Lucille Villiers. Lucille Van Clef. She and Lalumière popped up out of nowhere about twenty years ago, working for the radicals. Lots of the old radicals were discreet about their origins. The king's justice had a way of falling on the whole family, back in those days." Doyle began checking harness, running his fingers inside every strap that touched the horse. "Lalumière got hung one night in Lyon, and Lucille ended up working for the French Secret Police. Arguably the most beautiful woman in Europe. I could give you a list of men she slept with."

"And Annique?"

"Annique." Doyle sucked at his teeth. "Well. Been in the Game all her life. Raised by the Secret Police, really. Started at seven or eight, running errands for Soulier, back when he was Section Chief for the south of Europe. Couple years later they sent her out as a field observer. That's when they dressed her up like a boy. She was one of Vauban's inner circle, one of his five or six special ones. That's how good she is." He wiped his hands against his jacket. "I ran into her a few times in Vienna. Lovely thing, of course, but it's more than that. You'd notice her if she was plain as a rug. She's about twice as alive as anyone else. You can see it in her even now."

Adrian was adding hot milk to her coffee, handing her a roll, unobtrusively doing those things that were hardest for a blind woman to do without betraying herself.

"Thick as inkle weavers," Doyle said. "Pretty, ain't it?"

"Hawker's a good interrogator." He kept annoyance out of his voice. "Women like him. We can use that."

"Might work. She's young and scared, for all she's a professional. She's going to be looking for someone to talk to." Doyle flicked a look at him. "Hawker ain't gonna lay a finger on a woman of yours. He's just bedeviling you."

Damn the pair of them. "I'm putting Annique up next to you on the box. She has sense enough not to jump from up there. If you can get an arm around her . . . Her back muscles wind up a little before she attacks. Gives you some warning."

"Right."

"Try to get her to talk to you. Be nice."

"I like being the nice one." Doyle screwed his seamed and evil face into an innocent expression. "Wonder what they're saying."

". . . ABOUT two o'clock on your plate," Adrian was saying. "They have the first horse hitched. That looks like the last bags going up on top. We have five or six minutes."

"I will eat with dispatch, then." She kept her eyes down, directed to her hands. That had been the very first trick she taught herself. She pointed her eyes to her hands so her gaze did not wander about, staring at nothing, telling the whole world she was blind. Her hands she kept carefully beside her plate. She had burned herself already this morning, encountering the coffeepot. She did not wish to do so again.

The roll was indeed at two o'clock on her plate. She broke it into three neat pieces and ate deliberately, spacing the bites out. It had been a hard trip from Marseilles, and her stomach was not yet used to enough food.

"You have sense enough to eat slowly." Adrian approved. "You've been hungry before."

"You, too, I think."

"I was starving pretty much all the time till I got old enough to steal for a living." He chuckled. "Maybe I'd be a great walking mountain like Grey if I'd got fed regular."

"Almost certainly. You will sit back in the chair more, Adrian. If you wish to faint, do not knock my cup of coffee into my lap doing it."

The table told her of his movement. "Bouquets of womanly sympathy. Would you love me if I had Grey's muscles and walked around towering over all these Frenchmen? I wouldn't be half the agent I am if I had his height. Too conspicuous."

"I find myself not in the least sympathetic to the problems of being an English spy in France. I would not waste my love on such as you, in any case. You should eat something, especially if that man is to remove bullets from you today, as you say."

"I don't think food will help. Disconcerting when your surgeon dreads the procedure more than you do. When were you hungry, Annique? The Terror?"

She chewed and swallowed. It was harmless enough to speak of this. "At that time, yes, but not in Paris. I was living with the Rom, the Kalderash, for those years. That life is hard in the winter, if the times are troubled."

"Stolen by the Gypsies, were you?"

"That is a very false story, as you must know, being the so-intelligent spy that you are. The Rom never steal children, having many of their own, since they know as well as anyone how to make babies. It is not a matter of great difficulty, in case you wondered."

"I've heard that. I wouldn't try to hide that roll if I were you. No place for it under those clothes, delightful as they are."

"It is that this dress is not decent then," she said darkly. "I suspected as much.

"It's charming. Leave the roll next to the plate, please, and refrain from pilfering crusts in my presence. Roussel's over there handing up baskets to the coach. Enough food for a small army. One benefit of getting kidnapped by Grey, Fox Cub—you'll eat well so long as we manage to hold on to you."

"I will eat well for some time then." She had room in her stomach for a last sip of coffee or a bite more bread. Not both. She chose the coffee. She did love coffee.

Nine

Garches, near Paris

"IMBÉCILE." JACQUES LEBLANC SPREAD THE MAP flat, fingering across the roads of Normandy. "You waste my time with your whining."

"She is in Paris," Henri said sullenly. "They are on foot, without food, without money. The boy is wounded . . ."

"The boy is certainly dead. They abandoned him long since in some alleyway." Leblanc unrolled the map further. "By now they have horses. Even a carriage perhaps."

"The Englishman will go to ground. If Annique escapes him, she will go to her friends in Paris. Why would she—"

"She has friends everywhere. Be silent." Leblanc set two inches of Normandy shoreline between thumb and index finger. "This is the stronghold of smuggling. The path to England. Together or apart, injured or well, they must come here."

How long would it take the English spy to break Annique? Two days? Three? The Englishman was a hard brute. Even Henri was afraid of him.

This was a problem in simple logic. Allow three days for

the Englishman to break the little bitch and strip the location of the Albion plans from her. Then . . . Leblanc walked his fingers upon the map, town to town to town. Where had the plans been hidden all these months? Paris? Rouen? Near the Channel? They could be in England itself. The girl could have taken the plans to England for safekeeping when she left Bruges. There had been enough time.

It did not matter where they were. In the end—this was the Englishman's great weakness—in the end, the Englishman must cross the Channel. He had no choice but to go to the coast and fall into the trap laid for him.

Henri did not have enough sense to be quiet. "There is no proof she is with him. No proof she has ever left Paris. We should be searching the—"

"This is the Fox Cub, you fool, not one of your *poulettes*. She walked here from Marseilles, blind. Do you think she sits sucking her thumb in some corner in the *Quartier Latin* waiting for you? If she is not with the Englishman, she will still go to the Channel. She goes to Soulier. She thinks she will be safe with him.

Henri said stubbornly, "I think—"

"You do not think. Faugh. I am surrounded by idiots."

Events were escaping his control. Even now, Annique might be crawling to the Englishman, broken and begging, telling him anything he asked. Telling him about Bruges.

The map crackled. He closed his fist over Normandy. This was not disaster. Not disaster. He would scoop them up like bugs. The Englishman would be stopped. Even if he spilled some story of Bruges, who would believe what an English spy said? It could be quashed, every whisper of it. Every breath that spoke of it could be stopped.

And if he had the Albion plans on him . . . *ventre bleu,* but there was no limit to the gold a clever man could get for those plans.

It would not be like Bruges, with all his work, all his

planning, cheated from him. For what? A ridiculous few coins. An insult of coins.

He pressed his thumb on the city of Rouen and marked the road to the coast. "You will order patrols here, here . . . and here. Stop everything that moves and search it."

"We cannot stop every—"

"Look for a blind woman, for God's sake. That is simple enough for even you."

The Albion plans had dissolved from Bruges like a puff of smoke. He had torn that inn apart, looking for them. This time, they would not get away, not if he had to rip them from the belly of that bitch with his own hands.

"I will order patrols." Henri gave a terse, insolent nod. Another discourtesy he would eventually regret.

He would salvage this calamity Henri had created. He would retrieve the Albion plans. And he would shut Annique Villier's mouth. When she was dead, he would be safe.

"Here . . . and across here . . . place the customs. Let them do some useful work for a change. Send our men here." His fingers tented, spiderlike, above the names written into the blue wash that marked the Channel. These were the villages, tiny, fish-stinking, each with fifty huts and three dozen boats turned down on the sand. "She knows this coast from the days of the Vendée. She made allies among the smugglers, men whose names she never reported to me. This is where she will go, if she is free." He sat back abruptly and pulled a silk handkerchief from his pocket and wiped his forehead. The room was too warm. "Unless she expects me to look for her there. Perhaps . . ." He frowned at the south. "If we spread the patrols . . ."

Henri gazed at the oil painting that hung on the gold and crimson walls of the salon, a landscape that had once belonged to the mayor of Paris. "There are many possibilities."

He would deal with Henri. Oh, most assuredly, he

would deal with this disrespect. "Go. Go yourself. Give the order that any papers she carries are to be brought to me, unopened. To me alone. Do you understand?"

"To you. Unopened. Of course." Henri thought himself sly. If he laid eyes on the Albion plans, he would discover that he was, instead, expendable. "What of Annique?"

"Take her, if you want an Englishman's leavings. Use her to reward the men who find her. Then bring her to me."

"And the Englishman?"

"Kill him."

Ten

Normandy

BESIDE HIM, ON THE DRIVER'S SEAT, ANNIQUE maintained a dry and lofty silence for almost an hour. What finally broke her down was Doyle saying, in a very hurt tone, that she didn't need to slide her arse all the way to Calais. He weren't crowding her. The injured tone of voice and the vulgar word quite undermined her resolve. Even pressing her lips very closely together, she couldn't keep from giggling.

"That's better," Doyle said, satisfied. "I was wondering if you was gonna talk to me."

"I do not feel talkative. It is the being kidnapped, you comprehend."

"We've irritated you, have we?"

"You have. And I do not like to be so high up." The driver's perch was unpadded and far, far from the ground. It lurched frighteningly over every bump. She could not see the ruts and potholes coming, so she must hold on tight and brace her feet continually on the upcurved footrest. Her fingers had permanently taken the shape of the railing at the side of the seat. She would be unspeakably sore and weary by day's end, which was without doubt why she was up here. She would be in no condition to escape tonight. Grey had, as the English put it, fixed her wagon.

The coach jolted madly. She tightened her grip. "It is unsteady, this coach."

"I ain't going ter let you fall off." Doyle had such a wonderful accent. No one but a Frenchman born would have dared to speak French so vilely. "Been to a bit of trouble getting hold of you, after all. You know much about horses, miss?"

She had located Monsieur Doyle in the vast storehouse of her memory. He had many names. Her mother pointed him out to her, long ago in Vienna, and told her to avoid him, as he was tough and tenacious as a badger and probably the best field agent alive.

"Not so much," she said.

"Then we'll put you to work, and I can get some rest. You just . . . That's right. You just take this."

He handed her something. Then she worked out that she was holding the reins and the horses were jogging along with nothing controlling them whatsoever but her hands on thin strands of leather.

She'd spent a lifetime dealing with the unexpected. She gripped the reins as if they were ropes to a ship and she was in water in mid-Atlantic. *"Nom de Dieu."*

"You don't want to go choking up on the reins like that. Makes them horses nervous. What you wants to do is hold them bits of leather nice and loose like. Should really be in one hand, o' course, but let's us start out with the both of 'em, just at first. What you do . . ." He put his arm around her, taking both her hands. "No, loosen your fingers up there, and let me show you. What you do is . . . This gets threaded through here, see."

"Would you take these back? Please."

He shifted the straps in her hands till they intertwined

with her fingers. "This one over here," he twitched it in her grip, "goes to the left. That there's a bad-tempered devil on the left. Nancy, I calls him, on account of him not being what you might call complete in his privates. Old Nan's a great one for nipping at you when he wants yer attention. Now, suppose you was wanting to turn him to the left—not saying you does now, but if you was wishful to—you'd just pull nice and firm on this strap here. You feel that?"

"Doyle." She kept a firm hold on the abject terror the thought of these horses running away roused inside her. "It has possibly escaped your notice, but I am blind as a rock."

"Yes, miss. This other line here, the one you gots lying across your palm like—"

"Being blind, Monsieur Doyle, is not merely a lack of appreciation for the delightful blue sky and the field we are passing. It means I cannot do some practical small tasks. Like drive horses. This is a fact most self-evident that I tell you."

"Lord love you, miss, you don't have to see to hold on to these reins. Why, half the time I'm driving along with me eyes closed, just napping. The horses does all the work. The tricky part is remembering which of them lines is which, just in case somebody should climb up and ask you about it."

She clutched the pieces of leather till her fingers ached. This was not the small, creaky wagon of the Rom and a single, placid Rom horse, which was the only thing she had ever driven in her life. "I most extremely do not think this is a good idea."

"Best way for you to get around, miss. Driving. If you don't mind me advising you. Nothing like a pony cart for tooling around the country and no reason you shouldn't drive as well as any of them ladies in England. Why, from what I've seen, a full half of 'em driving must be as blind as you are, begging your pardon for bringing it up and all."

"You are a man of the most remarkable cold blood,

Monsieur Doyle. *Mon Dieu,* but your reputation is fully deserved."

"An' what would a nice young lady like you know about my reputation? When you gets to England, you just go out and get yerself a little cart, a pony cart, and you finds a pony with some sense to him, like this pair has. He'll take you round as pretty as you please without you do more than set your hands around the reins just like yer doing there."

"Get . . . a cart. A cart. But yes, I shall certainly do that if I ever go to England."

"Now, miss, don't go on like that. You knows we're taking you to England with us. Going there just as fast as can be. Getting closer with every mile." He shifted the straps lightly in her hands, steering the horses past some object in the road. "The sooner you stop fighting Grey about that, the easier it'll be on all of us. Makin' us all mortal edgy, you are, not knowin' if you're going to kill him tonight or not."

"Yes. Or no. Whichever it is." His arms were around her in a friendly way, but he'd let go of the reins again and left her with the whole carriage and these horses who might at any minute do anything at all. "Would you take these lines back, Doyle? Because I, of a certainty, do not want them."

"You just ease up on the reins a little, the horses'll walk right along and take us with 'em just fine. Holding on tight just distracts 'em."

"Lean back and go along most nicely, is your suggestion. Doubtless I am to do the same with all that Monsieur Grey intends for me. It is a very masculine way to advise me."

"Exactly, miss. And while these horses is walking so nice in the direction of the coast, what you gots to do, if you'll pardon me saying so, is learn Hinglish."

"Hinglish?" The meaning penetrated. "Oh. *Anglais.* But no. I do not just immediately plan to go to England, as it happens."

"Well, miss, that's just where you're going, if you'll

forgive the contradiction. So we'll teach you Hinglish. Ain't hard. Me youngest girl—she's just three—speaks it a fair treat."

It was easier staying on the box with Doyle's arm around her. It was even easier when he took the reins and held them, a little way above where her hands were, "Jest to show you how it's done, miss," and she could stop being terrified witless.

"Now take them." He must have made some gesture and realized an instant later she couldn't see it. "Them horses. In Hinglish we say, 'Them 'osses is slugs.' "

"Them is . . . But that is a terrible thing to call horses. Unless the English are fond of slugs, which is possible."

"Nah. Them's the buggers gets in the lettuce and crawls all over and eats it. Me wife, Maggie—I tell you about me Maggie yet?—she's a little spitfire, she is, and mortal proud o' that garden of ours. Me Maggie 'ates slugs. Sets out saucers of beer to lure 'em in and lets 'em die happy like. Goes against the grain, somehow, drownin' 'em in good beer."

She waited for her lips to stop twitching. Her mother had told her Doyle graduated from Cambridge. With honors. "I would agree, though I have never killed slugs. It is still a very strange thing to call horses."

She was learning that a better class of 'osses' were 'rum prads' and the Hinglish word for coach was 'bangup rattler,' when he took the reins from her and pulled to a halt.

The tenseness of her body must have shown how afraid she was. Doyle said at once, "Nothing to be worried about, miss. Jest looking for a place to stop for a bit. Might be here."

She felt a sense of humid openness and heard wind and the sound of a stream and humming flies. Birds sang in the distance. They were in the middle of fields then, away from any village, and there was a woods not far. They would operate upon the poor Adrian in the country where his outcries could not be heard.

"This is a good place?" The door of the coach swung open. She heard Grey jump to the ground and walk along the road.

"Might be." Doyle's voice was accompanied by a noise that puzzled her, till she identified it as someone scratching an unshaven chin. "What we got here . . . There's a couple or three rocks by the road, piled up casual like. That might be Gypsy work. We been following one of their trails a ways now—them scraps of cloth they tie in the trees up about level with a wagon top. So this rock likely means one of their campsites. Maybe back there in that bit o' woods."

They were both waiting for her to speak. The British spies, one and all of them, knew a great deal more about her than she liked. "What do they look like, Monsieur Doyle, these rocks of yours?"

"One great lump of a fellow, sorta roundish. That's in the middle. Then there's three in a line, running . . . Lemme show you." He tucked the reins somewhere and took her left hand and spread it back against his knee and made dots on her palm, showing her how the rocks sat, each with the other. "And then a flat one off here past your little finger, oh, a good foot or so to the right. Don't know whether that one's in the flock, or just a stray. Ain't no twigs or feathers or twists o' grass anyplace. Just the stones."

"You have read such signs before." They had found a Rom campsite, beyond doubt.

"The *patrin*? Seen 'em here and there, miss. Can't say I read 'em."

"Wagon tracks," Grey called from the fields to their right. "They're one in the other, dead center in line. Gypsy."

If Rom were encamped here, they would help her. They would not want to become involved in a quarrel of the *gaje* but neither would they like to see a woman who spoke Romany in the clutches of such men as these. If she lied ever so small an amount . . .

Doyle cleared his throat. "They're not here. Them

threads o' cloth been there a while. Months. An' the wheel tracks is old. We got the place to ourselves."

They saw too much, these two. She would have much preferred to deal with fools. "You are right about the *patrin*, the signs. There is a camp not far from here. A safe place. It will be higher on that stream we passed, higher than the road, so the water flows clean. The Rom are careful in this."

After a little discussion of the countryside, she directed the coach, not to a closest patch of wood which beguiled them, but up a long track that led into thickets and seemed to them less promising. She knew at once when they reached the clearing that was the Rom's safe haven. The smell of old campfires hung in the air. The herbs crushed under the coach wheels were the ones the Rom leave behind in their favored camps. Wild garlic, fennel, and mint grew here.

"It's a good place you've found us." Grey swung her down from her high place on the coach. "This is what we need. You have Gypsy blood in you, Annique?"

"Not from my mother's side, I am almost sure." She could smell his shirt, the starch and the vetiver-scented water that was ironed into it, which was wholly a French custom and not a British scent at all. They had such meticulous technique, these agents. "I do not know enough about my father to say—he died when I was four—but I think he was Basque. He spoke with my mother sometimes in a language I have never heard anywhere else."

He did not touch her, but something in her body reached out and greeted his body as if the two were old friends who had not seen one another for a long time. She did not like it that her body chatted to his in this fashion. She cleared her throat. "They were Revolutionaries, you understand. In those days, the radicals did not speak so much of where they came from and their families. It was not safe."

"I'd have called you a Celt, myself, with those blue eyes.

A Breton, maybe. Stay here a minute." Twigs crackled under his boots as he walked into the brush.

She opened herself to a sense of the clearing around her, as she did with new places. Sun warmed her skin. The stream was not so close as to bring a feeling of damp and coolness, but its voice was loud and comforting. The coach jogged behind her as Doyle released the second horse from its harness. He took both horses, hooves clopping on the leaves, in the direction of the water. The air was thick with the pollen of the trees, filled with old smells of charcoal and tobacco and the pomade the women wore in their hair. It was all familiar. This was a camp like the ones of her childhood. This was a home place of the Rom.

Life had been simpler when she lived among the Kalderesh. If Maman had never come to take her back, perhaps she would have made a life among them. By this time she would have a black-haired baby to dote upon and a swaggering young husband, instead of a kidnapper who was carrying her toward an intricate and unpleasant interrogation in London.

Grey came toward her. "Take this." He set a stick against her palm, a good sturdy one. She would call it a sort of quarterstaff, though she had never held a quarterstaff, as they did not figure heavily in one's daily life. But her father had told her stories of Robin Hood. This was exactly what Little John was accustomed to hitting the sheriff of Nottingham over the head with. Scaled down to her size, of course.

"This is very fine. Thank you." Possibly she might give Grey a whack with it at some time. "Will you take the bullet out of Adrian?"

His voice was tense. "That's what we're here for."

"I see." Never could she stop herself saying that. "You have much experience, perhaps, from the army?"

"None whatsoever. I'm going to unpack. Don't pick this time to wander off."

He was not pleased to be doing this piece of field surgery. He was worried sick. She could hear it in every step he took from the coach to the center of the glade, carrying things. That was where he would work, where Doyle was laying a fire.

She had not yet made her decision. She walked for a while, tapping with her useful staff, finding the old fire rings, coming to understand how the wagons lined up in this place. It had the feel of a rich camp. There would be, in those flowery fields beyond the wood, berries and many rabbits, even hedgehogs, if one were lucky. Her feet crunched the old shells of beechnuts. One would eat well here without stealing chickens.

The ground sloped gradually toward the stream. Anywhere she stood, that slope and sound of water told her where she was. It was comforting, that small certainty.

Once, she tripped, because she was thinking hard, and a tree root had been more clever than she was. She did not hurt herself badly. To fall from time to time is part of being blind. One must be philosophic.

On the highest side of the clearing were blackberry bushes, which she found by impaling herself upon the thorns. She ate a few and made her decision and went to listen to Doyle and Grey getting Adrian prepared.

". . . repaint the attic rooms the last week of November."

". . . files into storage in the basement . . ."

". . . everlasting whitewash. There's a lack of imagination that . . ."

They spoke of inconsequential things. A thousand times she had listened to men before battles, talking just this way. Grey's voice held nothing but calm confidence. Most certainly, to hear him, one would think he had taken several pounds of metal out of men in the last month, without exception a great success at it. Adrian had an almost French courage, as she had thought before. In his light words, she could hear his resolution to trust Grey, to put his life in those hands. In some time and place, Grey had earned the confidence of that cynical, knowing boy.

It would be a great pity if she had brought Adrian out of Leblanc's cellar and all this long way to die.

Most likely he would. Grey had not the least idea how to remove bullets. If she were entirely loyal to France she would be glad, for of Adrian she had heard some few things that told her he was a master at spying and a formidable enemy to her Republic.

Metal clattered. Doyle was setting the instruments in place, there, on the ground. She had decided to be disloyal to France in this matter.

"Grey, I would talk to you," she said.

"Later."

"Now." She walked off.

Tiens. This was the test of him, was it not? If he did not trust her to know what was important, he would not trust her with Adrian's life.

Ten paces downhill, she stopped. His steps followed her.

"I don't have time for this, Annique."

"I can take the bullet out of him."

She was treated to one Grey's long silences. Then he said, "I shouldn't be surprised. You were with the armies, weren't you? Where did you learn to take bullets out of people? Milan?"

"And Millesimo and Bassano and Roveredo and . . . and elsewhere." So many battlefields. "The safest place in battle, if one is dressed as a young boy, is in the medical tents. If I am busy mopping up repulsive liquids, no one hands me a gun and expects me to kill people."

"I see." Such a dry tone. She knew this about Grey. He had been an infantry major before they took him for the British Service. He would know about medical tents and the aftermath of battles.

"I came at first to clean, in those hospitals. When I was there . . . Grey, there was not one of those orderlies who could be trusted to sew up a pillowcase, let alone a belly. I am clever with my hands. It was not long before the surgeons knew me. By Rivoli they did not even look up when I came in, just pointed where they wanted me to start working. I have taken much shrapnel out of men, little pieces the surgeons had no time to hunt for. And when times became desperate, many bullets."

"Many bullets." She felt his breath on her face.

"I do not need eyes. Not for this." She did not know why she was trying so hard to convince him. Perhaps she could not save Adrian. Perhaps it was his inescapable fate to die when the bullet was removed. But it should not be for Grey to have his hands on his friend and feel the life leaking out. She could spare him that. "It is not a matter of looking, you understand. In digging out bullets, when one must cut away at the flesh, there is much blood. One cannot see. It is *always* necessary to go by touch, to feel within the skin and use a probe to find the path entered upon."

"Do it."

"I have much experience in—"

"I said, do it." He walked away without another word of discussion or question. She did not always understand Grey.

In the center of the clearing they had spread blankets upon the ground. There, Doyle had disgorged his selection of medical instruments. While she listened to Grey explain the change of plans—not once, for a minute, did his voice show any doubt as to her skill—she knelt and took stock of the fierce assemblage of metal. What dozens of instruments. Most, she swiftly tossed back into the leather bag. She kept only the smallest of the clamps and forceps and one pair of scissors and one little razor-sharp knife. This was enough for what she must do.

Everything smelled of fishes, for some reason, as well as old blood. She did not even want to set her hands upon these tools when they were so dirty. She sent Doyle to the running stream with soap, to clean them for her. She was feeling Rom at this moment. She would not wash them in a basin. The Rom do not wash in stagnant water.

Then she turned to touch Adrian, to know what was what with him. He had stripped to the waist. He sat on the ground while Grey cut away the bandage.

"*Chère* Annique, if I'd known you were going to cut into me, I'd have let you finish your coffee this morning." He caught her hand and lifted it to his lips to kiss. It was hard to believe he was not a Gascon. "How did Grey talk you into this?"

"It was entirely the other way around. Grey fought tooth and nail for the privilege of seeking bullets in you. But I was insistent." He would laugh on the gallows, this one. "If you have not taken the opium, you should do that. We must wait a time, you understand, after you take it. I would not have you discussing with me the price of green beans or the weather when I am working. I am easily distracted."

Grey said, "He won't take it."

Adrian's arm moved. He was shaking his head, she thought. "If I took enough to do any good, I'd be stupid for days. Leblanc's looking for somebody wounded. Make me groggy, and I'm dead."

"I bloody well hate it when he's right, don't you?" Doyle said.

"I'm always right. Annique . . . Fox Cub . . . I won't take opium. If I drank enough brandy to knock me out, it'd probably kill me. So it's nothing at all. Can you do this?"

"Oh yes," she said at once. "I have hunted out bullets, often and often. I am fast as lightning, me." *Mon Dieu,* could they know what it would be like? It is the stuff of nightmares to operate with no opium at all. Truly, Adrian was like her in this—the good fairies had not attended his cradle to scatter blessings upon him. "Always they run out of opium before they run out of men with holes in them. One copes."

"Nothing like practice. Here's this lot, clean." Doyle started laying instruments into her hand, one at a time so she did not slice herself.

"I am in the medical tents of the losing side, generally, so we have many wounded." She dried the scissors with a strip of bandage and clipped through the cloth, testing. They were sharp. "I have been diligently spying upon the Milanese and Austrians who lose battles with some regularity. It has been most odd, all these years, dodging so many completely French bullets."

There was a good supply of bandages. If she needed more than this, she would have killed Adrian anyway. "If you will lie down, Monsieur Adrian, I will be able to reach you. I am not a giantess."

She hitched herself close to Adrian, to a position where she could work. Her tools made a neat row on the blanket. She picked them up and put them down till she could find everything without thought. Then she laid a cloth across. It was better Adrian did not spend his time looking at this. Sharp, shiny metal is wearing to the soul. She lifted a stack of bandages into her lap where they would be handy. She must concentrate now and think only of what must be done.

Adrian's upper chest was nearly hairless, with hard muscles, set rigid in pain. He flinched when she first laid hands upon him, then took a deep breath and did not react again while she examined. The skin around the site of entry was noticeably hot. The mouth of the wound was damp and smelled of infection—the ordinary kind, not the rotting, sweet sort that means death.

Doyle settled on the boy's right, large and comforting. Grey moved to take the other side. They were not holding him down yet. Soon they would have to. She had operated without opium before.

"Monsieur Doyle, I will show you where I want your hands."

"There's one thing we'll do first," Grey said. "I'm going

to talk to Adrian. It'll take a few minutes. You get comfortable."

Almost, she hissed in exasperation. "You have had a whole morning to talk." Every moment they delayed made it worse. Did they think their Adrian was constructed of imperturbable courage? Did they think she was?

"We're going to try something I saw in Vienna. It may help." He leaned close, talking to the boy. "The way you do this, Adrian, is you just relax and listen to me. That's how we start, remember. You listen to what I'm saying."

It seemed she must wait until this was done. She called to her mind a picture of the blood vessels in the chest. They ran so . . . and so. With luck, she would avoid them.

This was her great gift, this memory of hers. Any page she had read, any street she had crossed, any face in a crowd—they all came back to her perfect and exact when she called. Other people forgot things. She did not. That was why Vauban had given her the Albion plans in the small inn in Bruges when Leblanc came to extort and threaten. She had put the plans into her memory and burned each page, one by one, as she read. Her memory was why Maman had taken her everywhere, even when she was a child. Her head was stuffed with the secrets of many nations.

Fortunately, her memory also contained anatomical charts. The upper chest is far from the worst spot to be hit in, if the bullet is not deep, which must be so, because Adrian still lived.

Grey plodded on and on with his so-necessary conversation. She did not pay attention, since it did not concern her and was very dull. He was saying, "We'll try this for a while, the first parts, anyway, and see how it goes. It's easy to get started. You're going to breathe slow and listen to what I'm saying."

"It feels stupid," Adrian said. "I'll try. But the gods know I feel like an idiot."

"You're not going to do anything stupid, Hawker. Only what you want to do. You're the one in charge. I'm just here to help you with what you're doing to yourself. You lie there and feel the breathing. That's how you do it. In and out. Now in. Now out. You feel the breathing. That's all you feel."

Grey repeated himself in an exceedingly boring way, which gave her no very high opinion of his powers of conversation. She finished thinking about the blood vessels in the chest and sat quietly, with her hands resting in her lap, letting her thoughts drift.

"Your eyes get tired in all this sunlight. You can close them." Having found another subject of stultifying monotony, Grey droned on and on.

The next thing she knew, somebody was shaking her. Grey.

"Yes. You. Wake up, Annique. That's it. Wide awake. You feel fine, Annique, and you are fully awake."

She seemed to have fallen asleep sitting up.

"Of course I am awake." Her legs had gone numb beneath her. "I am resting while you chatter so endlessly." She did not keep sarcasm out of her voice. "I had a difficult night."

"You are what is called an excellent subject," he said, incomprehensibly. "Adrian, on the other hand, is not. I saw this done a couple times in Vienna, but I've never tried it. There's a man there, uses it in surgery. Let's hope it works."

"You are through talking to him?"

"I'll keep talking. You ignore what I say and do what you have to. Very definitely ignore me. I don't want you nodding off again."

"Then hold him."

She showed them how she wanted him pinned. Doyle held his arm down and the shoulder. Grey took the other side, leaning his full weight on top, all the time talking and talking to Adrian—something about the pain being far away on the other side of a wall. Such bizarre stuff. She would ignore it.

"Do not let him move." Then she trusted them to do their work and did not think about it again. There were many thoughts to dismiss from her mind. Most of all she must not think of Adrian. Beneath her hands was muscle and bone and skin. Not Adrian.

She took a minute to explore the site from outside, testing the surface of the skin with her fingers. Good. That was the bullet. That lump. They had been incredibly lucky. It lay high in the chest, superficial, just below the collarbone, at the second rib, lodged against bone. The entry path was oddly slanted, as if he'd been shot by someone below him. The lead had not torn into the lung beneath.

The patient was still. Not limp—it was not like working on a man deep under an opiate—but he was most wholly and completely motionless. Good.

There was nothing more his body could say to her. She sat back on her heels and touched her way from instrument to instrument one last time. She would go in through the entry wound. That would minimize damage and clean it, too. She took up the long, slim forceps. Wordlessly, she rearranged Grey's hold and settled herself at a new angle.

Her left hand pressed the skin above the site, over the tiny lump of the bullet. Through her palm, she mapped the plateaus and valleys of the ribs. She snicked the forceps open and closed, twice, loosening up her fingers.

Now to do it. Fast. No hesitation.

She took a deep breath and went in with the forceps. Push. Spread forceps slightly. Push. Follow the path of the bullet through muscle. All her concentration flowed to the tip of the forceps, sensing the route, nudging along bone and fascia. Warm blood streamed between her fingers.

Push. Farther. Grit on metal. Her quarry. Open. Soft, soft now. Nibble at it. The tiny, slippery hardness. Catch it. Close the forceps. Yes! She had it. Bring it out. Fast now.

She could go fast now. The patient held his breath. His muscles—neck, chest, arms—like steel. Next to her, a voice gave firm orders about a wall of darkness, solid as bricks.

She dropped the ball in the palm of her hand and rolled it. The lead was flat with impact against the rib. It wasn't smooth. A chunk was missing. She must return. She made a single, unbroken motion of it, testing the bullet, going back in.

The missing piece would have been chipped off by the impact with the rib. She must go deep to look for it. Slide in. Keep to the path. Deeper. The patient gasped. Jerked. Go loose on the forceps, ride the movement lest she jab at him. Not her job to keep him still. Think about the metal.

He was still. Good. At the rib, delicate as a fencer, she probed. Blood vessels all up and down the ribs. Between them. She was searching for a grain of hardness where it should not be. Smooth, soft strokes. Soft . . . soft.

Deep on the lateral surface of the first rib, she found the brittle nub of bullet. The placement! *Mon Dieu,* the placement. It was as bad as could be. The forceps pulsed in her hand. The artery. Close. Deadly close.

"Do not breathe," she ordered. The muscles beneath her hand were stone. Quivering. The fragment rested directly against the artery. It pulsed. He must not move. Not move. She eased forward. No pressure. She must take it without the least pressure.

She closed the forceps and gently took hold and gently, gently brought the last of the bullet out. She fitted one piece of metal with the other. There was nothing missing.

"It is done." She laid the forceps onto the blanket, took bandages from her lap, and pressed them to the wound.

"My God," Doyle muttered.

The patient panted fast and shallow, hissing out through his teeth, an animal sound.

"Finished. Right." Grey sounded as shaken as she felt. "That's the worst of it, Hawker. Now we're going to build a wall between you and the pain. A big, dark wall. Thick darkness. The pain's on one side, you're on the other. Breathe in. Slow. Breathe out."

She herself had not breathed for a while, obviously. The ground swayed under her, which was an unmistakable sign.

Adrian—he was Adrian again to her—was losing blood. It soaked through the layers she held. Sluggishly, thank the *bon Dieu.* She had not nicked the artery. She had not killed him. This was not the hot rush of bleeding that meant death.

Never before had she operated on someone she knew. It was of a horribleness unimaginable. She would avoid this in the future.

"I got that." Doyle set her hands aside. Took over. He discarded the soaked bandages, twitched a clean one into place.

Adrian groaned and tried to roll. Grey, who thought everyone should do as he commanded, told him to hold still. Told him how to breathe. Again and again, told him how to breathe. It was most odd.

"We going to close this?" Doyle asked. "I got a hot iron. I can do it."

"No fire. He will stop bleeding soon." She wiped her sticky palms on her skirt. Adrian's blood. "We will let it drain, as the great Ambroise Paré taught. There is less of . . . of infection that way. No stitches, unless it bleeds and bleeds. Then one or two small ones to hold the edges together tomorrow."

"Lean on Grey, why don't you. He ain't busy," Doyle said.

"I am fine." She started to push her hair back from her face, remembered what was on her hands, and stopped. She took various deep, helpful breaths. "We are wise in this, we French. Paré taught that such wounds, we leave open . . . to heal from within . . ."

Grey abandoned his endless, one-sided conversation

with Adrian and abruptly stood to walk around. When he returned, he put a cold cloth to her forehead.

"You should not let me touch you." But she rested her cheek on his thigh in an intimacy which seemed wholly natural at the moment. The ground still wished to tilt under her. "I am entirely gruesome with blood. I have ruined this dress, though it was probably not decent in any case. But I do not have a great number. One must be provident."

He used the cloth to wash her cheeks, then folded it and held it on the back of her neck.

"You are doing this so I will not faint. I never faint."

"That's good. I'm sorry about the dress." He was apologizing for several things at once. She became certain the dresses he had given her were improper. "Thank you for saving Adrian's life."

"This was not so bad. Once I took fifty-two pieces of metal out of a man and he lived. An Austrian sergeant. He melted them down to make a paperweight, I heard."

"Sounds like a good idea." Grey was thinking a number of things. She could almost hear thoughts humming and clinking inside him. "Annique . . . I would have killed him."

"Almost certainly. The second tiny piece was close to the axillary artery. I felt it pulsing. Will you let me go free, since I have spared you from killing your friend?"

He did not hesitate. "No."

He was unreasonable, right to the soles of his shoes. "Then I will go wash blood off me and not sit here at your feet in this spineless fashion." She put her legs underneath herself and stood up, which she would probably have managed even without Grey's assistance. He put the useful stick in her hold and it supported her very handily without the help of any Englishman. She did not feel at all like fainting.

"Your bag's on the far side of the fire," Doyle said. "It's . . . No. More to the right. That's got it. There's soap and a towel on that rock. Yes. There."

"I am well provided for, then. I shall take these and go wash myself in privacy. Monsieur Grey may again talk to his Adrian with great tediousness. Certainly he has nothing of interest to say to me."

"No, miss," Doyle said pacifically. These English spies spent much of their spare time laughing at her.

"You will press down upon those bandages until the bleeding stops. As you well know."

"Yes, miss."

She batted away at the small bushes with her stick and found where the path descended to the stream. "And put a blanket upon him."

She was angry with herself. Stupid, stupid woman that she was, she wanted to stay with Grey and allow him to coddle her. He was destroying her, that one, with his kindness and his strong arms that held her and felt so full of caring, while he continued to be, inside, utterly ruthless.

He tempted her. He was a trap in every part of him. It would be so treacherously easy to place herself into his hands. But she did not trust him in the least. She had not yet lost her mind. Not quite.

When she came to the water it was pleasant, and warmer than she expected, which relieved her feelings somewhat. So did the deep silence on every side. As she worked her way downstream to find the bathing place for women, she reflected that these were thick woods around her everywhere. One could hide in them very well, at night, when one was escaping.

"WELL, that weren't so bad, then," Doyle said when she'd gone down the path and couldn't overhear. "Not like Adrian's a bloody Austrian sergeant with fifty-two pieces of lead in his gut."

"Name of God, Will, how long did she take?"

"Two minutes. Three, tops. I can see why those army

surgeons put her to work. Jerked that bullet out like a plum in a Christmas pudding."

"How many goddamned battles was she in, to learn that? What the hell kind of mother sends a child to an army camp to spy? How old was she? Eleven? Twelve?"

"About the same age we put the Hawker to work."

"Hawker wasn't a child. He was never a child."

"I don't suppose Annique was either. From what I hear, she was there when they hanged her father. She'd have been about four." Doyle blotted Adrian's chest with clean bandages. "He's not even leaking blood much. Get that blanket, will you? You going to do more of that talk-talk to make him sleep?"

"Every hour for a while. What the devil am I going to do with that woman?"

"Now, that I wouldn't care to speculate on. Spread your bedding over there a ways so you don't disturb Adrian when you do it."

"Very funny. I'll reconnoiter up the ridge and keep an eye on her so she doesn't sneak off. Call me if the boy wakes up. She's going to run for it tonight, isn't she?"

"All these woods and fields to hide in . . . yes. Hit you over the head with a rock first, I think." Doyle picked up the bits of lead that had been pulled out of Adrian, looked at them soberly, and put them safe in his pocket. "Hawk will want these."

"Good idea." Grey stared down the path she'd just taken. "She's already planning. I can feel her doing it. I don't think I can stop her. She is so ferociously competent."

"Be like trying to hold this one," Doyle gestured at Adrian, "when he wanted to run."

"You're saying it's not possible."

"Not easy. Not outside of Meeks Street."

Even if he tied her up, she'd find some way to get loose. "Leblanc's on our heels. If she gets away from us, he'll find her."

"Or Fouché might get to her first and pop her into a brothel. If she's lucky." Doyle began wiping the instruments and laying them back in the bag.

There was only one damned thing to do. "Put some food together. She'll be hungry, once she cleans up. And Will . . ."

Doyle looked up.

"Give her opium in the coffee."

Doyle bound a new pad of bandages on Adrian.

"You have something to say?"

"It'll work. She likes coffee." Doyle took the blanket and spread it over Adrian, easing the boy into a more comfortable position. "It had to come to this. I'll keep the dose low as I can. Go watch her."

Eleven

DOYLE HAD CONSTRUCTED AN OMELET OF FRESH eggs and butter from the inn's basket and chanterelle mushrooms from the woods. He was a good cook, Monsieur Doyle. But then, she thought, he did many things well besides pretending to be a coach driver. Grey sat next to her on the blanket, close but not touching. She felt his eyes on her though, continually. She considered escape plans for the evening.

"That innkeeper took a fancy to you," Doyle told her. "We got a pot of cream for your coffee, because you liked it so much this morning."

"I have a great allure for innkeepers, always." She set her plate down on the blanket beside her and picked up the coffee again. "They sense in me, you comprehend, a great cook, which is unbearably attractive to them. You are also that, I find. A cook. This is an excellent omelet for being made over the fire, which is most tricky to do. I would not care to attempt it."

She did not mention the coffee, which was not as good

as his omelet, being strong and very bitter. It was possible the events of the day had disrupted him, and he would do better this evening. Or maybe it was that he was not French and therefore incapable of understanding coffee properly.

"You want one of them rolls like you had for breakfast?" Doyle said. "Not too tired to eat are you?"

"But no. It is a nothing, this taking bullets out of English spies."

She doubted the dress she wore now was more decent than the one she had ruined. Grey told her it was green and covered everything it should. Doyle said it was the color of curled baby oak leaves and so entirely respectable she looked like a matron of forty years. She was not yet so foolish as to believe the words of either of these English.

When she had eaten as much of the omelet and some of the bread as she could fit into her, she settled against a tree and sighed in deep contentment and sipped coffee. It was relaxing, this, not to feel angry or afraid for a short time. She had learned many years ago to grab at any small moment of peace that presented itself. "Do you know, Grey, I like this place. It feels very old. Many, many of my people have been here."

"The Gypsies?"

"Yes. The Rom. I should not call them my people since I am no longer part of them. I cannot go back. Not anymore. There is no place among the wagons for a woman such as me." She hurt piercingly for a minute before she shook her head and put the thought away. "This camp, I think, is of great antiquity. The Rom must have been coming here as long as long. Hundreds of years maybe. That lovely stream . . . Rom would come a long way to camp here."

"You enjoyed that."

He was in a peculiar mood. He stayed close, intent upon her. It was as if he waited for something. He had finished his own meal and was drinking red wine with a complex woody smell. He had not yet offered her any.

"I enjoyed it most immensely. To wash . . . This is the first time in a month I have felt completely clean. It is one of the great pleasures of life, to be clean after one has been dirty so long. I went to the pool downstream. It is not broad, but deep, and the bottom is clean sand. They swim there, the women and children, I am sure. Farther down there will be rocks to wash clothes upon."

"Cold though, I imagine."

"I do not mind. I wished never to come out again, but I realized it is impossible to spend one's life in a forest pool, however pleasant. It is lovely soap Doyle gave me. What is it made with? Lavender?"

"I'm not sure. He stole it someplace."

"Of course. How silly of me." She drank coffee again. It seemed odd to sit beside Grey and talk of everyday things, as if they were old friends. She would not have expected it.

"You liked being with the Gypsies?"

"Oh yes. Maybe it was being young, I do not know. When I was one of them it was the only time in my life I was completely happy. I would wake up in forests like this or in fields full of crickets—you can just hear the crickets here, Grey, if you listen—and there was the whole day ahead with nothing at all that must be done at any time. Nothing whatsoever. Everything came to one in great naturalness, gathering sticks for the fire and the horses to water and always the fields and woods to search for food. Or, in town, dancing and begging. I was not much good at dancing, I shall tell you, despite certain lies I have told. But Grey . . . you cannot imagine what a juggler I was."

A pause. "A good one, I suppose."

"Doyle will have told you about my juggling, since I am sure he knows the entire story of my life. I was incomparable, I must tell you. I was even better with throwing the knife. Even now, without seeing, I could aim for that little bird singing up in the tree there—I do not know the proper

French name for him. The Rom would call him *bardroi chiriclo.*"

"That's a greenfinch, Annique."

"Ah, now I shall know. Well, even now, with the proper knife, I think I could hit that bird one time in ten, if I wished to eat finches, which I do not. One must be very hungry to eat finches."

Doyle spoke up beside her. "You don't like the coffee, miss? I think maybe I made it too strong."

"No, no. It is good indeed." She drank the last of it to the dregs and let him take the cup from her hold.

"Don't know but what I may end up drinking coffee meself, instead of tea, if I make many more trips over here," Doyle said. "You going to learn to drink tea in England?"

"I drink tea now, sometimes, when my stomach does not agree with me."

"You're getting better. You didn't even bother to say you're not going to England," Grey said.

"If you imagine I say what I am thinking, monsieur, then you are very foolish, which I do not consider at all likely." She leaned back again against the tree.

Adrian began stirring restlessly, so Grey went to him, and she was forced to listen to another extremely boring discourse on the subject of floating and sleeping. That was strange, when he droned on and on and Adrian became quiet enough to operate upon. She would ask Grey to explain this, later, when she was not so tired. It was annoying he should keep talking when she wished nothing more than to relax and rest. But after a while, she supposed, one paid no more attention to him than to the buzz of bees or a cricket calling.

It was very warm in the clearing this afternoon. Doyle went back and forth. The sound of his boots as he cleared away dishes and mended the fire seemed as right in this camp as the birdcalls and the shuffle of the horses, tied at the edge of the clearing. All the smells, all the sounds, were as they should be.

When she was young and dressed as a boy and following armies, sometimes Vauban would come to meet her. They would sit in the fields or in woods like this and build a small fire. He brought her food when he could. She was always hungry. She would eat and report to him every tiny thing she had seen, and Vauban would praise her and give her orders. She had felt safe at such times, for an hour or two. Vauban would have protected her with his life.

Sometimes Soulier came, elegant even when he wore rags or a soldier's uniform. Soulier smuggled her bonbons from Paris with such care they might have been secret documents. He made her laugh. Always, he had good advice for her. There was no one more cunning than Soulier.

He was in London now, Soulier, since he had become chief of all French spies in England. He played the role of the open agent, the agent that all men knew worked for the Secret Police but no one touched. It was an old agreement—who knew how old—that there should be one open agent in each capital. There must be, after all, a man the British could come to, to ransom sailors and agents and the odd soldier who had fallen into French hands, or to convey the most discreet and private messages from government to government.

Soulier must enjoy that work, as he had a taste for political games. He would enjoy also flaunting himself beneath the noses of Military Intelligence when they could not touch him.

"You are resting quietly, getting stronger. The pain is very far away." Grey's voice was only a murmur in the background. Something she could ignore. "You're safe, where nothing can touch you. The pain is far away. It can't touch you."

She was so drained from what she'd done to Adrian, she was drowsing in the sunlight, lulled by good food inside her and Grey's voice. He spoke in the accents of the South, which were so familiar. Her father had spoken thus. It was the language she spoke as a child. The language her dreams came in. She stretched and yawned and rearranged herself. The tree bark at her back wasn't at all rough. Soft, in fact.

After a while, Grey's feet came near to her and stopped. She yawned again. "You are an odd Head of Section."

"He's good at it," Doyle said.

Grey folded something smooth and warm around her. It was his coat, and it smelled of him. Then she knew.

"You have given me drugs."

"Yes, Annique," Grey said.

It was too late to do anything about it.

Twelve

The coast of Northern France, near Cayeux

"DO NOT GIVE ME FAMILY PARTIES OF DUTCH, with their three children and a grandmother." One hand on the reins, the other clenching a rolled list, Leblanc sat stiff in the saddle. "Or schoolgirls. Or two old men who tune pianos. This is useless."

"These have passed today. No one else." The corporal of militia stood stolidly.

"I tell you again, you are looking for a blind woman. Young, dark-haired. Very lovely. It is inconceivable no one would notice. There will be a man with her. Tall. Brown hair. Brown eyes."

"There may be another with them. A young man, wounded," Henri added.

Leblanc scowled him to silence. "Forget the others. We have to find the blind girl. She will come this way. She must."

Henri's mount crept forward, planning to take a bite out

of the corporal. Henri kneed it back into line. "Or they may strike south."

"She won't. She knows every foot of this coast. And it's the best route to England." Leblanc tore the list he had been offered into pieces. They fluttered to the ground and danced in the wind around the hooves of his horses. "How is she slipping past the patrols? How? Damn these peasants. Someone's helping her."

"No blind women came by my post," the corporal said stolidly.

Leblanc squinted across the barrens of pine and sand toward the slice of slate-colored sea. "That village?"

The corporal said, "Pointe Venteuse, sir."

"It has an inn?"

"*Oui,* monsieur, a fine one. Madame Dumare is—"

"You will take your men, Corporal, and you will go through every house in that wretched village. You will go through every hedge and outhouse and cow byre searching for that woman. Then you will search them again. You will do this until I tell you to stop."

"But—"

"Perhaps next time I will not hear so much of Dutch families. I will be at the inn. Henri . . ."

Resigned, Henri spurred forward.

"Let us make a lesson here. Pick two or three women and bring them to the inn for questioning. If the inn is indeed fine, I will spend the night there."

So. It was to be one of those nights. Henri shrugged and motioned four of the troop to fall in behind him. Husbands and fathers would object. They would object more tomorrow, when they saw what was done with the girls.

"Dark-haired," Leblanc called after him. "I want them dark-haired. And young."

Thirteen

TIME CRAWLED OVER HER AND AROUND HER. SHE floated in endless swirling waters. When the heavy, dark weight of them receded, she was sitting up with a man's arm around her.

"Drink this." It was Grey who said that, and what she was to drink was coffee. Very sweet coffee.

"I do not take so much sugar." She shook her head, annoyed and barely awake. "It is too much. Really." But she drank it because he put it to her lips and kept offering it to her until it was gone. Then he held her close to his chest as she spiraled into the blackness. It was like falling down into him.

Darkness gave way to the velvet times when she was full of mindless contentment and did ordinary things, but nothing was important in the least. She walked or stood or sat, and Grey was nearby, telling her what to do, guiding her through the moments of spinning bewilderment. Then she would lie down and sleep, in a bed or on the ground, wherever he had put her.

Once, she lay with the softness of a bed beneath her. Grey's body sprawled beside her, sleeping. The bed was warm with him, and his arm lay across her, heavy and relaxed. Desire uncoiled in her. Her skin stretched tight over a thousand humming feathers. She turned to him and slid herself against him, and it burned. Between her legs it burned and sang, and she pressed and pressed herself against him.

He woke. "Easy, Annique. You're dreaming. Don't . . ." He set her away from him. "No." It was a whisper in her ear. "You're beautiful, Fox Cub. Sleep now. Just sleep." But she held tight to him, wrapped around him. She felt, suddenly, an ecstasy that broke her into a thousand fragments. She cried out and fell, slowly, all the thousand pieces of her, into the warm, drugged ocean the opium had prepared for her.

Then she was in the coach, tucked against Grey's side, warm sunlight on her face. The *click click* of wheels and the jiggle and thump of the road had been with her a long time. Grey held her and stroked slowly down her back. It would be nice if he did that more. She slipped down to nestle into his lap. Now he would stroke her everywhere.

He ran his fingers softly across her forehead and into her hair. It was not enough. She rolled, inviting his hand across her belly.

"Like a cat," she heard him murmur.

Adrian's voice came softly, nearby. "She wants it. Opium hits some of 'em like that. She's going to make some man deliriously happy, one day."

"Not you," Grey said.

"Unfortunately, no. But then, it's not my flag she's running up the mast, is it?"

Grey gave a deep growl. The vibration buzzed through him and into her skin. She rubbed her cheek against him and breathed him in. Through the rough fabric of his trousers, the muscles and the bones of his thighs emerged into her mind like rocks from sand. It felt wonderful, touching him.

I should not be doing this. It was a faint voice, far beneath the dark waters of her mind.

"She's hurting." Adrian's light words drifted across her, words with no meaning. "Why don't you give her a touch or two and let her fall asleep happy? She won't remember."

"Why don't I kick you out in the nearest cornfield and let you walk home."

"I can look the other way."

"Shut up, Adrian."

"Your sort always makes it complicated. She's coming out again."

"Blast. You're right." The universe shifted. She was sitting up. She heard Grey say, "Make it a half dose. Or less. Less than that."

There was a glass to drink, very bitter. She did not want to take it, because they were giving her opium, but it was drunk before she woke up enough to fight. Then Grey let her lie down in his lap again.

"Go back to sleep." He rearranged her on the seat. She curled around his hand, trying to pull it between her legs, for the touch of him. It kept slipping away.

"Sleep. That's what you want. Nothing else."

She fell down into the darkness. The words fell in after her, melting on her skin like snowflakes.

HER face was wet, which confused her utterly. She was in the coach, and Grey was slapping her. Why was she so wet?

"I wish you would not do that." She tried to fight his hands off. "It is not at all necessary and very impolite."

"Wake up." He slapped her again. It was not painful exactly, but it was not a light tap on the cheek either.

"I am awake." She took hold of his wrist so he could not strike her again. Everything was confused inside her brain, as if it were foggy in there. This was Grey. Grey was in the coach with her and wanted her to wake up. Where were they? She could not at all remember. "You do not need to keep hitting me. I am awake."

"Good. I need you to be awake. Annique, the gendarmes are going to stop the coach. No, don't you dare go to sleep on me. You're going to stay awake and talk to them. Can you do that?"

She pushed the heels of her hands against her temples. Gendarmes. She was in France. Grey . . . Grey was the English spy. Leblanc was chasing her, hungry for her death. He had set the gendarmes after her.

She couldn't think. "Gendarmes?"

Grey switched to German. "Can you be Bavarian? We have to speak German. Can you do that?"

Terror peeled the layers of sleep off her. This was not Grey. This clipped, precise, intellectual voice. This German voice. Beside her in the coach was a man with Grey's shape and his smell and his warmth and his clothing . . . who was not Grey.

"Annique. Wake up and talk to me. Now."

She put her hand to his mouth and felt his breath move with the words. The feeling of Grey was there, the shape of his lips, the stubble of his cheek, his smell. But it wasn't his voice.

"What is it?" His words, but not his voice. Grey, speaking German.

It was horrible and bewildering to hear a different voice come from Grey's mouth. It was inconceivably wrong. She was alone in the dark and she had lost the familiarity of his voice.

"No. I am awake now." She shook her head.

She should not have shaken her head. It made her dizzy, and she could not think. *His voice has changed. That is all. He is still Grey.* She heard the ominous jangling that was armed men—leather and horse bits and guns slung across shoulders. Dreams and unreality clung to everything. She must wake up. *He is still Grey. Do not panic like a silly schoolgirl.*

Grey knew what must be done. He was the still point in chaos. She would do what he said, and trust him, and think later. "I will speak German." That was the easy part. She matched her accent to his. To a village she had lived in, a little farther east, midway between Munich and Salzburg. The lilting speech of hills and green valleys.

"Only German from now on, Annique. Your name is Adelina Grau. I'm your husband Karl. We've been married six months. Adrian is your brother, Fritz Adler. Your twin brother. You come from Grafing. I'm a professor at the University of Munich, going to London to give a series of lectures at the Royal Academy." He slipped something onto her finger. A ring. It was too large for her, with a smooth cabochon stone. Adrian had been wearing that. She knew its feel. She turned it inward so the gold of the ring appeared a plain wedding band.

"Adelina. Karl. My brother, Fritz." A hundred times she had done this. A hundred stories. A hundred different people she had been. Already she was trying to think in German. She could do all that was required of her. "The driver?"

"Blast. Yes. Josef Heilig. He's worked for me for ten years.

"Josef," she repeated. Grey was holding her upright in the seat as if he were afraid she would collapse. She would not, not in the middle of her work. Never in all her years had she given way when there was work to do.

The coach rolled to a stop with much jangling of harness and Doyle telling the horses Germanic things. Grey started huffing away, complaining. She should probably have asked what he was a professor of, but it did not matter. If anyone questioned her, or even looked at her closely, they were lost anyway.

"They are naturally officious, the French," Grey said in his crisp, citified accent. "It was not this bad in the old days. I tell you, Fritz, the French have changed, and not for the better. No one in Paris appreciates my work. Here's another crew of dolts in uniforms, come to impede our progress." All the time, his arm surrounded her, infusing her with the stubborn, indomitable strength of his.

When they were stopped, Grey gave her shoulder a last squeeze and flung the door of the carriage open. "Gentlemen, how may I help you?" His French was now Parisian, heavily accented with German, and he did not sound like Grey in that voice either.

Adrian touched her arm, letting her know where he was so she had one less thing to worry about. "We'll only stop a minute. Karl will take care of it, Adelina." His German was every bit as flawless as her own, the accent close enough. He spoke low, into her ear, "Trust him. He'll pull us out of this. He never fails."

Adrian was feeling better, she thought. His voice was strong. The arm that steadied her wasn't hot with fever. He was like a tough, wild animal, this one. He would live, if it happened the gendarmes did not kill them all. She wished saving Adrian's life was not such an ephemeral achievement.

Adrian continued in a whisper. A German whisper. "They're not suspicious. This looks like a routine document check. Seven men. Local troops, all of them with the weapons slung. Slouching in the saddle. Bored. We're safe enough unless they spot something. Nobody's going to offend Bavarians right now. They've just finished lunch, looks like. They'll be in a good mood."

How many times she had done this, assessing soldiers, holding out forged papers with a confident smile? In her Vauban days she had been part of a team like this. She remembered how it felt, five or six of them becoming a single organism, depending on each other's wit and skill. The old feeling came back to her now. She could sense Doyle, up on the box, and Adrian, beside her. All their attention was centered upon Grey as he strolled toward the soldiers. They waited to take their cue from him.

It was good to be part of such things again. She felt every perception stretched toward Grey.

Some of the gendarmes had dismounted to talk to him. She heard boots on the dirt of the road. In the midst of the shuffling of horses, Grey managed to sound very much the stiff, patronizing professor, a pompous man, important in his own small world. "Papers? Of course you may see our papers. Josef, hand me down the red case, the Cordoba. I see no reason for stopping travelers in the middle of—"

There was a courteous explanation from one of the gendarmes. He spoke slowly, as one does to people who have not the good fortune to be French.

Grey said, "We hardly look like smugglers, my good man. Let me tell you, we don't have smugglers at all in Munich, and if you would only . . . Yes, Josef, that one."

Adrian said quietly, "You're too pretty, Adelina. The lieutenant's seen you. He's coming this way, and he's very admiring. Trouble."

"If Grey does not want lieutenants to look upon me, he should not put me in this dress. I must be out of the carriage so I am below his eye level. Can you do this?"

"Natürlich," Adrian said at once. She didn't know whether this was easy or not. It didn't matter. The important thing was that this gendarme did not realize she was blind.

Adrian played his part skillfully, of course. They would see him being solicitous as he helped her from the carriage. They would not notice that he shielded her from view with his body and found her a place to stand where she could just touch the coach, where no one could come up behind her. It was useful, too, that young women of family were treated like idiots, so it did not seem unusual he should hover over her. He leaned upon the carriage beside her. For support, she thought. He would be weak, so soon after the bullet was dug from him. Three days, four . . . She did not know how long it had been.

"The subprefect in Rouen signed the *laissez-passer* himself," Grey was saying. "A pleasant man. He was most interested in my calculations upon the refraction of light in liquids. I gave him a copy of a lecture I delivered at Würzburg on the subject. He sealed my documents with his own hand. It is impossible that all is not in order."

"It is not that your papers are not in order," the gendarme said, very patient. "There is not the travel stamp from Marley-le-Grand."

"Travel stamp? What is this travel stamp? I was told of no travel stamps."

A pair of boots, no doubt carrying the admiring lieutenant, came closer. She kept her eyes down to the road and put her palm flat on the middle of her belly. "I think I will be sick." She spoke German in a firm, carrying voice. "I was better when the carriage was moving. At least there was a little wind."

"Ah." Adrian rose to the occasion. "Poor Adelinachen. Do you think something to drink would help?"

She shook her head decisively and the hand upon her belly subtly became the unmistakable, eons-old gesture of protection for a child beneath. There would not be one among these men who would miss the significance. French gendarmes were naturally courageous as lions, but it would be a brave lieutenant indeed who pressed attentions upon a woman in the throes of morning sickness.

"Perhaps some bread? Or a dry biscuit? I'm sure we have biscuits somewhere." Adrian was enjoying himself. She had known men like him, admirable spies, and a great nuisance to all who must work with them.

"Do not mention food. You are making it worse. How long will they stop us, Fritz?"

France had been at war with various German speakers

for the last decade. The chance someone in this troop spoke at least a little German was very good. The man most likely to do so was the lieutenant whose increasingly reluctant footsteps still approached.

"I don't think they'll keep us long. They will eventually realize a man doesn't take his silly young wife with him when he goes smuggling."

"I am not silly. I hope in England everyone does not scowl so much and ask for papers all the time." Dizziness swept across her—the drug trying to take hold. She stumbled and steadied herself upon the panel of the coach. "I wish it were not so hot. I do feel most dreadfully sick."

"Do not be sick upon the lieutenant, *Liebling*." Adrian switched to French. "Lieutenant, if we are to be stopped here much longer, is there somewhere I can get my sister out of the sun? In her condition—"

"I deeply regret the inconvenience to Madame." The lieutenant sounded young, she thought. Young and definitely uneasy. "It should be the smallest moment only."

"I was not told of the need for a local travel stamp. I was not informed . . . Excuse me, Lieutenant." Grey walked rapidly toward them. He need not have worried so much, she thought. She could handle this.

"Fritz, what does he say? I am not sure I can . . ." She kept her head down and put her hand delicately to her mouth and tried to look pale.

Adrian drawled, "Karl will be most annoyed if you are unwell again. Especially upon the lieutenant's boots."

The lieutenant understood German. He stepped back hastily. Then Grey was in front of her, so the gendarme could not see her face, and Adrian made some remark, taking the lieutenant's attention further away. It was a great pleasure to work this way with these clever men. It was like children playing, keeping the ball always in the air. The lieutenant did not have a chance against them.

"I was not informed of the need for a regional pass

stamp upon our passports." Grey spoke with fussy precision, shielding Annique behind him. "I was assured by my embassy in Paris they had acquired all the necessary permissions prior to our departure. Again, in Rouen, it was not made clear—"

"Yes. Yes. The stamp. It is a mere formality." The lieutenant's voice said he would much rather deal with Grey than with the young wife, *enceinte*, and a danger to his uniform no less than his dignity, however pretty she was to look upon. "You must correct this oversight at the mayor's office in Dorterre. That is all. It is a difficult time for your wife to travel, *non*?"

"Difficult?" Grey paused long enough to seem puzzled. "No, no, you misunderstand. She is young and strong, Adelina. Her condition is the most natural thing in the world. Women dramatize themselves at this time." He switched to German. "You will be better now, Adelina. No more getting sick, you understand?"

She gave her best young *hausfrau* nod. "*Ja,* Karl." Her skin was cold and seemed to fit her badly. She did feel sick. Sometimes she surprised even herself how well she could act. "If I could perhaps sit down for a few minutes. I am not—"

"No, Adelina. It is not good for you to indulge yourself. Exercise is what is needed. A gentle walk beside the carriage for the next mile or so will make you feel much better."

The lieutenant cleared his throat. "There's an inn at the next village. I know it myself. A most pleasant, respectable place. Madame could repose herself there until the heat of the day passes."

Having talked herself into it, she was now feeling decidedly unwell. "Karl, I feel so very—"

"Nonsense. I have made myself knowledgeable in this matter." Grey sounded insufferably complacent. All the while, his grip steadied her, unwavering, iron-hard, and full of comfort. "This is a perfectly natural process and should not cause the least discomfort. Mares do not become sick. Cats do not become sick. There is no reason for women to do so. I have explained this, Adelina. There is a monograph by my friend Herr Professor Liebermann on this subject which I will read to . . . Adelina, what are you doing?"

She broke free and groped her way along the carriage wheel, to double over, fists pressed across her stomach, and be sick with nothing in her. She had not eaten or drunk anything for a while, it seemed. This did not stop her from being abominably ill.

"I . . . we will not detain you further." The lieutenant sounded about fifteen years old and appalled. He retreated in haste. The whole lot of them, in fact—men, horses, and musketry—seemed glad to quit the area immediately.

Hooves clattered on the roadway. Grey, still being Bavarian, scolded, "Adelina, if you would simply concentrate your mind, you would not be sick. You must think of other things." He hid her from their view. Gently, he lifted her hair away from her face and held her upright, which was more than she could manage for herself.

"Fox Cub, that was one hell of a convincing performance." Adrian sounded exhausted. He spoke German still. So wise, they were. The cadence of a language carries farther than the words. One of the gendarmes might linger to listen and hear their voices change if they started speaking French.

"It's that poison we're feeding her. Adrian, get me . . . Good." Grey patted a wet cloth on her face. "Finished?"

She simply nodded. It was not that it was too hard to speak German. It was that she wanted to die.

"Drink this." Grey set something to her lips.

Not again. She knocked the glass aside and heard it shatter on the ground. She was too weak and dizzy to run. She could only put her back against the coach and cover her mouth with her arm. It would do her no good. There was no fight within her.

"Goddammit, Annique, there was nothing in that but water."

Adrian was lazily amused, as always. "He's telling the truth. This whole area's swarming with armed Frenchmen. We can't clutter up the coach with unconscious females."

"He's not trying to drug you," said Doyle, up on top of the coach.

"He leaves that to you, Herr Doyle. You are a sheep-swiving, swine-dog traitor, that is what you are." German is a lovely language for cursing.

"Now, miss, a nice young lady like you shouldn't even know them words. You folks going to mill around here for the next hour, chatting? Let me know so I can turn the horses loose."

"We're leaving." Grey switched back to French. "Adrian, get in the coach before you keel over."

"Ever obedient to your command, oh Exalted One." The coach dipped as Adrian climbed inside.

Grey came close. "Annique . . ." He molded her fingers around a cup. He poured, and the cup got heavy and cold. "It's water. Just water. God knows you don't have any reason to trust me, but I wish you'd drink it."

The reality of her helplessness closed in around her. They were such clever men, these three—hard and experienced and quite ruthless. Grey was the most dangerous of all. He made her believe he wanted to be kind. Every moment it was a fight to remember he was her enemy.

Perhaps he forgot also, sometimes. It was doubtless easier for the victor to ignore the realities.

She said, "I must drink, sooner or later. I have no choice." The cup held clean water with no taste but that of a metal flask. She drank what he had given her.

His hand on her cheek was like a flower falling onto her. "The first time, when I drugged you, it was wrong. I should have told you. I should have let you fight me. I made a mistake."

That soft touch. He had done that before. Memories were beginning to rise like bubbles to the surface of her mind. "I remember. I was lying beside you on a blanket. I wanted to touch you. I wanted—"

"It's time we left."

But she remembered. She had pressed herself against him and opened her legs and throbbed with mindless pleasure. "What did I do when I was asleep? What did I do with you?"

"You dreamed. The drug takes some women that way. It means nothing."

Were they dreams, the heat and the hunger and the shamelessness? *The drug takes some women that way.* In the midst of many turmoils, she must add one more. She became wanton when she slept with the drug. Even her body betrayed her to these English. Truly, it did not seem fair.

"I remember. Almost."

The hand slipped into her hair and held her. "Nothing happened. I'd tell you if we did anything."

She had done nothing? She remembered the smell of him under her nostrils and crying out without any restraint and twisting, twisting herself upon him. "I do not think it was a dream. I was wearing one of your shirts. I wanted it off. I wanted . . ."

The wanting escaped out of her memory and swept across her. In the turn of a moment, her skin was avid for him. She had never known that skin could be hungry for the touch of another skin. She turned to nuzzle his wrist. To taste him. She did not notice she was doing it till he jerked his hand away.

He breathed harshly. "Let's get you into the coach. You don't want this. You just think you do. You're drugged to the eyeballs." Now he sounded exasperated. "And you're falling asleep standing up."

"Grey, we have to go." That was Doyle.

Certainly he heard all of this, and Adrian, too, inside the coach. She might as well have been stripped naked, considering the privacy she had among these men. "I do not want you. And I am not asleep."

"Then I won't need to lift you into the coach. You can climb up yourself. That's right. I've got you. Adrian, don't try to help. You're going to rip your shoulder apart."

But Adrian carried her onto the seat anyway. It could not be good for him. She would scold him when she was awake. Grey put his arm around her. "Where are we?"

"Less than an hour from Dorterre."

"Ah. I was here two years ago." She tried to bring to her mind a map of this coastal region, but the image shimmered and melted away. She was not used to memories that did that. "I was in the smuggler villages. Hiding."

Grey settled her close. "Good place for it. What were you hiding from, two years ago?"

"The Vendée uprising. The last one. It was . . . very bad. I could not believe French soldiers would do such things to French women and children. And I had been given such orders . . ." Confusion swirled in her mind. Fragments of pain. Memories. "I disobeyed my orders. I would not spy on those poor people, so I ran away and hid. Everyone was very angry with me." She rubbed her face against her arm. "I talk with this drug. I will have to remember that."

"Those aren't state secrets, Fox Cub. The whole world knows what Napoleon did in the Vendée."

"I should not say so much, anyway, when my head is not clear. Did you know you do not sound at all like yourself when you speak German? It startled me altogether for a moment. It is as if there is suddenly another person in the carriage. Do not do it again."

"I'll try not to. Why don't you go to sleep."

And she was falling into sleep once more. Had he given her more of the drug, or was she being dragged down by what she already carried within her?

"I remember what we have done together. I am almost sure it was not decent." But she let him comb her hair back with his fingers and tuck a blanket around her and arrange her at ease along the seat. "I will decide what to do about it when I am awake. Perhaps I will try to strangle you once more. Though you have the most beautiful body imaginable. Like a large animal."

Adrian murmured, "What complex and interesting nights you two must have."

"Shut up," Grey said.

When she was almost asleep, Grey pulled her against his chest, cradling her possessively. Her body was used to it. She fitted against him as if there were a place there formed especially for her.

Fourteen

"ANNIQUE." GREY SHOOK HER. "WE'RE IN TROUBLE. Wake up."

She clawed through feathery blackness and came alert. She was afraid, instantly. Something bad had happened. Very bad. She heard it in his voice. The coach had begun lurching in the ruts and gullies, going fast.

"There's a troop of men behind us," Grey said. "Seven or eight at least. They're keeping their distance, but it's just a matter of time. We can't outrun them."

On the opposite seat, Adrian moved back and forth, quietly and swiftly. "I'm done." He clicked something. The catch of a bag, she thought.

"They're in mufti. They don't ride like army. They don't act like customs. They're Leblanc's," Grey told her.

"He has tracked us?" She rubbed her face.

"Just bad luck, I think. Leblanc's flung a net along the coast and caught us in it. We knew this might happen." Grey was busy with small metallic sounds. She could smell gunpowder.

They would fight. They were three men, against so many.

A muffling of trees on either side caught and held the echo of the horses' hooves. They were in deep woods then. Horsemen could not make a concerted rush upon them on a narrow path in the woods. One or two would approach from the back. Doyle, outside, would die almost immediately, with the first shots. Grey and Adrian would fight for a time, and then die. The thin panels of a coach are no defense against bullets.

She would huddle like a dog on the floor of the coach. In the end, if she was not killed by a stray bullet, they would find her and take her to Leblanc.

To cower on her knees, with so little dignity. Anger and fear congealed in her throat. Never, never had she hated her blindness more than at this minute when she was so helpless and so useless.

Grey put his hands upon her shoulders, squeezing, as if he tested her strength. He must feel her shaking. He would know how little it meant. "You'll do."

A brief, impersonal touch to her arm. That was Adrian. "Listen, Cub. We're liabilities, you and I. There's an old monastery a quarter mile ahead. We get off there."

"We'll deal with the men and come back for you." Grey's voice went stern. "Annique, don't make a mistake. You don't want to meet whoever's following us."

"You are right." She had no friends in France who rode in packs on horseback. Only her enemies were so strong.

"There's nothing in any direction but miles of woods and barrens and the sand. No houses and no help for you. Stay with Adrian. Don't try to go off on your own."

He was protecting her, even though she was an enemy agent. That was the core of Grey of the British Service. To protect. She said simply, "I will go with Adrian and take care of him as best I can. You have my promise."

Adrian and Grey were both silent at that. They smiled to themselves, she thought. Men could be such idiots.

"You can take care of each other," Grey said. "Here's your monk house coming. We won't stop. Adrian?"

"Ready."

Adrian crouched, holding the door open. The valise he held bumped at her legs.

Grey had such strength. Without effort, he braced his legs between the two seats, to lean above her. "I want you alive. Don't do anything stupid.

"I am not a stupid woman."

"If you run, I'll track you down. I'll be damn annoyed when I find you." He tightened his hold. "There's been no time. Whatever you've done . . . Oh hell." His mouth was brutal as it closed over hers. "We'll talk about this later."

But she did not try to talk. She went mad for him. She found his hair, laced into it, and dragged him to her. She consumed him, mouth to mouth. She fought the awkward angles of their bodies, the lurching of the carriage, and went to him. She could not get close enough.

She had one minute. Then he took her head between his hands, hard, and set the last kiss on her forehead. "That's settled, then. I'll be back. We'll finish this. I'm not letting you go."

She had wondered what it would be like if Grey once let himself reach out to take her. Now she knew. He would be vehement and direct and very certain of himself.

The carriage slowed. "Now!" Adrian called and jumped. She heard him hit the ground.

"Grey . . ." she said.

"Be careful." He swung her through the open door. She tumbled into the sickening drop before she had time to feel afraid.

The road slapped her. She kept the cry of pain inside and spun, over and over. She stopped, dizzy and hurt, on slimy, cold ground. Rocks and slick mud were under her. Before she could move, Adrian's fist tangled in her clothing. He pulled her, fast, into scratchy bushes and pushed her underneath him and collapsed on top of her.

The coach rolled away, speeding up. The sound of wheels was eaten by the trees.

"Your shoulder?" She made the smallest whisper. Had he torn his wound open?

"Good." The words fell into her ear almost without sound.

She pressed close to the ground and lay her face into the dirt so the white of her flesh would not give them away. Adrian had also lived through battles. She heard him breathing beside her, face down, hidden.

Silence. Then the jingling of harness and the beat of hooves rose in the distance. Came closer. She could disentangle the sound of six horses, trotting one by one, in a line. After a space, three more followed. She held her breath, pretending to be soil, pretending to be rocks and bushes, until they passed.

When they were gone, she pressed her ear to the ground and waited till even the faintest thud of hooves had faded. Then she waited longer. The hum of insects returned, and the birds singing among the scrubby branches of the pine woods, and she still waited. She wished Adrian had chosen a place less inhabited by sharp sticks. And little bugs.

Nine men. Even Grey could not overcome so very many. He was going to meet his death in these cold woods.

She set her forehead against the cold earth and squeezed her eyes shut tight, for she was crying. It was over, this incident in her journey, and this man, who had torn the heart from her body. She would not meet him again or struggle with the feelings he aroused in her. She knew what Grey had said with that kiss. What he said was farewell.

The mist condensed into a cold drizzle. There was nothing to be gained by staying where she was. She had Adrian to care for, sick and weak, and as much a fool as most men, for all he was very deadly. If she did not stay with him, he would probably die. She said, "It is time to move. I am cold."

"Me, too."

"Can you walk? No, give me that. Are you bleeding?"

"Not much."

She touched his shirt. He told the truth. "Which way? Can you walk?"

"I can walk as far as I have to."

She took the bag from him. It was heavy enough to contain half a dozen weapons and no doubt did. These English went about armed to the teeth. Adrian put his arm across her shoulder to guide her around the many ruts and to steady himself. It was smoother going when they left the road and entered the old courtyard of the monastery. Their coming disturbed birds and sent them upward in a flurry of wings. That would be uncomfortable for these small birds in this rain.

"The chapel still has a roof on it. We'll go there," Adrian said. "Straight ahead."

The odor of fire clung to this place. Perhaps the Revolutionaries had burned the monks out a decade ago. Or the monastery might have been destroyed in the War of the Vendée, by one side or the other. Once the soldiers were gone, it was not easy to tell which side had burned what.

But no one had bothered to torch the chapel. She pushed the door open and heard the echoes of an enclosure within, with no rain falling. The windows must be broken, though, from the draft of cold air that blew in her face. When she walked forward, her feet kicked aside rubble, dry pieces of wood that had probably been chairs and carved statues. That would make tinder to start the fire.

"There's shelter at the back," Adrian said.

There was a space between the altar and the wall of the church where the wind did not reach. She left him there, sitting on the stones, wrapped in his coat. He had no strength to waste, so she did not argue when he told her he would do this thing or that. She just ignored him and did them herself.

It was not easy in her darkness to do those things needed to make a camp, but it was not impossible, either. In her youth, she had pitched camps in many uncomfortable places. The rubble on the chapel floor yielded stones for a cosh and the long stick she needed. Outside was a huge, wet tangle, thorny as a jungle, where the monks once had a garden. On the paths still paved she made her way between the burned timbers and fallen walls. There was bracken in the corners, dry enough to bring in to sleep upon, and enough charred wood to make a dozen bonfires. She even located an apple tree. No blackberries though. The birds must have eaten them all.

There was not the faintest suspicion of fighting in the distance. Whatever had become of Grey, it had been done silently or very far away. She indulged herself, crying as she worked in the rain in this empty garden.

In the end, she dried her face upon her sleeve and finished the tasks she must do, carrying firewood and bracken. She was muddy and very wet by the time she finished, but at least it did not rain inside the chapel. She knelt against the altar, which was marble from the soapy feel of it, and set the small cosh she had prepared next to her knee. She would make a fire. Even before she was blind, she had learned to make fire in the dark.

"It is melancholy, this. I do not have an English spy's liking for such places." Wood shavings caught fire in the shelter of the curve of her hand. She fed in tinder—dry scraps that might have been some carved angel, ages old. Someone had stomped it to small pieces, none longer than a finger, but she could make out the shape of wings.

She lay the angel bit by bit into the fire, feeling the delicate, dry lightness, the old paint and gilding upon the surface. "Do they have any chance at all, do you think?"

Adrian sat on the piled bracken, his back to the wall.

"They're very wily. Very experienced. I don't think the man breathes who can find that pair in this weather in wild country. Grey's half deer when he's in the woods."

"The rain is lucky for us, then." She balanced slender shards of the wood onto the fire, not burning herself. There is a trick to it, which she well knew. "I can hear the sea outside, if I listen carefully. It is a mile from here, no more. There, that has our fire going nicely."

"I could do all that."

"Of a certainty. But my hands like to be busy. I shall set a trap for rabbits in a while. I smell them back there in the old garden."

"Leave it, unless you're starving. You're already wet clean through. There's a cloak in that bag, one of mine that I brought for you. It'll keep you warm tonight."

"It shall keep us both warm. With this fire, I shall be dry soon. Where is that bag of yours? I shall have a look at that, if you please."

"There's a loaded pistol on top."

"Even if I could not smell it I would know there would be a loaded pistol on top of any bag you carried."

The bracken rustled at her.

"It is not being a spy that makes you so stupid," she told him. "It is being a man. Now me, I have been playing what you English call the Game for . . . oh, a dozen years perhaps. Ah. The catch works thusly. I see." She set the bag open. "In all those years, I have had a loaded gun in my hands precisely three times. And to make it three I must count this. I shall give this silly gun to you, to hide under your pillow."

"You may put it down very gently right there."

"You do not trust me with it only because my eyes do not work, though I am unspeakably clever." She shook her head. "Alas. There is any amount of human folly, do you not think? So this is the cloak you speak of. But it is very nice. It shall go on top of us. You shall put your coat underneath, and we shall have less of this admirable vegetable poking at us."

"You're a remarkable woman, Fox Cub."

"I am, although you do not yet know it, because you have never tasted one of my omelets. *Mon Dieu,* but you carry many useful things with you. And knives. It is a good knife, this."

"I like it."

She touched her way through the last things in the bag. There was a coil of fine-woven silk rope, thin, but strong enough to hold a man's weight. It was light and smooth as flowing water, and there were yards and yards of it. "Adrian, I will tell you . . . we are much alike, we two." She ran the rope reverently through her fingers. "Even though you carry that noisy pistol with the powder that is certainly wet already. This rope . . . I shall set such a snare with this. You shall help me."

"Rabbits, Annique?"

She laughed. "But no. Weasels."

Fifteen

THE FIRE HAD BURNED DOWN TO EMBERS. THE wall of the chapel protected her back, and she held Adrian close to her to keep warmth between them. One cloak, like a blanket, spread over them both.

"There are pictures on the walls," Adrian said. "I've been lying here looking at them. Where the plaster's left, it's painted with . . . I guess you'd call it a meadow. Flowers all over. Thirty or forty different kinds. The columns have vines of blue flowers running right up 'em."

"It sounds pretty."

"It is. Right above us on the ceiling, there's a white bird with the sun behind it. That's up there getting smoky from the fire."

"I think we have been sacrilegious. I did not remember this was a house of God when I was roasting apples."

"The gods moved out of here a long time ago." Adrian hesitated. "You can't see what happened here. Believe me, cooking apples is nothing compared to what was done in this place."

"Do not tell me, then. I have seen enough elsewhere that I can imagine it."

"We both have." He moved restlessly, with a crackling in the bedding beneath them. "I wish you'd go to sleep. Unless you've decided to pull all these damp clothes off and make wild, passionate love."

"No, Adrian."

"I was afraid not. Be a good girl, then, and try to sleep. It's not your watch. It's too soon to expect them back. Much too soon."

"How long will we wait for them?"

There were many things they did not need to say out loud to each other. "The rest of today. Tonight. Till tomorrow at noon. If Grey hasn't come by then, we'll leave."

Rain dripped persistently at the far end of the chapel, near the door. There was a leak there, and a wide puddle of water. "He will not come, will he?"

"He's been in worse corners than this. You French don't know half the things he's done."

The cloud of misery that had been weighing upon her lightened somewhat. She must remember that Grey was no ordinary man. He had been in many dangerous snarls, and always he had untangled them and escaped. Perhaps he and Doyle were even now enacting some fiendishly clever plan, and he would come looking for her again as he promised. She would not put it past him.

"I know almost nothing of Grey. I have not interested myself in the British, as there are any number of other nations to spy upon. It is a grave lack in my education. You, little brother, I know something of, from the time you worked in Milan."

"When did I become your little brother? I thought we were twins."

"We are, but you are seventeen minutes younger. Because of this, I have always bullied you unmercifully. I work these things out when I am playing a role, you see. I used to blackmail all your candy from you when we were children in Grafing, and I told tales on you and got you into trouble. Even now I tell my friends about your mistresses so the young ladies are all shocked with you. I am a terrible person when I'm your twin."

He chuckled weakly. "You're a terrible person even when you aren't, did you know that?"

"I have several terrible people to be, within me, when I need them." Twigs scratched her annoyingly as she stretched. "What does he look like? I have not seen him, you know."

"Skin like shoe leather. Wide across the shoulders. Big barrel of a chest . . ."

"Not Doyle, as you understand quite well. I have seen Monsieur Doyle several times in Vienna when we were with great attention not noticing each other. What does Grey look like?"

"He is the Head of Section for the British Intelligence Service. He is not for you, my child."

"*Bien sûr.* I am also, you understand, not for him. But I would still like to know what he looks like."

"Tall and battered around some. Not handsome." That was all he had to say.

"I hope you are more eloquent in reporting to your superiors, for of a certainty I am no wiser than I was three minutes ago." She grimaced toward the unseen ceiling. "Which was doubtless your intention. You are right, though. It does not matter."

There was no picture of Grey in her mind. He was strong arms to harbor in and broad hands with calloused palms that had touched her everywhere. He was sternness and great certainty in deciding what must be done, so much certainty that the air around him was charged with it. He was the cleverest of spymasters, frightening when he was one's enemy. He was the smell of clean soap and a roughness of his chin when he had not shaved for several hours. Those things, and a voice speaking the French of Toulouse, were all she had. Strange to know so much about him and not to know what he looked like.

Adrian said, "Have you fallen in love with Grey? That wasn't wise of you."

Sometimes, she was not wise. There were many people who could have told him this.

He said, "You aren't going to deny it, are you? Not to your twin."

She listened to the fire for a while. "When one says, 'I will not let myself feel anything for that man,' it is already too late."

"Why, Annique?"

"I do not think such stupidity can have a reason." She had most assuredly been stupid. "To love . . . it is a great madness for those in our profession."

"You're right about that." He shifted again, uncomfortably. "It was a woman who put that bullet in me. Did you know?"

"One cannot tell from looking at the wound, as it happens."

"A remarkable girl. Something like you, in a way. A great player in the Game."

"You should still not let her shoot holes in you. You are also very good at this Game you play."

"We're all daunting as demons. Did Grey get to you yet, or are you still a virgin?"

She should not have been surprised. There was nothing this one would not say. "You make numberless assumptions, many of them wrong."

"I don't think so. Has he?"

"Has no one told you that you are nosy beyond belief?"

"You don't have to answer."

"But you will speculate upon this endlessly, whatever I say or do not say. And you will do it aloud. There is no shame in you, Adrian."

"None." She heard the smile in his voice.

She sighed. "*Tiens.* Your Monsieur Grey has done nothing at all to me, except that kiss which you saw, and perhaps some other careless bagatelles in these last few days, which I do not remember very well. It does not matter much, one way or the other, whether one has performed that particular act or not . . . And you may stop your foolish laughing, which will only make your shoulder ache."

"If Grey doesn't hurry up and take you to bed, I swear I will. You should find out what you've missed."

"Very little, I suspect. This business of man and woman is not a club with secret passwords. Me, I know all there is to know of these things and—"

"That's what I thought. You've done nothing. Grey is six or seven kinds of a fool."

"This is a very indelicate conversation, and I do not believe I will have it with you any longer."

"If you get the chance, make love to him. He's not a master of the art, like me, but—"

"You may keep watch, you, in a more serious manner. And do not pander. It is unbecoming." She pulled the cloak up so it covered him more securely.

"I'm warm enough."

"Then you shall stay so. I am glad I did not make love to Grey. He annihilates any common sense I have, which is disturbing to me as a Frenchwoman, for we are a logical race. I am more a Frenchwoman than a spy. Did I tell you I am decided to retire from spying?"

"Really? Governments all over Europe breathe a sigh of relief. Will you do it any time soon?"

"The moment I deliver you to safety and perform one small final task I have set myself, I shall slip away to become obscure and harmless as a dormouse. Probably in your own England. It is a big place, according to the maps. I do not think your Service will find me."

"It's hard for a blind woman to hide." He was warning

her. Always, just an inch beyond their conversation, hovered the uncomfortable truth—that they were enemies.

"I shall manage. When we leave here, I shall take you to my smuggler friend up the coast, if he is not in prison again. He can be trusted utterly. We are here in his very domain, which is most fortunate for us. I do not think we could travel far, we two."

"You know where we are." He was amused.

"If this is the monastery of St. Honoré, I do. I hold many good maps within my head, little brother. It is a talent of mine. Also, I know the coast here well. When I was a child, we came to visit just this smuggler. He is an Englishman like you. One of my mother's lovers. I have a picture of Englishmen not quite accurate, perhaps, from having met only spies and smugglers in my—"

A sound that was not wind or the fall of rain or the faint rumble of the surf slipped into the pattern of the night. A distant pounding. She stopped talking instantly.

Horses. They came from the direction of the coast. In a single surge of motion, Adrian was up, kicking the fire apart, smothering it.

The beat of hooves grew louder and slowed. The riders turned aside, coming into the monastery.

"It is better if we go separately," she whispered. *I will be his death. Adrian must abandon me and run.* "You will go first. Out the back. I have cleared an escape route as far as the wall."

"Of course. An escape route. In between picking apples, you cleared an escape route. I'd expect no less." Laughter rippled in his voice. For Adrian, disaster would always be a game.

The monastery courtyard filled with clatter and men talking between themselves. They had come to search the buildings. The metallic scrape beside her said Adrian had gathered up the pistol and was checking it. Then came a small miscellany of sounds as he rooted through his bag.

His knives would be finding their way to their accustomed spots about his person. One, in a sheath, landed in her lap.

"Take that and put it away," he said. "This is what we're going to do—"

"We will run. You go through the garden. I will—"

"Shut up, Cub, and listen. I leave first. I'm going to take these Frenchmen for a stroll in the woods. No telling what accidents might befall them there." He could have been talking of a pleasant evening's entertainment—stopping at a café, then on to the theater. "You, *ma petite*, will keep your head down and stay put till they've gone after me."

If he walked silently into the rain, he would be safe. Instead, he would lead the hunters away from her. "Do not—"

"Money." He snaked a smooth, cool purse into her bodice, between her breasts. "Buy something pretty. When you get to England . . ." He was fitting his boots on, fast. ". . . forget about hiding. Go to the British Service and turn yourself in. They'll make a deal with you for the Albion plans. And they'll keep you safe from Leblanc."

"I will not, of course."

"Listen carefully. In London, go to Number Seven Meeks Street, not far from Lincoln's Inn Fields. Meeks Street, off Braddy. Remember that."

"My memory is excellent. But I will not do it."

"I'll see you there. Stay alive. Grey will kill me if you don't." He pulled his coat from the bracken, awkward and rustling as he put it on, because one of his arms was not working.

He was most probably going to his death, so she used his true name. "Good luck, my Hawker."

"Why are all the best women French spies? Bad planning on somebody's part." He set his open hand, briefly, on her hair. "I would kiss you good-bye, sister mine, but I don't think I could stand the comparison with Grey. When I'm gone, count to fifty, get out the window behind you, and take that escape route you've laid out through the garden. I'll be headed the other way. You have a chance, I think."

Men approached the chapel. She could hear them. She took his sleeve to hold him one last minute and whispered, "The village of St. Grue is five miles north, up the coast. The smugglers are run by an Englishman named Josiah. The password is jasmine, like the flower. Tell him you are from me."

"That's where I'll aim. Good luck, Annique *mia*."

She heard his footsteps down the length of the chapel, then a scuffle as he climbed through one of the empty windows. A moment later, shots came. Two. Three. Four of them. He had showed himself to the men in the courtyard. Somehow, weak as he was, he must have made it over the wall. Men shouted and ran, yelling that he had escaped. Horses set steel on stones, riding for the gate.

She stayed quietly where she was and listened. Perhaps they would all be fools . . .

Sadly, they were not. One horse still shuffled on the stones outside. One man had remained behind to finish the search.

So. She would deal with him. She lifted her cosh and took her staff from where it leaned across the top of the altar. She had swept the floor clean in the path she must take. It was entirely silent to creep the length of the chapel and press herself flat against the wall behind the door. The searcher was in no hurry. Long minutes passed before she heard boots on the stones outside. The latch lifted and the door creaked. He crossed the threshold.

Paving stones crashed to the floor as the snare fell. He yelled. She was on him at once, using the cosh. It took only two blows to make him most thoroughly immobile.

She and Adrian had discussed at length where a man would fall, tangled and fighting in the web that came down upon him. It was a pleasure to discover how correct they had been. He was sprawled unconscious upon the doorsill itself. Her prize was breathing, so it was not even a murder on her conscience.

Altogether satisfactory. That was one man less to hunt Adrian. It had been worth the hour it had taken her to weave her trap.

She knew him by the smell of his clothing before she felt his features. How remarkably persistent Henri was turning out to be. She cut strips of his shirt with Adrian's knife and tied him up before she extracted him from the strings of her trap. Then she dragged him the length of the chapel to the pillar she had picked out. He carried a useful knife, which she collected from him. She also helped herself to his money, of which there seemed to be a good deal. There is no rain which does not water someone's turnips.

When she had finished, she wiped her hands on her dress—truly, she did not like touching Henri—and considered her alternatives. Should she go . . . or stay? Adrian might return. Grey would come, or Doyle, if either lived. Or Henri's comrades might come looking for him. There would be visits from everyone, in fact, who was not lying in his blood out in the woods. This would be a most busy place, this chapel, if anyone survived.

Most certainly she should leave immediately. She had Henri's horse. Within a few miles of this spot were fifty friends who would help her go to England. She was ruled by grave responsibilities. Whether she gave the Albion plans to England or remained loyal to France, she must not let them fall into Leblanc's hands. It was stupidity beyond measure to stay in this chapel on such an eventful night.

If Grey came, he might be wounded. He might need help.

And so her decision was made. There were various small businesses to attend to. She walked outside into the cold density of rain, to lead Henri's horse to an inconspicuous spot in the briar jungle behind the chapel. It tried, several times, to bite her and succeeded once. Then there was her trap to set once more, with rocks and rope, above the door. It was Ovid, after all, who said that one's hook should always be cast, for there will be fish in the pool where one least expects it.

HAWKER crouched in the sand, feral and silent. They were closing in—not Leblanc's men, but a gaggle of dragoons on patrol. Nowhere to hide. He was too weak to run.

But somebody else was out here in the dunes tonight. Smugglers. The sound of gunfire had flushed them out. They had as much to fear from the dragoons as he did. And they had a boat.

He flogged his body into motion, staggering toward the breakers. Mushy sand dragged at his feet. Nothing to see in this black fog. Nothing.

Follow the sound. Annique walked around like this all the time. He could do it for a hundred yards.

The boat was already yards out in the water, oars stroking with a regular slap. He splashed after it. *"Attendez. Aidez-moi."* Damn cold stuff, seawater.

Clomping and shouting their way over the crest of the dunes, came the dragoons. Gunshot skipped across the water. He should have learned to swim. It couldn't be hard. Dogs did it.

Waves knocked him down. His clothes weighed like lead. The ground disappeared beneath his feet, and he sank like a stone. He barely felt the arms that pulled him on board.

"Ain't one of ours, Josiah," an English voice said. Sharp corners bit in as they rolled him over. A bullet pinged into the side of the boat.

"Frenchie by the look of 'im."

"Throw 'im back." Sussex voices reached a consensus. He was lifted roughly and shoved to the gunnels.

"Slime-gut, buggering pus-suckers." He skimmed back to consciousness. "Password's . . . jasmine."

"That's the king's English, that is. Stow 'im aboard, lads, I won't leave even a Cockney drown." The voice of command was an older man with a Yorkshire accent. Someone leaned close. "Cover 'im up and let's get out of here."

He was pushed into the bottom of the boat and became limp and unknowing as a fish.

BIRDS chittered back and forth, discussing the coming day to see if they liked it, which was something they did before it became truly light. She sat beside Henri, listening to him grunt and thrash. He was trying to get out of the knots she'd tied. He would not succeed.

When a single horseman entered the courtyard, she took up the cosh and got into position.

The second fish in her net fought more strongly than the first. She was not gentle with her cosh. This man, returning so soon, meant the hunt for Adrian was over. He must be dead, somewhere out in those trees. She was crying when she tied the man's hands behind him.

Then she checked to see whether she had crushed his skull, subduing him. He was unconscious but breathing. He was Grey.

She did not often have a chance to indulge in her extensive collection of swear words. She did so now. Did Grey have no care for himself at all? Did he not know how dangerous she was? Nothing could be stupider than for Grey to come to this place, sneaking about, wearing another man's coat so that she did not know him. She would tell him so when he woke up.

She went quickly to wet a cloth in the nearest puddle. By the time she got back, he was groaning. She had not hurt him lethally, then, doubtless because his head was of solid, stupid rock. She washed his face with the cloth to bring him fully awake and as repayment for the several wet cloths he had slapped across her.

"Annique? My God. You're the one who set that trap?"

"But of course. My friend, I must tell you. More than two hours ago, men rode into this monastery. Leblanc's men. Adrian led them away, except for Henri, who is over there." She waved in the general direction of Henri, who was wriggling noisily by the pillar she had attached him to. "Adrian has not come back. There were shots . . . He is so weak. And there were at least three of them."

"He'll make it. He's the sneakiest man alive. The men chasing us are great blundering dolts in the woods. City men. Untie me."

"Doyle is . . . ?" She couldn't finish the question.

"Leading them in circles. They won't get Doyle. He's been doing this longer than you've been alive. And we killed a couple. Get these ropes off my hands."

"I do not think so." She did run her finger over the ties she had made, but it was to check that they were quite secure. "I wish Doyle very well. You also, Grey. I wish you the good luck in your travels." She spoke to him, this last time, in the intimate form of the language, the one used between friends and lovers. "I part company with you now, as has been my intention for some while. This should not amaze you."

"Don't do this, Annique. Let me loose."

Oh, but Grey was furious. He did not like to be helpless, this one. But there were other things in his voice . . . Worry for her. Caring. She could not be completely mistaken about that. She would not hurt like this if he did not care at all.

"I cannot stay long," she said. "Leblanc's men may become bored with chasing the excellent Doyle and return. And there will be gendarmes, before many hours pass, who will ask themselves why this wood is completely full to the brim with dead bodies everywhere. Do you need money? I will give you some of Henri's, if you like."

"Let me get you across the Channel. I'll set you free on

the other side, I promise. I'll give you a head start. Whatever you want. Don't do this on your own. You don't have a chance."

She smoothed the coat on his shoulder, where there were admirable muscles. She could indulge herself also in stroking his cheek. That was even better—the touch of skin upon skin. "Do you know, when I am with you I am not afraid at all. It is a magic altogether curious that happens inside the heart. I wish I could take it with me when I leave."

She should not waste her time sitting and talking to him. They both had numerous tasks to accomplish before dawn. But she had not engaged in so many dissipations in her life, after all. She could allow herself a few minutes. "I am frightened of this next journey. The noise of the sea makes it hard to hear what is around me. I must go a long way through this desolation, which is chaotic and full of men trying to kill me. I would avoid it, if I could. I am not an idiot."

"Think. Just stop and think. If by some miracle you get to England, you're going to fall into my hands anyway. You're just delaying the inevitable." He was working very hard to get free, but she was no amateur at the craft of tying people. "I'm not going to hurt you. I swear it."

"It is sad, my Grey. We are constrained by the rules of this Game we play. There is not one little place under those rules for me to be with you happily. Or apart happily, which is what makes it so unfair." She sat more comfortably, pulling her knees up, resting her arms across them. "I have discovered a curious fact about myself. An hour ago I was sure you were dead, and it hurt very much. Now you are alive, and it is only that I must leave you, and I find that even more painful. That is not at all logical."

In all the time she had known Grey—well, it was not so very long after all—she had never searched his face with her hands to know what he looked like. She could do it now. His hair was short, but soft to hold between her fingers. He had strongly marked bones in his nose—it had been broken once, she thought—and skin of an uncivilized roughness. The ridge of his eyebrows was most pronounced. Not pretty, Monsieur Grey. She had not thought he would be.

"I shall leave you the knife of Henri," she said, "though I could use it myself. It is in apology for those bumps I have given you with this useful small cosh of mine. You must cut your way free when I am gone. I shall gift you also with Henri, who, I must tell you, I am beginning to find boring in the extreme in his attentions. I have still not murdered him, as you see. I am all benevolence."

"You're going to get yourself killed out there."

"It is very possible." She had one last minute to stroke his body, to hold on to the warmth of him. He was strong and worthy of respect, and gentle, and her enemy. Her choice of him seemed as inevitable as tides in the ocean. One drowns in the ocean. "Do you know the *Symposium*, Grey?" She set her palm against the stubble on his cheek. Men were not like women at all, to the touch. "The *Symposium* of Plato."

"I'll find you, wherever you go. You know that. I'll never give up."

"You will not find me. You shall not know at all where to look for me. Pay attention. Plato says that lovers are like two parts of an egg that fit together perfectly. Each half is made for the other, the single match to it. We are incomplete alone. Together, we are whole. All men are seeking that other half of themselves. Do you remember?"

"This isn't the goddamned time to talk about Plato."

That made her smile. "I think you are the other half of me. It was a great mix-up in heaven. A scandal. For you there was meant to be a pretty English schoolgirl in the city of Bath and for me some fine Italian pastry cook in Palermo. But the cradles were switched somehow, and it all ended up like this . . . of an impossibility beyond words."

"Annique . . ."

Swiftly, softly, she leaned to him and covered his mouth and kissed him. It seemed to surprise him.

"I wish I had never met you," she whispered. "And in all my life I will not forget lying beside you, body to body, and wanting you."

"For God's sake . . ."

She stood up and jammed the knife in a crack between two stones some distance away, where it would take him a while to get to it. "Adrian was right. I should have made love to you when I had the chance."

She walked out of the chapel, ignoring his words behind her, which were angry in the extreme, and taking care not to trip on the bits and pieces of her trap that were strewn around the entryway.

Henri's horse was glad to see her. It did not like being so enclosed by briars. There was less trouble than she would have thought to mount, and no one in this dead monastery would see that her dress was hiked up far beyond decency. She gave the horse its head to find a way out of the courtyard and onto the road. Then all she could do was point toward the sound of the sea, hold on to rein and mane very tightly, and kick hard. It would be dawn soon. There was enough light for a horse to see. At the water's edge she could follow the line of surf north.

She had come a mile when the road straightened and sloped downward. Henri's horse picked up speed.

A blow slammed her. Shock. Pain. Falling. She had an instant to know it was a tree branch, hanging over the road, that had hit her. That the horse had done this on purpose.

She fell. Cried out in fear. Her head hit the ground, and the world exploded.

Then, nothing.

The horse, having demonstrated the vicious streak that allowed Henri to buy him cheaply, gave a satisfied grunt and trotted off in the direction of St.-Pierre-le-Proche.

Annique lay in a ditch by the side of the road, her face upturned into the drizzle.

SHE hurt. Tendrils of pain reached into the nothing and gave it shape and form. She was pulled unwillingly to a place where pain knifed into her. Her head, in particular, hurt.

It is better to be unconscious. That was her first thought.

Pain filled her head like fire. Like fire. Like . . .

That was her second thought. Between one instant and the next, she knew.

Light. Light diffused through her closed eyelids. In terror and awe, she opened her eyes and saw pale dawn in the sky. Light everywhere. Light across a whole mass of swirling clouds.

So it had happened. The doctor in Marseilles, with his unnecessary Latin, was right. The horrible bit of something in her skull had shifted off her optic nerve and was now wandering about, preparing to kill her.

She lay, getting ready to die, as the doctor had said she would.

It was entirely typical she should have a view of stubby pine trees to look at for her last minutes of life. Typical she should be stretched flat in soggy, cold mud. She tried to compose her mind to a nobility suitable for such a serious moment. What she thought upon, however, was her stupidity in trusting Henri's horse and how uncomfortable she was and how hungry her belly felt and how radiant were those tiny drops that quivered down the needles of the pines . . . the drops that slid along the pine needles and fell one by one onto her face.

She waited. Minutes passed. Nothing happened, except that she became more wet.

It came to her that she was not going to die. Or at least, not just immediately. She sat up. In ordinary times, the ache in her skull would have occupied her attention to the exclusion of all else.

"But this is bizarre." She found herself looking down at her hands, so automatically did her eyes go to where she'd rested them when she was blind. Amazing to see her own hands again. To see this dress she wore—pale green, smudged with dirt. To see . . .

She could see. She was no longer the blind, ridiculous worm. She was herself. She was Annique, the Fox Cub. Spy extraordinaire. "I can . . . see." She felt hollow with amazement, a shell containing only joy. "I can do anything." She scrambled to her feet. She wanted to dance. To fly.

The ditch was full of pinecones, which had been uncomfortable to lie among. She found five of them, tightly curled, heavy, and palm-sized.

One. Two. Three. She tossed the simple circle she'd learned from Shandor, when she was eight . . . that first night she'd come to the Rom and been so lonely.

Catching was easy as breathing. The Two and Two. The Half Shower. The Fountain. So beautiful. She craned her neck far back, swaying to keep under her catches. Her head ached like blazes, but it did not matter in the least.

Bon Dieu, but she was stiff. There had been a time she could sometimes juggle five. Today she was happy to keep a circle of four in the simplest of patterns, a child's juggling.

She wanted . . . oh, how she wanted Grey at this moment. She wanted to show him this. Her juggling. Her little art. The trick she had mastered only for the joy of it.

The pinecones were bright and happy in her hands. Nothing lost after all these empty months. Hands and eyes working together. The wonderful eyes that could see for her.

Grey would never see her juggle. Never.

She became clumsy suddenly and missed a cone, so she

let the others go. They landed, left and right, hitting neatly on each other, as juggled things do.

She set her face against the tree trunk. It was the same tree that had knocked her into the ditch. In the thick, muzzy silence of the wood, her breath caught in her throat and tears slipped from her eyes. She cried, sad and unspeakably happy.

The coast of Northern France,
near St. Grue

THE HOVEL FRONTED THE BEACH. AN OVER-turned fishing boat flanked its door. Leblanc ignored the sobs that came through the wood shutters from inside, ignored also the girl child, held between two burly dragoons, snarling and fighting. His attention was all for the man kneeling at his feet.

"When did she leave?" he demanded.

"With the fishing fleet. At dawn." The fisherman's voice slurred through a cut and bleeding lip. "In the boat of the English smugglers."

"Where do they go? What is their home port?"

"Who can say? They have many safe harbors, up and down the coast. They—"

Leblanc's riding crop slashed the man's face, sudden as a snake, and left a line of blood. "Where?"

"Dover. They go to Dover." Panting, the fisherman bowed his head.

"Dover, you say?" Leblanc moved his gaze to where the

girl was stretched, wriggling, between the soldiers. "Be very sure."

"It is their place, so they have always said. I do not know if they tell me the truth. They are English."

"It is you who must tell the truth." Leblanc studied him another minute. "Henri!"

Henri appeared at the doorway, tucking his shirt into his trousers. "There's nothing in the house, just some clothes she left behind. That's all."

"No papers?"

"None."

Leblanc went white around the mouth. Abruptly he turned and stalked back to where the horses waited. He took reins from the trooper standing at attention. "She can see. She's made a fool of us all." He mounted. "Come."

"What do you want done with these?"

Leblanc stepped into a soldier's cupped hands and swung into the saddle. He looked from father to young daughter, and to the house where a woman wept. Then he smiled. "We will reward them, of course." He pulled out coins and tossed them. "They have been helpful. See that the other villagers know of this." His horse kicked up sand. The dragoons rode across the coins, following him.

The fisherman watched them out of sight.

"You told them." His daughter collapsed to the ground, crying, now that the troopers were gone.

"Someone would have told them, in the end, after they hurt more women." He stooped like an old man and began to gather up the coins, running his fingers into the sand to find any buried deep by hooves. "Help me with this. Your eyes are better than mine."

"You betrayed Annique."

"Do you think she would expect us to fight him?" He did not meet her eyes. "It was what she told me to do, if that man should come here. She made me promise."

"If he finds her—"

"He will not." He brushed dirt off the coins and put them into his pocket and turned to the house. "Stay here and look for the money. I must go to your mother." He stopped at the doorway. "He will not find Annique. She is the Fox Cub. And she made me promise."

Seventeen

Dover, England

AT TEN O'CLOCK IN THE MORNING, ANNIQUE and a great many flopping halibut came ashore at Dover. She wore the second-best dress of a French fisherman's daughter and a pair of sturdy boots. A shawl, knitted from the wool of the kindly-faced black sheep of the salt marshes, wrapped her shoulders. Adrian's knife was strapped to her thigh under her dress.

She had eaten bread and cheese in mid-Channel, in the rocking darkness, with the smugglers. It was always interesting to talk to men of what they did for a livelihood, and now she knew more about hiding casks of brandy than she had known before. They waved at her now in a friendly fashion as she left, even Thadeus, the oldest, who had been dubious of her when she came aboard.

She stood on the quay amid piles of flounder and mussels and felt a moment of complete happiness. England. It was very beautiful, England. She had admired its white cliffs, riding in, with the sails behind her.

The noisy town of Dover stretched above her with its

stone houses stacked one upon the other up the hill and the castle above everything. Around her, gray green water washed the pilings, splashing tiny explosions of light, spinning bubbles of silver and snow white. In baskets of fish, the scales shone in iridescent ripples.

After months of darkness, brightness assailed her on every side. Color whirled and danced around her till she was dizzy. She was drunk with it. The line of stark shadow on a white stone wall cut like a shout. A crimson dress in the doorway of a tavern dazzled. Sometimes she could barely think, her head was so full of color and shape. She was lost in this riot of light, struck dumb by the beauty of a gull hovering over a sparkle of water. Never, never would she take the light for granted.

This was to be her new country, this England.

She had three pounds, sixpence, in English money hidden under her shift, her negotiations with the smugglers having consumed the rest of Henri's valuables. She had no luggage and no roof to shelter her tonight. The thought came to her that in nineteen years of life, not one material object—not a scrap of paper, not a comb, not a gilt trinket—had succeeded in clinging to her. When she walked away from the wooden quay she might have been Aphrodite, rising newborn and naked from the sea. She would start with nothing. It had all been stripped away.

She had been a spy for as long as she could remember. That was over. Whatever she did with the Albion plans, she would spy no more for France.

This was her last turn at the Game. She would go to London and find safety with Soulier and make her choice. In a week, or two weeks, she would make her decision about these Albion plans that would try the patience of a paving stone, and perhaps give them to the British after all. Then she would slip away from Soulier and drop into England like a spoonful of water into the ocean. The deadly men who hunted her, both English and French, would never find her.

She would seek out an obscure place and become plain and simple Anne, perfectly ordinary Anne, and take up work which did not decide the fate of nations. She would, perhaps, keep a cat. It would be restful, such a life.

The rocks lining the wharf made a complex landscape of terraces, escarpments, crags, and valleys. They looked most exactly like the rocks of France, which was a philosophic truth of some depth, probably. As she walked the track up from the docks, she saw that in one of the wood shacks, someone had put yellow flowers in a blue jug on their windowsill. Flowers yellow as bright silk. Yellow as sunrise. It was her welcome to England.

Dover city was a seaport like any other, a place of strong smells and many prostitutes. She did not wish to linger here and, in any case, she must go to London and meddle with great affairs.

She had met a man, once, who juggled balls of fire. The secret, he told her, was to keep them in the air and never truly touch them. That way, they did not burn the fingers.

The Albion plans were like that to her. She could not take one decision and hold it in her hands without being burned, but must keep them all in the air.

To give to the English a few dates and tides and routes was useless. The French would learn of this—the Military Intelligence was a most perfect sieve of secrets—and change the dates and invade anyway. Or the English would be uncharacteristically stealthy and lay an ambush to welcome the invasion. That was not a satisfactory outcome. She could, of course, pass to the English the great compendium of the plans. The French would not dare to invade then . . . but so much knowledge would turn the course of many battles for years to come. She would stop the invasion, at the cost of many French lives.

If she did nothing, of course, this town of fish and harlots would be a pile of rubble in the spring. There would be no brave yellow flowers in any window, nor any glass in them, nor any hand to set the blue vase upon the windowsill.

She could have named countless statesmen and scholars who would have known exactly what to do in this situation without thinking at all. It was a great pity the Albion plans had not landed in their laps.

Perhaps answers would occur to her while she walked to London. Montaigne, who was both wise and a Frenchman, had said that traveling produces a marvelous clarity of judgment. This had not yet occurred, but it still might, since there were many miles to London. She would buy a loaf of bread to carry with her when she left Dover. It is a false economy to starve oneself when one must walk a long distance.

She was in the vegetable market near the docks, admiring oranges—they were so perfectly round, with the shallow dimples and a color strong enough to warm the hands; she had never appreciated oranges before—when she noticed the squint-eyed man beside a pyramid of apples, watching her. When she wandered away to visit vegetable marrows and onions, he followed. Such interest.

She had been careless, sauntering around this town. If she had still been a spy, under orders, she would have realized sooner she was being followed.

Tiens. This was not good. Was this the English authorities already finding her, or did Fouché's long arm reach for her across the Channel? Or was Squint-Eyes only a common rapist or thief? In any case, she did not want to encounter him.

She ducked under the red and white striped awning of a stall and dodged staid matrons and baskets full of cabbages. *Mon Dieu*, but she missed boy's clothing. A boy her size could run like a deer without anyone taking note. A woman collected stares. They marked her path behind her, as heads turned in her direction.

Out of the market, then, and away from these many eyes.

She found small streets. She had not yet seen any part of Dover that was beautiful, but this section was distinctly unlovely. She ran hard now, taking left and right at random in this twisting maze of narrow lanes. The squint-eyed man, who must be French for the speed of his feet and his cleverness, was still behind her. Gaining on her.

She could not avoid a confrontation. Better to choose her own ground for it than to stumble into some blind alley.

Let it be here. She skidded to a stop and lifted her dress to tug Adrian's knife from the cloth that bound it to her thigh. It fitted reassuringly into her grip, a sneaky, five-inch blade, balanced for throwing, utterly characteristic of Monsieur Adrian. She pulled the kerchief off her hair and tossed it aside, shrugged out of her shawl, and lowered the knife against her skirt.

The alley walls rose up on either side in ragged, poorly laid brick. Piles of rotting garbage heaped the cobbles. The alley lay between mean stone houses, the windows small and shuttered, the doors locked. No one would come to help her if she screamed. No one would see what passed here.

Squint-Eyes rounded the corner and halted, startled to find her waiting. He glanced around quickly, then at her, suspicious, and saw only a woman alone. He groped under his jacket and fingered out a skinny dagger and began a slow advance.

She held her ground. Let him come to her. "Why do you follow me? I do not wish to speak to—"

Behind her, a boot gritted on stone. It was a tiny, sharp, malevolent sound, and it terrified her. She whipped around. Henri Bréval blocked the light. He blocked her escape. She was trapped.

She had walked into this like an idiot. She faced her death.

Not like this. She threw herself against the brick wall, protecting her back, keeping both of them in sight. *I am the Fox Cub. I have not walked a million miles through hell to die at the hands of these canailles.* She hissed short, short breaths through her teeth to drive fear out. It was not hopeless. There were only two of them. She would stick her knife into Squint-Eyes, push past, and run for her life. A simple plan, but a good one. Henri was no greyhound in the chase. She would be lightning.

She readied her little knife.

Henri smirked. Out of sight, someone approached with deliberate, unhurried steps. Her stomach turned cold and sick. It could not be . . .

From behind Henri, from the shadows, stepped Leblanc.

Panic broke across her like a wave from the cold sea. Leblanc, with his throwing knife and cold malice. Leblanc, who could not afford to let her live. *I know what happened at Bruges, but I cannot say one single word. It is Vauban's death if I tell.*

Down the length of the alley, Leblanc saw her fear, and he smiled. But he did not draw his knife and throw and kill her. He motioned Henri forward. He was so certain of her silence that he could toss her to his henchmen like a bone for the dog. She would not be given a clean death.

Three men. Three knives. She had no chance. No chance.

"Come, *poulette.*" Henri beckoned with little flicks of his knife. "Come, we only want to talk to you. Only talk."

Here in England there would be no talk. No underground cell. No torture. No leisurely destruction of her mind and spirit. On this foreign soil, Leblanc was the intruder. His influence was nothing. Here, Leblanc would forgo the Albion plans and settle for her death and the concealment of what he had done in Bruges.

"I let you live, Henri Bréval." Her voice shook all by itself. No pretense was needed. "Remember that. Twice, I let you live when I could have killed you."

"My thanks." He gave her an ironic salute. She could read her short future in his voice. Leblanc had promised Henri the rape of her before they slit her throat. Already

Henri saw her helpless and struggling beneath him. He was cutting her clothes away in his mind.

Let him fill his thoughts with that pretty picture. It would make him unwary. She risked a glance behind. Squint-Eyes held his knife extended, as if he offered a cup of tea. Had no one told him she knew how to fight? This was the weakest of them. She shuffled away from Henri, toward Squint-Eyes.

"You shrink from me?" Henri smiled. "You will only make me angry." He had decided to make a game of it, drawing his pleasure out.

"I beg you. *Je vous en prie.* Henri, I will do anything." She gained a long pace. Two.

"So shy, little Cub?" He snaked the knife at her playfully. Leblanc should tell him not to enjoy himself so much.

"If you will only listen to me. Only let me explain—"

In the middle of a word, she twisted and struck at Squint-Eyes. She cut downward, fast and precise, to slice the tendon at the base of his thumb. He squealed. His knife wheeled away, glinting red, into the gutter. He fell to his knees, clutching his hand and shrieking.

It was a small, expensive victory. Henri attacked instantly, slashing, driving her back from the mouth of the alley. There was no way to break past him. She had no chance to run.

There would be no more games from Henri.

Pitiless sunlight shafted into the narrow alley, glinting off the steel Henri held. Leblanc was a monstrous, dark presence. In the dirt behind her, Squint-Eyes wept like a woman. She retreated, knife held close to her waist, her other arm extended for balance. She had seconds, only, before she was defeated. She would use them to cripple Henri, if she could.

So she launched herself at him. He evaded. In the moment he was off balance, she tossed her knife to her left hand and jabbed, fast as fast, where he would not expect.

His hand was a small target, but she hit it. Slashed. Opened a crimson streak across his knuckles. Blood spilled down his fingers.

He will have a scar to remember me by. She backed away.

"Salope!" He shook his hand, and drops of blood scattered vivid on the cobbles. When he brought the knife up, it was wrapped in a red grip. He held it at the height of her heart. "I will hurt you. I will carve your face to pieces before I kill you."

He slashed at her eyes.

She saw a silver blur. Jerked back. Instantly, he cut again. Steel whisked by her ear. Cold terror shot through her. She turned and ran down the alley.

Leblanc came to meet her. His knife was a cold, gloating streak, slicing, slicing at her. Never quite touching. Making her jump and dance. Forcing her back toward Henri.

No escape. No possible escape. Her lungs pumped pain after pain. She tried a feint that didn't work. Nothing worked. Leblanc was a master with the knife. *I cannot win. I am a child against him.* He forced her back and back. Back to Henri.

She retreated. Her back touched the wall, and Henri closed in. *This is the end. It will hurt. It will hurt very much, dying.* She braced upon cold brick, her knife before her . . .

Black pain hit her belly. Henri's fist knocked her breathless. He twisted her knife hand to an unbearable agony. "Drop it." Her hand opened. Her knife fell. It was over for her.

Henri's muddy brown eyes exulted. The point of his blade lay at the pulse in her throat, at her breath. He didn't press it home.

She thought, *He will rape me before he kills me.*

HE was in time. Barely.

Grey heard the sound of a scuffle and a woman moaning

in pain and took the last thirty paces at a flat-out run. Turned the corner into the alley . . .

A man hunched on the cobbles, nursing a bleeding paw. He was the one crying. Leblanc lurked at the far end of the alley. Annique was pushed to the wall with Henri's knife at her throat.

Attack. Grey roared and charged in. Rammed Henri midbody. Pulled him off Annique before he could slit her throat.

They went over together and slammed the wall, jarring bone and flesh. Henri's knife spun away, end over end. They hit the ground and rolled and grappled, smashing against the bricks and boards of the wall. For all his size, Henri wasn't good at body-to-body, rough-and-tumble fighting.

They were on their feet. Close up, inside Henri's ape-long arms, Grey punched—one, two, three—short, stiff-armed punches to the belly. Henri turned red in the face, then went pasty white when Grey cracked a knee into his groin.

He backed away. Henri folded, boneless, to the ground. The fight was finished. It had taken less than a minute.

He kicked Henri's knife away, out of reach. He'd make sure the Frenchman was out of commission for a while. He jerked Henri up from his knees and bounced him off the far wall, aiming the shoulder foremost. Lots of small, breakable bones in the shoulder.

He would have finished the job, but Annique kept leaving the bastard alive for some reason. He'd defer to her judgment.

A startled cry. He spun round.

Leblanc swayed, his face twisted in pain. His blade rang and jittered on the cobbles where he'd dropped it. The hilt of a throwing knife stuck out of his expensive coat, and blood ran down his sleeve.

Annique had put the knife into Leblanc—into his arm,

not his throat—before he could throw. No telling which of them Leblanc had planned to kill.

Leblanc broke and ran, skittering down a side alley, trailing blood, clutching his shoulder, fast as a rabbit. He had a thirty-foot head start. Henri Bréval staggered to his feet, scooped up his knife left-handed, and headed in the opposite direction. The whining fellow at the mouth of the alley wobbled off, still mewling.

There was nothing to do but stand and swear and watch them get away. He couldn't take prisoners when he had no men to control them. And if he turned his back on Annique, she'd disappear like smoke.

She sagged against the wall, breathing hard. If he'd come into that alleyway five minutes later . . . The thought of her, bleeding her life out in this filth, hit like a body blow.

Idiot, idiot woman. What the hell were they thinking, everybody who went around praising her to the skies and calling her a master agent? She let herself get backed into an alley. She'd done minor injury to one man, hadn't followed in for the kill, then just about missed Leblanc altogether. She could throw better than that. She was game enough, but she lacked edge. If she'd been his agent, he wouldn't let her off the front steps without a keeper.

"He has taken Adrian's knife away with him," she said clearly. "How am I to cut vegetables?" She stared down the alley where Leblanc had disappeared.

Those were the first words he heard her speak in English. She had a beautiful voice—fluent and husky, the French of her buzzing under every syllable. A caress of a voice. The woman couldn't breathe without enticing him.

"But I would not have wanted to cut vegetables with it, would I, if it had Leblanc's blood upon it." She put her fist over her mouth and began to giggle.

Battle nerves, that laughter. She'd need a wall behind her to hold her up for a while.

He'd lost his knit fisherman's cap during the fight. He

bent and picked it up and beat it on his trousers, watching her. She'd run as soon as she pulled herself together.

"He would not have wanted me to cut vegetables with it, in any case, the man who gave me the knife. He would be delighted where that knife is. He does not like Leblanc—my friend does not—the friend who has so many knives." She pushed glossy strands of black hair off her forehead and peeked up at him. For the first time, he saw Annique looking out of her eyes.

She didn't know him.

Frank and charming, pale as parchment, she smiled. "Thank you very much. Thank you very, very much."

He played the black knit cap through his fingers and waited for her to recognize him. That would be the end of the joy in her. He'd drag her out of this maze of streets and wipe the brightness from her and carry her off to London. There was a bleak, nasty fight coming in a few minutes, inevitable as sunset. He'd win. She'd lose.

She ran her eyes over his face, his hair, his shoulders, the whole length of him in his smelly fisherman's jersey and trousers. Appraising. Approving. She said, "It is a strange thing. I can speak five languages, and I cannot think of a single way to say how grateful I am that you have saved me."

Why don't you know me, Annique?

She trembled with the shocky aftermath of terror, and laughed, and thanked him politely again and again, and she didn't know him at all.

My God. You've never seen me, have you? You don't know my face. You don't know the color of my hair or the shape of my nose. I could be anybody.

She didn't know who he was. If he left her free, and followed her, she might lead him straight to the Albion plans.

Could it be done? The more he considered it, the better it sounded. She knew where the plans were. He was sure of it. Somehow, after that bloody debacle at Bruges, Annique had been left holding the Albion plans.

She didn't bring anything from France. He'd been following her since she stepped out of the fishing boat at the docks, empty-handed. Could the Albion plans already be in England?

Where are the plans, Annique? Are you headed for them right now? Going to take them to Soulier, I bet.

If she led him to the plans . . . It was the cleanest way that could be. One instant of shock, and it would be over. No long, well-practiced interrogation. No poisoned intimacy as he stripped her secrets away, hour after hour. No clever, painless coercion that would leave them both feeling sick.

At Meeks Street, in his comfortable prison, he'd loosen her hold on the plans, inch by inch. He was expert. He'd take them from her. He'd get dirty fingerprints all over her soul, doing it.

He could leave her free. It was tempting on every level. If he left her free, he'd have days with Annique when she wouldn't be his enemy. Maybe she'd keep looking at him like he was some kind of white knight. Maybe that was what he wanted.

She knows my voice. But I can change my voice.

Growing up in deepest Somerset, he and his brothers had run tame in the stable, copying the grooms' speech and getting clouted for using it in the parlor. Broad Somerset still came easily to his tongue when he went home.

He pitched his voice deep and spoke in the familiar West Country cadence. "Are you hurt?" He didn't sound like himself to his own ear.

"Not in the least, thank you. It is very brave of you to attack so many men, three of them, when they were armed."

He shrugged. He wouldn't talk much. She couldn't recognize his voice if she didn't hear it.

"You are modest as well. But it is because of you I am

not gutted like a herring, for which I am unendingly appreciative. It is heroism on your part, to throw yourself into a fight with such eagerness, when you do not know me at all."

"Anybody'd do the same." He kept expecting the next word to wake her memory and tell her who he was.

"Perhaps. There is much altruism in the world." She pushed herself away from the wall and staggered over to pick her shawl up from the dirt. "But it does not always arrive promptly and with such useful muscles. A friend gave me this, that her mother knitted for her." She shook out the shawl. "It would have been found beside my body, if you had not come."

He made a noncommittal noise. He could fool her for a day or two, if he was careful. That might be all he needed.

"I have been very lucky this morning, have I not? I cannot begin to think of how I will thank you."

She smiled at him. If she kept being grateful to passing strangers, somebody was going to bundle her into a bedroom at the nearest inn and lock the door and let her prove exactly how grateful she was.

When she walked unsteadily down the alley, stumbling and setting her hand on the wall from time to time, he walked with her, keeping an arm's reach away. He didn't try to help. He didn't lay a finger on her. A single touch, and she'd recognize him with her skin.

HER sense of direction had not deserted her. She backtracked down one long street and made a right turn, and they came to the small market square with wharves behind it. At the side was a line of stone benches. She sat and closed her eyes and felt the world spin around her. When she opened her eyes, the tall man in the black fisherman's sweater was still there.

It overwhelmed her continually, the intensity of seeing.

She could have counted the individual dark hairs upon his cheek, and every one of them was beautiful.

He wiped his hands upon his sweater that smelled so of fish and said, "You don't look well."

His accent was different from the English smugglers she knew. His voice grated harsh from his throat. That would be from those years at sea, probably, or heavy drinking ashore.

"I am fine." But she shook in every fiber. It was good to have a clean place to sit. "It is only that I have been frightened to the core, you understand, thinking I would be killed, which could terrify anyone and is a thing I have never become used to."

The sailor was a large man, and obviously strong as an ox, which was doubtless useful on boats. He might have been twenty-eight or thirty. His brown hair was cut close to his skull and lay in layers, like shingles. His eyes were a dark, colorless mixture of shades, like the sea itself, a sort of gunmetal gray. The lower half of his face was dark with stubble. None of this should have made him handsome, and yet, to her, he was.

She liked sailors, in general, and had spent much time chatting with them in various ports of Europe, discovering what they knew about coastal defenses and the movements of naval vessels. Most sailors were more talkative than this one.

"I will not bore you again with gratitude, but it is only because you have been capable and brave for me that I did not die today. If you will look away for the smallest time, I will take out my money, which I have hidden." There was a tavern across the street. Near the docks of a city there is always a tavern. "That house does not appear respectable," she said, being frank about the women who were inside it, "but the smell of its beer is good. I was traveling for a time with a man who would have called a mug of beer a 'heavy wet,' though he did not get around to teaching me that. I will buy you a heavy wet."

"You will not buy me a drink. You shouldn't have anything to do with that place, and you know it." He considered her some more. "I'll get us both something. Stay here. Don't move, not an inch, till I get back."

One corner of the market was full of food sellers, and that was his goal. She watched him stride through the crowd. He expected every man to step out of his way. And they did. His clothing might say able-bodied seaman, but his confidence spoke of command. He was first mate, she thought, or captain.

And, most likely, he was not exactly a fisherman. He walked confidently in this market of Dover. She had heard much of the English press gangs from her smuggler friends. The English navy would take any such man from the port towns, so tall and strong, with his hands marked with pine pitch and tar, and drag him off to their naval ships to be poor and uncomfortable. Unless he had powerful protection. The smugglers had great influence along this south coast of England.

Almost certainly he was an English smuggler like her friend Josiah. Smugglers were cunning and capable men and it was not altogether surprising she should owe her life to one. How interesting life in England was turning out to be.

He was so tall it was easy to follow his progress amid the booths of the market. He picked a stall, and the woman dropped her other customer like a three-day-old mackerel to hurry to serve him. She was old enough, that woman, that she should not have been so foolish for a pair of broad shoulders. Or perhaps she was not so foolish. When he left, he flipped her a silver coin, not asking for change.

He brought back whelks, held in a cone of broadsheet paper. They looked exactly like the ones she had eaten in the fisherman's hut in St. Grue two days before, though these were English whelks. He carried also two mugs of tea, hooking the two handles with one finger very deftly.

The tea contained milk in abundance and great heapings of sugar, neither of which she wanted, but he had saved her life for her and she would have happily eaten a bouquet of meadow grasses if that had been what he offered.

He sat and drank tea and watched her winkle the whelks out with a peeled wood stick. Two housewives sauntered by, with their shopping baskets and white aprons and pretty bonnets. They shot her smuggler glances. The harlots came to the tavern window and whispered with one another, letting their dresses slip low on their shoulders. And well they might. He was a large and excellently made man. She would indulge herself in smugness for this few minutes while he sat beside her.

"I am Annique. I have not told you that yet." No, the tea did not improve upon acquaintance. "Annique Villiers. It is my life you have given me. That was not some slight quarrel you interrupted, monsieur, *je vous assure*." She chewed. "*Peste*. I will speak only English now. I am determined." She was very hungry, and the whelks were fresh and admirably clean of sand. "I would most certainly be dead if you had not happened by. Leblanc must kill me, you see, to shut my mouth, as I know certain discreditable facts about him. Leblanc is the one I put my knife into. Henri, who would also be happy to kill me, is the one you were kind enough to throw among the garbages."

"You should keep out of alleys."

"*Bien sûr*. I shall most certainly do so in the future." She ate the last of the whelks. "But I will be safe in a few days. Leblanc will not find me again, once I leave Dover. There is much of England to hide in."

All this time she had been tossing whelk shells onto the pavement, the way everyone else did. She hated to throw the paper there, so she crumpled it up and put it in her empty tea mug.

She was delightfully filled. She wanted nothing more than to curl up like a cat and sleep. But cats do not have agents of many governments chasing them. "I thank you for whelks and for the tea, which is very English. I shall have to drink a great deal of it to properly appreciate it, I believe. Will you tell me your name? It is hard to say thank you with such great sincerity to someone whose name I do not know."

"My name is Robert Fordham." How solemn he was with it, as if he were trusting her with a secret. Perhaps he was. It could be that this town was posted with numerous handbills from the Office of the Customs, seeking his capture. He did not know that she had kept many secrets and could be trusted with his. "I'm pleased to meet you, Annique."

His expression was somewhat grim, all this time. He was captain, she was almost sure, and in the habit of worrying often and deeply about the safety of his small smuggling ship. This was someone who would lead men as naturally as he breathed or hurl himself into an alley to save the life of a stranger. In the army of Napoleon he would already have risen to high rank, though not in an English army, naturally, which was enslaved to the old order of things.

A seagull flapped down beside her feet and began upending the shells she had discarded, checking inside. There were multitudes of seagulls pillaging the market. The women who sold fish fought them continually.

It was time, she knew, to get up and be upon her travels.

"Monsieur . . . No. I will break myself of the habit of speaking French in a day or two. Mr. Fordham, I am grateful until I have no words, and I am a person who has many words. You have my good wishes, for whatever they are worth." She had no map of Dover in her head. She carried no exact maps of English cities at all, really. She shaded her eyes and looked up at the sun. London was north, so she would walk north. It always surprised her how often the obvious works. "I hope, if you are ever in danger, someone comes to your rescue."

"So do I." The man rose when she did, and walked with her. "Where are you going?"

She gave him the truth, since he had saved her life. "To London. I have an errand."

"The London stage leaves from the Bear and Bells, at the center of town. The easiest way is back through the market—"

She laughed. "I have only three pounds, Monsieur . . . Mr. Fordham."

"Robert."

"Robert." She liked that name. She said it in her own way, the French way, so that it sounded correct to her. "I have three pounds and sixpence. It would be silly to squander it. I shall walk."

He frowned. "You can't walk from Dover to London."

"But yes. I have walked the whole way here from the south of France, except for some distances when I went in a coach, and I shall tell you, the times walking were the more agreeable. It is a nothing, this walking to London."

He was so tall he was able to take slow, deliberate steps and still keep pace beside her. "You'll take the Canterbury Road then. I'll show you."

He said little as he unwound the town for her, street to street, and finally pointed the way onward. The Canterbury Road led straight uphill and did not look easy, which made it typical of the roads she had encountered in her life. When she turned to thank him, he had already turned away. He had not waited to say good-bye.

She saw him striding purposefully in the direction of the docks, his black cap and shoulders showing above the other people on the street. He was good to look upon, strong and brown and muscular from carrying illegal cargoes around. It is a healthy life, to be a smuggler, if one does not get hanged for it.

"It is unfair, this," she remarked softly, to nobody. The people she would most like to avoid—Leblanc, for instance—she encountered everywhere. Someone like Robert Fordham walked away an hour after he saved her life.

Doubtless he was married to a woman in one of those stone houses and had three small children with slate-colored eyes. He would be hurrying home to them at this minute. She amused herself on the long climb out of Dover, wondering which house might be his and what that good woman, his wife, had fixed him for his supper.

These white cliffs about her were oddly light colored, as if they were made of old snow. At every height birds flew. The ocean behind her was blue this afternoon, like the warm waters of the south. She walked away from Dover, remembering the cliffs of Italy and France, thinking of the Roman historian Tacitus, who had written about England, and wondering where she would go after she had seen Soulier and then completed her business in London. She must find safety, of course, but also earn a living, since she was no longer to support herself by stealing secrets. Perhaps she would become a cook.

She was still in sight of the sea when she realized she was being followed.

GREY CAUGHT UP WITH FLETCH WELL OUTSIDE Dover on an open, uphill stretch of the Canterbury Road. The sea was a flat, blue line on the horizon. Fletch had hitched a ride in a vegetable cart, keeping a good ways back, curled up in the cabbage leaves with a pocket spyglass. Imaginative man, Fletcher.

It was Fletch's horse under him. No point in being Head of Section if you couldn't borrow a horse now and then.

He pantomimed scissors as he passed the wagon, cutting Fletch loose from following Annique. Being the peaceable man he was, he ignored Fletch's return gesture. Fletch would get his bloody horse back, eventually. He clucked the gelding to a brisk walk.

He saw the moment she spotted him. Awareness slid across the distant figure, like the stillness of a deer scenting its stalker. Half a second, and she relaxed, just as subtly. She'd figured out who he had to be. She did it all without turning back to look. A hell of an agent, Annique Villiers.

When he came up level with her, she said, "You are following me."

"No, I'm not. I'm right beside you." He dismounted and strolled along, holding the reins.

He'd never been more impressed by her. In that dull homespun, with the shawl pulled up over her head, she blended into the brown and dun countryside like a quail. She'd become a dusty farm woman. A man could ride right past and never get a glimpse of her beauty.

"That is sophistry, Robert Fordham. Why are you following me?"

"To protect you. Until you get to London."

"The problem is that I talk too much." She sighed and kept walking, looking straight ahead. "If I would keep my mouth closed, I would not get in these situations. You are all that is kind, monsieur, but I do not need your protection."

She'd called him "monsieur" in France. He didn't want to rouse those memories. "Robert."

"Robert," she agreed readily. With every minute that passed, to her every sense, he was becoming "Robert." He was becoming familiar. Soon it'd be impossible for her to see him as anything but Robert. "Robert . . ." His name, in her mouth, was a caress with a long, warm roll of the *r* at both ends. "I have played dangerous games all my life, and no one has succeeded in killing me yet, not even Monsieur Leblanc, who is strenuous and resolved. I would very much rather you left me alone."

Never in this world. "No."

"No? That is all you will say? *Eh bien,* if I talked as little as you do, I would be in considerably less trouble."

She stopped to pick one stalk from the long grasses that grew beside the road, carefully selecting it from among the others. She started off again, peeled away at the stem with a thumbnail. "I will explain something, Mr. Fordham. I am beyond measure grateful to you for saving my life, but I will not sleep with you."

He'd had a taste of this devastating directness while he held her prisoner in France. "I didn't ask you to. Are you always this blunt?"

She shrugged. "It is this English. It is impossible to be subtle and beautiful in this language, which is not delicate like French. Besides, I have spoken almost no English since I was a little child. Only read it." She gestured with the grass stem. "I must say this, even if I am indelicate. I will not lie with you, Robert. You waste your time . . . unless it is your pleasure to hurt someone and force them."

"I don't hurt women." That was a lie. He'd hit Annique hard enough to leave her doubled over, gasping. He had an ironic truth to give her though. "I'm not going to touch you."

"Then I do not understand why you are here."

"There are three men trying to kill you."

"Many more than three, Robert." She thought about that for a hundred yards, nibbling on grass, glancing at him keenly once in a while. "Do you know, I believe you are sincere. But it is not necessary. I am the old hand at this." She took the grass stem out of her mouth and rolled it back and forth between her fingers. The fluffy head on the end went whirling out and out like some child's toy. "You are . . . Oh, you are very tall and strong and brave and a good fighter. But these are entirely committed and evil men who pursue me. It is my own acts which have set them after me, not any concerns of yours. I would not like to see you get hurt."

The idiot woman was worried about a husky brute of a man, instead of taking care of herself. "I don't get hurt easily. May I give you a ride? Harding here . . ." He had no idea what Fletch called the horse. His Latin teacher at Harrow had been named Harding. ". . . would be happy to carry you."

"You have not listened at all to what I say. I will tell you that England is an even stranger place than I had heard. I do not believe Englishmen toss aside all their concerns to walk to London with some woman they have met in an alley. It is not reasonable."

Tricky, this business of lying to Annique.

"You remind me of someone I knew once. A woman." He hoped the hesitation sounded like looking at old memories instead of inventing as he went along. "Not in England. She was French. I treated her badly, and I can't go back and undo it." That was close to the truth. What he'd already done to Annique ate at him like acid. Maybe regret came through in his voice. "It's too late."

" 'But that was long ago and in another country,' " she quoted softly, " 'and, anyway, the wench is dead.' " She darted another shrewd glance at his face. "I wondered why you studied me so strangely back there in the town."

"You look like her."

"I do not want to look like someone else. I have troubles enough of my own without a . . . a doppelgänger making more for me."

Maybe it wasn't convincing. He waited, remembering to keep his breath even. Making himself look at the horse, at the ground. Men telling lies like to look you in the face.

"I have made mistakes," she said after a long time, "which haunt me at night and which I cannot erase." She ran her thumbnail down the long stem of grass, frowning. "You saved my life. All the same, I cannot believe—"

"I was leaving Dover tomorrow." Rational, logical Annique. Give her a practical, sensible reason, and it would convince her. "Headed home for a visit. To Somerset. I have to go through London anyway. I'd be glad of the company."

He made himself stop there. When it came to lies, as Hawker always said, "Don't embellish."

"Ah. It is not so big a change, that, to leave one day early. To you it would seem like fate, perhaps, when I am presented under your nose. I am not inclined to believe such things myself, but I know many people who do."

She looked out over the fields, thinking abstruse, clever Annique thoughts.

Take it on trust, Annique, just this once. Believe me. Lead me to the Albion plans. Make it easy for both of us.

Then she nodded. "I will travel with you to London, if this is what you must do to clean yourself of the past. I owe you that much. But Robert . . . you would be wiser to return to your ship and your family and forget this woman who has long since made her peace with God."

"If I get you safely to London, that's enough. That's what I have to do."

She must have caught the determination in his words, but it didn't frighten her. Good. He was damned sick of frightening her.

"*Bon.* We will travel together then, till London. I will be grateful for the company."

She turned her face to the north, to the length of road, measuring distances under the sky. He was seeing the real Annique Villiers at last. This was what she'd been for all those years, trailing across Europe in the raggle-taggle tail of the army, in boy's clothing, nibbling something plucked from a field. A pair of larks sprang up from the field beside them and flew a complex pattern toward a stand of trees. She brightened, gazing after them, delighting in the moment, squirreling another memory away inside her.

"I will like England." She started walking again. "I have been here only four hours, and already I have met three men trying to kill me and one who bought me whelks. For better or worse, this is not a country that ignores me."

Nineteen

The Green Parrot Inn,
Dover, England

"I WILL SLIT HER THROAT." HENRI'S FACE WAS marbled into an ugly map of bruises. His hand, on the tabletop, was swathed in white cloth.

"Ass! Do you think the English have no ears?" Leblanc glanced around. Fishermen stuffed themselves with onions and fried fish. At a table in the corner, a woman drank gin. No one was listening. "You will get your chance soon enough."

"First, I will deal with him. I will gut him like a mackerel and leave him flopping in his blood."

"As you did before?"

"No one reported this English spy was in Dover. How was I to expect—"

"Cease! You whine like a dog." Leblanc hunched over his watered rum. His arm ached unbearably. He was in England, wallowing in this dockside filth, in danger. He might be stopped and questioned at any moment by stupid, clumsy British authorities. Annique had escaped him. This was Henri's fault, every bit. "She goes to Soulier, in London, to tell him lies about me. He has been her objective all along. I am sure of it."

"But she does not carry the papers. We could have stayed in France, if it is papers you want." Henri doubtless thought he was clever.

"Forget the papers. What is important is that she dies. She must not reach Soulier."

"We are in his territory. When he hears what we have done . . ."

"She is my agent, assigned to me. I can do what I like with an outlaw who crosses the Channel without my orders." Leblanc finished the glass in one swallow. What he would not give for an hour in privacy with that bitch. One hour. "I have sent word to Fouché what she does. When the *Directeur* of the Secret Police supports me, I do not give a fart for Soulier. Faugh. Who can drink this?"

"There is brandy." Henri looked for the serving maid.

"It is all pig wash. Rum, gin, beer, brandy—they are horse piss in this stink of a country. You will take six of the men and go east, along the coast. Send the others west. She is squatting by the fire in some fisherman's hut, thinking she has outsmarted me."

"Why would she hide in some small village where everyone peers and spies and chatters? She will go to London. To Soulier. When he learns we are in England—"

"Enough." Leblanc slammed the empty glass on the table.

One fisherman, and then another and another, shot looks in their direction. The whore at the corner table hastily dropped a coin by her mug and left. Even the innkeeper eyed them with suspicion.

Leblanc held rage behind clenched teeth. He could not order these scum hauled into the street and beaten. He, Jacques Leblanc, friend of Fouché, had no power here. Everything . . . everything . . . was in ruins. He had lost any chance of the Albion plans. That bitch whore, Annique, would run to Soulier and complain. He should have killed her, her and Vauban, too, there in the inn at Bruges.

Henri would not cease. "I only say that we must watch the road to London—"

"I am not a fool, Bréval. I, myself, will watch the coaching inn to see if she takes the stage to London. You will search the coast. And you will not concern yourself with papers."

The Albion plans were lost. The payment that should have been his—lost. His very life was threatened. Annique had many sins to pay for.

Any minute, she would learn of the death of Vauban. She must not reach Soulier and babble in his ear. "She is to be killed on sight. They need not be gentle." Let her suffer a lifetime of pain in every second it took her to die.

"Soulier is fond of her. He will be furious."

"When she is a corpse, it does not matter what Soulier is fond of."

Twenty

In the light of the thin new moon, Robert groomed the horse Harding. He brushed his way with care and thoroughness from mane to withers to rump and tail. From bite to kick, as it were. She thought the horse Harding liked it. He looked smug.

"You are indulgent to that horse." She watched the outline of him against a gray sky. "He has done no work whatsoever except to walk a little."

"I like taking care of animals."

She supposed a life surrounded by fishes and smuggled brandy would not allow time to care for livestock. "Is he from your home, the horse Harding? Perhaps one that your brother bred, who is so fond of horses?"

"Spence? No, Harding isn't one of his. I picked Harding up in Dover. Spence would like him though. If I brought him home, he'd try to win him in one of his card games. He'd cheat, most likely, since it's just family."

"It must be interesting to have brothers and sisters. I have often thought so."

For four long days Robert had laid his whole history out before her, like a gift. It was as if he'd waited all his life for the chance to tell his story to a grubby French spy walking on the dusty roads in Kent. She knew now of the house in Somerset where he had grown up, where his mother and father and the older brother Spence and a young sister still lived.

She could picture it, that huge old farmhouse with the horses in the stable and the chickens his mother was proud of, who each had names and were of a special breed from Constantinople and not at all like other chickens. Robert had, she knew now, a house of his own called Tydings where an aunt looked after him, and another brother in the army and three other sisters, younger than he was, but married, who did not live at home.

It was a joy and a burden to know all this. She would remember it when they parted and it would make her infinitely sad.

They were encamped far back from the road, deep in the stubble of harvested fields. She turned the embers with a pointed stick. She had built such clean, invisible fires a thousand times. There was little smoke. No sparks flew into the night to show where they were.

Robert finished with his pampering of Harding and came to sit beside the fire with her. "That's a pretty tune. What is it?"

"What? Oh. I had not realized I was humming. It is a children's song." She sat back on her heels. "Let me think . . . In English it would go, 'Let the gutters flow with the blood of the aristocrats. Let us wash our hands in their entrails. Let all who stand against the voice of the people perish like rats.' There is much more of it."

"Good God."

"Most exactly. It is a pretty tune, though. It is sad that my voice is like a jackdaw, as many people have told me. We used to sing that one, jumping rope. 'The fat aristos shall perish, one and two. The traitors shall die, three, four.'

We were all without exception bloodthirsty when I was six. That was the year we took the Bastille. It is strange to know all those boys I played with are in the army now, or dead."

"An interesting time."

"It was to stand at the pivot of history, to be in Paris in those days. Dreams were as solid as the stones of the street. A thousand possibilities. That is what you English do not understand. We French will not stop until the whole world is conquered for the Revolution. Napoleon puts his harness upon those dreams and drives them for his own purposes. You do not know at all what you are up against."

"You think the peace won't last?"

She knew the peace would not last. The Albion plans set a date for the invasion. She knew the very road troops of the *Grande Armée* would march upon. Some of them, a third part of the army, would murder and pillage their way down this one. "It is Napoleon's passion to conquer, not to rule. There will be no peace." The fire made a comfortable hiss and sputter as she flipped ember after ember. She had seen houses and villages burned till they were just this. Embers. "He prepares again for war, even as we sit here."

"Maybe he'll pick some other country to invade, one with less water around it and a smaller navy."

"And a better climate." It had rained upon them today for a time. And yesterday as well. She did not like to be wet so continually.

"One of those Roman writers said something about the rain in England. Deformed by rain . . . something like that." It had surprised her at first that Robert Fordham, smuggler and yeoman's son from Somerset, should have the education he did. Perhaps he read much when he was at sea.

"That is Tacitus. He said the sky in this country is deformed by clouds and frequent rains, but the cold is never extremely rigorous. I do not suppose matters have changed much in a thousand years. Certainly there is still rain."

He had taken off his black sweater to groom the horse

Harding and unbuttoned his shirt far down his chest and rolled up his sleeves over his forearms. He was brown, as men become who work upon the sea, with a roughness of skin from wind and salt water. In the dim yellow light of the fire, he was a dark and massive form, with the strongness of rocks and tree trunks, uncompromising and very beautiful.

Once she could have admired him, or admired the strength of his horse, and it would have been the same. She had still possessed innocence of a sort. Her time with Grey had made her wiser and infinitely more foolish. Now when she looked upon Robert Fordham, she brooded and yearned like a schoolgirl and felt the most shameful heatedness inside her.

She did not make herself turn away and gaze upon something that would disturb her less. She had become weak.

The fire developed nicely. Soon it would be useful to cook upon. "It is not right that we French should invade here." She glanced across at Robert. "Oh, you smile, but that is not obvious if one is French. Of a certainty, you English would be better off without your foolish German princelings who spend so much public money. You should have a republic and voting by everyone."

"Is that what Napoleon would bring us?" Robert said softly.

"That is how it would begin." Her life would be simpler if she did not think so much. "Napoleon would make some things better here. But at a great cost. When he comes to this green island, he will burn all those pretty farmhouses we passed today."

"You can't stop it, Annique."

But she could. It was her choice whether those farmhouses would burn and the plump farm women and the barefooted children burn with them. It had become her decision when Vauban set the Albion plans into her hands in that inn parlor in Bruges, six months ago.

If she betrayed the Albion plans to England, she would be a traitor. She would die for it. Vauban would be pulled from his bed to go to disgrace and death upon the guillotine. And France would be at great peril from the detailed knowledge she gave to the British. But the children in that white farmhouse would live.

Or perhaps not. She could not know. Perhaps different children, equally innocent, would die instead. This meddling in the fate of nations was a grim affair.

Even a year ago, she would have gone to London, to Soulier, and laid everything in his lap and followed his orders. But she was not a child anymore, and her answer could not be that simple.

She turned a small square coal of glowing orange over carefully on its side, giving it most considered attention and accomplishing no purpose whatsoever. She need not decide today, after all.

Robert searched into the basket he had acquired an hour ago from that very farmhouse down the road. Under the red flowered cloth that was tucked across, it contained the most lovely things—sausages and bread and small brown eggs. This was one more thing she did not know how to deal with.

She watched him investigate. "I would not have dared to ask for these foods. You are very courageous, did you know."

"Braving the dread Kent farmer in his lair?" He spread the cloth between them. "They're not so dangerous."

"He might have set his dogs upon you. Me, I do not like dogs."

"I'll remember that."

The hairs of his chest were gold where the firelight struck them. She imagined how it would be if she reached across to his shirt and opened the last buttons and drew it off of him. She could almost see herself doing this.

He would feel furry, with those hairs, but his skin would be of the toughness of leather. Grey had worn a leather coat. He had wrapped it about her, keeping her warm as she wandered in and out of the drug. If she lay her cheek upon Robert, he would feel like that leather, with softness that went no farther than the outermost glide across his skin. He would be hard muscle underneath, as Grey was. His hands would be like Grey's hands, too, rough from the work he did, only great carefulness making them soft upon her. If he put his hands upon her breasts . . .

She closed her eyes. Her body clenched immodestly and moistened. She did not know whether she was desiring Grey or desiring Robert. She was most probably going mad.

"Bread. Sausages." Robert took bread from the basket as he named it and laid it on the red cloth. The sausages he skewered on a forked stick. "I've had enough hedge berries and sour apples. It's no life for a man."

"*Bien sûr.* But you have paid that farmer. I do not have the money to buy such a meal, having only three pounds—"

"And sixpence. Yes, you told me. I have a good bit more than that."

"You are to be felicitated. But I cannot take this food and not pay my share. And I cannot pay my share."

"You face moral qualms."

"They are everywhere if one goes looking for them. Though perhaps I am being silly."

"Sounds like it to me. And eggs." The eggs were in the bottom, in the nest of straw the farmer's wife had made for them. "There was a man who could tell eggs apart. At Delphos."

He was trying to distract her. He would discover that did not work. "The story is from Montaigne. It goes, 'He never mistook one for another, and having many hens, could tell which had laid it.' I am not sure I believe that. But then, I do not know any hens with such intimacy. Montaigne does not help me to know what to do about this food, though he was very wise, of course. I have already taken whelks from you. I am not accustomed to being fed by strange men."

"Do you think I'm trying to seduce you with boiled eggs?" He picked one and offered it to her, holding it up in three fingers.

"Do not be the fool." She suddenly felt very cross. She

took the egg from him, and his fingers did not touch hers, not one tiniest bit. She could have been a cloud of vapor for all the interest he took. "You are not in the least trying to seduce me, you."

"No." He smiled. He was perfectly friendly, and he did not desire her in the least. It was a great annoyance. "Lovely Annique, if you were camped out here with your Gypsies . . ." She had told him that part of her life, since he had told her about growing up on his farm in Somerset. ". . . would you sneak over to that nice farmer's henhouse and steal some of his eggs tonight?"

"Not eggs. The Rom do not eat such things. Did you know you can tell a cooked egg from a raw one when you juggle them?" She tossed the egg in the air and caught it a few times. She had showed Robert her juggling while they walked. It had impressed him, she thought. "The chickens should be nervous."

"Then pretend you're stealing this food from me. That settles your moral qualms."

"You make the specious argument. But it is a complex one." She cracked the egg upon the side of the basket and threw the shells into the fire.

"Here, thieve some bread from me, too. It's a good fire. Learn that from the Gypsies?"

"I do not think I ever made fires at all when I was Rom, or had anything to do with them much. The women do not like children poking their fires, getting ashes in the food. This trick . . ." She circled her stick around the hole she'd dug into the ground which contained the fire and kept it below eye level and invisible in the night. "This I learned from an old soldier in the Tyrol. For all I know he is still out there in the army, surviving. He was almost unkillable himself, but I do not think he was much good at fighting. He avoided it most remarkably for a man in uniform. He did not like to kill people, he told me."

"Did you kill any, when you were being a soldier?" He

glanced up from roasting sausages and, as it was so often, his expression was unreadable.

"Do you know, I don't think I ever killed anybody at all, except doing surgery on them." She stirred at the fire. "Some men I was angry at may have died eventually, because I put knife wounds in them, but that is a thing one can do nothing to prevent. There is altogether too much killing in this world, I think."

"I have to agree with that."

"That was the last thing of importance my father told me before they hanged him. That killing is the stupid answer, not the wise one. I have found it to be true."

"You've never killed?" His eyes were sharp upon her, searching, weighing.

"Never that I know." She looked at him, over the fire. "But I will tell you something that is not so pretty about me, Robert. That man, the first one who attacked me . . . I cut the tendon at his thumb. It does not mend, such a wound. He will not use his right hand again to hold a knife or for anything else. Not ever in his life. I am not a nice person, me."

"Perhaps his next victim would disagree with you. There, you've set me one of your moral conundrums. Have a sausage while I think about it." He held it out to her on the end of the stick so she could wrap bread around it and pull it off. This was as close as he would come to her.

He would not touch her. He had not spoken of a wife, but it was most probable he had one and was being faithful to her. She was a lucky woman, his wife.

She had learned Robert Fordham by heart in these days they had walked so far together. She knew the path of every wrinkle across his forehead. There was a curved, faint scar on his left hand from some fishhook he had treated carelessly. She knew, right to the center of her, how he moved. She could not breathe sometimes when he twisted to look behind them on the road, and his muscles danced like poetry.

This was the gift her memory held for her. She had

Robert inside her now, even the lines of the palms of his hands. She would not forget him. "We will be in London tomorrow."

"Before noon, if we keep up this pace. Were you planning to spend the night under a bridge?"

"There, or in an alley. I will not sleep much. My small business will take only a few days. Then I will leave quickly. A city is not kind to a woman alone and without money."

"I'll show you a place I know near Covent Garden. A safe place."

How much she wished to stay with him in his safe place near the Covent Garden. She took a bite of her sausage and chewed. "It has allspice in it, this sausage. I find English cooking interesting at times. Robert . . ." She was glad it was dark. There are words one can say in the dark that cannot be said when it is light. "You may not come with me into London. Early tomorrow, when we enter London, I shall send you from me, on your journey to Somerset."

"No, you won't."

She sighed. "You know, do you not, that I desire you."

"Yes."

"I was certain you did, for I have not been concealing this very cleverly. At first, I did not perfectly recognize what had happened to me, and later it became too confusing. It is not important, you understand."

"I know."

"This comes to me because you have saved my life, I think. And because of a man who was with me in France. I did not tell you about him."

"No, you didn't."

She ate slowly, trying to find the right words. "He was a kind of madness that struck me because I was alone and friendless and in great danger. He changed me. He left me . . . I suppose you would say he left me ready for you. When you saved my life in that courageous way and are so handsome and strong, I fall into a foolishness." She thought for a while. "I came to love him in a complicated way. I still do. But I find it is not any protection against desiring other men, which is awkward and humiliating. My mind is in a state of great turmoil. You must not pay too much attention to what my stupid body is doing."

"I won't."

She waited a while before she said the next thing. "I have not wanted men before. Not even one. It is a grave moral weakness to desire two men. I had not known I was this sort of person."

"You aren't." His words were clipped, dry, and unsentimental. "You haven't done anything, so you aren't that kind of person. Forget it."

A smuggler would see things so simply. "That is an interesting philosophy and most likely true in its way. You must go away from me, Robert. You have fulfilled your commission to your conscience when I cross the London Bridge. I do not think I can stand much more of this."

"I'm not going to touch you. And I'm large enough to fight you off if you forget yourself."

She did not laugh, because that would only encourage him. "If I live to be very old, perhaps to a hundred or so, I may understand this thing that is between men and women. What I do know is that touching or not touching does not matter between us. We have gone beyond that. Tomorrow we make an end. It is also not good for you to be in this state, I think."

" 'Men have died from time to time and worms have eaten them . . .' "

" 'But not for love.' I am less sure of that than I was a week or two ago when my life was inexpressibly simpler. I do not think one dies. One may well go insane, however."

"I'll take my chances." He pulled his own sausage off the stick and folded it neatly in bread. He wasn't laughing at her exactly, but there was an amused look behind his eyes. "I'll see you settled safe in London. We've come this far together, what does an extra day matter?"

He made it sound sensible. Did he know in the least how easy it was for him to convince her of anything?

"It is at times like this that I miss my mother." It was easy also to speak simple truths to him. It was a sign of how dangerous he was to her. "It has been six . . . no, five weeks now since she died. I keep thinking, 'I shall tell her this,' or 'I shall ask her this,' and then I remember I shall never see her again. Maman knew all there is to know about men. She was very wise. She would tell me not to stay near to you at all, not for one hour."

"I'm not going to hurt you, Annique."

She couldn't help laughing, though her mouth still had sausages in it. "That is what he said to me. Almost exactly that. The man in France who was unkind to me and whom I loved in a way—he said that. You are a bit like him, did you know?"

The flames made his eyes glitter. "Am I?"

"It is that your bodies are alike. A little, anyway. He is even larger than you, I would say, and immensely strong. Though you are strong, too, of course. But you are different in spirit. He had no softness in him at all, not truly, not anywhere inside him, which is as it should be in a person in his position. He is older than you, too."

"Older?" Robert stared at her, fascinated.

"He is very senior in his work. He must be eight or ten years older than you, I would think. He is fiercely determined, as well, though you are that yourself, a little, except that he does not go about it so nicely. Also he does not smell of fishes. That is from your sweater, you comprehend, which is a beautiful sweater and skillfully knitted but in need of washing—"

The bullet hissed by. It brushed her hair like an insect. Then the blast of sound slapped her skin.

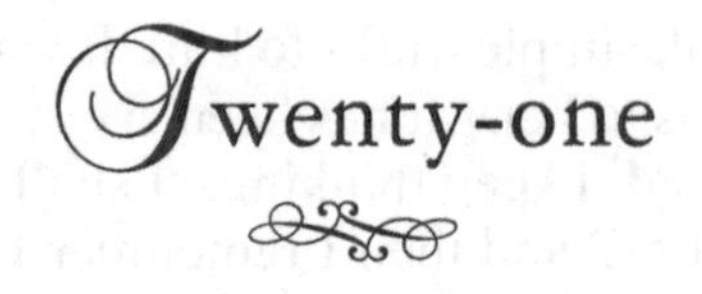

Twenty-one

REFLEX THREW HER FLAT TO THE GROUND. SHE scrambled away. There were no trees. No brush. The field was flat and without shelter. No place to hide. Nothing but darkness to protect her. She heard Robert roll away from the light of the fire.

A man rose out of the black and silent fields, silhouetted against the stars. The first gun had missed. He tucked it into his belt and traded the second pistol to his right hand and raised it.

She scuttled backwards. Spears of wheat stubble tore her skin. Her knife was under her skirt. Couldn't get to it.

The barrel of the pistol followed her. He took careful and deliberate aim.

No chance to run. She rolled sideways. Fought the cloth of her skirt. Too slow. Too slow. For everyone, there is a last time, when they are too slow. Finally she held her knife. Drew back. Picked her target. Threw.

The explosion of the gun cracked the night. There was a flash of light. She sucked in a breath. She could not feel where she had been hit. Perhaps it was as they said, that dying did not hurt.

No. She was a fool, entirely. The man had missed a second time. Unless he was a walking arsenal, he was without guns for the moment. Her hands were wiser than she was. Already they scrabbled and dug for a rock. Found one. She pushed herself up from the ground, cradling it for the throw, straining to see.

The dark figure crumpled and folded in upon himself. He fell with the clumsiness of something from which the spirit has already departed. She was quite sure, when she went to look, that she would find him dead.

Robert ran past her, a pistol in his hand. She had not known until just this minute that he had a gun with him. He ran like water flowing, absolutely silent, to where the man lay on the ground. He bent and picked up the man's head by the hair and then let it flop limply back.

He straightened up and looked toward her. "You're not hurt?"

"The bullet did not touch me. Is he dead?"

"Very." He cleaned his hand by rubbing it on the ground, then went to take one of the sticks from the fire. When he waved it back and forth, it flamed up brightly. He walked back to hold it over the rag doll thing lying on the field stubble. When he knelt, he stuck it into the ground to give him light.

"You don't have to look at this," he said.

But she kept walking forward. "The men Leblanc has sent to kill me . . . Some of them I have known since I was a little child. So I must see." The dead man was small and dark, about thirty, and he had been shot directly through the center of the forehead. She did not think it was a merely lucky shot.

"Do you know him?" he asked quietly.

"He is entirely a stranger to me." She looked away.

This man was gone from the circles of the world. He

would do nothing, ever again, for good or evil. A final and sickening end to all he might have been. She should not care. In the aftermath of battles she had seen many dead men lying upon the ground in just this way, all of them more worthy than this assassin of women. But never had she become used to death. Never.

Robert knelt and inspected her knife where it emerged from the corpse. "You missed by five or six inches. Not surprising, given the—" He paused. Then his breath hissed out through his teeth. "You didn't miss. This is exactly where you hit Leblanc."

"At the insertion of the deltoid. It disables the arm, you see."

"Annique," he said in a strange, tight voice. "When someone has a gun pointed at you, you aim for the throat. Not his arm, not his knuckles, not his bloody toenails. His throat. Do you understand that?"

"But of course." It was not the time to argue with him. Instead, she faced into the night and did not watch while he retrieved her knife and cleaned it on the dead man's shirt. He did not offer the knife back to her, which was a delicate consideration on his part.

He muttered as he emptied out the pockets of the dead man. "Nothing. Nothing. Roll of string, tobacco pouch, house key." One would think he killed men every day, he was so cool about this searching of them. Certainly, smugglers were desperate and violent men. "Another key. English money. French money. Gribeauval pistols. Those are first quality. The jacket's French. His shirt, too. He's someone who followed you from France."

"But, of course. I have offended the English, certainly, but not yet sufficiently so they will kill me."

"He's not going to tell us anything else. Pack up. Leblanc may have ten more men lurking out there in the dark." He was already up and striding away, untying Harding's halter.

It took her two minutes, no more, to be ready, because she had left places in a hurry on many occasions. Since her blindness, also, she had the habit of neatness and always remembering where each small object had been put. She was ready when Robert mounted and rode forward and reached his arm down to her to draw her up into the saddle before him.

It was fortunate she was small. Harding could carry them for some time, though it could not be comfortable for him. "I did not know you had a gun. Where was it?"

"In my coat pocket. A cuff pistol by Manton. I didn't show it to you because I didn't want to frighten you." Harding picked his way through the rough, plowed fields. Then they were on the road and could pick up speed.

The night was clear, with the curve of the moon in the east. It gave light enough that the trees drew long shadows across the road. Above them were ten million stars.

"Will they hang us, if they catch us?" They hanged men in England for stealing bread. Certainly they hanged them for killing people.

"No."

"You seem very sure."

"I am sure. That, you don't have to worry about, Annique."

He sat straight and stiff in the saddle. Perhaps, like her, he was still sickened and awed by the presence of death. Perhaps he had his ears tuned for the sound of hoofbeats behind, which would mean they were being followed.

"Will the farmers come to look because of the shots? Or will they be afraid?"

"They won't be afraid. They'll think it was someone poaching deer."

He was right. This was England. Safe, peaceful England, where no one would think shots meant murder in the darkness.

He shifted the reins. "They won't find him till morning. We'll be long gone."

They trotted, jolting painfully. Finally, they slowed to a walk and she could let go of Harding's mane, which was a relief to both of them she was sure. She leaned against Robert's chest. His arms went tight about her, as if he feared she would suddenly disappear from between them.

"Thank you for protecting me," she said. "I am sorry you had to kill him, even if you are accustomed. It is drastic, to kill a man."

"I didn't mind. I haven't taken very good care of you, have I? If he had carried more accurate guns, you'd be dead. I'm sorry."

"It is the contrary, *mon ami*. You have saved my life twice now. That woman you feel such guilt about—the one in France long ago. Upon her behalf I will tell you that the account is closed. You may sleep well at nights."

"Not yet."

So stubborn a man. This one would always shoulder his responsibility and that of another dozen men as well. His band of smugglers was lucky in its leader. "As you wish. I am not wise enough to be your conscience, so I will not try." She yawned. Now that she had stopped shaking with fear, she was sleepy. "To me you seem a good enough man for most ordinary uses."

He shifted in the saddle, moving her to be easy against him. He was getting used to holding her, she thought. He smelled of the gun he had fired, and of fishes, of course. If she had married a fisherman and gone to live in his village, instead of becoming a spy, it might have been like this for her, riding home from some journey together. Except that she would have washed his sweater more carefully so he did not smell so much of his profession.

"My mother was right."

"Was she?"

She felt the immense strength that was Robert behind her and on every side of her. Safe as houses—that was what the English would say. She yawned. There was no hurry to speak. What she had to say was not, after all, so earth-shattering a bit of wisdom. "She said that the bodies of all men are alike in the darkness. I did not quite believe her, but I find she was correct. This is remarkably like being held by that man in France. Why is it only Kent?"

His hold tightened further. "Why is what only Kent?"

"The others are Yorkshire or Cheshire or Wiltshire or something shire. Why is it not Kentshire?"

"They can't all be shires."

"Oh. That accounts for it."

She could hear his breath move and his heart beating. He pulled his coat around her more so she would be warm. He had saved her life, and she was very tired. She let herself pretend, just for this little time and in the secrecy of her mind, that she was married to Robert and they were going home together.

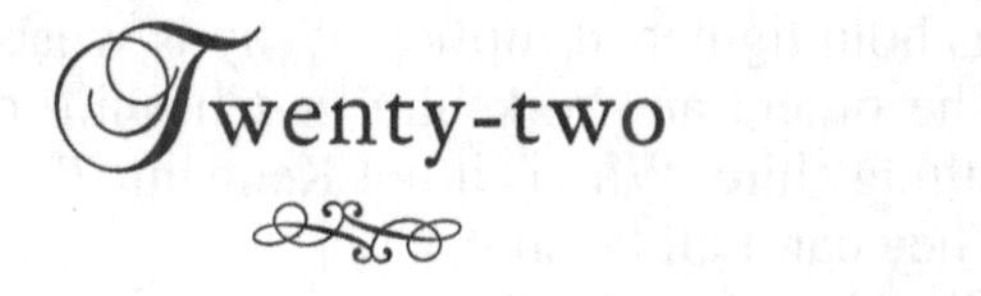

Twenty-two

SHE SLEPT, HELD IN STRONG ARMS, WHILE Robert and the horse Harding brought them the last of the way to London. He was taking her where she would be safe, he said, and she was content to let him do so.

She had awakened in the dawn to the sound of wagons on cobblestones and women in white kerchiefs selling ladles of milk from the huge cans on the back of their carts. The sky was still pink when he brought her past the Covent Garden, which was not a garden at all but instead a market of incredible size, full of flowers and vegetables and chickens in cages, complaining. He bought buns there, from a street seller who handed one up to her, still on Harding's back, and spoke an English she could not understand at all. It was sweet and had raisins and cinnamon in it.

Beyond the market, the streets were quieter. Robert guided Harding into a long, well-tended alley between houses now, little more than a walkway, that angled into a mews, a passageway behind the houses where carriages and horses were kept. Then through alleys again. She could match none of this with the map she carried in her head, which did not mention such small lanes. They were going west and north, away from the rising sun. In the green square they crossed, the windows of every house were still shuttered and the curtains drawn. The only people in the square were two maidservants carrying baskets piled with bread, who looked at them curiously as they rode by.

"Your friends are bourgeois." She assessed the neat, stuccoed facades. "They will not want such guests as we are, even in their kitchen, I think."

"They'll take us in."

He imposed her upon his family, then—an uncle or cousin. Only with family would he be so certain of a welcome. She regretted the lack of a family of her own from time to time. Maman had said quite absolutely nothing about her past or Papa's, not even the town they came from. Now she would never know.

Another alley led them to the middle of a self-satisfied street with linden trees trapped in fences. Dull and respectable was written on every door. She had spent little time in places like this. She did not expect to be comfortable here. Whatever he believed, his respectable relatives would not welcome a questionable and not-so-clean woman to their home.

"Here we are." Robert slid from the horse across the rump. He had great skill in riding for a man of the sea, she thought. He must be as stiff and tired as she was, but the arms that lifted her down were steady and strong as tree limbs. He held her even after she had gained her footing.

It was a large, white, solidly built house . . . a rich one, on this quiet street. He tied the reins to a post, and they went to the front door, like guests, up seven stone steps. Stern, unamused-looking iron barred the windows. A careful and suspicious householder, then. She was cautious herself, as a rule, but she did not think she would like people who barricaded themselves in such a determined fashion against the hazards of the world. The knocker was in the form of a curled rose—brass, richly detailed, highly polished.

Robert knocked loudly. After a minute a boy opened the door. He was expensively dressed, but in shirtsleeves. Not a servant then, but perhaps a member of the household. He was taller than she was but perhaps three years younger. Though it was early, he did not look in the least sleepy. He began to smile in a way that said Monsieur Robert was indeed welcome here.

The bars on the windows plucked at the back of her mind. None of the other houses upon this street had bars on them. Odd. Even this early there should have been a servant at the door, not a young boy in a fine linen shirt who examined the street so alertly and stepped back at once to let them in.

Robert pushed her rapidly across the threshold into the house, into a dull, tasteless parlor, stiff with disuse. The door that closed behind her had strong locks on it. Expensive locks. Very faint, below the smells of cooking and beeswax, the house held the scent of gunpowder. A house should not smell that way.

"Robert . . ." She tried to turn, and his hands tightened and did not allow it. "I have decided not to stay here. I do not . . . Stop it, Robert." But he was very strong.

The boy locked the door behind them. "The others made it back safely. All of them. We didn't expect you till later." He went to unlock the other door on the far side of the parlor.

What others? Robert was expected. But he had not told her he was going to London. Robert was not a man who told light and easy lies.

"I do not understand. I don't like this . . ." It did not matter what she said. Robert thrust her ahead of him through the second door, into the house.

The boy followed and locked it behind them. "Galba wants to see you."

Her mind splintered, brittle as shattered ice. Galba? No. She was confounded, utterly, at what was happening and at the change in Robert. He forced her swiftly, firmly forward, down a wide hall with a bare wood floor and the strong smell of fresh bread and eggs and ham coming from behind one of its closed doors. He didn't say anything at all.

At the end of the hall a door stood half-open. Inside, a man sat behind a large, cluttered desk. On every side of him, papers and folders and binders were stacked in bookshelves. One high shelf held a violin case. The barred window showed the garden at the back of the house. The man stopped writing and looked up as Robert impelled her into the room before him.

She already knew. She could not understand or believe, but she knew where she was. The number beside the door had been seven. This was Number Seven Meeks Street. This was the innermost stronghold of the British Service.

The man set his quill neatly back into the pot of ink. He was perhaps sixty, solid and square, pale-skinned, his hair gone stark white with age. He had eyes bright and pitiless and intelligent as a crow's, but intensely blue, the only color in that face. His gaze fixed upon her as if she were an object of the greatest interest to him, and he had been awaiting delivery for a long time.

This was Galba, unmistakably Galba, who was master of all English spies.

"Did anyone get hurt, coming home?" Robert held her pressed against his chest, surrounded by the brute strength of his muscles as she shook uncontrollably. Now at last, when it was too late, she recognized him. The knowledge of who he must be swept across her and the hopelessness of it all and the fear.

"Adrian did minor damage to his wound," Galba said, "climbing in and out of boats. Doyle showed up yesterday. He was in a French lockup for a while. No harm done."

"We've been lucky." Robert pushed her, stiff and unwilling, forward. "Sir, may I present Mademoiselle Annique Villiers. Annique, this, as you no doubt have already guessed, is Galba."

"Mademoiselle, I am very glad to meet you at last."

"She'd better sit down." Robert pushed her into the cushioned chair that faced the desk and stood behind her. He kept a warm, large, remorseless hold upon her shoulder. "She's scared."

How had this happened? The world had turned upside down so suddenly. How did she come to be here, defenseless and trapped, in this quiet, secret house?

It was Grey who held her, and it was Robert. Grey had only ruthlessness within him where other men carried hearts. Not one thing she knew of Robert was true or real. She was being held by Grey's hands, which had fought with her and comforted her and knew all there was to know about every part of her body. They were Robert's hands, whose image was graven in her memory as if chiseled there. The same man. She did not think she could hold this knowledge in her soul and not be destroyed by it.

Someone slid into the room behind Grey and took up a station at the side of the room, leaning negligently against the wall. He was thin and young, black-haired, wearing the clothing of a London dandy. She did not know him until she saw his eyes. Then she knew. It would be years before the rest of him caught up with the age of those eyes. He smiled at her, rueful and a little pitying. Adrian.

Doyle also would be somewhere in this house. She had the most formidable enemies ranged against her. There was no role she could play, no fabrication she could create, that would fool these hard-eyed, patient men. She was the mouse in a houseful of cats. Not a chance for her.

Galba tapped lightly on the desk to draw her attention. "Mademoiselle, I want you to believe we wish you well. I will do you no hurt whatsoever, not under any circumstances. You're understandably frightened. We will give you time to get used to the situation."

It would begin now, the questioning. They would be courteous for a while.

"It is not so new to me, this situation." Her voice did not break, thank the good God. "I have been before in the hands of men who want things from me, Monsieur Galba. I do not fool myself. It will hurt eventually."

Behind her, she heard Grey mutter, "For God's sake."

Galba opened a book on the side of his desk, flipped past a few pages, then closed it with a snap. "I cannot believe your mother let you grow up thinking the British Service tortures people in this house. It is inconceivable to me."

"I do not think my mother said anything at all about the British Service. She did not work against you directly, ever. Nor have I."

"Has anyone, anywhere, ever made such an accusation against my service?" There was anger underneath Galba's voice.

The methods of interrogation of the British Service had become a matter of some urgency at this moment. She prodded and prodded at her brain until it could work a little. The Military Intelligence of the British had a bad reputation. But Galba's people . . .? In the field there were deaths and violence—these were not the games of children they played, after all—but nothing in her vast store of memory spoke of torture.

"I have not heard of it," she admitted.

"Then don't prate foolishness at me. Even terrified, your mother's daughter should have more sense." Then, immediately, he shook his head and made a wiping-away gesture across the desk. "I retract that. You're exhausted and shocked, and you've been dealing with barbarians like Leblanc. It undermines your judgment. And in one way you are correct. I intend that you will cooperate with me in the end."

Her skin was cold everywhere except where Grey touched. She wondered if she might possibly faint.

"Have you fed her at all today?" Galba was looking at Grey. He continued without waiting for an answer. "I'm stupid to ask. Of course you have, knowing what awaited her." He made the same impatient gesture. "But you haven't let her wash or given her decent clothing. Take her away and let her compose herself. She can't think when she's in this state, and I can't concentrate, seeing her like this." Beneath bushy white eyebrows, piercing blue eyes studied her. "Mademoiselle Villiers, we will not talk seriously until you have recovered your equanimity. Not until tonight, or perhaps tomorrow. You will need time for lengthy reflection."

She sat, numb and unmoving, till Grey took her under the arm and levered her out of the chair.

"One thing more . . ." Galba had become grave. He moved the inkwell upon his desk a finger's breadth to the left and stared at it, his lips compressed and twisted at the corner, as if the inkwell had blighted many hopes. "We heard of your mother's death, but not how it happened. Will you tell me?"

Pain rang within her like a bell, cold and sharp. After weeks, the hurt was not less, thinking of Maman's death. "Her carriage fell from the cliffs. Into the sea. And she was lost." Maman, who had dared so much and escaped so many evil chances, had died because some stone rolled from the crest of a hill. A pointless death. It was an irony of the gods. "Near Marseilles."

"You are sure she is dead? Beyond doubt?"

She nodded.

"I'm very sorry," Galba said quietly. "Go now. We will talk later."

Grey led her away. Her exit was followed by Adrian's

wry gaze, but Galba sat looking down at the book in his hands, his face set and utterly still.

It was Robert who walked beside her down the hall and opened the door to the stairwell that led to the basement. It was Robert, looking as he always did, who smiled reassuringly at her, as if all were correct and excellent with the world. But it was Grey's grip on her the whole way.

Twenty-three

IF ONE WISHES TO DO SECRET AND UNPLEASANT things to people, Annique thought, cellars are the logical place. It was not altogether surprising Grey should take her to one. It was not damp or sinister, being one of those basements half in, half above, the ground. The corridor was carpeted, the walls papered in a delicate pattern of blue flowers. All was deceptively ordinary. But the arched windows, high in the wall, were barred with iron grills that sank deep into the brick.

No escape. How thorough they are. She and the knowledge she carried were wholly at the disposal of the British Service. Doors, closed and threatening, waited on either side of the hall. He would take her behind one of them.

"They aren't torture chambers." Grey was annoyed. "Left side is workshops. Storage rooms on the other side. That one's full of papers. Not an oubliette in the house. I'm not Leblanc."

"You are more subtle than he is. Infinitely, evilly more subtle." She wrapped her arms around her to control the shaking. He opened the last door on the right and went in before her. She did not know what would happen next, but she could not imagine Grey hurting her. Or Robert. Whichever one he was.

"You are not real." She stood in the empty hallway. There was nowhere to run, after all. "I have been tearing my heart to pieces for a mountebank scarecrow. A puppet. I am the girl in the story who falls in love with a clockwork figure in the tower. I have thought myself very clever from time to time, but I am more stupid than dirt."

Grey came back to the door. He had Robert's face, but he was not Robert. "I'm not made of clockwork."

"You. You do not exist at all. You are a nothing, Monsieur Grey. You are a shadow and a cloth flapping in the wind."

"I am Robert Greyson Montclaire Fordham. Everything I told you is the truth—my parents, my brothers, the house in Somerset, the trout pond, the pony I taught to do tricks. I was Robert Fordham for twenty-six years before Grey ever existed."

"You *lied* to me. You are nothing but lies to your back teeth."

His grin showed exactly those teeth at her. "Then we're well matched. Are you still afraid?"

"Of course I am afraid. I would be an imbecile not to be afraid."

"You're already over it. I won't hurt a hair on your head and you know it. Come." He took her hand and pulled her with him into the room which was, amazingly, a bath. It was shining clean and luxurious and surprised her considerably more than a dungeon would have.

"This is a bath," she said stupidly.

"So it is. I hope you find that endlessly reassuring."

"I do not want to be reassured. I want to escape."

He laughed. He had betrayed her and decoyed her into this house and captured her and now he laughed at her. He was most definitely coldhearted as a clockwork.

She was confronted by a small, paneled room. The two arched windows were barred with iron latticework. She couldn't see out of the milky glass, but, from the angle of the sun, she could tell the room faced south. A red rug from Turkey slanted across the black and white tile. A fire was just starting in the brick fireplace set in the wall. Beside the fire, a cheval glass reflected everything.

The bath was a huge, high-sided, oval tub of polished mahogany. Odd pipes emerged from the wall, with spigots upon them.

"This looks like an expensive brothel," she said, knowing something of the matter, "except for that," she gestured toward the pipes, "which looks like part of a brewery I saw in Munich once. What do you do with this?"

"It's a bathtub. What do you think I do—stew prisoners in boiling oil?" He stomped over and opened spigots. They gave out water, which was logical, though she did not see how it could be hot. "My official torturer takes Wednesday off to practice on small animals. You'll have to make do with me. If you're wondering about the water—the other side of the wall is the kitchen stove and a hot water tank. I have ingenious drainage instead of servants running around with pails."

Servants who might be bribed. They have thought of everything. "I see."

"I thought you would. I'll have this full in a minute. You get your clothes off." He thrummed with hungry tension. Inside her, an answering tension arose.

"Do you think it is this simple between us? That you will ask, and I will take off my clothing?"

"I think it's damn complicated between us. Always has been." He shut the taps off and tested the water. "Not one bloody thing's been simple so far. Why should this be?" When he came to her, he took hold of her carefully, as if she were breakable. He turned her to face away from him, toward the mirror. "We'll take this one step at a time." He set his hands to the shawl she was wearing and unwrapped it and dropped it on the floor. "This is the first step."

"Why are you doing this? Why?"

"Taking your clothes off? Desperation. Madness. If you take a good look at me you'll see I'm about to break apart." His voice was tight and fierce, deep as a growl, unsteady at the edges. "Now we take your dress off. That's the next step. Lots of knots to untie, aren't there? Stop me if you have any real objections."

"I do not even know what you want with me."

"You'll figure it out, clever girl that you are."

"I do not mean at this moment, here. I mean . . ." She made the mistake of looking in the mirror. "I mean . . ." The mirror showed a perfect ragamuffin with parted lips and wide, staring eyes. Robert was in the mirror with her. His fingers were silk soft on her back, letting her dress loose.

"How can you be both of them?" Her voice came out young and bewildered. "Robert, how can you be Grey? I look at you and look at you, and you are both of them, and I think I will die of it."

"Very unlikely."

"I cannot do this with you when I do not even know who you are." But she lied. It did not matter which man it was who made her feel this way.

"Let's see if you can." He plucked away at the knots.

She did not want this. She desired it with all her heart. She managed to do both at once, very strongly, with her mind entirely empty of thought the whole time.

He undid the last knot. In the mirror, he opened her dress and folded the edges back like petals and pulled it downward. No hurry. No hurry at all. Her dress slid away from her, a long, dark column collapsing.

He said, "You can't imagine how much I hate this dress. I've wanted to rip it off you every minute of every day, morning till night. I've dreamed of doing this."

"Robert did not want that." Her voice had become husky.

Her mind filled with imaginings so strong they were tongues of heat, lapping her thighs, licking inside her. She was melting like wax in his hands.

"Robert wanted it so much his teeth ached." He lifted the pale shift from her shoulders and slid it off, uncovering her breasts, inch by inch. "I'm Robert. I know."

Her hands clenched convulsively when the linen brushed by, falling. But she let it slip away. Let this happen to her.

She was naked and more naked. The brothels had mirrors like this. She had not known why. Now she did. It pulled at her mind, seeing herself naked with him. It made her only a woman with all her clothes off and the dark shape of a man behind her. Such elemental simplicity. It was obvious what she would soon do, that naked girl in the mirror.

She looked down so she would not see herself submitting in this idiotic way. The rug was rows of jewel-bright flowers. Around her feet spread the dark pool of her dress and her white shift. Grey knelt on the rug, on all those flowers, and unwrapped the rags that had held her knife, which she did not have, and had not once thought of using, anyway. Then her stockings fell, and she was stepping out of her shoes. His touch was velvet on her legs. She could not think at all.

"God, you're beautiful." His breath feathered across her skin as he stood. "Let's put you in the tub while the water's hot." He pushed her gently in that direction, fingers on her bare back. "That's right. Off you go."

Maman would tell me to do what he asks. That is the path of the clever spy . . . to use her body to entice and control. But she was the one enticed. She did not become naked before Grey to be devious.

She stepped into the bath. Water steamed around her. All the little waves stroked at her as she lowered herself in. She slid down far into the water, sinking in it to her chin, and kept an eye on Grey.

Grey sat on the carved bench at the side of the room and

untied his cravat. The bench had griffins on its arms and he hung his cravat over one of them, across its nose. He laid his jacket beside him on the bench. "We'll wash your hair."

"If you go away, I will wash anything you want me to." All her many years as an agent had not prepared her for this. A decade cavorting with lions and demons in hell would not prepare one for this.

He smiled Robert's smile, slow and warm. "Do you know that you become a complete vagabond the minute you set foot on the road—grimy and rumpled and chewing grass stems? I watched you get dirtier and more disreputable every ten paces. You have the most amazing protective coloration."

She swallowed. "When one is a vagabond it is necessary to look and act like one and smell like one. I learned that before I could talk."

"You're not a vagabond now. You need your hair washed." He thumbed the studs out of his cuffs and set them aside on top of his jacket. Then he began working on the buttons of his shirt, going from the collar downwards.

He would make love to her here. Would he carry her to the rug by the fire and lay her down in front of that mirror? She would see him twice—in truth and in the mirror. Would it feel like two men making love to her, Grey and Robert? She was completely daunted by this entire situation. She decided to spend a long time in the bathtub, thinking it over.

He tugged his shirt free from the band of his trousers and pulled it over his head. For the first time, she saw him unclothed.

He had the body of a soldier. The thin, white line on his ribs was a saber cut. The pitted marks were shrapnel, four or five pieces. There were other scars. Men had tried and tried to kill him. They had all failed because Grey was tough, right to the fiber, and also smarter than they were.

He jerked a boot off and shied it across the room to thump on the bricks of the hearth. Then he did the same to the other and stood and stretched. A hundred muscles slid under his skin. He was very beautiful. She wanted to rub across him everywhere with her mouth and the sensitive skin of her face. It was not fair that he should do this to her.

He strolled toward her. She would have sworn, without the smallest lie, that his eyes glowed like hot coals.

She huddled further into the water which was not a substance useful to hide in. When he leaned against the tub, his bare chest was so close she could have straightened and touched him with her lips, without the smallest difficulty. He cupped water with both hands. Drops spilled down through his fingers, silver and sparkling.

"My advice is, close your eyes," he said.

She had not quite worked out what he meant before he dumped water upon her.

He said, "Not good at taking advice, are you?"

"I have been told that." She sputtered water out of her mouth and wiped her eyes with the heel of her hand.

When he dipped another handful, she was more ready. Water poured in sheets across her face, again and again, until she was most thoroughly wet. She waited and dripped while he made lather in his hands from a soap that smelled of bay leaves. That was Robert's smell, not Grey's. She would smell like Robert when he made love to her.

When they made love . . . "You do not need to do this. I have been washing my hair entirely by myself for years and years."

"It'll be a change then. Keep your eyes shut when I put the soap on. I'm out of practice."

She did not resist, but sat like a dolt while he scrubbed her hair efficiently. It was useless to reason with him. He was, as she knew, a man of unending ruthlessness.

"Hold your breath," he ordered.

This time, she was wise. She grabbed a lungful of air before he pushed her down, under the water.

"*Espèce de chien.* You drown me." She shook her head fiercely, getting water everywhere. Upon him too. "You had only to ask and I would . . ."

His fingers wove into her hair to hold her still. The first kiss, fierce as fire, was to silence her. Then he began little kisses, one after the other, along her lips . . . demanding and demanding till she kissed back. This was the only safe way to deal with a man of unending ruthlessness.

"I want you so damn much," he whispered into her mouth. "It hasn't stopped, not for a minute, since I saw you in Leblanc's cellar. For days I've thought of nothing but stripping you naked. I'm nine-tenths mad with it."

He tasted of cinnamon. It was ironic that a man like Grey should taste ordinary and domestic. It let him slip, somehow, through her defenses.

When he loosed her, she floated in the water, dizzy with wanting him.

Something fitted into the tub next to her. Then, on the other side. He was above her, naked, and eager for her as a stallion after a mare. He lowered himself into the tub. His skin was solid and warm and shocking as it slid against her. Altogether unfamiliar. This might have frightened her if she had been capable of any emotion at all, except being entirely overwhelmed by this turn of events.

She held tight to the rim of the tub. "You cannot do this."

"Watch me."

"I mean, you cannot do this in any case, but it is also physically impossible. There is no room."

"We'll find out. Hold on to me instead of the tub." He put her hands on his shoulders. He made it seem sensible and natural. Water sloshed wildly as he circled her ribs and raised her up. Then he was underneath her, lifting her smoothly, and she was above him.

He smiled. "We fit just fine. See? Relax a bit, and I'll . . . Yes. That's right." He centered her body upon his, and her legs parted. He guided her hips down upon him as if he had done this a thousand times with her. "Damn, that feels good."

It was . . . extraordinary. She straddled him, riding him in the water, her legs wedged tight against the side of the tub. She was open. The maleness of him knew exactly where it belonged. It nudged at her, wanting to go in. Entirely ready to do so.

Time jogged to a stop. Nothing—no preconception, no advice—had prepared her for this.

His eyes were level with hers, inches away, filling the universe. "You're still bruised." He barely touched her ribs. "Here and here. I'll be careful with you."

He was a fighter with fists as hard as stone. He would be gentle with her. There could be nothing more devastating to her senses than that alliance. "It is not fair that you do this to me when I am a prisoner."

"Is that what you're telling yourself? That you're doing this because you're a prisoner?" He picked up soap from the dish on the little table and turned it over and over between his palms. "Then you just climb out of this tub and start yelling. Galba will be down in two minutes to rescue you. Hawker will cut out my liver and Doyle will stomp it into the ground. Or you can lay me out with one of those pokers over there by the fire. That should appeal to you." He spread soap on her shoulder, taking his time. There were plans for her seduction in every small movement. He was a man of many successful plans. "You want this."

"I do not . . ." She felt him draw the line of her collarbone with one soapy fingertip. "I do not want this. I will not." When he returned to her shoulder, he made small circles there, playing among the nerves. He was barely touching. Was there anything in the world except his eyes? "I should not."

"You keep working on that and let me know." He smiled. "Did you ever have long hair, Annique?"

"When I lived with the Rom. It grew very long, all down my back."

"I'd like to see your hair long." He traced curvy lines on her chest, in the foam of soap. The prickle and slide wiped her mind utterly clean of thought. "It would flow down like this." He showed the path long hair would fall. Down her shoulder and over her breast. Just the way it would flow down her, his skillful, slippery fingers flowed. "You have midnight hair, full of silk and hidden stars. You snare me past redemption."

She had been told many times that she was beautiful, generally by men who then asked her price. This was different. It was Grey who found her beautiful. She had never cared before. "This is not wise. Not for either of us."

"I know. We're about to be very, very stupid."

"We should stop."

"You do that. I'm not going to." He shifted in the water. Hard, male warmth slid against the parts of her that were secret and sensitive and not used to this irrational business. Hunger blossomed and burned. It spread everywhere inside her.

"I cannot think when you do this."

"You don't need to think. You already figured this out. Remember Plato? I'm the other half of your egg. We're getting back together."

"Maybe. I do not know. It was easier to talk about Plato when your hands were tied." He explored her breasts, drawing trails of fire with little explosions of surprise at the peak. She swallowed hard. "It is beautiful, what you do to me. When I look at you, it is so beautiful it hurts. Like the curve of a wave or a leaf falling. Have I told you that?"

"Not in so many words." He brought a nipple toward him so he could kiss it. "I like the way you nubble up here, all pink. Shows you like what I'm doing. You taste good." Another kiss. "Soapy but good. I think I'll do this for a while. Stop me when you stop liking it."

She did not stop him. She let his mouth lead her through shock after shock into a spinning wildness. Heat burned in pulses. She groaned and threw her shoulders back and leaned toward him, yes, with all of her body. It was a yielding of everything.

She was part of the madness now. She was committed.

He knew the exact moment she gave in. He stirred strongly where they were nestled together between her legs. "I feel you enjoying it. You stir inside when I do this, down where we're touching. You'll like the rest of it, too."

"I am . . . deciding." Warm water lapped and eddied between them with every move. Hot shivers gripped and tugged at her. "Do not hurry me. I am still deciding whether . . . or not. Maybe not."

"You keep thinking that. But it's late for you. You haven't been able to stop yourself for a while."

He was right. She could not have drawn away from him to save her life.

He stroked down her belly to where she ached for him so much. He tangled his fingers in the small curls there. He did not touch within her. He could, at any moment. It was torment, knowing he would choose his own time to touch her there. Ribbons of longing spun through her, pulling and pulling. She moved upon him. "This is . . . I should not . . ."

"When you're ready." The flat planes of his abdomen were hard, quivering with tension where she braced her palms against him. His voice had deepened. Gone hoarse. His eyes were the color of smoke, with flame beneath. Hot. Ravenous. "We'll wait till every part of you wants this."

"No." She could not stare into those eyes or she would be lost. She bent her head. Her hair hung in tendrils that swayed when she shook her head. "I . . . No."

He took a deep breath and held still. He was ready beneath her, ready as iron. "What is it, Cub?" Careful, his hands shaking a little, he lifted her chin and searched her face. "I swear, I wouldn't have you like this if I didn't think you wanted it. What's the matter?"

"I do not . . . I do not do this with English spies . . ." It came out in short, frantic breaths. ". . . who do not give a fig for me. And who . . . confuse me."

"You don't do this with anyone, according to the best available evidence. A man knows, at this point." He lifted strands of her wet hair and pulled them back from her face, left and right. She had to look at him. Laughter and stark hunger and tenderness poured from him . . . and a shrewd understanding that scared her witless. "Give me a little credit, Cub. You want this. If you didn't, I sure as hell wouldn't be deflowering you in a bathtub."

"I . . ."

"From the first, I've known. You. Only you. Inevitable." His fingertips skimmed her cheek, then over her lips. She shuddered. They both knew what he was doing to her. "We'll make it work. Trust me. Do you want to talk for a while?"

"I cannot. You distract me."

Oh, but he thought that was very funny. He made the water shake with his laughter. "I think I'll distract you some more." He kissed one breast, then the other.

She ached. Already, she swayed in his hands, unable to stop herself. But he wanted the words of surrender also. He tormented them both with his foolish scruples. She was not so naïve to acquiesce to a man while he laughed at her.

She no longer cared whether it was wise or disastrous or merely inevitable. *I need him. I will have him.* He would see the surrender she made to him.

She gripped the side of the tub and rose up. He was ready. She thrust herself downward, hard.

A deep cry wrenched out of her. She felt tearing inside. The stab of pleasure hurt. It was honey sweet.

"Good . . . God." Grey surged upward to meet her. "Wait." He locked his hands to the bones of her hips and kept her tight to him, panting, face contorted. "Wait. Wait a damn minute."

"Yes." She held most totally motionless, stunned past thought.

"That was . . . That . . ." He sucked in a tremendous, shaky breath. "Annique, men like to be prepared for this sort of thing." He held rigidly still, savage with need, shuddering with laughter. "You'll be the death of me, woman. Does it hurt?"

"No." She shook her head. "Yes. Not exactly. It feels different."

"I imagine it does." His hands clenched. Released. Stroked the length of her body. Clenched around her again. "Don't move, or this is going to be remarkably . . . brief." He took another deep, ragged breath. "I'd planned something slow and elaborate."

Elaborate. He need not have worried. Inside her, things were extremely elaborate. She made some sound.

"I've been looking forward to this for a long time," he said.

She wanted to tell him that she had, as well, waited for this. But she could not speak.

"Stay still now. I'll try to go slow." His fingers slid down to open soft, sensitive parts of her. He eased gradually deeper into her. Pain by pain. Pleasure by pleasure. He was smooth as the water swirling past, compelling as the pull of tides.

Thought quenched. She gasped and started to move upon him.

"Softly, love. Wait."

"I . . . I cannot."

"You can. Gently with yourself." He pressed her hips down to him, holding her still. His other hand caressed persuasively, building a restless anxiety within her. "We're in no hurry. See. It doesn't hurt when you hold still. I do this, and there's no pain at all."

She did not try to answer. She had misplaced the ability to translate between French and English. An overmastering rhythm gripped her. She was frantic to ride upon him. It was impossible to keep still. He would make her insane. She made fists and hit upon his chest in great strokes, like a bell tolling, as she rocked. Upward. Down. He opened his hold and let her move upon him, deeply. He gasped each time.

Again. Again. A wall, solid and heavy as bricks, but made of burning light, grew around her. And crashed down. Over her. Everywhere.

He must have felt what happened within her. He thrust upward, deep inside. Yes. And yes. She threw her head back and cried out, altogether lost. Except that she must hold him, tight, tight to her.

It did not hurt. Nothing could hurt when she was like this.

Pleasure rushed in. Filled her. Jolts of it hit, spaced by the moans she made. It was limitless pleasure, orbed and blazing, that glowed and burned inside her. She felt herself closing over him again and again.

Time flowed once more. The edge of that glory slid across her and away. She collapsed, inch by inch, shaking and pulsing, onto him.

His arms wrapped around her. She lay her head upon his heart. It beat like a horse running, strong and even.

"I am glad I did this," she whispered in French, "whatever comes after."

She felt everywhere light as feathers, but when she tried to move, she found she was, on the contrary, heavy as lead. It was a good thing she had someone beneath her or she would probably have drowned.

Twenty-four

HE CLOSED THE DOOR SOFTLY BEHIND HIM. Anaique slept on the couch in the study, wrapped in a white Turkish robe—his damp, sweet, vulnerable, and deadly French agent, exhausted from making love with him.

Miraculously and at last, she was his. He could solve everything else, now that he'd got that right. He wanted to grin like a fool and caper around the halls. Pity a Head of Section couldn't do that.

"There's nineteen beds in this house," Doyle was waiting for him, leaning against the wall, arms folded across his chest, his ugly face set in lines of amusement, "if you count the cots in back of the kitchen. None of 'em's good enough for you. You do it in the bathtub. God's cat."

That was the trouble, living with spies. They figured out every damn thing. No privacy. "We need to get her some clothes. I can't keep her in a bathrobe."

"Maggie'll bring over some bits and pieces. They're close enough in size."

"Except Annique is what I'd call plum-size, very tasteful and understated." Adrian came up, light on his feet. He wore his gentleman's togs—charcoal jacket, dove-colored waistcoat, ruby stickpin in his cravat. He didn't look like a man who'd had a bullet picked out of him ten days ago. "Maggie, on the other hand, is more—"

"And you, me lad, can stop right there," Doyle said.

Grey needed a look at Tacitus and Montaigne. One final confirmation. They'd be on the shelves in the library. He started upstairs. "Where's Giles?"

"I sent him to mop up." Doyle allowed a short, innocent pause. "Seems the bathroom's an inch deep in water somehow."

"Send him to the office when he's done. I shot a man in Kent. We have to notify a magistrate."

"This spree of lawlessness you've embarked upon . . ." Adrian trailed them upstairs, shaking his head. "Fletch sends his compliments and suggests you return his nag. I take it the beast is tied outside."

"Right. More work for Giles. And remind Ferguson to serve coffee at dinner, not tea. Annique doesn't like tea. I'm glad you two made it out of France."

"I'm glad she didn't crack your skull on the way up from Dover," Doyle said equitably. "For one thing, you can sort this mess that piled up while you were depopulating the countryside. First off, Military Intelligence knows we got Annique. They want her."

"They can go to hell."

"With bells on. However, Colonel Reams has invited himself to dinner. A conference, he calls it."

"Then I'll tell him to go to hell myself.'"

Doyle and Adrian followed Grey down the hall and into the big front room. Sun poured through the curtains, glinting off the collection of blades Service agents had hung up on racks over the years. Big leather chairs faced the fireplace. The *Times* lay open on one table, a deck of cards and a long clay pipe on another. Hundreds of books were jammed and stacked in bookcases that covered two walls.

Grey said, "I need Montaigne and Tacitus."

"Who are . . . ?" Adrian said.

"A Frenchman and one of them Romans, respectively." Doyle wandered to the shelves beside the fireplace. "Dead a good while, which makes me wonder why I'm looking for them. Now Montaigne . . . when last seen he was somewhere around here." He stretched a spatulate hand across books. "Try over there for Tacitus. Bound in red, if I remember. Fletch told us about Annique's eyes. There's a doctor with a cartload of degrees wants a look at her. His report's on your desk. The good news is that it's probably permanent. And some news that's not so good. Leblanc's in England."

"We met. He tried to knife Annique in an alley in Dover."

"Old news then. He brought twenty men across the Channel, give or take. The military's been rounding 'em up along the south coast since Monday, which is how they found out about Annique."

"Soulier's spitting tacks, bless his devious French heart." Adrian propped himself on the arm of a chair and pulled out an eight-inch throwing knife and began to pare his nails. "Leblanc has come to our fair shores without orders and without reporting to Soulier. Much fluttering in the dovecotes of French intelligence."

"An' wouldn't it be nice if Soulier killed Leblanc for us." Doyle worked his way down the shelf. "No love lost there."

"You can pass this along—Leblanc's wounded, upper right arm. Henri Bréval's cut across the knuckles. I may have cracked his collarbone. The rest is Annique's work."

"Lethal chit," Adrian said. "And you've brought her here to wreak havoc upon Service personnel. How exciting."

Doyle grunted, looking amused.

"Speaking of our lethal chit." Adrian inspected his nails.

"I ask myself . . . Why the tub? She's agile as a little eel, of course, but you don't want to go taking the first poke at a virgin in a couple feet of water. Makes 'em nervous. With a virgin, what you do is pick a flat spot. Dry, for one thing. Soft, if you can manage it. Then you—"

"I can do without your expert advice on deflowering virgins." Grey felt his face get hot. "This isn't a topic for discussion."

Doyle slid a lazy glance. "You been told off, lad."

"And . . ." an edge came into Adrian's voice, ". . . you don't leave the girl to sleep it off alone. You stick around to be there when she wakes up."

"God's chickens," Doyle muttered.

Hawker didn't like the way he was treating Annique. Fair enough. He didn't like it much, himself. "She needs to dig away at the bars for a while to convince herself I've got her trapped. Then she'll take some time getting used to the idea. She won't want me there while she does it."

"And you don't get kicked in the guts if she gets testy," Adrian said dryly.

"That, too." Mostly, he wouldn't be tempted to make love with her again while she was still sore.

Tacitus was on the bottom shelf, bound in red, in three volumes. It was in Volume One. When he paged through, the passage leaped out at him. ". . . deformed by clouds and frequent rains, but the cold is never extremely rigorous." She'd got it right, word for word. That was the positive proof, if he needed it. But he already knew what he dragged into Meeks Street this morning. He slid the book back into the shelf. "We lock up the house, double-lock it. Every key turned."

"Already done," Doyle said, "the minute she walked in."

This might be the safest place in England. It still wasn't safe enough, not for what Annique was carrying. "Leblanc has men and money. He wants her dead. How does he get to her?"

Hawker's knife stilled. "There's the old standby . . . snipers."

Doyle moved along the shelf, checking titles. "We put on extra guards. We watch the neighborhood. She stays away from windows."

"Then there's setting the place on fire. Land mines in the garden. Rockets."

Rockets. He massaged the bridge of his nose. "How hard is it to get rockets in London?"

"Not easy," Doyle said. "Could be done."

"Artillery through the front door. Prussic acid in the next shipment of coffee beans." The knife disappeared into Hawker's sleeve. He pushed himself to his feet and started pacing the Bokhara rug. "Satchel bomb over the wall. Cobras down the chimney. Poison darts. Tunneling in from the basement. Armed thugs at the back door. Your standard mysterious package delivery."

No one more inventive than the Hawker. "You can't get cobras in England, for God's sake. Talk to Ferguson about the food, though. That's a possibility."

"I know where to get cobras," Adrian said.

"You would." Doyle pulled out a book. "And here's our old friend Montaigne. Why are we looking at Montaigne?"

"I want a reference. The man at Delphos who could tell eggs apart. Where is it?"

"Crikey. Well, you picked one I know. 'Essay on Experience.' About in the middle. I had to copy it out once, at Eton. Forget what I did to earn that particular punishment."

"You're looking up one of Annique's clever sayings?" Adrian had taken himself over to the window. He was studying Meeks Street, probably working out ways to kill somebody.

"One of mine."

"Here it is." Doyle read, " '. . . yet there have been men, particularly one at Delphos, who could distinguish marks of difference amongst eggs so well that he never mistook one for another, and having many hens, could tell which had laid it.' Is that what you want? Why are we interested in French philosophy?"

"She knows that line."

"She's an educated woman. I suppose she—"

"I offered her three words, and she came back with the rest. I picked a bit out of Tacitus about the weather, obscure as hell. She knew that one, too. I'll bet I could open any of these books, anywhere, and she'd recite the page for me. She has them by heart. When did she do that?"

Doyle flipped the pages under his thumb and closed the book and set it down. "It shouldn't be. You're right."

"She's been traipsing around Europe, following armies. When did she go to school and sit down and learn these books word for word?"

"She didn't. I should have seen this." Doyle looked disgusted with himself. "She has one of those trick memories. I've heard about them. Never actually met one."

Adrian slammed the wall with the flat of his hand. "Maps. She told me she had maps in her head. I wasn't listening."

"That's why they sent a ten-year-old into army camps." Doyle's eyes narrowed over a hard expression. His oldest girl was ten. "They couldn't pass up the chance to use that trick memory. They dressed her as a boy and put her to work in those hellholes the first minute she could survive on her own."

She'd survived. What was it like to live like that, remembering every freezing night, every forced march, every death? Never forgetting. No wonder she filled her brain with philosophers. "She's carrying it all," he circled his hands as if he were holding her, the smooth forehead, the soft, dark hair, "inside her head."

They stood, looking at each other, absorbing the implications.

"Do the French know what she is?" Doyle answered

himself. "Not Fouché. He'd have her locked in a cage. Or dead. Probably dead. Who knows about this?"

"The mother had to know." Adrian was pacing again, crossing between the long windows and the fireplace. "And Vauban. Both of them dead now. It's likely Soulier knows. He picked her up and put her to work when she was half grown. What do you wager they used her as a courier—Soulier and Vauban—back and forth across France, keeping messages in her head?" He tapped his fingers as he walked, one by one, against his thumb. "Not Leblanc. He doesn't know."

The mother, Vauban, and Soulier. The three of them using her to pass secrets around. She was the perfect hiding place. Somebody—Vauban probably, back in Bruges, for some god-awful reason—had decided to use her to store the ultimate secret. "She has the Albion plans."

"Will you stop that?" Adrian swung around and confronted him. "I don't give a damn what Leblanc said. I don't give a damn she was in Bruges. She didn't kill our men in cold blood."

"I agr—"

"Vauban wouldn't send that girl out to kill under any conceivable circumstances. No chance. Not the remotest. She wouldn't stick a knife in somebody's throat for a pile of gold. How could you spend two weeks with her and not know that? I saw it in six minutes."

"I agree. It isn't in her."

"She . . . You agree?"

Nice to catch Hawker off guard for a change. "I watched her not kill four men between Paris and London when they were doing their damnedest to kill her. Very convincing. There is no murder in the woman."

"Oh. Well then." Adrian tugged his jacket straight. "Sweet reason prevails."

"But she is carrying the Albion plans." He held his hand up. "No, listen to me. I've seen them inside her. She gave herself away fifty times, walking up from the coast. She knows the invasion route, foot by foot." She hadn't thought to hide that knowledge from a sailor she'd trusted, who'd saved her life, who had nothing to do with spies and secrets. "At least some of the troops will be taking the Dover Road. I watched her figure out exactly where people are going to die when Napoleon invades, which streets, which hillsides. I saw the villages burning in her eyes. She has the plans."

Adrian was mutinous but silent.

"A heavy weight for someone like her," Doyle said.

"It's eating her alive. She could be that Spartan boy with a fox hid under his shirt, gnawing away."

"We don't have any choice, of course." Doyle picked the stack of playing cards from the table and began shuffling them from one big hand to the other. "We take the plans from her. She's lucky it's us doing it and not Military Intelligence. Reams isn't above using torture." He spread the cards in a fan and closed them up again.

"Is that a problem?" Adrian flung it over his shoulder and started pacing again. "We haven't misplaced the thumbscrews, have we? Myself, I like a heated knife and that thin skin between the toes. Sensitive spot on women. I always say there's nothing a clever man can't do with a knife."

"You're annoying Robert," Doyle observed mildly.

"Duly noted."

Annique had recruited a pair of strong protectors. Good.

No sound came from the study downstairs. She'd be awake by now, exploring the edges of the box he'd locked her in, soft-footing around the room with her robe knotted over that miraculous white body and her mind all sharp-edged and racing. She'd be scared. He couldn't do this to her and not scare her. Even if she was just standing there, part of her would be battering against the bars, frantic to escape. It was his job to keep those bars in place.

"No force. No pain." But they already knew that. "No

threat. No coercion. We don't even have to argue hard. She's going to talk herself into doing what we want. Why do you think she's in England? She's about to give us what we want. Freely."

Doyle turned the idea over. "She didn't just come to hide. She didn't come here looking for safety. She's here to stop the French fleet from sailing."

"Being what she is, she can't do anything else. She's going to weigh the damage those plans can do to France against the hell that the invasion will be. She'll give us the plans. When it comes down to another one of Napoleon's bloodbaths, or helping England, she's going to go with England. Whoever gave her the plans must have known that."

That was something else he'd find out. What the hell had happened in Bruges, that Annique ended up with the Albion plans? "I almost wish we were using coercion. Then she could hate me, instead of herself."

"Oh, that's deep, that is," Hawker muttered.

Doyle said, "Waste o' breath, warning you. Always was."

Twenty-five

Cockle Lane, Soho

THE TWO MEN PUSHED BRUSQUELY PAST IDLERS at the tavern door. Henri limped, keeping up with Leblanc. ". . . watching Meeks Street. They report she entered the house with Grey himself. Grey of the British Service. It is disaster."

"You should have killed her in Dover. Why am I surrounded by idiots?"

"Do you not see? The man we held in Paris . . . it was this same Grey. *Sans doute.* The description is unmistakable. The one who attacked me in Dover—it is Grey. He has been with her since Paris. Since you put them in the same cell." Henri clenched his fist and flinched. "*Bougre de Dieu.* I am crippled by that man."

"You are worse than crippled. You are an imbecile. There is no proof the man was Grey." Leblanc kicked at a black dog that sniffed along the gutter edge.

"We held the Head of the British Section in our chateau and did not inform Fouché. We let him get away. If this comes out, I do not want to face Fouché."

"You will not face Fouché." Leblanc's gaze flicked across Henri. He slipped his hand under his jacket, to the knife that rested there. "You have brought the men up from the south? The money? All is prepared?"

"Done. All done. It is always a mistake to use women. You all trusted that bitch, and now she spreads herself for this Grey and squeals our secrets. It must be stopped."

"Not by you. You are useless to me with a broken shoulder. I need men who can shoot a gun." Leblanc looked up and down the deserted street. An alley opened to one side, shaded and crooked and private. "Come. We will take this shorter way."

Twenty-six

"But these are lovely clothes." She held up a walking dress of figured silk. "And you say they are English. Life is very strange, I find."

She still wore the white bathrobe that reached almost to her feet and was large enough to surround her twice. It belonged to Grey. He had enjoyed wrapping her in something of his.

His bedroom was a snug place, with blue brocade curtains and a very large bed. It was untidy with his things in a pleasant way. The lovely clothing was spread out across the bedspread.

"Dress for dinner." He chose the pale green dress with an embroidery of flowers upon the bodice. "This one, I think."

The gowns were beautifully cut, the apparel of a woman of taste and refinement. The boxes at her feet held shifts and pantalets, all completely new and as delicately immodest as any she had ever seen in Paris. It was not usual for a prisoner to wear such clothing to dinner. She had been a prisoner several times, and she knew.

"These are given to me by a friend of yours? That is kind." She did not like it that he knew a woman of whom he could ask such favors. "When one considers how many respectable women there are in the world, it is remarkable I am not sometimes presented with more modest underclothing."

"Isn't it?" His expression was hungry and knowing. She was entirely sure he looked forward to seeing her wear these silk and lace nothings. He already pictured himself taking them off of her and laying her down upon his bed. He was Head of Section for England, assuredly, but he was also a man.

She found she was not at all in the mood to lie back and make love upon that big bed with the blue covers. She wanted to hit him with something, not in a lethal manner, but hard.

She picked up a shift and turned away before she loosed the robe. It fell to the floor, and she pulled the shift on, all in one movement, so quickly he would have only a glimpse of her being naked. That was her reply to the look in his eyes. He would comprehend. He was a man given to subtleties.

"This is an agreeable room." She pulled the green dress over her head and smoothed it down her hips. It fit well. His woman friend was almost precisely of a size with her, except with a larger bosom. A lovely and womanly bosom. "I notice it contains a great many deadly things. I would not trust me here if I were you. I would keep me in your dungeon, which you insist you do not have."

"No dungeons. I have a comfortable, boring room I put dangerous people in. I won't show it to you because I don't want to frighten you out of your wits. I promised Galba you'd behave sensibly."

"At least I shall not attack you with any of these tempting objects you have left strewn about. Not at this moment." She tried to reach the buttons on her back, but he nudged her gently around and did them up for her. "Thank you. It is difficult to dress in fashionable clothing, unaided. One would expect life to be better managed."

He watched her as if he were trying to take her heart apart like a puzzle box. As he was her interrogator, it would be his task, for a time, to take her apart piece by piece. It is inexpressibly frightening to be the puzzle box in these cases.

He did the last button. "Maggie bought a comb. It's on the dresser."

"The Maggie of Doyle? Do you tell me these are her clothings? I am very surprised." She thought about Doyle, who had been to Cambridge and bought his wife such dresses. And such underthings. "I think she is not at all as I pictured her."

Grey did not wait for her to take the comb but picked it up himself and began to use it in her hair. He combed and smoothed after it with his hand. It was a common action, strong and simple as a sunset or standing in the sea. A man did such things for a woman who belonged to him.

In the mirror, her mouth was ripe as fruit, and her eyes were soft and foolish. She looked altogether like a woman who had just given her virginity to someone. The bathtub part of it was no longer obvious, since she was not dressed in a long white robe. Grey had transformed himself into a gentleman, here in the heart of his power. He wore an evening jacket that was the blue black of midnight and a waistcoat with thin stripes of burgundy and white. A heavy signet ring gleamed dull gold as it slid in and out of her hair with each stroke of the comb. He was not handsome. Men such as Grey ate handsome dandies for breakfast twice a week. If she had been a foolish young girl, she would have been dazzled.

"When I escape from this prison," she said, "I shall find a boy of the Rom, younger and darker and handsomer than you. I shall make love to him in barns and haystacks until I do not feel this way for you." She said it to hurt him and to free herself from him. She did not like what she saw in her own eyes in the mirror.

"I hope you enjoy yourself. You won't change what's between us, Annique, not with fifty Gypsy boys."

She wished he did not speak so many excellent truths to her. She stepped from his hold and began to straighten the clutter upon his dresser, lining everything up. "One does not love one's jailer. It is a fallacy jailers have, that their prisoners like them, but it is never true. If you had not trapped me, I would have walked away by now. In a week I would have forgotten you altogether." *Or in a month, or a year. Or never.* "There is nothing between us except a hunger of bodies."

"There's that, too."

"I do not want to feel anything for you. Do you understand? Can you imagine what it is to have not even a shift to wear? To be so dependent upon a man that I must ask him for clothing? This is not a good basis for friendship."

"I know. It makes it harder. Will you sleep with me tonight?"

He would ask. Not demand. Just ask. She did not know how to fight such cunning. "Can I say no?"

"Of course you can. There are five or six empty bedrooms, one right across the hall. I can put you in there." He took back the space between them till they were almost touching. "I'll leave my door unlocked. Will you come to me?"

"I am very stupid."

"I think that means yes." He was smiling.

She gave him his victory. "I would come to you sometime in the night, tiptoeing down the hall, and open the door and crawl in beside you. Already, I am listening to the argument your body makes to mine. If you carried me to that bed, even without taking a moment to be persuasive, I would want you like flames."

"The hall gets chilly. Sleep with me tonight, in that bed."

He cradled her cheek into the warm hardness of his palm. He was so aware of her . . . even the infinitesimal nod of her head, he felt.

"You have to say it."

"Yes." She was without shame.

"I'll hold you to that." He drew her against him, body to body, and nuzzled into her hair, breathing the scent, making a growl deep in his throat. It grappled at her heart, that he desired even her smell.

His hands also hungered for her. They molded the soft dress to her buttocks, stroking, taking pleasure in the shape of her body. She closed her eyes to be in the darkness with the strength of him, and his hunger, and the massive beating heart. There was nothing but sensation. Heat ignited between her legs and spread sweetly. She glowed inside her skin, in ripples. She was drunk with it. She was . . .

She was Annique Villiers, and this man was her enemy.

She pushed away from him, breathing hard. She had been moaning little noises and not realized. Truly, she was a fool.

"I make . . ." She had to start again. "I make mistakes with you. I lose myself."

"You're not used to being confused."

"Do not patronize me, monsieur. I have gone ever so slightly mad where you are concerned. It could happen to anyone." She stomped across the room, barefoot, to sit on the edge of the chair. The Maggie of Doyle had provided her silk stockings with a white pattern. Exquisite. She would wear exquisite stockings to go mad in. "Perhaps I shall regain my senses and sleep alone tonight. Who knows? You cannot bemuse me and entangle me forever."

"We're entangling each other."

"But one of us is the jailer. You want me to forget that. That is why you are so gentle. Me, I would rather you were sincere and badgered me with questions. Then I would remember I am a prisoner. If I had any pride, I would not crawl into your bed and play the whore."

Silence struck, forceful as any bolt of lightning. Tension crackled in the air between them. She felt his anger like hot sparks on her skin. "Is that what you're doing? Playing the whore?"

She would not look at him. "I have been taught to do that, if captured."

The man who gazed down at her was entirely Grey. Not one speck of Robert. "Prisoner and jailer? If that's all we are, then let's get down to a little badgering. Tell me about the Albion plans. Who gave them to you? Ah. That's almost perfect. You look surprised and offended. Very good."

Chill wrapped her suddenly, because he was angry at her and because he was a man who could see through lies. She had nothing, really, that belonged to her now but her lies. She tied her garter and secured the stocking into place. "I have never seen these plans everyone is so fond of believing I carry around with me like a cat her kittens. I do not know why—"

"You carry them in your head."

Cold covered her. Froze her heart. She could not move. *He cannot know that. He cannot. No one knows that.* "I do not understand what you mean."

"Every page, every list, every map. It's all in there in your memory, knocking up against Racine and Voltaire and Tacitus. That's why Leblanc's never going to find them. He doesn't know where to look."

Slowly, she slipped on the shoes he had brought for her from somewhere. She must keep moving. Her brain would not work, not even one tiny bit. *He knows. He knows. How can he know?*

He studied her and waited. "I didn't mean to strike you dumb."

You have stood before gunfire. You have stolen dispatches from under the very noses of the Prussian high command. You are the Fox Cub. Do not sit like the tongue-tied idiot. It was great fortitude that allowed her to shrug. "You theorize. That is sloppy. And it is a very silly theory."

"What are you going to do with the plans, Annique? Stand on the shore and wave when the French fleet sails in? You know where they're landing, of course."

Her mouth was dry as sand. "I do not say I know nothing, because I am a woman of unparalleled intelligence, but certainly I know nothing of invasions. You have fallen into a great pit of nonsense."

"You hate Bonaparte. You've probably hated him since the Vendée. You came to England to stop the invasion. You walked from Marseilles, blind and alone, because you know what's coming."

"I tell you again, I know nothing of those plans. I am a loyal Frenchwoman."

He let it lie between them for a while before he said, very gently, "In the end, when you have no other choice, you'll give me the Albion plans. You can't do anything else."

Something within her cracked and crumbled. Her courage, perhaps. Grey knew. He had added so many little pieces together—Leblanc's malice and her incautious words—and he discerned everything. One sniff, and he knew all that was in the kitchen. The secret of her memory. The choice that confronted her and tortured her. The decision she must make. He knew even what she would decide. He was one of the great spies, the equal of a Soulier and a Vauban.

He saw when her courage broke. There was nothing he could not see inside her.

"Damn." He crossed at once to where she sat and lifted her and held her. "I've scared you. I promised myself I wasn't going to do that." Her cheek pressed the lines of his brocaded waistcoat. He pulled her to him, and his arms became iron. "We'll talk. We'll just talk. I'm not going to make you do anything you don't want to. But Bonaparte's scheme is madness. We both know it. It's going to hurt France as much as England."

He was so wise about her. He would gnaw away at the foundations of her spirit like a mouse at the wainscoting. She had no defenses against him. "I do not wish to speak of French politics. It is an intricate and depressing topic."

"Fine. We're not talking." He set his chin on top of her head. "Just hold on to me for a while."

With her eyes closed, in darkness, it was like being back in France, being blind, knowing Grey by the touch and smell of him. After a time, a clock sounded in one of the rooms along the hall. Seven strokes. His back muscles tightened under her hands, and she knew the little truce between them was over. Truces were of that nature. They ended, sooner or later.

He let her go. "I shouldn't have made love to you this afternoon. I've made you doubt your own judgment. You'd trust me better if your body weren't hungry for me." He looked down and traced the shell of her ear with his fingertip. "See? When you feel even that much, you pull back, thinking I'm trying to manipulate you."

"Are you not?"

He opened his hand, as if he released something. "I don't know how to convince you. I want you so much I can't think clearly."

"What will you do with me when I will not become the traitor for you?" She let her arms drop away from him.

"It's not going to happen that way."

"That is a comfortable belief for you, surely."

"Do you want promises? I have a few. Whatever happens, I'll protect you from Leblanc and Fouché. I'm not going to hurt you, even if I keep scaring the bloody hell out of you."

"I am desolated to disappoint you, but you are an amateur in this business of frightening me. I have met experts."

"And it just gets worse from here on in. You are so bloody complex. I wouldn't love you if you were stupid, but it'd be a lot easier on both of us." He took a deep breath. "Come downstairs and eat. They've already started."

Twenty-seven

IT WAS A WHOLLY MASCULINE *DÉCOR*, THIS HOUSE at Meeks Street. The halls were hung with antique maps and architectural drawings in dark frames. The tables she passed held file folders and empty coffee cups and men's gloves tossed carelessly into a wide bowl. There was no clutter of flowers, no potpourris, no bibelots.

The dining room was next to that study where Grey had let her sleep this afternoon. She was learning her way around the house which was her prison. Eventually she would know it extremely well.

At the mirror in the main hall she stopped to inspect her toilette one last time.

"The dress is good on you. Sweet. Innocent." Grey scowled. Not at her. She was merely in the line of fire as he considered his own thoughts. "You're harmless as a Bengal tiger, thank God. How much do you know about Colonel Joseph Reams of British Military Intelligence?"

Her face betrayed nothing, but her stomach clenched. Françoise, who had been one of Vauban's own, and her friend, and a spy of great skill, had been questioned once by Reams—taken and questioned only on flimsy suspicion. She had needed months to heal. "I have heard of him. One or two small things."

"Then you know what we're dealing with. You'll have to meet him."

It was well known that Reams of the Military Intelligence tortured women like her, spies, and took pleasure in it. She had let Grey lull her into complacency. Now she was wisely terrified again. "He comes because I am here. The Military Intelligence takes interest in me. I should have thought of that."

"Do you trust me?"

"No. That is . . . perhaps. In some ways." Could he not see she was frightened into idiocy and leave her in peace? "That is a strange question."

"Trust me this much. Reams can't touch you. He has no power under this roof. I will not let anyone hurt you."

"That is what Galba said. I would believe it more if it were not said so often."

"You have my word." For him, that settled matters. He had been an English officer before he was put in charge of many spies. Perhaps she did trust him.

He opened the door to a gem of a room, perfectly proportioned, papered with Chinese scenes of pagodas and distant mountains. Curtains of white jacquard silk were drawn close so one could not see the bars. A simple dinner had been laid upon the table. She gave her attention to the men, and the one woman, who sat there.

". . . avoid a confrontation," Adrian was saying as she walked into the room. "Lazarus may even be hoping—"

He stopped speaking and sprang to his feet. The other men rose too—Galba, at the head of the table; Monsieur Doyle, whom she recognized easily from years ago in Vienna; the boy Giles, who had opened the door to this house for her; a thin, brown-haired man she did not know. Grudgingly and at the last minute, the last of them stood, a short, pink-faced man. That was Colonel Reams, she thought.

"Mademoiselle, I hope you are rested." Galba drew her to the table and made a great show of introducing her to Doyle, who was calling himself Viscount Markham, and his wife, Lady Markham, who did not look like a woman named Maggie. She was, amazingly, French, with the accent of an aristo, which is not a thing expected of a Maggie. The thin man with the aspect of a librarian—most certainly a spy of considerable deadliness—was the Honorable Thomas Paxton. Next, Galba presented Colonel Reams, who did not look at her, but sneered rudely. Galba then allowed her to meet Adrian and Giles.

Grey put her into the chair between Galba and Adrian and went himself to the left side of the colonel, which is the weaker side of an opponent and advantageous for attack. "Colonel," he said, sitting down.

"Major." A terse and unfriendly acknowledgment from Reams.

They hated each other, Grey and the Colonel Reams. The others were also not fond of the colonel. She, who had been trained to notice such things, saw that Doyle and Adrian and the scholarly Paxton sat as men sit in an unfamiliar tavern, loose in their chairs, their arms upon the table, their feet planted, ready to spring up. Every man in the room watched Colonel Reams carefully, though they did not seem to do so. It was a dinner party awash in well-practiced stratagems.

Adrian murmured that she was not to worry as Grey had matters entirely in his hands. He served upon her plate chicken and potatoes and green beans, pretending to consult with her but in fact paying no attention whatsoever when she said she wanted nothing.

Galba resumed the conversation where it had left off. "Your culpability will be known, Adrian. Lazarus is no fool. Have you considered the consequences?"

"If we don't intervene, Whitechapel will be knee-deep in bodies by the end of the week. What I want to do is—"

"You need to keep yer nose out of it, is my opinion," Colonel Reams interrupted. "Let 'em bite each other's buggering cocks off and choke on 'em. Since we're shut of that nonsense—"

"You are so earthy and forthright, you army chaps," Adrian coolly cut in.

"I want to know why this French whore trots in here like she—"

"But this isn't some manly, thigh-slapping dinner in your barracks."

Grey made an inconspicuous hand motion, and Adrian subsided. "You're a guest here, Colonel, and there are ladies present. Adrian, serve Mademoiselle Villiers some wine."

Grey was making a point, so she let Adrian fill her glass for her.

The colonel snarled and swiveled to confront Galba. "You tell me why there's a bloody slut of a French spy sitting at the dinner table."

Galba allowed an eloquent silence to punctuate, then said, mildly enough, "We will not discuss this now, Colonel. Or in those terms." He turned back to Adrian. "I'm wary of intervention in Lazarus's own household. It is provocation on our part."

"Not our part. My part. I'm acting on my own. Annique, you will not grow up to be big and strong if you don't eat your vegetables."

She rearranged what Adrian had put upon her plate with her fork and listened to him wax eloquent in favor of some scheme, doubtless dangerous and complex. She did not eat. She could not have eaten anyway while the Colonel Reams seethed at her in that fashion. The wine smelled like an excellent Bordeaux.

"Your decision?" Galba glanced at Grey.

"It has to be attempted. We'll deal with Lazarus afterwards. Will goes along to do the heavy lifting."

Adrian exhaled impatiently. "It's a second-floor window. She . . ." His eyes slid across Reams. "The package I'm collecting weighs four stone. I could fetch it out under one arm."

"And that's all you have," Grey said. "Your shoulder isn't healed. Do this, if you have to. But Will goes with you." Thus Grey made judgments of important matters, sending these deadly men out to steal, taking care they should be safe.

It would be easy to fall in love with such a man. He felt her eye upon him and grinned, just in a flash, like a man at his sweetheart, and also like a tomcat who has been much satisfied by a tabby. It was a compliment, but an embarrassing one, though of course no one at the table knew what he had been up to with her.

Then he was speaking to Doyle, all business. ". . . pull in two extra guards. Galba's in the guest room, but Pax leaves before dawn."

The quiet Paxton stretched across the table to fetch back the wine bottle. "I'll take the usual route. If you have messages, give them to me tonight."

"You already have mine." Galba took up his wineglass. "Good journey." It was unobtrusive, but Grey and Doyle and Adrian lifted their glasses as well, and they drank as one.

How it brought back memories, this meal. As a child in Lyon she had carried bread and wine to tables like this and sat as the quiet mouse while men and women made such preparations and left, one by one, to walk alone into danger. Later, she had been one of Vauban's people, his very inner circle. That silent toast . . . Her friends had made those for her. It was lonely to look upon this as an outsider.

"Upon that note . . ." Galba's chair creaked. "Mademoiselle

Villiers, we must clarify this situation for all concerned. I regret giving you so little time to compose yourself."

She set the fork down and ceased annoying the vegetables. "I am all attention."

"Do you wish to accompany Colonel Reams and place yourself under the protection of Military Intelligence? I did not think so. No, Colonel, you may speak later. Your choice, mademoiselle."

She shook her head.

"Then you shall not. You will remain with us. However, I would prefer that you were not distracted by illusionary alternatives. You are planning to escape, I believe."

"One explores many possibilities." She did not try to look young and naive, as that would be wasted here. Instead, she composed her face as if she were at the opera, attentive but uncomprehending.

Grey appreciated it. The flicker in his eye was all amusement.

Galba was less easy to read. "Let us make your situation plain. You are not without intelligence, but you underestimate your worth on the playing field. That is not uncommon in someone your age. Robert, you may take Mademoiselle Annique to the front door and open it for her."

Colonel Reams hopped to his feet like a red and angry bantam. "She's a French national. You have no right. The girl's mine, damn it." He should have been absurd with his jiggling paunch and a napkin clutched in his hand. He was not ridiculous to someone who might soon be in his cellars for questioning.

Then Grey was at her elbow, shepherding her from the room, his body between her and that spewing of rage, his path direct and unswerving toward the colonel. It was Reams who backed away. He swung round to snarl into the bland face of Galba, whose dangerousness was of an order the colonel did not recognize.

The clamor of his outrage trailed them down the hall to

the dim, stiff parlor where Grey unlocked the front door. The cool evening wind enveloped them.

They stopped just inside the doorway, and Grey looked alertly at the houses opposite. He was considering the question of snipers, she thought.

"The colonel fears you will let me walk out of here. He is a stupid man, is he not?" she said.

"He's a self-serving son of a bitch."

"That also." She looked upon the quiet street in the dusk. "You have opened this door for me as Galba told you to. You wish to show me something. I have an idea what it may be."

"Of course you do." He gestured toward the large black carriage waiting directly in front of the house. "That's Reams's carriage. The healthy young men inside who are taking such an interest in you are from his private detachment of marines. He's brought three."

"Three? It is an honor of sorts, I suppose."

"You have a reputation among spies. We can ignore them, however, because Reams can't touch you. Remember that. Now, look to your right, farther up the street." Grey's arm around her was not to keep her from running. It was for comfort. "Number Sixteen, with the window at the front where the lamp is. That's Soulier's agent keeping an amiable eye upon us. She grows herbs in her back garden and presents us with sachets of lavender every year at Christmas. She has visitors tonight. Large Frenchmen. They're at the window now, watching us."

He let her absorb it for a while, then said, "When Soulier gets orders from Fouché, he won't have any choice."

The sky was opalescent with sunset. The linden trees planted in the little strip of garden in the middle of the street rustled very slightly in the wind. They both knew that a death order from Fouché might already have reached London. "It is a difficult time for Soulier."

"So it is. We have no word on Leblanc yet. He's probably

already in London. Let's finish this. Look left." A cart and horse waited in the street. Pickaxes and shovels and piles of bricks disordered the pavement. Two men, long after any reasonable hour, repaired a brick wall in front of one of the houses. "Our local Czarist agents."

"I am learning Russian. It is a country France has not invaded yet, but I wish to be prepared."

"I suppose that memory of yours helps you learn languages. Who else have we got? The French Royalists are up on Braddy Street, two or three lots of them, mostly keeping an eye on each other. It's hard to tell the Royalists apart. Sometimes they're not even sure."

"Is that all of them?" She felt profoundly tired. It was inconceivable so many men should interest themselves in her. It was sheer perversity. They could not possibly know what she carried in her head.

"One more. At the corner. See the crossing sweeper? He belongs to Lazarus."

"Lazarus? Ah . . . the Lazarus of Adrian. The one he goes to steal from tonight. I do not know the name."

"He's not political. Lazarus rules the criminals of this town. He deals in precious objects. He'd sell the knowledge in your head, and you, to the highest bidder." His grip tightened on her arm. "You would give him that knowledge within a short time. He is . . . skilled."

"This is an interesting neighborhood." She didn't try to keep the fear out of her voice. Grey had brought her here to frighten her and deserved to know how well he had succeeded. "They will all speculate upon why I am in your headquarters, beautifully dressed and not held by any duress. That is what you want, no? To show them you have done me no harm?"

"Soulier will be relieved."

"Do not be slighting. Soulier used to buy me meringues in the Boulevard St. Michel when I was small enough to ride on his shoulders. He took me to the opera when I was eight. I wore a white dress with a blue sash. He taught me how to pick locks. It will give him no pleasure to kill me."

Within an hour Soulier would know she was here. He would wonder if she had become a traitor. Grey did this on purpose. So clever of him. "Let us go inside. I feel cold."

Reams was still shouting and pounding the table when they returned, using English words she had not yet learned. Without glancing at him, she took her place at the table beside Galba and picked up her napkin to put in her lap.

"Oh good. You're back. Your food was getting cold." Adrian lounged in his chair, his expression benign. "And the colonel is repeating himself."

Reams swung his head like an enraged bull, glaring up and down the table. "She goes with me. Now."

She was certain Reams could not give orders to Galba. Almost certain. Why, oh why, had she never learned more about the British?

Galba didn't raise his voice. "The jurisdiction is moot. Come, Colonel, sit down. Let us not fall out over one French operative whose usefulness is still questionable."

She concentrated on looking like someone whose usefulness was questionable.

"Military Intelligence has priority. Damn it, she's mine till I'm through with her." Reams's gaze crawled across her. His fingers curled hungrily. This was a man who had expended much imagination planning exactly how he would interrogate her.

Galba folded the wineglass between his hands. "Your organization will have access to all documents we obtain. But she remains with us."

"I say—"

"This is England, Colonel." Grey was rock and adamant steel. He took a step toward Reams. "This time, you don't have a troop of armed men at your back." He took another step.

Reams retreated. Only one step. But everyone had seen

him flinch, as a dog before the wolf. They all knew he feared Grey.

"Damn you." Panting and red-faced, he whirled and slammed his fist onto the table in front of Galba. Silverware rattled. Glasses danced. "You'd better get yourself another pretty slut to play with. You're going to find out I *do* have the authority to take her." He marched out, not glancing back, and young Giles jumped up to run nimbly to get the doors unlocked in his path.

"That's got his truss in a twist, don't it?" Doyle remarked amiably. "I hope you weren't listening to none of that, Maggie, 'cause it weren't polite."

"Poisonous little beast." Lady Markham, who was Maggie, took a sip of wine.

Annique let her breath out slowly. She felt as if she were made of ancient paper, ready to crumble at a touch and blow away in the wind.

Adrian talked in her ear. "Reams gets so few chances to harass beautiful female spies. He's very disappointed." He took one of her hands and began chafing it between his. "For us it's routine. We abuse women most days of the week. And why am I the one holding your hand, when what you want is Grey, who . . . Yes, he will eventually show up." Then Grey was beside her, and she turned toward him and buried her face into his waistcoat.

"He can't touch you. It's all bluster." Grey stroked her hair. "Weren't you listening to me when I said you were safe?"

"Robert, take her out of here," Galba said.

"She'll be fine. Give her a minute."

"We can grant her few amenities, but privacy is not beyond our means." Galba looked away. "Marguerite, I apologize for exposing you to this. You are aware of the exigencies that force me to tolerate Colonel Reams."

Doyle chuckled. "Hell, Maggie don't understand half them words the colonel says, do you, luv?"

"I most certainly do. I have learned many vulgar words from you."

They were all so carefully not watching her. She could not collapse in fear and self-pity under the eyes of so many English agents, and an aristo. She ceased clutching Grey. "Do not concern yourself. I am most perfectly fine."

He did not release her, however, for which she was inexpressibly grateful. "I'm sorry to put you through that. We had to show him you're under my protection. Under Galba's."

"I am all complaisance to be displayed like a performing monkey." She looked very hard at her plate. "Though I do not like loud, angry men arguing over who shall take me to his basement and torture me."

"He can't get to you," Doyle said quietly. "He can't get past us."

"Mademoiselle," Galba said, "I'm sorry we distressed you. We shall postpone the rest of this discussion."

How polite he was. The noisy colonel with his many threats was the least deadly of the men in this room. Now she must face the others. "There is no purpose in waiting."

"Perhaps not. Do you wish to retire elsewhere to eat in peace?"

"It is not necessary."

"Will you try to drink the rest of your wine?"

She shook her head.

"I'm not trying to cloud your judgment. One glass of Bordeaux is unlikely to do that. No? And none of the rest of this will tempt you either, will it? Bring the wine, then, and let us go into the other room."

Adrian pushed back pocket doors that separated the dining room from the study. This was the room where she had slept on a sofa earlier. Evidently she was to sit on the same sofa now. Grey had brought her glass of wine along. She did not drink any, but it gave her something to occupy her hands. Behind them, in the dining room, Giles cleared the table, stacking the dishes in a dumbwaiter in the wall.

No one spoke to her. They settled into the comfortable chairs with the ease of long familiarity. Paxton pulled back the edge of a curtain and looked out past the bars to where the last light was fading. His eyes were on the sky, assessing, like someone who would take ship soon. Adrian began a low-voiced discussion with Doyle, being technical about ropes and roofs. Galba settled into the broad red chair a few feet from her and watched the fire. After a few minutes, Giles brought in a tray with cups and a silver pot. It was coffee, even though this was England and she had expected to be assaulted with the Englishman's idea of tea. She wondered whether this was the usual custom for these men or whether it was a part of the evening planned for her. Grey stood behind her, so close his jacket brushed her back.

"Shall we talk together, mademoiselle, or do you need more time?" Galba asked.

"I congratulate you on the economy of your threats. I do not suppose you have said twenty words to me all evening, and I am entirely quivering with terror of you."

The old man made a sound of annoyance. "It is useless to attempt to reason with you. Robert, take her upstairs. We will return to this when you are calmer. Tomorrow—"

She dared to interrupt him. "Monsieur, for this discussion I will never be calmer."

"Then, in the name of sanity, drink some coffee—Giles, get her a cup—or stand up and scream, or punch Grey in the stomach, or do whatever is necessary to compose yourself. The thought of dealing with a woman of your caliber, terrified, appalls me."

She knew, almost certainly, the path she must take in the next hour. "I will not drink coffee. Nothing at all. Let us talk instead." She set the wineglass firmly on the table, away from her.

Grey's hand moved lightly to the nape of her neck, beneath her hair, warm against her skin. He did this to strengthen and reassure her. She had the thought that it does not take much to convince a woman she is in love if one is even a little kind to her when she is alone and frightened.

"I would like to call you Annique, if I may," Galba said.

He would wish to be informal when he threatened her.

"Pull yourself together and answer Galba," Grey said softly.

"Of course you may call me Annique."

Galba's lips twisted. "I will not presume upon it. Annique, have you considered your options carefully? Let me recapitulate your dilemma. At the front door are jackals from several nations. Somewhere, not far from here, Jacques Leblanc is making plans to kill you. That is what you face, if you escape. Waiting for you also are your French masters. Robert tells me you no longer wish to serve Fouché. Is that correct?"

"I would rather not." Her voice was a dry rustle of sound, not much louder than the fire.

"Is this ideological? Or is it because Fouché is so lacking in imagination he will require you to work as a courtesan?"

She did not answer. One does not explain one's motives to one's captors.

Galba shifted his weight in the chair as if he had become uncomfortable. The boy brought him coffee in a demitasse so small it disappeared in his hand. They waited while Galba drank. He took his time, as if he delayed to seek words. "I do not fault your mother's choice. She was a great patriot. But that path is not for everyone. It is not for you."

"No."

"Besides your French masters and what awaits you beyond the front door of this house, you have a final alternative. The British Service."

"We're not as final as all that." Adrian slipped onto the couch beside her. "Cub, I owe you my life four or five times. I pay that kind of debt. I won't let Galba do anything horrible to you."

"I saved you only twice, I think. And yes, you will let him do things entirely horrible to me, *mon frère*." It warmed her to be defended by Adrian, as they knew it would. As he knew it would. "You have done many things you did not want to do. Hurting me will be harder for Grey, who has some conscience, which you do not. But both of you will do it."

She faced Galba. Grey's hold tightened upon her, perhaps because of what she had said, perhaps because he felt the change in her. For she was angry now, instead of wholly abashed with fear. "You speak of choices. Why do you tease me with what I would do if I were free? There is a game children play here—button, button, who has the button? The English have the button. What will you do with it?"

She thought Galba was pleased. He preferred it when she was not afraid.

He finished his coffee and set down his cup. "I propose an exchange. What I require is the knowledge stored in your brain. What I offer is a way out of the trap you are in."

She said nothing, waiting.

"Give the Albion plans to England. I will spread the mantle of my protection between you and Fouché. I will crush Leblanc. I have the power to do this. I will give you a new name and a home, anonymous and safe, where no one can pursue you." Piercing blue eyes fixed on her face. "Give me the plans, and you will be free of the weight of the thousands of deaths that are coming with this invasion. Whatever happens, it will no longer be your responsibility."

It was as if Galba lifted the lid to her soul. It chilled her to know she could be tempted with a few well-chosen words. She wished to be free of this heavy choice so very much. Almost, she wished to close her eyes to the damage England could do to her country with those plans, and give them away and be rid of them. Galba saw that cowardice in her, and she was shamed.

"This is an equitable bargain, Annique. Will you accept it?"

Doyle and the others looked elsewhere, pretending to be concerned with their coffee or a spot on the wall. The fire crackled in the fireplace. She had glanced into that chimney earlier. It was guarded halfway up by crossed iron bars set in the bricks. Every mouse hole in this house was closed. There was no way out.

They would free her from this terrible choice. They were so wise and cunning. They knew precisely what to offer.

She folded her hands into her lap and looked at him, straight. "Monsieur Galba, I do not wish to be questioned by any of the men who haunt your doorstep. I do not wish to return to Fouché, who is not a gentle master. But I will go to Paris and whore for him as my mother did, before I will turn traitor for a fat, white, sly old English spy like you."

Adrian gave a crack of laughter and was up, striding to the window. On the other side of the room the woman Maggie smothered a giggle. Grey found a new hold upon her shoulder. A firm one.

The flowers woven into the rug were of a sort she did not recognize or which perhaps did not exist. She considered those flowers closely, since there was nothing and no one in that room she felt like seeing at that moment.

"A French patriot," Galba said. "The very essence of irrationality. At least we are clear where we stand." When she risked a glance upward, it was extraordinarily difficult to read his face. He might even have been amused. Cats probably were amused when the mouse squeaked at them and struggled.

"The conversation becomes predictable from this point. Giles . . ." The boy was stacking cups on the silver tray. He, too, laughed and was impudent enough he made no attempt to hide it. "Giles, take Mademoiselle— No. We will stop this Frenchified nonsense and give her thoughts a better direction. Take Miss Annique and introduce her to Tiny as a guest. Then put her in Grey's bedroom and leave her."

Grey pulled her upright, helping her to stand, taking care of her.

Galba stood. "Good night. We will talk again. We have much to discuss."

They knew she held the Albion plans. They intended to take them from her. Under all the cordiality, that was what had been said. It was best to establish this reality between them.

"Good night, Monsieur Galba." She curtsied, as a girl of good family would, to an old man. "We will hold all the discussions you wish. But I shall not eat or drink while I am in this house. You have only a short time to set about subverting me."

Twenty-eight

"AN IMPRESSIVE WOMAN," PAXTON SAID WHEN the door closed behind her. "I congratulate you on bringing her out of France."

"Maybe Fouché planted her on us to drive Grey insane." Adrian was still chuckling.

"Could be," Doyle said. "She's that good, we'd never know."

"I'd know." Damn, but he was proud of her.

"If you know her so well, tell me how we pushed her into this stupidity." Adrian pushed the curtains closed, lapping them so there wasn't even a strip of light out onto the side yard. He was dead serious again when he faced them, and angry. "She's the one I should be hauling out of second-floor windows tonight. She's wrong, you see." He shot a look at Galba. "I'm not going to let you do 'entirely horrible' things to her."

"Nobody's going to hurt the girl, unless Tiny takes a bite out of her on the way upstairs." Doyle raised an eyebrow at

Galba. "Did you expect that to work? Against a political idealist the age of that child?"

"I had hoped to establish an extended dialogue and prevent exactly the sort of bravura performance we just enjoyed. Unfortunately, she had this farce planned before I even spoke to her."

"You think it's a bluff?" Doyle asked. "I don't."

Galba glanced in Grey's direction. "Robert?"

"Not a bluff."

"Adrian?"

"Not a bluff. In fact, she's calling ours." Adrian jerked a thumb. "Grey's."

Galba nodded. "That is my own opinion. I called it bravura, but it is, in fact, admirably rational. She will not eat. It's the only conceivable weapon left her. I assume she will not even take water."

"No water. Nothing." He closed his eyes, going over the conversation, trying to remember when he'd felt her resolve harden. "She was planning it when she refused the coffee. She made the decision when she heard your offer. For a minute, she wanted to say yes. She's not going to let herself surrender that easily."

"So she has given us less than two days to persuade her by reasoned argument or demonstrate we are villains," Galba said. "Captive and with no weapons, she has wrested control of the situation from our hands. Admirable."

Doyle sprawled in the big chair next to the fire with his feet up on the firedogs. Maggie was on the low ottoman, leaning against his knee, companionably close. She stirred and sat up. "Are you saying that girl means to starve herself to death if you don't let her go?"

"I won't let it come to that." He picked up Annique's wineglass and rotated it softly. The wine made a circle, a whirlpool of spinning red lights with a dimple in the center.

"She has been preparing for this eventuality all her life," Galba said softly. "We are her enemies, Marguerite, and we have her cornered. She is desperate and passionate and, most especially, she is very young."

. . . *And bloody careless with her life.* He set the glass down impatiently. "Damn Socrates, anyway."

Adrian started to speak, then stalked over to help Giles clear away the cups.

Galba tapped the carved panel inset in the arms of his chair. "The Albion plans are a grave responsibility for one so young. Eventually, we will relieve her of that. In the meantime, we must present her with alternate methods of confronting us."

"I should take her home with me before you end up killing her in your stupid Game with your stupid secrets." Maggie scowled. "You will be satisfied, I suppose, if she suicides herself to escape you."

"We won't let her do that, Maggie. It ain't dead simple getting hold of pretty French girls this side of the Channel." Doyle pulled his wife back against him and wrapped her in bearlike arms. "And Robert wouldn't like it."

"Then Robert should not push her to desperation," she said tartly.

"We're all in on it." Adrian retrieved Paxton's empty glass. "Grey takes her to bed. The rest of us slink around being friendly and insidious. We're so wily it makes me sick."

"Wily," Doyle agreed. "That's us."

Adrian expressed his opinion by picking up Doyle's coffee cup, still half full, and walking off with it.

"Hawker." Grey got a tight-lipped, angry glare from Adrian. "Don't make her less than she is. She's not just friendly, pretty Annique. Remember that. She's the Fox Cub and this is the Game."

"With points about even, so far," Doyle said. "So I don't feel as brilliant as I generally do. Also, I don't like Reams breathing down our neck. He's got jurisdiction, when it comes right down to it."

Reams wasn't going to touch Annique. "There're ways around that." Grey clenched and unclenched his fists. Unfortunately, he wouldn't get to use them on Reams.

"The colonel could fall off his horse, I suppose." Adrian stopped stacking dishes to think. "Or eat something that disagrees with him. Or find a cobra in his bed."

"There's a lot of that happens," Doyle agreed.

"Or he could cut his throat, shaving."

"We will not call upon your peculiar expertise, Adrian." Galba rose heavily and walked across the room to the large walnut desk. He fished in his waistcoat pocket and drew out a key. "Nor is that her best protection from the colonel." He frowned. "Pax, I have information to disclose that I do not wish to burden you with, where you must go."

Paxton gave his slow, deceptively gentle smile. "I need to pack. And sleep, if I can." He collected the bottle of Bordeaux from the sideboard as he walked by. "Good night, all. As for you, young man . . ."

"I know. I know. Ferguson needs me in the kitchen." Giles took it good-naturedly. He clattered the last of the dishes into the dumbwaiter, closed the hatch, and followed.

"I shall find something to do as well, I suppose." Maggie brushed her skirts and prepared to stand.

"I'd like you to stay, if you will." Galba fitted his key into the side drawer of the desk. "I value your insight, Marguerite. It will also save Will the trouble of repeating this conversation to you, later."

"I admit nothing." But she smiled as she approached the desk where Galba was laying out file folders. "What is this, then?"

Grey stood. These would be the files about Annique, the ones that had never passed through his office. He'd wondered why there was a skilled, important agent, with no file on her, anywhere. The hairs on the back of his neck prickled.

Two of the three thick files Galba laid on the blotter were old. The original buff had darkened to a dull brown.

On the opening lip of all three was a long, crimson line. That meant they were to be opened only in the presence of a Head of Section.

Grave-faced, Galba picked the topmost. "What is in these files has been the most closely guarded secret of the British Service for twenty years. The time for such secrecy is past. It ended six weeks ago." He pushed the folder across the desk. "In extremis, you may use any of this. It will trump Military Intelligence."

It was Annique's file. The one Grey had never seen. The name, Annique Villiers, was the third of twelve aliases scripted in bold ink on the upper right corner. The folder was three inches thick, filled with close-written reports in many hands. Most of the papers, even the faded ones, were crisp and unwrinkled. They hadn't had much handling. Not many people had read this file.

He hesitated, then flipped it open. Summary notes were always inside the left cover. The first line told him everything. Adrian was reading upside down. He drew his breath in sharply. "Ye gods." Doyle, leaning over his shoulder, took it in with a single glance and cursed.

He kept reading. No wonder this was secret. No wonder.

Doyle took a lumbering step toward Galba. "I should have been told."

"Nobody was told."

"They were operating in Vienna. My fief. Damn it, I should have been told."

Galba said, "You know the privileges of detached status. Will, you *made* those rules."

"You don't use 'em against *me*. I came close to . . . Good God, why didn't you tell me? One word would have been enough. One word."

"Your actions and your enmity were part of her protection."

Annique's file. Grey turned over page after page, feeling the anger twist in his chest. *This is going to break her heart.*

"She doesn't know. Why the goddamned hell doesn't she know?"

"I do not deny culpability." Face grim, Galba relocked the drawer and pocketed the key. "I disapproved, but I sanctioned it. The simple fact is, her mother chose not to tell her."

Unbelievable. "I understand it when she was a child. But when she was grown—how could she not tell her?"

"There are no excuses. She never told Annique. Now we must."

"We tell her everything. Every damn thing." He slapped the file. "We give her this. Complete. Every word. She has the right to know."

"She has the right." Galba sank heavily into the wing chair by the fire. "I knew this was coming. I pity her profoundly, but I cannot take this cup from her."

"Tomorrow." *Not tonight. Let me give her one night, before I have to do this to her.*

Adrian was flipping angrily through the second folder, page by page. "Twenty years of lies. We haven't left you a rag against the wind, have we, *ma pauvre*?"

"It was wrong." Doyle rubbed the back of his neck. "I don't care how valuable she was to us. This was wrong. And we did it."

Maggie wasn't familiar with Service files. It took her longer to read notations and decipher the story. "I cannot believe this. How could a woman do such a thing to her child? They were close, Annique and her mother?"

"Very close," Doyle said.

"You will hurt her unbearably. With her mother newly dead . . ."

"I know, Maggie luv. It's bad enough what we're doing to that girl. Now we kick her in the guts with this."

"We're not going to drop it in her lap and yell, 'Surprise!' We'll go slow . . ." Adrian, for once, looked unsure. "We'll . . . we'll what? How do you say something like this?"

"She will not believe you," Maggie said. "Even before you hurt her so badly, you must convince her."

"The proof's in her own mind," Doyle said. "Her mother must have slipped up once or twice in all those years."

Once she was told, Annique would remember. She'd lie awake at night and remember every lie she'd been told.

And he had to decide how to tell her. "Maggie's right. We have to convince her that it's true." He took the file Adrian was looking at and extracted a single sheet. He smoothed it flat for everyone to see. "Here. We start at the beginning. Tomorrow we take her to St. Odran's and show her the original of this in the parish record. Can we do that with Leblanc loose?"

Doyle hesitated, then nodded. "It's a small risk. But we have enough men to keep her safe for that long."

"Good. We show her the parish record, then bring her back and give her the files. We explain." He looked up. Galba's shrewd, deep-set eyes met his. "You explain. I sure as hell can't."

"I have been considering the proper words for ten years. Perhaps I'll find them tomorrow."

Twenty-nine

Annique was waiting for him in his bedroom, on his bed, on her belly. She was on top of the covers, reading a book. She was naked.

She looked at him through her eyelashes. "I am glad you were not devoured by that animal which has draped itself across the doorway. What is it, that thing?"

In all England, all France, all the world, there was no other woman for him. Only Annique. He had her naked in his bed. One of life's perfect moments.

"We think it's part wolfhound. Doyle found it down by the docks, likely off some ship or other."

"I would say it is rather wolf and possibly also part elephant. It does not like me."

"Good. Then you won't go wandering around the halls after dark. Maggie brought some nightclothes."

"I saw them. They are very lovely, of course, but I thought you would prefer to see that I am totally harmless when you approach me. It is necessary, as I understand these things, that a man not be nervous at such times." She propped herself up, her breasts just brushing the crimson leather cover. Her smile was knowing, and her eyes were shy. Men would kill to possess this woman.

He came to her, unwinding his cravat, sliding it out of his collar, tossing it onto the chair in passing. He felt infinitely powerful. She made him feel that way. "I'm glad you're so willing. I suppose you're preparing for one last beautiful night of lovemaking . . ."

Her eyes widened slightly. "Perhaps."

". . . before you start dying of thirst."

Her brows contracted in annoyance. "I had not intended to bring that up. Such matters are not conducive to romantic behavior."

"Casts a damper over everything, doesn't it, all that dire nobility of yours."

"I have changed nothing with my decision. I merely strip away the veneer of civility. I do not need to justify my behavior to a—"

"Then don't. The best minds in the British spy service are going to talk you out of it tomorrow. We spent the last hour plotting. We have plans."

"Oh." She looked stubborn and apprehensive. Also relieved. Nine-tenths of her was hoping to be persuaded out of that idiocy.

He said, "I have plans, too." She had only to look at him to see what he had in mind.

He jerked the last button loose and pulled his shirt over his head and dropped it on the floor, then stripped his trousers off. She started to sit up, but he set his hand on her shoulder to keep her as she was. He liked her this way . . . naked, laid out on her belly. She was exquisitely lovely, and she couldn't attack. "Have I mentioned you're the most beautiful woman in the world?"

"From one cause and another we have missed saying such things to each other."

Those sleek cat muscles of hers told him how nervous

she was. Willing, but nervous. He could use that nervousness. He could make it explode inside her like foam in a keg. He'd send her wild tonight. Beyond thought. Beyond restraint. "I like the curve here . . ." He ran his hand down the long, taut muscles that paralleled her spine. "It's like the countryside back home. Long and rolling."

"I am like countryside?"

"Somerset countryside." He stroked her buttocks. "With little hills."

"But truly, men have strange minds."

He stroked her again. "Did your mother tell you that?"

"I find that my mother did not say anything to the point. She did not wish me to be a courtesan, you understand, and therefore did not instruct me in those arts." She glanced at him from the corner of her eye. "Except for a few trifles. I believe they are not known to respectable English girls, who are very uneducated. I will show you, if you like."

A pang of pure lust shot through him. His lady was not at all innocent in some ways. He foresaw many long, interesting nights while they worked out exactly who would be in charge in this bed. "Later, maybe."

"There is one in particular that sounds interesting. I am curious to see how it works."

She would drive him insane. She'd do it on purpose.

"We'll save it for those long winter nights ahead. Have I told you I love you, Annique? It started about the fourth time you tried to maim me. I never did find time to say the words."

"It is the right time now. We are at leisure, and I am not armed." She was sad under the teasing. He'd put a stop to that fairly soon. "I find it gratifying in the extreme to be loved, especially by a man like you. I shall become quite puffed-up and conceited with it, I think."

"You go right ahead and do that." The sweet flesh of her back had decided to stop being nervous and go soft. The tremors in her were just beginning. "This is where you say you love me back."

"Ah . . . love." She pinched a crease into the linen pillowcase beneath her. "You must be disappointed, *mon ennemi.* I desire you. This is not love."

"Just desire."

"You are the first man for me. There must be a first man for every woman, when she is innocent and fools herself into believing in love. This is true even if she is destined to lie with seventy thousand in her lifetime."

She lay there, wanting him. Scared of it. Wondering if that made her a whore or just a fool. Halfway wondering if she was trading herself to an enemy spy, for safety. Not trusting herself to know the difference between wanting and being in love. If her mother weren't already dead, he'd strangle her himself.

And that was enough worrying from the Fox Cub tonight. In ten minutes he'd make her forget that nonsense. Give him fifteen, and she'd forget her own name. He slid the book out from underneath her and tossed it away. Her breasts cuddled softly into his palm.

When he touched her, he felt the shudder, felt the throb in her flesh.

You're mine, Annique . . . every exquisite, dangerous inch of you. "I haven't worked it out yet, but seventy thousand would keep you fairly busy."

He raised her up some, kissing along her neck to confuse her, to quiet that busy mind of hers. She bent her head to watch him while he touched her, watched her nipples squeeze up into hard little buttons between his finger and thumb. She'd already started breathing fast. She was responsive as hell. Good. With a woman like Annique, he needed all the advantage he could get.

He kissed the top of her head. "Seventy thousand's a lot. Maybe I can convince you to settle for a few less. How about a hundred? Or a dozen?" He lured her chin upward, drawing her jawline. "Or one?"

When she lifted her eyes, they were deep blue and vulnerable as spring flowers. "One?"

"Me."

"Oh." She breathed onto his shoulder. "Well." He could feel each separate breath. Neither of them moved. Slowly she let her forehead lower till it rested against him. Her tongue—a soft, warm touch—tasted him. Tasted his skin.

He knew for sure, then. This hit her as hard as it hit him. They were both lost. No way back for them.

His hand shook with the effort of keeping control. Slow. He had to go slow. He didn't trust himself to touch her anywhere but her hair. Her neck. The shell of her ear. *Let's not roll her over and dive in like a sailor on shore leave, Robert. She's new at this, and more ignorant than she wants you to know.*

He took her face in light, outstretched fingers. Finger to flesh, tied together by the current between them, he drew her up and up until she was kneeling on the bed. And he was kneeling. Hunger and magic danced in the air. He set his lips to her lips. He'd never had a chance to enjoy her slowly, to savor her when there was nothing ahead but a night of lovemaking. Now, he did.

Her mouth was soft and hot. Hungry. The gateway to a universe of desire. She shuddered as he licked and bit and demanded.

He broke away and whispered, "Who are you thinking about, Annique? Those seventy thousand men? Or maybe a Gypsy boy?"

Dear God, but she was ready for him. He knew it by the slick of sweat on her skin, by the quivering of those sleek, beautiful muscles, even by her smell. Her whole body was his for the asking. Nothing held back. Nothing forbidden.

"I am not thinking of any Gypsy boy, my Grey." Her voice was husky. "I am thinking of no one but you."

She put her arms around him and drew him down beside her on the coverlet. She whispered, soft in his ear, wickedly, "And Robert, of course."

Thirty

ONE FEELS FOOLISHLY JOYFUL THE MORNING after taking a lover—tired but exhilarated, as if one had danced all night and successfully stolen a Prussian dispatch or two.

She considered herself in the mirror of Grey's bedroom. She looked smug, she thought. "Maman did not tell me not to let men buy me dresses, as other mothers advise their daughters. She told me not to let men pick them out."

"A wise woman." Grey had told her to wear the lavender walking dress for the activities of this morning. The color made her look fragile. The excellent plainness of the design was, on her, entirely *jeune fille*.

More puzzling was the knife he handed her. She tossed it from hand to hand a few times, then slipped it into its place in the sheath he himself strapped onto her wrist. He acted as if it were altogether normal to make love to a captive spy at dawn and then arm her in this deadly fashion. She could not imagine why he did this.

"This is Adrian's," she said, because the knife was flat

and matte brown and balanced precisely as Adrian's other knife had been.

"He says to take better care of it." He rummaged in the armoire. "Wear this, I think." It was a straw bonnet with lavender ribbons, which meant she was going outside. Truly, this was an altogether odd first morning of captivity.

She pondered this as they left the room and headed for the top of the stairs. Voices came from below. Soon enough she could look over the banister and see Galba in the hall on the ground floor, being courteous to a skinny old man, very fashionably dressed.

". . . my nephew, Giles," Galba said, which was something she had not known about Giles. "He's assisting us till Devlin recovers. Giles, this is Lord Cummings."

"New doorkeeper, eh? That's keeping it in the family." The visitor spoke in the high-pitched whinny of an English aristo. "I'm sure you do a fine job holding off the villains, young Giles. Fine job. I imagine in a week or two you'll be back to Eton, telling them all about your adventures in London."

"Harrow, sir," Giles said.

"Umm. Yes. Best years of your life. Cricket and . . . so on." He tucked his cane under his arm. "See here, Anson, we must talk."

Galba walked around him and continued toward the parlor. "You're here on a Sunday, Cummings. It must be a matter of urgency."

The aristo trotted in his wake. "What's this nonsense Reams brought me? You're refusing to hand over a French agent?"

She was engulfed in a mad instant of fear. She was to be given to Reams. That was why she had been dressed to go out. Aristos still ruled here in England, and they had immense power.

Then Grey poked her in the back, which told her she was to continue walking and for some reason dissolved the foolish panic altogether. Grey would not give her up. Not for a thousand English aristos.

Galba said, "Essentially, that is correct."

"Nonsense. Oh, I know what happened, of course." The aristo gave a fruity, aristo chuckle. "Reams barged in and made an ass of himself. Offensive to everyone in sight. Not quite a gentleman, the colonel. But useful. Useful. We have to tolerate men like him in wartime."

Galba said, "I will tolerate Reams. What I will not tolerate is his interference in Service affairs."

The popinjay's noisy suit swished with each step. "Quite right. Quite right. Here your men snabble themselves up a bit of French crumpet. Reams goes blundering in, ruffling feathers, demanding a taste. Nuisance of a man. Now you and I have to smooth the whole fracas over. Tell you what. I'll bundle our bit of French fluff off where she won't be fought over. I brought a couple marines with me, don't y'know. I'll drop our game pullet off on my way home, and we'll call that the end of it."

Grey continued down the stairs and along the hall, pushing her ahead of him with the greatest sangfroid.

In the parlor, Galba stood in front of the mirror over the heavy and hideous sideboard and put on his gloves. "Miss Villiers remains with us."

"Devil take it, man. This isn't one of your political games. This is a military matter."

"And I say it is not. Will you dispute prerogatives with me, on behalf of Colonel Reams?"

"Are you claiming jurisdiction over a piece of French tail your Head of Section has a fancy for?" The aristo stabbed his walking stick into the rug. He looked, every minute, less the peevish fool. They played a game of power, these men. "When this gets out, your Service is going to look—"

"*Is* this going to get out? We had hoped for an end to the leaks in your office."

Grey chose this moment to push her forward.

"Ah, Robert. In good time." Galba reached out. She had no choice but to let him bring her forward and place her firmly under the nose of this aristo and into the midst of their game. "Annique, allow me to present Lord Cummings to you."

"Your niece? A charming child. Charming. Anson, we should continue this in your office." The Lord Cummings was not interested in her, except to be polite a moment because she was pretty.

"But no." She gazed upward through her eyelashes and curtsied like a schoolgirl. "I am Anne Villiers, my Lord."

"Villiers. Villiers? This is . . . ?" The aristo's face hardened. Oh, most excellent. He had been made to appear ridiculous by the Colonel Reams. "Reams said she was a . . . Reams said she was . . . older."

"Reams was mistaken," Galba said, very dry. "I hope you slept well, mademoiselle."

Grey answered for her. "She slept fine."

So. It was to be obvious to this English lord that she had become the mistress of Grey. She swiftly considered several alternatives and decided to be very young and shy. That was a role with many possibilities. By thinking of some of the things she had done last night in bed with Grey, she made herself blush, a deception of great skill. She was proud to achieve it, especially before Grey, who would appreciate the genius that called it forth.

She still held her bonnet, so she let it swing by its strings, as a child does. It would do no harm to play thus with the aristo.

The Lord Cummings cleared his throat. His eyes flickered from her to Grey, who scowled, to the front window where carriages waited. "It could be temporary custody. Only temporary. She'll be treated well."

"No," Grey said.

"I give you my personal assurance." He shifted his cane

from right hand to left. "See here, Major, you're infantry. You understand how important—"

"No."

"I'll make it clear to Reams he's not to . . . That is, I can see she's young. I'll tell him to treat her with every respect."

Of a certainty he would. He would know it meant nothing. He would give her to Reams to rape and torture, and he would feel badly about it for much of one evening. He would regret it for five minutes the next day. Then he would forget her altogether. The British called this "deploring the necessity."

Grey said, "Be damned to that."

"She is a French agent, privy to military information. We—"

"I don't care if she has naval codes stuffed in her corset. That bastard's not going to get his hands on her."

"Enough, Robert. You've made your point." Galba rested one hand on the high back of the crimson sofa, making a barrier, acting as if Grey were imminently dangerous and must be restrained. "Military Intelligence has no legitimate interest in Miss Villiers. Her work has always been political, and never directed against England."

It was time to play her own part. She took a hesitant step toward the aristo, working on tears. "Please. The colonel frightens me very much. Please do not send me to him."

Cummings did not look directly at her. Oh, but she knew the men of his type. He gave his orders in some pleasant office in London. Never did he involve himself with the torture of women in basements or directing artillery fire into towns to bury children under the rubble.

"She was one of Vauban's cadre. Vauban dealt directly with the traitor in Military Intelligence. I'm bleeding secrets from my whole department, and she may know the name of the man who's doing it. Give her to me." The aristo had abandoned all pretense of being a fribble. His words were hard as horseshoe nails.

"Your bloody incompetence doesn't give Military Intelligence the right to pirate my operation." Grey matched snarl for snarl.

"This is a military matter. It falls in my jurisdiction. The sooner Reams cracks that name out of her . . ."

She thought like lightning. "But it is Reams's own office where the traitor is. It is his—"

Everyone turned. She lifted her hand to her mouth, as if she had said more than she should. *Dieu.* She should bite her lip and stammer like a schoolgirl. This aristo expected no more from her.

The lordship had gone perfectly rigid. "What do you mean, it's Reams's office?"

"Hush, Annique," Grey said quickly. "You shouldn't talk about that." One would swear they had worked this out beforehand, he did it so smoothly.

"But you must not give me to Colonel Reams." She selected a tiny sliver of her fear and blew it into her voice. To build a role out of the blocks of emotion already within one—this was a great art. "If you send me there, I will not live to speak. Do not do this to me."

"Reams won't touch you." Grey was grim as stones. She did not think he was acting. "This is a waste of time. He's frightening Annique," he said to Galba, "and we're going to be late."

"I demand to know what she meant by that." The aristo almost danced in frustration.

"Our investigation has only begun." Galba picked up his hat from upon the hideous sideboard. "Too much has already been said. Leave her to us, Cummings. It's in neither of our interests to release her to Colonel Reams."

The Lord Cummings did not speak at all. Much internal calculation was going on behind his eyes. She had been correct to conclude he was no fool.

Galba collected a pair of small black books from the marble top of the bureau. "Now I must ask you to excuse us. As Robert says, we are late."

"You can't take her . . . I mean, where are you taking her?"

Galba raised his eyebrows. "Is it possible you have forgotten what day this is?"

"Day?" Lord Cummings was bewildered.

"It is Sunday, as I pointed out. We are going to church. A pleasant morning to you."

Thirty-one

THE HACKNEY AWAITED THEM AT THE CURB. SHE followed Galba decorously down the steps, and she did not let an eyelid twitch with all the vast amusement that was bouncing around inside her. Grey held the door, and Galba helped her tenderly in.

"The men are in place?" Grey slid in next to her. As the coach started, he opened a panel in the upholstery, removed a gun, checked it, and returned it. Then he reached past her and did the same on the other side. This was a hackney carriage very well supplied with guns. He had one in his coat as well. She felt it bumping against her thigh.

"Will's been up since five. He assures me we're adequately covered." Galba filled the seat across from them with his large, square body. She should not have called him fat. He was simply one who took up a great deal of room, like an old tree, strong in its fiber. He had his own gun, a small one he held just clear of his jacket pocket.

"Well, that was fun." Grey scanned the streets on the

right as the carriage rolled along. Galba was watching the other side. "Annique wasn't what he expected."

"Reams is an imbecile."

"Whatever else happens, Cummings is going to flay Reams alive for making him look like a fool in front of you. Annique, why did you say the traitor is in Reams's office?"

He looked at her, straight and level. She was jolted into remembering that Grey was not just a lover in her bed, he was the Head of Section for England and master of many spies. She must decide, this moment, what she would give to the British.

A hundred yards of pavement rolled under the horses' hooves. Were there depths of treason? Small trivial treasons and large ones? She waded in dirty water, deeper and deeper.

But she had only one choice, unless she wished to visit Colonel Reams's interesting cellars. "The lordship is wrong in one thing. It was not Vauban who dealt with the traitor in your Military Intelligence. It was Leblanc."

Grey and Galba stayed silent. Silence is a potent weapon in interrogation. After another hundred yards had passed, she said, "Our spy is in Reams's office. He has been in the pay of France for three years, recruited only for money. We have deposited to him hundreds and hundreds of pounds through an account at Hoare's Bank. His name is Frederick Tillman."

Grey hit the cushion beside him, an eye-blurring boxer's jab. "Got him! We got the bastard! Tillman. Reams's brother-in-law, for God's sake. His second-in-command." He grinned, tight and fierce. "This is going to bring Reams down."

Galba smiled.

They were very pleased. She sold one small secret for a little safety. She did not feel delighted.

Thus it began. Not with a dramatic decision to reveal the secrets of the Albion plans. With the name of a minor and greedy weasel. The British would corrupt her one secret at a time, upon this excuse and that, until she was wholly their creature. She knew how such things were done. She was no match for these men in determination, or in wits, either.

Grey needed no more than a glance to read what was happening within her. "It's not the thin edge of the wedge, Annique. You know exactly what you're doing."

That was true, so she felt better. In Fouché's files in Paris, Tillman was marked as untrustworthy and expendable. He had outlived his usefulness. Any French agent might reveal his name, at need. "He is an inferior sort of traitor, your Monsieur Tillman, who works only for money. He sells us British secrets, then sells French secrets to the Romanovs, and everyone's secrets to Hapsburgs. He betrays several masters." Her fingers were making creases in her dress, which was a bad habit, so she stopped. "There is no proof I can give you. Only the name that is in my head."

"I'll get the proof. Now that I have the name, I can get the proof." Grey put an arm around her. It was not the touch of a lover but the comfortable hold of a comrade before battle. All the time his eyes kept watch through the window, seeking in every corner, as if this were indeed a journey onto a battlefield.

Galba, too, studied the street. "Nobody's following us yet. Robert, your assessment—does Cummings dare to challenge me directly? He brought twelve uniformed boobies with him. He's a politic, cautious man, but he is also enamored of seizing the moment. Will he take her by force? We are prepared for all eventualities but that."

Another street passed. Grey took that long to think about it. "He intended to. That's why he brought that gaggle of marines. He changed his mind when Annique dropped her little grenade. He can't risk backing the wrong player. Besides, he's afraid I'd shoot him."

"You would."

Grey did not need to answer. His silence was like the flatness of a polished knife.

Not far onward, they reached a church, small and old, crowded between houses, with the name St. Odran on the front gate. Sooty stone went upward in many sharp points, some with knobs on the top, and it had small, bright windows.

"We are really going to church?" They had said so, but she had not taken that at face value.

"Contact with the established religion will leave no outward scars." Galba collected his hat from the seat beside him.

She walked through the church door between two men, armed to the teeth, and saw, almost at once, Adrian in the back row, looking like a tomcat at a tea party so little was he suited to this place.

"You will kill me with bafflement, you," she whispered to Grey.

"Look reverent," he advised, and he left her to sit beside Galba. He went somewhere behind her. After that, she felt him watching her most of the time.

Galba sat imperturbably through the long, incomprehensible service. He was transformed, as soon as he entered, into the very portrait of a prosperous city merchant, a shade cunning and foxlike, but fitting wholly into this assemblage of petty bourgeois. He had about him an air of conscious self-satisfaction, as if he were a proud grandfather taking his pretty young granddaughter to church.

So she played the pretty young granddaughter, as she had played so many roles, and held an English prayer book when he handed it to her. After searching her memory, she concluded this was entirely the first church service she had ever attended. She stood and sat and knelt with everyone else and tried to relate these activities to what was happening at the front of the church and failed.

While she was sitting and the man in black talked at

great length, she paged slowly through the *Book of Common Prayer* and put it in her memory, for one never knows what will become useful. She felt bewildered through all of this, without pause, until finally they stood and chanted and everyone except them started to leave. Grey joined them. After a few minutes, they were the only ones in the tiny church.

The minister finished shaking hands at the door of the church and bustled to see them. He greeted "Mr. Galba" and "Mr. Grey" and then took her hand.

"This is Miss Jones," Galba said. Such names, the British Service chose. It had struck her from time to time that the men of this Service had a peculiar sense of humor.

The clergyman smiled upon her benignly. "I married your mother, you know. You want to see the entries, I understand. I've put them out in the vestry. Do follow me."

She was completely on the other side of the church, walking in a puzzled daze, before she realized that the old man in black was not claiming to be some husband of her mother, but rather the clergyman presiding at a marriage.

Maman had married someone? She was not completely amazed, except that it had happened in England. But her mother had done many interesting things in her life, so one more was not impossible, even in England.

A vestry turned out to be a small room. One came to it through a narrow door set between stone columns and, once there, found it dusty and full of cabinets. On the table a large book had been laid open. It filled the entire table.

"Mr. Galba tells me your mother passed away recently. Allow me to offer my condolences. I remember her well, though she wasn't one of my regular parishioners. A most beautiful young woman. You have a great look of her, by the way. This is the record."

He pointed to one line. In the dim light that came through the diamond-shaped panes, she saw that on September 3, 1781, Lucille Alicia Griffith had married Peter Daffyd Jones.

There are not so many Lucille Alicias in the world. It appeared that, indeed, her mother had been married to someone.

"The christening." The minister lifted one huge page, turned it, and trailed his index finger down the entries. "Here. This is it." Small, neat, spidery script, a bit faded, read, Anne Katherine Jones.

She had been christened. How odd. Galba took the minister away and talked to him.

"Do you accept this as authentic?" Grey asked her.

"What?" She had not thought of that. She drew her fingers across the page. The powdery slickness under her fingertips told of undisturbed inks. No trace of discontinuity. No telltale roughness. The colors were properly faded, and they matched. The binding was untouched. The smell, old. "It is real. I just don't understand."

"Not a forgery. Not a substitution. You accept this as genuine."

She nodded. "I was in England as a child. I remember it, just on the edges of rememberings. But I did not know I was born here, in London. Why would I be born in England?"

"We all get born someplace. Let's get out of here."

Outside, Adrian waited, his back against the wall, watching everything with the impartial, carnivorous attention of a hawk. He passed a few words to Grey.

"One scuffle in the churchyard," Grey said to Galba as they got into the coach.

Galba held his gun across his lap on this trip back. Grey kept his at his side, resting on the seat. The coach skirted Booth Square to take a different route home. She felt the presence of men out on the streets, shadowing the coach on all sides, protecting her. She had a sense of moving in an ocean of events, pulled by tides she did not understand.

Meeks Street had been emptied of its assemblies of spies. She was escorted up the stairs by hard-faced men, looking serious, and Doyle, looking amiable and completely relaxed. She was so preoccupied she scarcely noticed she was walking back into her prison.

In the parlor, while they waited for Giles to unlock the door to the inner portion of the house, she said what had been on her mind since she left the church. "Peter Daffyd Jones." Grey and Galba turned. "Has anyone told him my mother is dead?"

Grey said, "He's dead, too, Annique. Peter Jones was your father."

It was impossible that they did not know. This was common knowledge about her. "My father was Jean-Pierre Jauneau, called also Pierre Lalumière. He was a hero of the Revolution. He was hanged in Lyon with the other leaders of the Two Sous Rebellion when I was four."

"Pierre Lalumière was Peter Jones. He was Welsh. Stay still a minute. I think I'll disarm you for a while."

She pulled back her sleeve and held out her arm so Grey could unstrap the sheath. "This makes no sense. My father was Basque, or perhaps Gascon. Do you tell me my father was Welsh? Why should he be a Welsh? Nobody is Welsh. I have never known a single person in my life who was Welsh. It is an utterly stupid thing to be."

"I'm Welsh," Galba said. "Come upstairs."

"That does not wholly amaze me, for I should suppose there are many in England, which is nearby, but there are not any in France that I ever heard of. Why should someone who is Welsh live in France? Why should he pretend to be French?"

She was halfway up the stairs when the first of several realizations hit her. She stopped dead. "*Sapristi.* If that is true, I am legitimate." She put her hand on the wall, not to hold herself up but to reassure herself that something in the world remained solid and reliable.

Grey waited beside her, so she informed him. "I am not a bastard."

A shadow of amusement crossed his eyes. "Does it matter so much?"

"I don't think so." She felt inside herself and did not notice anything different. "It is just that I had not thought of myself in that way." She climbed two more steps, and a thought struck. "I have a name then, one that is rightfully mine." Another thought followed. "Jones? That is a name? But no one on earth is truly named Jones. It is preposterous."

Grey obviously expected her to continue upstairs and then to walk the length of the hall to the front of the house. They came to a wide, light room with five tall windows and a view, through white curtains, over the street. She had not been here before. It had broad leather chairs and a fireplace and racks of swords on the wall and many bookcases. An oval oak table was empty except for a few files in a stack. She could smell coffee and tobacco and the leather of the chairs and the fire. Homey smells. Meeks Street was a house of many such comfortable places.

"Jones is a perfectly ordinary Welsh name," Galba said.

Giles had come upstairs behind them with a tray, carrying coffee and bread. He gave coffee to Galba, who took it, and offered to Grey, who refused, and set a cup on the table next to her without asking. They were insidious, these English.

These English. Another realization came upon her. "I am half Welsh." She could not help feeling dismal about it.

"You are fully Welsh," Galba said. "Your mother was born in Aberdare."

The map flashed into her head. Aberdare was in Wales. "Maman was not truly named Griffith, was she?"

"She was."

"But that is an ugly name. One cannot pronounce it. It is

no wonder she called herself Villiers, which is euphonic. At least Griffith is not laughable, as Jones is."

She had eaten nothing for a day and had no coffee, and now she felt dizzy and light-headed. Many unpleasant truths stared her in the face. She was not prepared for this. No one on earth could be prepared for this. "You are telling me my mother was named Griffith, and she was Welsh. I am not French. Not one little drop." No one contradicted her.

After a while, she said, "We spoke English when I was very little. Maman called me Annie Kate, before she called me Annique. I had forgotten."

So serious, their faces. This was all true, not some elaborate lie. She remembered the language her father and mother had whispered to each other in the night when they were alone. She had the certainty that if she remembered hard enough and asked, she would discover it was Welsh.

"I am Welsh. It is like saying I am a giraffe or a teapot or an Algonquin Indian. I have become impossible and ridiculous."

Galba stood waiting, as still as a tree that had been planted there.

"You need to know the rest." Grey walked to the table and slid the files there toward her, in a pile. They had wide red bands across, which no doubt meant something. "I saw this for the first time yesterday. I didn't know before."

The file on top was labeled with many aliases, some she recognized. Among them were Pierre Lalumière and Jean-Pierre Jauneau, but the first name written was Peter Jones.

Peter Jones . . . Son of Katherine and Owen Jones . . . Cambridge University . . . Recruited into Service . . . Assigned to Brittany surveillance . . . Grade 7 . . . Commendation and promotion . . . Assigned to Nimes . . . Chief of Station, Lyon . . . Detached Agent

> status . . . Commendation . . . Grade 11 . . . Commendation . . . Commendation and promotion (posthumous) . . .

This was the file of an agent of the British Service who had been born Peter Jones and had taken the name of Pierre Lalumière. He had been a detached agent and a grade 17 when he died. His pension was assigned to his widow, Lucille Jones.

The file held hundreds of pages, old papers with their feel and smell entirely authentic. This was political reporting he had made upon the abuses of the Old Regime and on the intellectual ferment that became the Revolution. The secret societies. The political clubs. She leafed through. Pierre Lalumière, who was so honored in France that every schoolboy knew his name, had been a British and a spy.

The folder below was her mother's. She picked it up, finding it thick.

> Lucille Alicia Griffith . . . daughter of Anne and Anson Griffith. Born Aberdare, Wales . . . Recruited into Service. . . .

Pages and pages. Maman's political reporting from Paris. Secrets of the Austrians and Russians from Vienna. Details that were the most deep secrets of Fouché's Secret Police.

The oldest part, deep at the back of the folder, in her mother's tight, spare writing, was the long, dreadful story of the time of the Terror. Notes on top, in another hand, said that Maman had pulled more than three hundred men and women from the machinery of the Revolutionary Council. So many lives saved. Innocents and not so innocent, but none deserving extinction. Annique had not known her mother had done this.

The death of Lucille Alicia Jones was entered on the

left-hand side of the folder in ink fresh and unfaded. She had been a grade 20 when she died, on detached service. Her pension was assigned to her daughter, Anne Katherine Jones.

She did not want to look at the last folder. Her own. It was very thick indeed. All the letters she had written to Maman, all her reports, her whole lifetime of spying, was in it.

She had laid so many secrets in her mother's lap and never asked where they went. Now she knew. The French got only the dregs. The best had gone to the British. It had always been the British, all those years.

"You're convinced this isn't fake," Grey said, when she stopped and closed the file and sat unmoving over it.

"It is genuine." She stared at a book lying on the shelf. If someone had asked her what it was, she could not have told them the word for it. "Maman was remarkable. There is no French agent so deeply planted within the British. She had access everywhere, my mother."

"She was unique," Galba said.

"Even Vauban. All those years I was with him, I told her everything we did. Now I see it written in this file. I was so clever and pleased with myself, and I gave everything to her. René, Pascal, Françoise . . . and Soulier. Soulier, who trusted me with such messages . . . I betrayed them all. Vauban would spit upon me for being so stupid."

Then she could speak no more. It was hard to see because of the water in her eyes. If she once started crying, it would pierce like icicles.

Grey took the files out of her hands and made her stand up and pulled her to hide against his chest. She did begin crying then. It hurt just as much as she had thought it would.

There were many times in the past it would have been perfectly simple to be killed. If she had been sensible, she would have died then and never come to England to this room to see everything of importance shatter to bits.

She had many tears in her, but at last she pushed away from Grey and dried her face upon her forearm, clumsily and quickly, like a child. It was time for her to think and not just hurt. Although she would continue to hurt as well, probably forever.

"I am curious." It was a crow's squawk. "I am curious to see what you will do with me now that I am made nothing in this way. In one hour, you have destroyed me. I have been a traitor all my life. All my life, everything I did . . . It was for nothing. Nothing."

Grey slid a plate across the table toward her. "Annique, eat something."

She did not move.

"If nothing matters," he said, "it doesn't matter if you eat."

It was coffee and rolls. He was right, of course. None of it mattered. She put her elbows on the table to steady herself and drank coffee and then ate most of a roll so her capitulation would be complete. When she was finished, she put her head into her hands.

The floor creaked as Galba moved. "Annique . . ." He had to repeat it before she looked up. "Annique, I am in some part the author of this injustice. I did not intervene. I am profoundly sorry."

Which was English too complicated for her. "I am the offspring of a mermaid and a sea cod. And they were married. I had no idea. Why did my mother lie to me?"

"At first you were too young to burden with this secret. Later . . ." Galba spread his hands. "There is no excuse. Later, she chose to keep it from you. The last time I saw her, you were twelve. We argued about this, fiercely. She told me you were a child of single heart and she would not tear you in half. I don't think she expected either of you to survive this war. Grey, she's not even hearing me."

"Leave her here with me. She needs time."

"Do not talk about me as if I am not here." But she had become insubstantial as smoke. If she was not French, she could not imagine what she might be. Maybe nothing.

"I apologize." Galba sighed. "Annique, you are not the offspring of a halibut and a mythical sea creature. Your parents were two of the finest people I have ever known. Your mother had great respect for you. She knew someday we might sit in this house and face this moment."

He waited for something.

"She doesn't know." Grey took her face between his hands, so she had to look at him, and spoke slowly. "We have to tell her. Galba's name is Anson Griffith. If you were more familiar with the Service, you'd know that." He waited. "He was Lucille Griffith's father. Your mother's father."

Her mind was flat and barren as a tidal beach. None of the words made any sense. Maybe she had forgotten how to speak English.

Galba grunted. "When she can think again, bring her downstairs. She shouldn't be alone."

Grey stroked her hair, slipping it through his fingers. "She'll be fine in a few minutes."

"I will never be fine again."

"Yes, you will, my little halibut. You're incredibly tough, did you know that?"

Thirty-two

SHE COULD NOT GUESS HOW MUCH TIME PASSED. She did not hear Galba go out. When she looked up again, she was alone with Grey.

He stood by the window, lifting the curtain with the back of his fingers to stare into the street. She made some sound or changed her breathing, and he turned toward her. She saw then what was in his eyes. He would have rolled England up by the corners and moved it to Greenland, if that would have helped. He would have done that for her.

She had become pitiable. She had never been the clever Fox Cub. She had been the dog to fetch secrets to Maman. She had felt so smug in her cleverness all those years, but she had always been the dupe. All her life, the dupe.

Blood beat like drums within her ears. The world pulsed red at the edges. "Lies." The chair scraped behind her and toppled and crashed as she pushed it aside. She pounded her fists down. "Lies and lies and lies!"

Her mother's file lay on the table. She took it with both hands and threw it across the room. Papers disgorged in midair and flapped and scattered. "Nothing but lies!" She swept her father's file from the table with the back of her hand. It spread out in a long, smooth line across the rug—pages and pages of his upright, precise writing.

That left her file. She ripped the cover in half. Everything emptied out across the table. Reports that should have gone to Paris. Her letters. The letters she had written Maman. *Dieu.* The silly, loving, trusting words she had written . . . all her little secrets. Everyone here had read them.

Dozens and dozens and dozens of letters, written in little minutes on the edge of battlefields, creased from being carried next to her skin. Paper dirty because she had scavenged it from the garbage, paper stolen from the officers' tents, paper bought when she had no money for food. All those letters filled with the careful, rounded script of an obedient child.

She grabbed them and tore again and again and again till they fell out of her hands, between her fingers, small, small pieces that fluttered like leaves. Scraps fell with lines of writing turned in every direction. And she knew every word. That was the pain of it. She knew them all. With each falling scrap, in a little flash, she remembered where she had been when she wrote it.

> . . . moved the gun emplacements to Liège. Twelve eighteen-pounders and thirty of the lesser kind, the six- and four-pounders. They are short of ammunition for the greater guns. I counted . . .

> I am lonely here, Chère Maman, and hope for one small visit, if you . . .

> The Chasseurs have been released toward Santo Spirito, leaving under cover of the snow flurries with . . .

• • •

> . . . so I have shoes again. There was a brief encounter with the dogs that eat the dead upon the battlefield, but . . .

> . . . for the 157 horses held by heavy cavalry and light horse artillery. The commissary strength is 59 pack mules in theory, but of these, at least a third will founder if we are forced to retreat as seems . . .

> I am feeding one of the cats that lives in the ruins of the innyard. It has white patches . . .

Paper curled in her fists. Her hands shook.

Grey said nothing and did not try to stop her. She could destroy every file in this room, and Grey would not stop her. None of it, none of it, made the least difference.

The fools had left cup, plate, saucer upon the table. They exploded, one after the other one, when she threw them upon the floor. They were not so smart, these English.

"I hope they were expensive dishes." She looked at the pieces and the crumbs and the spots of coffee all across the rug and the spoon lying on its side. Her head ached horribly.

"Very expensive. Crown Derby."

"I would feel better if I killed someone. I am almost sure of it. You are stupid to leave knives all over this room." She had held her hand back from murder for her whole life, but it was never too late to start. "After I finished stabbing you, I could burn this house down. It would not be so hard. I could burn all your thousands of files you love so passionately."

"Start with these." He pointed at the limp, desolate heaps of paper on the floor. "I'll help."

She would not cry again. Probably she would never cry again in all her life. She wanted to hold Grey and fall to pieces in his arms like a weakling, but assuredly, she also wished to kill him.

The hearthrug had a hundred little holes in it where

sparks had fallen for many years. "My father was a great man."

"A very great man," Grey said. "We argued about him at Harrow, in the common room at night. What he wrote. What he and the others did in Lyon. I was halfway a Revolutionary from reading him."

Beside her was one of those strong, heavy chairs in which the room abounded. It was old and worn from spies sitting upon it. For Grey and the others, this was their refuge, their place to talk and read and forget their work. The heart of the house. These wise and terrible men had brought her here so she would be enclosed in their concern, in their most sheltered place, while they destroyed her.

She swallowed. "It is hard to believe my father was an English."

"Welsh."

"Do not nitpick at me. It is a difference only an English would notice, as trout are enthralled by the difference between a trout and a pickerel."

The fire on the hearth was newly lit. They had built a fire to comfort her because they had no other help to offer. They knew she would be cold. When one's heart is ripped entirely from the body, it leaves one quite cold.

She wrapped her arms around herself, but it was not like being held by Grey. "I was taken by Russians, once, when I was fourteen." Talking cut like knives in her throat, but it hurt less than staying silent. "I had been betrayed, as one often is. They knew my name. One of them, when he heard it, knew whose daughter I was. All of them, all of the officers, had read Papa's books and knew how he died. And they let me go. The interrogators had barely started on me. I was not even scarred."

Grey was stiff with his anger at those long-ago Russians. "No scars. How nice." He could be sarcastic sometimes.

"My life was spared, in lands far from France, because men knew my father's name."

He had decided she was safe to approach again. He came behind her and put his hands on her shoulders. It was warm, being held. "Your father was a brave man."

"I was there, do you know. The day of the march. They carried no weapons. Not a pocketknife. The loom workers who were starving walked to the town hall to face men with guns, knowing that some of them might die. They asked only for the honest wage. Only that. Every French schoolboy knows the names of those who were hanged." The lump of ice that was her stomach began to melt. "I have always been proud to be his daughter." That had not changed. The most important truths had not changed. "He did not make that march because he was a spy for England. He did it for those men. He loved France and died for her. "

"He was a man capable of loving more than one nation."

"My father would not have lied to me. If he had lived till I was old enough to talk with, he would not have lied to me."

"Your father would have sent you to England when things went bad in France. Before the Revolution. You'd have been safe in a girls' school in Bath." He let that sink in. She would have been a schoolgirl in some provincial town. That would have been her life. It was a thought to chill the blood.

Grey knew her. He had taken her to his bed, and held her while she was vilely sick, and walked with her all the long road from the coast. He knew exactly what he said to her.

"I would not have liked a school in Bath. You are being subtle with me, and I wish you would stop. I am disgusted with cleverness. I am drowning in it."

Wind played with the curtains and slipped under papers all over the floor, making them lift and settle like birds getting ready to sleep. One paper turned over altogether. One of her so-many letters. She had written, always, by every courier, when she was off spying. Because Maman worried.

She had believed, right to her soul, that Maman worried about her.

He saw where she was looking. "Have you asked yourself why your mother lied to you?"

"To make me her puppet. To use me. You have never seen me in the field, Monsieur Spymaster. I am useful beyond measure."

"You're not a child, Annique. Stop acting like one. She could have told you the truth and still used you. You'd have done whatever she asked of you."

"I do not want to hear this."

He went on relentlessly. "She didn't have to lie to you. She could have told you the truth when you were eight. You'd have been even more useful to her. Think about it. Why did she lie?"

"I hate you." That, at least, required no thinking. That, she could have done in her sleep.

"She lied to you, so you didn't have to lie. She gave you René Didier and the house in the *Quartier Latin.* She gave you learning to cook in Françoise Gaudier's kitchen. She gave you being one of Vauban's people. She gave you those years."

She closed her eyes. Grey made no demands, not even that she speak. It was possible to stand and absorb these thoughts and consider what her life would have been if Maman had told her the truth.

She had seen clever ceramics from Dresden, painted and glazed to look like apples and lettuces and cauliflowers. Wholesome and edible to the eye, cold as skeletons to touch. She would have been like that, if she had grown up playing a double role.

"Maman was wise," she whispered at last, "and very alone. I had not realized how alone." She looked around the room. "I should pick up the papers."

"Leave it for Adrian to clean up. He wants to slay dragons for you. Come downstairs."

"No. Take me to your bed. I need you."

Thirty-three

IN THE DEEP OF NIGHT, SHE DREAMED.

The prison courtyard was dark, full of bobbing lanterns and loud voices. She could not get to Papa. He was in the wagon with the other men. They grabbed at Papa. Shoved him.

"It's the little girl," someone said.

"Dieu. *Get her out of here."*

It was not right. Papa should not look like that. Jerking like a fish on a string. Kicking and swinging. His face was . . . ugly. Not like Papa. Black and ugly with his mouth open.

They tried to grab her. Darkness around her and stone walls. She ran and ran, back the way she had come, into the prison. "Maman. Maman. Où es-tu?"

In the long corridors of the cells, she heard screams. Thin, high screams like a pig being killed. Soldiers were everywhere with their high leather boots and their guns. She clawed her way through. In the middle, Maman was on the floor. She was naked. There was red blood on her mouth.

The man had pulled his breeches down. White, hairy thighs showed under his jacket. He was hurting her. Making her cry.

She would make them stop. "Arrêtez. Arrêtez. Maman. Maman."

Someone picked her up. She could see nothing but the blue coat with brass buttons while he carried her away.

"Maman . . ."

She woke in bed, sweating and cold.

Grey held her. "It's a dream. It's only a dream. Go back to sleep." He spoke French and pulled the blanket over both of them.

She shivered. "She found them later. The men who hurt Papa." She was only half awake. She put her arms around Grey, slipping back into sleep. "She told me once. The judges and the soldiers from Lyon. The men who killed Papa. During the Terror she found them, and they died for it. Every one."

Thirty-four

GALBA COUNTED ELEVEN CHIMES FROM THE clock in the front parlor. Another hour had passed. Still no sign of Robert and the others.

There were no clocks in the study. This was one of the places they occasionally kept prisoners and contained no glass, no sharp points, no wire and springs, nothing that could be made into a weapon. Even the plumed and bannered army of chessmen, Venetian and very old, was papier-mâché.

His granddaughter set her index finger upon a scarlet miter. "I will not move the bishop, I think."

She'd advance the queen, he thought. She'd send it scurrying around the board instead of manipulating pawns and knights and rooks. Emotionally, right to the core, Annique was an independent agent. When she joined his Service, she'd never be Station Chief or Head of Section. She was not another Carruthers. And she was a truly dreadful chess player.

"I am not good at this." She slid the queen forward. "I would rather play cards."

"But sometimes you win at cards."

"I thought, when I first came to know you, that you had no sense of humor whatsoever . . ." She managed to add the next word, though it was obviously prickly as a cocklebur in her mouth. "*Grandpère.* I now believe you have a diabolical one. I do not enjoy being related to you. It is like being granddaughter to one of those large monuments in Egypt that no one can read the writing upon. You are about to tell me I am in check, are you not, with that annoying pawn of yours?"

He'd had ten days with her. She delighted him and filled him with boundless regret that he'd never known her as a child. When she tilted her head like that, he could see his Anna in her, his wife, long dead. Her face was the face of Peter Jones. The passionate warrior. The dreamer. She had Lucille's charm, all of it, and made it distinctly her own. But her brain—that cool, amused, assessing brain—that came from him. She and Robert would have formidable children.

"Check, Annique."

He was coming to understand her moderately well, his Lucille's daughter. It had puzzled him, at first, that she could be such an effective agent and yet so unguarded, so open and direct. In ten days, his spontaneous, unstudied, frank granddaughter never slipped up, not once, in all that chatter.

"So." He did not intend to let her sit brooding about Robert. "We were talking about the nature of secrets, were we not?"

"Yes." She slid her knight into his trap.

He didn't immediately fall upon it. It would be more instructive if she had time to apprehend her mistake before he moved. "We agreed, did we not, that secrets are intangible, but commodities? That they may be bought or sold or stolen? They may be owned?"

"Certainly they may be owned." There. That flick of an

eyelash. She had realized her knight was doomed. She was probably beginning to suspect her bishop was the next to go. He would teach this woman to play chess yet. "We are agreed upon it. I wish my conversations with you did not consist of me agreeing with things you have said and then concluding things I do not at all want to believe."

She was so strictly disciplined under that frivolity. Not once did she glance to the front of the house. There were no signs even he could detect that her whole spirit was poised, waiting for the carriage to return.

Robert and the others were taking a long time. The negotiations with Lazarus must be more difficult than expected.

"If a secret may be owned, it can change ownership," he said.

"Oh, surely. Secrets are most promiscuous. I have eloped with a few myself, in my time." With a thoroughly French shrug, she accepted the loss of her knight and sent her queen to cunningly waylay his bishop.

"Can they also remain faithful? Do my cuff links remain mine, though resting in Robert's dresser drawer?" He moved a knight. "The drawer does not own the secrets."

"Hah. You say, in effect, the secrets in my head do not belong to me. I disagree." She scooped up his bishop, muttering, "This does me no good whatsoever. You merely toy with me, I think."

"So I do." He moved a pawn. "Check."

"But where? You do not . . . Oh." She bit her lip. "I think that is cheating. You have not moved your rook for such a long time I forgot him altogether." She set her finger on the queen. "I see clearly how to escape this trap so it is probably more subtle than is believable. *Grandpère*, my head is not a dresser drawer. I do not care who has put the secrets into it or who needs them. They are mine now. I will decide." She moved the queen.

He set the last pawn into place. "Exactly. They are no

longer French secrets. They are yours. You must dispose of them according to your own conscience. That is checkmate in three moves."

She glared at the board. It took her a minute to work the moves out, twice that long for her invincible stubbornness to admit she was beaten. She gave an exclamation of disgust and stood up. "I do not know why I continue to play chess with you, since I never win."

"You play because I ask you to, Annique."

He set the white king and queen, side by side, into their velvet-lined nests in the box, then the red queen and king. It was always a pleasure to touch these old chessmen. His Annique picked a rook, a bishop, and a pawn from the table and began to juggle. The pieces hovered before her like hummingbirds while her hands flew in circles around them.

He stopped, fascinated. The girl was such an odd compendium of talents. She used just the tips of her fingers, soft as the wind.

"I am teaching Adrian to juggle." Her attention was all on the chessmen; absorbed, unselfconscious, cat-quick. "It will help him with his throwing knives and also amuse him. Doyle will not learn. It does not accord with his persona, he says, though not in those words. Grey has not the time, since you work him without mercy at all hours of the day and night."

"Is it hard to do that? Juggle with the different shapes?"

She caught them. One. Two. Three. Then tossed the bishop by itself so it spun in the air. "But they are the same, these pieces. There is a weight inside—small stones, perhaps, from the feel of it—and it is alike for all. One juggles the center of balance." She set the three pieces down in a row on the edge of the board so he could put them away.

He should have brought this child to England ten years ago. What Lucille had done to her, what he'd allowed, was nothing short of criminal. It was one more regret among many he lived with. "Find the center of balance and everything falls into your hand."

"That is one way to think of it. I must tell you, though, that I am not so easily manipulated as these chessmen you use so well." She gave her street urchin grin. "Do you know the small thing I missed most when I was blind?"

He put the red bishop, rook, and pawn each into its place in the box and closed the lid. "Juggling?"

"Juggling, too." She was looking past him, out the window. "I missed pigeons. I could hear them everywhere, but I could not see them. I am very fond of pigeons. I admire of them that they are large and yet they do not continually bully the sparrows. They also keep their tongues within their teeth and do not argue politics at one continually through the day and night. Do not be the natural historian and tell me pigeons do not have teeth."

"I would argue instead that pigeons do not have politics." Now he must choose something else to distract her till Robert and the others returned. They were on a small errand, this business with the criminals of the rookeries of East London. But he'd lost agents doing small errands. And Marguerite was with them. "To the piano, Annique. It is time for your practice." He pulled the cord for Giles to come and unlock doors.

"They do not know, any of them, the hideous things you do to prisoners in this house." Her eyes danced when she said that. She was comfortable with him, feeling at home here in even these few days. His granddaughter was a woman of strong, uncomplicated loyalties. She was binding herself to him and his organization and to England every hour. In another week, or even a few days, it would be done.

Giles was another lure. The two of them walked ahead of him down the hall toward the front parlor, heads together, murmuring. She was enchanted to have a blood relative her own age, a cousin. She listened endlessly to the dullest family gossip, marveling that all these people should be related to her.

She'd already forged an unbreakable bond with Robert. His daughter and his granddaughter had both chosen remarkable men to love. The Griffith line was safe.

But not its music. That had been misplaced along the way. He followed her into the parlor to find her standing, outlined by the sunlight of the front windows, scowling mutinously at the piano.

She was beautiful as the dawn, of course. One of those troublesome women born to drive men mad. That old devil Fouché was right in one thing—it was high time this agent exchanged boys' clothes and the battlefield for the salon and politics. She was too valuable to waste on the military side. "You will wish to portray a young woman of good family someday. You should have learned to play the piano badly years ago. I don't know what your mother was thinking of."

"I am not musical, me."

"Neither are the young ladies of good family. They worship at the shrine of Euterpe, but they hear her not."

"Which is to say 'they cannot play.' You make my head ache with your classical allusions and your piano lessons and your endless arguments." She propped sheet music on the stand. "You are very certain I will stay here and work for you and give all my secrets to England."

"I am certain. You've spent ten years wading through the carnage Napoleon has made of Europe. You are neither a nitwit nor a savage. Rather than see Kent raped and burned, you will give me what is in your head."

"And shift advantage to England, so I may see British soldiers burn the little farms of Normandy."

"Or perhaps you will save the Vendée from being burned again by Napoleon. No one can know the final consequences of his actions."

"No one can know . . . It is foolish what you say."

She was so very young. He forgot that, sometimes, talking to her. "For thirty years I have contrived and schemed to command events. What I have learned is that the future is not a performing dog. Nothing happens as we plan. Expedience is the most delusive of guides."

"And yet, one must choose." She turned a page of music and then another. "I must choose."

"Then stop trying to read the future and do so. Do what is right to do, here, in this minute. And *that*, granddaughter, you are perfectly capable of discerning."

The knowledge she carried, the unbearable weight of it, showed in her eyes. Just a glimpse. Then she hid it and thumped herself down on the piano bench and flipped the wood panel up from the keys. "Even if I could understand you, which I do not, I would not listen. You will say anything, you and Grey, to get what you want."

"You are not a woman one lies to with impunity. Whatever we say, you will decide for yourself. Wisely, I think."

She would choose correctly in the end. She could never be of the cult that worshipped Napoleon. Not Peter's daughter. It would be her terrible duty to betray France. His job, and Robert's, to reconcile her to the guilt of it.

"I speak politely to you because I have been taught respect for age and white hairs." She let off a few loud discords to make her point. "You become sure of me. It is a mistake on your part. I am a woman of infinite cunning. I will give to you precisely as much information as I wish, no more. And I will do it for my own reasons, in my own time."

A formidable woman, as Paxton said. Thank God Robert knew how to deal with her.

She began to poke through Bach's "Prelude in C Major." Her hands could never be clumsy, of course, but she was utterly without an ear for music. He chose the red sofa, a deliberately uncomfortable piece of furniture, and closed his eyes and accepted his penance.

The notes ceased abruptly. *"Ils arrivent."*

They were coming. She stood and gripped the back of a chair, keeping well away from the window and its chance of snipers. Vauban had trained her supremely well. The young girl longing for her lover's return was wholly subsumed in the experienced agent who never made mistakes.

Now even he could hear the horses. Out front, Ferguson stumped up the basement stairs to greet them as the hackney pulled to a halt. They were back, safe. From the corner of his eye he saw Annique truly relax for the first time in hours.

He is back. She pressed her hand to her stomach and felt the knots untie, one by one. Was she not foolish to worry about Grey, who had survived battles, when he went upon a trifling errand? Being in love made her an idiot.

Galba pretended not to notice her weakness. She was disarmed, utterly, to be the recipient of such delicate politeness.

Marguerite came in first, Grey and Adrian following. She looked extremely pleased with herself, so it was even more clear that all had gone well.

"Done." Adrian tossed his cane on a table and spun his hat down on top of it. "Smooth as silk. I told you it would be."

Marguerite's fingers worked at the ribbons of her bonnet. "I saw the child myself, on board, still sleeping. She is recovering. Everyone is agreed to let her go with her father, though the man is a rogue."

"Walk in. Steal someone. Walk out." Adrian's eyes gleamed. "I love this work."

Doyle was the last one in. He portrayed some low English type in a leather coat and a neckcloth with brightly colored dots upon it. "Lazarus is annoyed. Mostly at that young fool."

"I've annoyed him before."

"How you managed to stay alive as long as you

have . . ." But his Marguerite brought him a glass of wine from the sideboard and kissed him upon the mouth, right there in the parlor. It was a serious, married kiss that looked as if it had been practiced a good while.

"You like him dressed rough, do you, Maggie?" Adrian dodged back from the small fist Marguerite raised in his direction. He was like a buzzing fly when it amused him to be. "Must be like having an affair with the groom. You should try that sometime when he's off wandering in France."

"You, Hawker me lad, are going to get your comeuppance one fine day," Doyle said. "Maggie don't need no advice who to have affairs with. Woman with a mind of her own, she is."

Marguerite chuckled. "I prefer my lovers more *soigné*, but a woman my age cannot be particular. I think this one will clean up nicely when I get him home."

Adrian went to help Giles pour wine. "Lazarus didn't slit my throat, the smugglers owe us a huge favor, and the Service walks away clean. Ye gods, sometimes I even amaze myself."

And Grey had come to her, come as if there were no one else in the room. He put a glass into her hand and closed her fingers around it. How could she think at all when he looked at her this way, as if he wished to drag her to his lair upstairs and make her naked?

Adrian lifted his glass. "To espionage. The bladeless sword . . ."

". . . without a hilt." Galba made the answer. "My congratulations. You've done well, all of you."

She toasted with the others. How easy to sink into the camaraderie here, to pretend she was one of them.

It was time and past time she escaped this house. She was disconcerted by many of her thoughts nowadays. Day by day she could feel her certainties seeping away. Each night she slept curled in Grey's arms, warmed by his rumbling breath as he slept. She felt herself slowly become Welsh, as a caterpillar might lie, puzzling in its cocoon, dreaming and changing. Soon she would not want to leave. Soon, perhaps, she would trust the British and give up her secrets to them. She felt them waiting for that, Grey and the others.

Marguerite strolled across the room, drawing her fingers through her hair. Sunlight dappling her blue dress as she passed the windows. Thin curtains swayed with the wind, molding the bars, blowing loose. Outside a coach approached. It slowed.

A shaft of uneasiness pierced her. Wrong. Something was wrong. In profile, passing the window, Marguerite could be any woman. Any target. "Marguerite!"

"Maggie," Doyle said sternly. "You're making a shadow. Get away from the window."

The carriage outside. Slowing. Wrong. Wrong.

Adrian already had his hand on Maggie. The bullet shattered the window, and Maggie fell like a stone.

That shot was the signal. The world crashed apart. Windows burst inward, one after another, in thundering blasts. Splinters of glass flew like a million spears in the air. She hit the floor. Hid her face. Broken glass cascaded down on top of her. Her arms stung and began to bleed. The curtains writhed like mad ghosts. More shots. Chaos.

"Maggie!"

Adrian's voice cut across Doyle's cry. "Not hit. She's not hit."

Which was a lie. She could see blood upon Marguerite's head. But she knew what Adrian meant—that Maggie was not killed.

Outside, horses neighed in terror. Hooves rang on the cobbles.

Rattling concussion pounded and pounded and tore the room apart. The ceiling caught the force of a direct hit. Plaster thudded down around her. She wriggled and crunched forward. Women's clothes were no good for this. No protection from the glass. She cut herself. Lead smacked the rug an inch from her face. She crawled forward, right there, through the path of that bullet. Shots hit the bars and bricks and marble sill and bounced off, striking at random. Death riding little slugs of metal. Everywhere.

A pause. Then three shots came in rapid succession. Another pause. That was reloading. She crawled fast toward the front wall.

There'd been nine separate blasts in the first volley. Three in the second. Shotguns and rifles, not muskets. Probably three or four men only.

She made it to the wall, to Maggie, who seemed to be unhurt, except for a cut through the scalp. Her face was bloody. But everyone was bloody now, from the shower of glass. Maggie had sensibly rolled to the wall under the window, which was the safest of all places at that moment. Adrian crouched over her, guarding her with his body, his knife upraised like a cold, black flame.

He had an extra knife to toss to her, *grâce a Dieu.* She wedged in next to him, putting her body also between Maggie and the bullets. There was time now to be afraid. Time to consider the doors to this room. Soon, men might break through. She wished she had two knives.

Doyle scuttled toward them, pistol drawn. "You hurt, Maggie?"

"No. Only crushed."

Another battering volley. Lead hit the wallpaper and gouged holes six inches deep. The piano took a direct hit and died noisily.

"That's my girl." Doyle stretched to peer through the broken window. He shouted to Grey, "One coach. Men inside. One on top. Nobody on the ground."

Doyle kept out of her line of throwing, Adrian did also, a courtesy of great value in this tense moment. This was the advantage of working with men of some experience. She was also relieved beyond measure that no one was bleeding much or thrashing with a wound. How much longer that could continue, she did not know.

Two shots in rapid succession. Then more. The red velvet sofa whooshed and sucked air. Feathers joined the plaster dust floating in the room. Galba had folded himself tight in the corner, keeping out of his operatives' way, his lips thinned, his eyes frigid and distant.

"Four shooters. One driver," Grey announced. He calculated the interval of the shots, as she had. He was flat, elbows braced on the floor, covering the front entrance. It was a classic position, the way Grey held that gun, pure army. The manner in which he ignored the bullets slapping into the floor around him was also purely army and showed that he had been much in combat. He rapped out, "Out of here. Everybody. Into the hall. Giles."

Giles had his keys out. He half stood to open the door. He was young enough, that boy, to think he was immortal.

"Down, you fool!" Grey grabbed him and shoved the idiot behind what was left of the sofa. "And stay down." He waited, counting. A double blast shook the room.

Smooth as if he could slip between bullets, Grey launched himself at the wall, at the bracket that had held the jagged remnant of a lamp. He grabbed the brass sconce and twisted in a wide circle. Inside the wall, smoothly, the bolt pulled back, and the door swung free.

"Giles. Anson. Out," Grey ordered. "Into the safe haven. Doyle, take the front. Annique, can Maggie be moved?"

"She is not hurt." She raised her voice above a volley of gunfire. "Except cut." A spindly table chose this minute to rock and crash to the floor, carrying with it the last still-intact lamp globe.

"Get her out of here. Adrian, with me."

Maggie, once no one was kneeling upon her, showed every ability to crawl with commendable speed. Halfway down the hall Galba opened a door and pushed Giles ahead of him. The safe haven room was windowless, small and dark, but it would give some security from the bullets. She pushed Maggie through and slammed the door behind her. She stood with her back to it.

Grey met her eyes as he passed. He nodded one swift approval and headed to the back of the house, leaving her as the last guard of those within the safe haven. Wholly and completely cold was her Grey at moments like this, most entirely deadly.

So. This was her post. She knelt, hunkering down as far as was practical. Bullets spat through the front window, down the hall, and pockmarked the plaster. She did not like the thought of one hitting her. Her knife—good. It was completely familiar. All Adrian's knives were of the same balance within the weight of a pea.

She had a good view of the front door. Doyle, in the parlor, would take the first man through. She would take the second and perhaps give him time to reload.

The piano was hit again, more bass this time. Then pistol shots began outside, a sound like the popping of pine logs in a fire. Grey had circled the house and was shooting into the coach. Doyle took this as a signal to raise himself and fire out the window. He dropped to the floor to reload. She heard the coach rolling away, and in a minute gunfire ceased altogether.

Silence. Her ears were dull and stuffy. Plaster dust, feathers, and gunpowder hung in the air. The walls of the parlor dribbled plaster and strips of wallpaper. She waited, unmoving. Doyle, too, stayed in position, his back to the wall, gun held close to his chest. In the safe haven behind her there was no sound. So much experience they had, all of them.

"It's me," Grey called from outside. "Hold fire." And when the front door opened, it was indeed Grey, not anyone she should throw a knife into, so she stood up and breathed out, long and slow. She had not thought the attackers would loiter when men began to shoot back at them.

The door of the safe haven opened behind her. Galba emerged into the hall, stiff and angry. "Is anyone hurt?"

Grey walked toward them, his pistol primed and pointed to the rug. "Stillwater has a sprained ankle. Ferguson got cut on the arm. Nothing serious." He touched her face, turned it to see where she was bleeding. "You're fine." He said it as if she were one of his men. It warmed her that he should think of her that way, that he did not make of her a civilian like Maggie and Giles. He set his gun on the hall table and took out his handkerchief to stop the bleeding on her forehead. Doyle came to take Maggie away, picking pieces of glass from her hair, his huge bearlike hold tight around her. Outside, she could hear men swearing imaginatively.

Leblanc had come all the way to London to kill her, braving the wrath of Soulier, knowing the the British Service would take great interest in the events at Bruges. Now, more than ever, he would be desperate. He committed this outrage on a street where children played, where women might come out of their houses at any minute. What a dog of a man he was.

"Someone," Galba said, "has offended me. Leblanc?"

"Leblanc." Grey's eyes were the color of granite.

"That was Leblanc." She was sick to know what she had brought upon this house. "That was his first try."

Thirty-five

GREY PUSHED HER DOWN UPON THE BED AND pressed his mouth to the cut on her forehead. He ran his tongue across it.

"You search for glass?" she said. "You do not need to. The cuts are clean. I washed thoroughly, and Maggie and I combed one another's hair to remove it all. Now that I talk to her I find she is an interesting woman, even though she is an aristo. Did you know her oldest daughter speaks four languages and she is only eleven? Doyle took Maggie down to that indecent bathtub to wash her."

"So he did."

"I hear what you are saying beneath your voice, but I am sure washing is all they will do in that tub."

"I wouldn't count on it." Now her elbow fascinated him. He set his teeth there, lightly gnawing away at her. It was one big shock after another when he did that. He drove her to the edge of madness, sometimes, before he entered her and released the hunger he had built.

"I had thought an aristo would be more respectable." She

would speak of nothing serious, tonight. She would only laugh. *For one little hour I will not think of what I must do.* "Are you certain you are not French? This seems very French to me, somehow."

"English since the *Ark*. What would you know about how Frenchmen make love?" He ran the sharp edge of his teeth along her shoulder.

"I have heard things, me, though I have never heard of the things that you do. I do not think there are even names for them."

His hands slipped beneath her and lifted her up so her breasts crested under his mouth. He made tiny bites till she clutched at the sheets, holding on, twitching even before he touched her.

"You start talking French when we're in bed. Did you know that?" His voice became deep when he was aroused. He sounded like the bottom keys on the piano.

"I did not notice." Yes, she said it in French.

She was a stretched drum, thrumming with vibration, as he kissed his way along her ribs, exploring each with his tongue. She heard herself crooning softly. Maybe it was in French. Who could say?

Having brought her so far, he settled down beside her so they could talk. He liked to talk in bed. She, herself, was not in the mood for talking at such times.

The candles were out. He had drawn the heavy blue curtains back from the window. Moonlight slid over him, outlining every bone, each muscle. Across his deltoid an old knife cut had healed into a straight white line so flat she could not feel it with her fingertips. She would miss that scar when she left him. If Soulier did not kill her, she would miss it for all the long years of her life.

"You're worrying." He drew his thumb across her lower lip. "I want you to stop that. I want you soft and supple as noodles, not worried and fighting me."

"If I were fighting you, *mon ami*, you would know it."

"Maybe you're fighting yourself." His thumb continued down her throat, past the joining of the collarbone, between her breasts, down the entire journey to her belly button. His expression was unreadable. "You'd run from me, if you could. Even this minute."

He saw too much, always. How could she not love him? "Grey, I . . ."

"It's in your eyes every time you pass a window. You're thinking how to get out. What's out there you have to do?"

"This and that. I do not want to talk about it." She had only an hour or two left with him. She would not spoil it.

"And we're back to being enemy agents." He slipped his arm under her shoulder so they both lay looking up at the ceiling. "I wish to God we'd met some other way. You could have come to Littledean—that's my village—on May Day. You'd be walking along the way you do, chewing on some piece of donkey's meal, and I'd see you—"

"Am I dressed as a boy? It is depraved of you, to notice a boy in that way."

"You have on that green dress you wore at dinner the other night."

She wiggled closer, warming her skin against his. "I am foolish to walk the fields in such clothing."

"This is my dream. I get to say what you're wearing. So . . . You're walking by the forge. We have a big party on the green at May Day with races and dancing and a bonfire and everybody gets drunk. You stop to see what's going on. I toss a couple louts out of the way and ask you to dance."

"I say, 'Yes, thank you.' "

"So you do. Then I swing you around till you're too dizzy to stand up . . . between the dancing and the cider. After a bit, I lure you off into the woods and slip you out of your clothes."

"I do not go into the woods alone with men. I learned that before I even had breasts, as much as I ever got any."

"Are you fishing for compliments? You have splendid

breasts." Swiftly, he rolled on his side and leaned over her, tracing the air above her breasts. Not touching. "Perfection. Well, two perfections, really."

The feeling of him not touching her . . . Lovemaking is of the mind, not a grappling of anatomies. There was nothing Grey did not know about leading her mind where he wanted it to go.

"We walk in among the trees, past the old mill, down the spinney," he said. "There's green places in the woods full of flowers. I spread my coat under us, on the grass."

"We lie together," she whispered.

"Till dawn. And I tumble headlong into love with you. Do you stay with me, Annique? Or do you get up and brush yourself off and walk away?"

The Head of Section for England stripped himself to his soul in front of her. He was easy to love. "I do not want to hear the end of that story. I would rather go back to dancing on the green."

"Or making love on the forest floor. That's a good part, don't you think?" He bent to her breasts, breathing upon them. If he expected her to talk with him, he should not do such things. Her hands wrapped themselves around his forearm where the tendons and muscles were tough as leather. He was a stern man in every way. Except with her, sometimes.

His breath moved across her face, across her closed eyelids. "If we were in Littledean, you'd wake up with bits of flowers in your hair. You wouldn't want to run anywhere at all. You might even fall in love."

"I was a little in love with Robert, when I knew him, before he turned into you and locked me up."

"I can't let you loose. Leblanc would kill you."

"Perhaps." It was not possible to shrug, lying down.

"What do you know about him? What's this secret he's going to kill you for?"

She had the Head of the British Section in bed with her suddenly. She hated it when that happened. "You are persistent." She dropped her hands from him. "Let us discuss gun emplacements in Toulon instead. I can be extremely witty about the gun emplacements of Toulon."

The next instant the spymaster was gone, and it was Robert who smiled down at her hungrily. "Later." He nuzzled her breast, sucking, and the pang of it came between her legs. She wanted to groan and curl around the sharp longing that struck her there. "We'll get to gun emplacements later. I have a whole list of secrets I'll seduce out of you."

"You. You do not seduce anything out of me. You do not talk politics at all, not even when I become entirely mindless, and you could make me agree to a theocracy ruled by mice."

He laughed at that, her so-serious Grey, whom she could make laugh. "Galba's the one for political theory. I'm a practical man, and you have a very pretty belly button. Have I told you that? Like an acorn cup. Just the right size."

"The right size for what? Oh, for doing that with. But that is not erotic, that only tickles." She began to breathe fast. "I keep expecting you to corrupt me with argument, and you do not."

He kissed his way down and down her belly. "I'll get around to corrupting you."

"What was I speaking of?"

"Politics. No. Lie back a bit. We're not in a hurry. I'll see if I can change your opinion about belly buttons. More important than politics anyway."

"It is a fault in you to be of such cynicism. You are . . . You . . . I have decided it is, after all, erotic, what you are doing."

"Mmmm . . .?"

She trembled because Grey kissed the soft skin in the inner curve of her thigh. "I will tell you . . . I am abjectly susceptible to this particular thing . . . you are about to do."

"Are you now?"

"I did not think I would be, when this was described to me. It sounded . . . rather silly . . . at the time."

"Silly. Well then." He began to kiss between her legs.

She could no longer speak. He transformed her to a creature of liquid fire, all desire. Her hips thrust in rhythmic, shuddering motion. She became only a hunger, only the need to be joined with this man.

She heard herself whispering, "So beautiful. You are for me, beautiful. Only you . . ." When he made her like this, her mouth was not sufficiently connected to her brain. It said more than she meant to say.

He waited until her breath sobbed in and out, until she clutched at him, at the bedclothes. Then he loomed above her, looking down.

"We can talk politics, if you'd like."

She gasped. "I do not . . . No. Let us not."

"Sure about that?"

She needed him, such need that she shook with it. The skin of his chest was slick and salty on her lips. It was impossible not to taste, not to draw her tongue over harsh, curling hairs, over sweaty skin, over the flat, dark, alien nipple. He shuddered when she did that. She felt it. They had such power, each over the other. "You, Monsieur Grey, are the devil."

He smiled, slow and complacent. He had forgotten with whom he dealt.

She employed one of the wrestling tricks René had taught her all those years ago. Grey was not expecting it. He flipped over most satisfactorily onto his back, and she climbed on top, straddling him.

"The women of my family," she bent to whisper in his ear, "know exactly how to deal with cunning foreign spies like you."

He did not look disconcerted. Perhaps he had known that trick, after all. His hands enclosed her hips, one side and the other, deep and strong against her flesh, and he thrust upward. Between clenched teeth he breathed out, "Yes. Just like that. That's right. Yes."

He was a man who controlled sternly the passion that lived at his heart. In bed, he set it free. It was not his practiced skill or his huge, hard body that drove her to madness. It was the fierceness of him.

She felt it now, gathering like the wildness of a thunderstorm. He was not slow and careful, but a fury like a beast. No more thought. No questions or answers. She wrapped her legs about him and rode the storm. Rode the thunder. Masculine power jolted through her. Power unending. She took indescribable pleasure from him and arched back and cried out into the night.

MUCH later, when they were quietly side by side, snuggled against the cold that came in from the window, she lay her head upon his arm. Her last hours with him were slipping away. He would sleep soon. Then she must go.

He said, "I could protect you from Leblanc if you'd tell me what's going on."

She did not even bother to answer, just shook her head. Outside, a mist rose over the city, glowing in the distant streetlamps. The cobbles would be damp and slippery when she had to run.

She stretched so her lips were next to his ear. It was, after all, the last time. "I will tell you a truth, Grey. What I have for you is love, deep to my heart. Only love could hurt this much. I wanted you to know that."

"You're saying good-bye to me again. I wish you'd stop that. I'm not going to let Leblanc get to you."

"I just wanted to tell you."

"Go to sleep, Annique.

"Leblanc will kill someone in this house if he is not stopped. He knows where I am, and he is very dangerous. It would be far better if you let me go, to face him on my own."

"Never. Go to sleep."

SHE SLIPPED DOWN THE STAIRS LIKE A SHADOW, naked, wearing only shoes, her clothing bundled under her arm. It would be ten or fifteen minutes before Grey stirred in his sleep and felt for her and realized she was gone from his bed. She had that long.

At the end of the hall, a single yellow flame burned in a glass chimney. But she had counted these steps. She could have walked this path blind. Surprises of glass crunched in the carpet under her feet. Ferguson had not been able to sweep it all up. For this one night the monster dog was not stalking the halls, slavering and famished, seeking human flesh.

The door to the front parlor was closed, locked with its expensive Bramah lock. But Grey had opened this door from the other side with a hidden lever. In this devious house, doubtless there was a release on this side as well.

There is a truth of locks and hidden places. If the same mind contrives two, they are alike in flavor. In the parlor, the release was a sconce on the wall. Here . . . ? The mirror at the end of the hall flickered with the shadow of her pale, naked body, as she made her silent search. A narrow marquetry table clung tightly against the wall, so tightly she could not squeeze her fingers behind it.

It was the back left leg that lifted to the side. A hidden bolt snicked. The door to the parlor clicked. Cool air touched her face, blowing in from the glassless windows.

Ferguson's broom leaned against the wall. She brought it with her. Two minutes had passed since she arose from bed.

She did not pause to congratulate herself. Softly, she picked her way across the parlor. The floor had been roughly swept. She made no sound, walking through. Broken furniture was pushed back against the walls. The hideous sideboard was unscathed. It was typical of battles that the ugliest things emerged unharmed. The piano was a ruin of twisted wire and splintered wood. No scales would ever again be practiced upon it. One heartening thought amid much destruction.

How many broken rooms had she walked through when she lived among armies? She had seen houses as wealthy as this, shelled and looted and left open to the weather. This parlor had the smell of a battle ruin—gunpowder and plaster dust and, faintly at the edges, blood.

One image filled her mind, plucked from the confusion and fear this afternoon. An image of the window.

The bars were lines of solid black against the gray fog, lit by the streetlamp outside. She slid her fingers along the sill. Yes. She'd seen shotgun blasts hit here again and again. In the deep crevice, the middle bar shifted in its mooring.

She would bend this bar. This birdcage would open, and the bird would fly free.

Ferguson's broomstick was still in her hand. She wedged it hard against the metal and pried. Pried again, panting with effort. The lead that secured iron into marble rattled and crumbled. It was moving.

Another try. She set her foot against the wall and racked

herself, calling on every muscle, on desperation, on all the strength of her will. With agonizing slowness, the bar bent.

Again. Gasping, she set a new hold. This was not the first obstacle she had approached. Like many others, it was convinced, reluctantly, to move aside.

Again. This time, when her hold slipped, she stepped back. Panting, she measured the gap with her outstretched hands. It was enough. Just enough. Men who put bars across windows never believed how little a space is needed to squeeze through if you are small and know exactly how to do it.

Ten minutes. It had been all of ten minutes by now. Quickly, she tossed her bundle of clothing into the night, to the paved space in front of the house. She sent her shoes following.

Giles and Ferguson had knocked out the last of the glass, preparing for the glaziers tomorrow, but malicious splinters lurked everywhere. She sliced the palm of her hand, climbing to the windowsill. Naked, lubricated by fear and blood, she squirmed between the bars.

She had always been thin, and the long, dark road from the south of France had fined her down even more. But it was not easy getting through. Iron edges scraped skin. Unyielding stone and metal bruised muscle and bone. It was necessary to close her mind firmly against pain.

Soon Grey would awaken and find the bed empty. That was also a pain she must close her mind to.

And she was out.

She crouched on the windowsill, drew her legs under her, and launched herself outward, past the kitchen stairwell, with its little sharp spikes, to the paved space beyond. She hit and caught herself with outstretched hands and turned it into a roll. A kaleidoscope of pain. Stone blocks, glass, sharp edges battered at her. At the end of her roll she flopped flat, arms outstretched, sick, dizzy, half-unconscious.

It took a few seconds to come back to herself. The paving was icy under her bare back. She hurt with many varied, individual pains.

The house at Meeks Street stretched above her into the night. Behind it hung the gauzy ball of the moon. When she turned her head, the streetlamps were a long row of globes hanging in blackness, each one smaller than the last. They wavered, shimmering, because she was crying. She had no time to cry. None at all.

Fourteen minutes.

She struggled to her feet, naked except for goose bumps. The spies stationed in this street would see her, a hunched and pale ghost, as she scrambled into her clothes. First the white shift went over her head. Then the dark, concealing dress. She contorted to button it.

She must move fast now. Grey would search for her. Already, men must be creeping forward down this prim street. Stockings. Shoes. She had planned her escape in detail. One has much leisure to make plans, when imprisoned.

She took one last breath. The air of Number Seven Meeks Street smelled of sulfur and charcoal, as a battlefield does. Then, running, she crossed the road to a narrow walkway between two houses. The low fence was a mere hop, and the mews beyond led to Braddy Street.

Men waited for her there.

She dodged them. She ran, flat out, till her sides ached with each breath. Stopped suddenly and slid into a back garden. Became a passing wind that did not even awaken the dogs. Crept down the alley to another street. Ran again, in a different direction.

This was the Game she played so long and well. Again, she was the little fox who outwitted them all. But tonight she was not joyful with it. Tonight, the game she played hurt and hurt and hurt with every step she took.

The night was filled with spies. Some she outran and some she evaded and some she fooled altogether. But the best of them kept pace, and tracked her, as she had known they would. In the end, she let them trap her in a corner behind a shop. They were large men, firm and skilled, and they did not hurt her much. They were French.

ADRIAN held the lamp so they could see the gap in the bars. "Leblanc might have her. Or Soulier. Reams left four marines up on Braddy Street. The Russians are still sniffing around. And Lazarus. Those are the most likely."

"Lazarus is angry at you." Grey chipped the words off from the great, cold fear inside him. Among other criminal enterprises, Lazarus bought and sold women. They all knew what Lazarus did to women.

"If it's Lazarus, we have time. He goes slow at first. He won't hurt her much tonight. He'll just . . ." Adrian started to say more, then looked at Grey's face and stopped. "I'm not welcome there right now, but I can find out if he has her."

Galba was swathed in a brocade dressing gown, the knot tied askew. He touched the bars. "Giles, get some chain and close this. Robert, what are the chances she'll run the gauntlet and escape out of London?"

"None." He shifted Adrian's hand holding the lamp. Annique's bloody fingerprints showed stark red on the windowsill and up and down the bars, still damp. "She won't make it a mile. If Soulier doesn't bag her, Lazarus will. He knows she's important to Adrian, and he has a hundred thieves and murderers to set on her trail."

Galba said, "Where do we send the men?"

He looked into the night, making himself cold and analytic. A gibbering madman rattled at the back of his brain. He was going to kill someone tonight. "We go to Soulier. Get dressed, Hawk. We may not have much time."

Thirty-seven

ANNIQUE HAD KNOWN SOULIER ALL HER LIFE. He had been Papa's friend. It was Soulier who came when Papa was hanged and carried her away in his arms from the king's prison. Years later, Soulier had been one of Maman's lovers.

When she had been the youngest of Vauban's cadre, Soulier had visited often in Françoise's house in the *Quartier Latin* to sit at the kitchen table and laugh and drink and plot with René and the others. She'd scampered to bring cakes and pour them coffee in big cups or little cups, depending on the time of day. He had chucked her under the chin and named her Fox Cub and she had called him Old Renard. They had been very witty together.

"Entre. Entre donc, petite," Soulier welcomed her, just as if large men did not accompany her. They went to stand against the wall, regarding her every twitch. Six men. Did they imagine she would spring and attack Soulier with her teeth? Someday she would discover where this rumor of her bloodthirstiness had been started.

Soulier had not changed at all. He was thin and exquisite, somehow like a cynical old magpie, one who has seen many nests robbed and many eggs broken. She must lie to him tonight. It would be very difficult, lying to Soulier. One does not become director of spies in the stronghold of France's enemy by being a fool.

"Come. Yes. Here to me. My child, I was pierced to my heart to hear of your mother's death. It hurts me still. She was a great and beautiful lady and my friend. To die so suddenly, in such an accident. I am grieved beyond measure."

In the midst of her plots and contrivances, she had forgotten Soulier would mourn her mother's death. She had not thought once of his sorrow. It would seem she had become cold and unfeeling these days, as well as a traitor. She gave him the only comfort she had. "It was swift. There would have been a single moment only when the carriage tilted. Then . . . a fall into the sea."

"Seconds only, and she is gone. The brightness of her snuffed out, and we are left, missing her. You most of all. Coming so soon after the other . . . But we will not talk of this. It is too new and painful."

"I cannot quite believe it, even yet."

"It is good you have kept yourself busy. That is always best at such times." He beckoned. "But let me look at you. You have become a young woman since we last met. You will be more lovely than your mother, even." He made a gesture toward her face. "It is there, waiting within you. I am glad you were able to escape the British."

"I am as well, though I am fled from the frying pan to the fire, as the English say."

"As to that . . . Fouché is annoyed with you, I'm afraid. But sit. Sit. Or you will make me play the polite host and stand up, and I am far too indolent to do that. Come next to me, in this armchair. I do not wish to shout at you across the room. Yves, bring the boule table, yes, here between us and set the lamp upon it. Just so. Now we may be cozy. Were you coming to see me, child? Somehow I do not think so."

It was a great irony that she had escaped Meeks Street and put herself into the path of the French exactly so she would be brought to this house. "It is a long story. Where shall I start?"

"With Monsieur Grey, perhaps, and why you have chosen to travel with him across France and England. I am one of many wondering why you have done this thing. Do not hurry. Think upon it a while. I would wish your little history to be perfect."

"Me, also."

"I have every faith in you. It is even possible you shall tell me the truth." He spread his elegant hands. "What will you take with me? Wine? Biscuits? Coffee? I shall send this great side of beef who stands here so idly to the kitchen to make himself useful. I do not even know whether this is early or late in London. A city that does not have proper bakeries to tell one that morning is come . . . How shall a man know?"

She lifted her hand, palm up, to show equal bewilderment. She felt herself being very French. Strange how she slipped back into it when she was speaking French. "Do you know, I have been almost starved in this dreadful country. Coffee, really good coffee, I would like. And a morsel of bread one can eat. You would not believe what the English eat for breakfast."

"I have lived in this country for five years. There is nothing I would not believe of these English. Yves, tell Babette to prepare the little meal for us, and coffee." Soulier meticulously adjusted the shade of the lamp, making the light fall across her face, unmerciful and bright. "We shall drink coffee together, and you will explain to me why you have been such a naughty girl that Fouché has sent me the orders he has. And why Leblanc has pursued you here from his proper station in France."

Leblanc was one of many topics she did not wish to discuss tonight. "Events are of such a complexity . . ."

"It is said you become the lover of Grey, the Head of Section. He is an admirable man, Monsieur Grey."

She knew what they were all thinking. To Soulier and his agents she was become a nothing, an unreliable who spilled her secrets in a man's bed. She was humiliated before the only audience that mattered. "We are lovers." She had known it would be bitter to turn traitor. She had not prepared herself for the shame that washed across her.

Calm, wise eyes studied her. "We used to chuckle at you, Vauban and I, that you played the harlot so well and were so fastidious and virginal beneath it all. We thought, when the time was right, that René would drag you into the bushes some evening and make you wiser."

She had to smile. "René teased me about it, always. He made such promises—a pasha of the East could not have fulfilled them."

"A wild man, that one. So much laughter in him. He is wasted upon the Russians. You were all scattered when Vauban retired. I do not think any of you remain in France but Leblanc."

She let her hands fall, empty, into her lap. Leblanc. Always Leblanc. "He was never one of us."

Soulier snapped his fingers. One of his henchmen came quietly to kneel by the fire and build it up. She had shivered when he named Leblanc, so Soulier warmed the room for her. He saw everything.

His cane leaned beside him, a slim ebony wand tipped in silver. He played with it, twirling it between two fingers in his familiar way. "Was Grey your first? One's first love is sweet and strong and fresh. My home city has a wine of that nature. Beaujolais. One drinks it raw and new, in great quantities, when one is young, before one turns to finer wines."

She cleared her throat. "He was the first."

"That will make a fine memory to carry with you when you leave England. Not the wisest man to pick. But I do not think he gave you any choice, eh, *petite*?"

"No, monsieur."

"You will call me Soulier, as always. Things have not changed between us because you have been foolish with an Englishman. Though you have enraged Fouché completely, I am afraid."

Yves, who was the chief of Soulier's men in England and not stupid in the least, had returned to place a silver tray on the table between them. There were small flaky rolls, very hot, wrapped in a napkin, and a silver coffeepot, and wide, cream-colored bowls of a size to settle kindly within two hands. It was wholly French, such a breakfast.

Soulier poured coffee into a bowl. "You shall have much of this hot milk and just a touch, only, of sugar. I remember what you eat in the mornings, which Babette has decided this must be. She is infallible, my Babette, so we shall call it morning. We shall wait patiently till evening to let you taste a wine I have been saving, which you will someday develop the palate to appreciate."

She took the bowl of hot coffee and the roll from his hands. Presented with these things, this way, there was nothing to do but dip the roll into the coffee and eat it bite by bite, as one does at home when one is entirely safe. This was Babette's message to her and Soulier's as well.

"So I shall live to this evening. Perhaps even long enough to develop a proper palate for wine."

"If it were in my hands, you would live as long as Methuselah. Of course I shall ignore these orders, which Fouché has given when something he ate did not agree with him. He would not thank me if I took so literally every small word that drops from his lips."

"Thank you." She had known, in all the French secret service, only two men brave enough to ignore a death order from Fouché. Vauban was the other.

She finished the roll and drank milky coffee in long, slow sips, holding the bowl with both hands.

"It has been a long road for you, my cub, all the way from Marseilles, with Leblanc so incomprehensibly murderous. The men I sent were not quick enough to find you and rescue you." He shook his head. "For that I am greatly at fault. You have felt abandoned, I think. And then you fell into the hands of the British. Will you tell me what secrets were the price of refuge in England?"

"I will answer whatever questions you put to me, monsieur."

"Annique, *chérie,* you hurt me."

"Soulier. Yes. I will tell you, Soulier."

"That is better. You have been the guest of the British Service for many days now. What have you told them?"

It was not time to speak of the Albion plans. Not yet. Not yet. She would speak of little betrayals first, as was believable. "I have confirmed the names of Vauban's old agents, though they knew us all. I gave them Frederick Tillman, who is in British Military Intelligence for us." She swallowed. "There is more."

The agent Yves stalked across the room to attend to a draft that worked its way through the curtains. He did not glance in her direction, but he condemned her with each angry footfall. He was the first of many who would despise her.

No. Not the first. She despised herself. Tonight was the end of her long loyalty to France. She had deserted Grey as well, and the British Service. After tonight, she was loyal to no man, to no nation. She who had believed herself loyal to the death, once upon a time.

Part of her watched her hands tremble upon the bowl of coffee. Part of her was pleased she played so skillfully the repentant sheep, returned to the fold. Such excellent technique she had. So skilled an agent.

She was quite sick of Annique Villiers. She set the

bowl down because it was not possible for her to drink it, after all.

And Soulier saw so much. "I have said this and said this, Annique, but you passionate young ones never believe." Soulier stabbed his cane to the floor, emphasizing. "All men can be broken. All! You. Me. That self-righteous young fool who stomps himself across my *salon*. Anyone. The British Service has men who can suck the pith from your soul without leaving a mark upon you. Grey is the most expert of them. You had no chance against him. *Petite*, please, look at me."

She did. One obeyed Soulier.

"You will tell me, one by one, the holes you have put in our defenses. I shall repair them. I have seen many mistakes in my life. This is not such a huge one."

"There is more. You do not know . . ."

"I shall amend all. Fox Cub, this has happened before, many times. France does not tumble down like a house of cards when an agent is captured. A few operations will be closed. This agent or that will be moved and given a new name. I shall amuse myself sending some of our fat colleagues scuttling for cover, *hein*? It will do them no harm. We become complacent. Now we shall be the tidy housewife and sweep the dust out of our corners."

The Albion plans were not a matter of small housekeepings or moving this agent or that. Such treason was not forgiven. Soulier would receive orders even he could not ignore.

He said to her softly, "I shall bring you to Paris, and you will grovel before Fouché, which he will enjoy greatly because you are a pretty girl. He will give you most unpleasant work for a time, to prove your loyalty. A year. Perhaps two." He dissected her spirit, accurately, with remote kindness. "You will do as he says. No. Listen to me. You will do this. You will accustom yourself, and you will live. It will be easier to accept this when you do not come so directly from your English lover's bed, still warm from him." He saw the involuntary flinch and reached across the table to touch her arm. "I understand better than you imagine, child. I will do nothing to smudge your memories of Grey, but the interlude has passed. You have been foolish. Now you will be sensible."

She pulled away from his hand. "I will not whore for Fouché."

Soulier sighed and turned away and made a small adjustment to the wick of the lamp. He was elegant even in this tiny, domestic office. "Sadly, it does not depend upon your consent, *petite*. I will do what I can to make it bearable. But this is painful for both of us. Instead, you shall tell me why Leblanc has conceived this irritation with you that sends him mad in this way. What has possessed him?"

Greed and evil. "Who can say? He is a man of many unpleasant schemes."

"Assuredly. But his schemes have never tempted him to murder you, not even when you were twelve and maddening as a sack of mice. Why now?"

She could say nothing at all. It was a deadly dance she made with Leblanc. They held each other by the throat. She accused him of nothing. In return, he would keep his silence about Vauban and that day in Bruges.

Soulier's eyes never left her face. "You do not care to speculate? No? That is interesting, I think. And what is this?" A servant girl, an English by the look of her, entered and stooped to whisper a few words in Soulier's ear. "How rumor bestirs herself in this town of London. You are sought."

"Leblanc?"

He had come to kill her. He would take her from this parlor out to the streets and kill her.

"Do not look like the stricken doe, Annique. I shall not let him stain these pretty carpets with your blood. Instead, I shall ask him why he does extraordinarily stupid things here in my island kingdom." He listened again to the maid, then gave her quiet orders. "Leblanc is only the first of our morning callers. Your lover, Grey, approaches as well, almost upon Leblanc's heels."

Grey had found her. She fought the sudden, absurd relief that filled her. This was not rescue. It was confusion beyond belief.

The cane in Soulier's hands inscribed a neat circle on the floor. "This will be entertaining. I must admit Grey to this house. I am the open agent in England and here under his sufferance, so I must behave myself."

"You should send him away. He is dangerous."

"He is that, certainly. But perhaps he will chat with me about Leblanc's schemes, since you have so little interest."

At the front of the house, doors opened and closed. She tried to imagine what would happen when these three spymasters met and could not, except that she would probably die at the hands of Leblanc. All was disaster and unbridled turmoil. There was no plan she could conceive for dealing with it.

Then Leblanc entered the room, and she was so simply terrified she could not think at all.

"Jacques." Soulier's voice was noticeably cool. His men, waiting quietly in the background, became alert. "You condescend to visit me. Come. Babette shall prepare coffee for you as well. Or if you would prefer wine—"

"I have come for Annique. Give her to me, and I go."

Leblanc held his right arm stiffly to his chest. So it pained him still, where she had put her knife into him. His face was pasty against the dark English coat he wore. But it was not wholly pain that made him pale. He was in great fear. Was it that Grey was moments behind him? Or did he think she had broken her silence about what had happened in Bruges? He should know she would not betray Vauban.

Soulier said meditatively, "You are abrupt tonight, Jacques. And yet I find we have much to discuss. There is the matter of the attack upon the headquarters of the British Service—"

"I have no time to prattle with an old man. I am an officer of the First Consul of France. I do not concern myself with appeasing English spies. When France is threatened, I take action. I—"

"And I am an old man," Soulier said, "who does not enact dramas at three in the morning. You see Annique? She sits with Fouché's death order hanging above her and this irresponsible knifing in alleyways you attempt. She does not play me melodramas at this ungodly hour. Sit down."

"Annique is mine." His eyes said he had come to kill her. "Assigned to me by Fouché. Do not come between me and what is mine, Soulier."

"Pah! You are upon my territory, you and your men you have brought to England without my permission or my knowledge. You have done various insane actions in my domain. You shall explain them to me, and perhaps I will not raise my voice loud enough to be heard in Paris."

"Do not cross me. I have an agent to discipline and a death order to—"

The door opened, and Grey came in.

He had come to her, here in the bastion of his enemies. He wore the authority of his office and the controlled deadliness of a soldier. He had never looked more menacing.

Soulier inclined his head. "Monsieur Grey, I bid you welcome. You will forgive me for not rising. It is an old trouble with a wound. You have come to assure yourself that Annique has come safely through the perils of the night. As you see, she is unhurt."

Ignoring him, Grey stalked forward.

Unperturbed, Soulier continued, "I make you my sincere and humble apology for the damage to your headquarters. Do not, I beg of you, send men to enact the same stupidity upon us in Paris. It is the work of this one *crétin* who rampages madly in England. He will be brought under proper control."

Grey lifted her half out of her chair to kiss her, passionately and possessively, hard upon her mouth. It surprised her, but she was more immediately concerned with receiving and hiding the knife he passed to her. As a declaration of affection, the knife did as well as any number of kisses.

His expression was murderously grim. If he killed someone, she hoped it would be Leblanc.

"Why is he here?" Leblanc's voice rose to a squeak. He stabbed his finger at Grey, sputtering. "What are you doing? What are you plotting with this Englishman? You accuse me of madness. This is the madness." He looked from man to man, at the circle of Soulier's agents. "Remove this Englishman. I have Fouché's authority, and I say this."

No one moved. Soulier said, "You will doubtless explain why you give orders in my house, Jacques."

"It is you who overstep yourself. Even you cannot consort openly with English spies. You make treason here."

"I do the unusual, perhaps, but I feel in my bones this is an unusual night. Monsieur Grey and I know one another of old, though we have not met face-to-face . . . as you did when you held him in your cellar in Paris."

Leblanc spat on the rich carpet.

Soulier smiled. "Does Fouché know you held the Head of the British Section and had not the wit to recognize him? We will hope he is in a good mood the day he hears that."

Leblanc was red now as he had been pale before. "My position is secure. Do not challenge me, old man. I have become a power in France, the confidant of Fouché."

"Then perhaps Fouché will be sympathetic of your blunders."

Soulier and Grey exchanged cool glances. "Jacques is correct in this much. This is unprecedented, what we do here. Tonight we step out of our assigned roles, you and I, and face one another. I am a man who has no love of the bizarre. What my colleague so rudely demands, I ask more politely. What do you come here for?"

"Annique."

"You may not have her. You must realize that."

Grey said, "This is England, Soulier."

"And the woman Carruthers is your agent in Paris. Let us not speak of force. You will not enter my stronghold and remove my agents. In return, the woman Carruthers will knit placidly in her white house with blue shutters in the Faubourg Saint-Germain. It has been understood for a decade between Galba and Fouché that one square upon the board shall be sacrosanct in each capital. This is ours. Annique stays with me."

"She's not safe." Grey jerked his thumb at Leblanc. "That bastard's going to kill her."

"Not within my house." Soulier touched fingertip to fingertip, his elbows on the padded arms of the chair. "Monsieur Grey, no harm will come to Annique. With the death of her mother, and my old friend Vauban dead as well, I stand as protector to her. I will let no . . ."

Vauban? What had he said? *It cannot be true.* She felt the room jar, as if it were a carriage that had stopped suddenly. "Vauban is dead?"

They stopped and looked at her. Grey said, "You didn't know?"

Soulier said carefully, "For weeks now. Did you not hear? The last day of July. He died peacefully in his sleep, my child. His years were fulfilled. We were—"

Gunfire cracked. A shock. Heat stung her cheek. She was on the floor, flat on her face, with no memory of throwing herself there. Gunpowder hung in the air. She had not been hit. She felt no pain, only cold and fear.

Frantic scuffling. The thud and grunt of men fighting. A chair clattered. The pistol bounced across the floor.

Soulier was on his feet, his cane revealed as a thin sword blade. His guards stood in front of him, shielding him.

Leblanc pulled his knife. In a blur of speed, Grey wheeled and kicked and connected. *La savate.* She had not known Grey was a *savateur.* Leblanc staggered and screamed and launched himself upon Grey, stabbing.

They went down together. A lamp fell. Dishes crashed to the floor. She could not throw her knife into the tangle of two men wrestling. The guards, idiots, did nothing.

It was a fight of lightning swiftness, a fight of cats in an alley. Leblanc raised steel that glittered like ice. Struck. Grey caught his arm. The blade sawed back and forth and flipped, end over end, to clatter at Soulier's feet. Grey's fist struck. Leblanc collapsed, bloody, on the floor.

She knelt, gasping, the knife she had not used still in her hand. Grey was not hurt. Not hurt. Not one tiny bit hurt. He was safe.

The guards ran forward, not sure which man to hold. Soulier's voice came calmly. "Assist Leblanc to rise, Yves. Just so. Continue to assist him. Monsieur Grey, I am inexpressibly grateful. Annique, my very dear . . . you are not injured? I see you are not."

She got to her feet, shaking so badly she searched for something to support her. The scratch on her cheek . . . She wiped at it with the back of her hand. A nothing. When she turned to look, behind her on the yellow silk panel of the wall, the bullet made a neat, round puncture, black at the edges.

Leblanc hung heavily in an implacable hold. He looked . . . diminished. He was only a thin, ugly man in rumpled clothing, bleeding from his nose. Not the important spy of France. Not the bogeyman of her childhood.

Her voice came as if from far away. "Vauban is dead. I did not know."

Grey came up behind her. "I would have told you. I thought you knew."

There was a humming in her ears. So strange. She felt as if she were floating. Because she knew everything. She could see it all. So obvious. "Vauban dies. And it was a week, not more, that Maman's coach falls unbelievably from a high cliff. I was to ride out with her that day."

"My God," Grey muttered.

Behind her eyes, fire pulsed. She faced Leblanc. "Was I so hard to kill you must take Maman as well? Or did you think I had shared the secret with her?"

"I don't know what you mean." Leblanc's gaze slid away. His pupils jerked in tiny twitches. He was guilty. Guilty and afraid.

He killed Maman. The world went blood red. She dropped her knife and went for him with her bare hands.

He gagged as her hands closed on his throat. She would tear him apart. Rip his flesh to pieces. She fought the guards who pulled Leblanc away. She fought Grey when he held her arms behind her back and did not let her sink her claws into Leblanc.

"Arrête, chérie." Soulier's voice reached her.

"I will kill him." She kicked Grey, who kept her from Leblanc. "I will kill him fifty times. Murderer! Assassin. Animal!" She would shred him to bits.

"She lies. Do not listen to her. It is all lies."

"So far, she merely promises to kill you," Soulier said. "I am almost inclined to allow it. But we will hear what she has to say first. Calm her, Monsieur Grey. She will hurt herself."

She would wipe this piece of filth from the universe. She would grind him to suet. "Son of a maggot. Murderer."

"Annique, stop." Grey's strength closed around her, and she could not move. "Tell me."

The smell of Grey, the steadiness of him, filled her senses. Fury trickled away. She was empty. She slumped against him, chilled and sick, panting for air.

Vauban was dead. He would never again fold together the pages of her report and nod, all gruff, and say, "Good work," in front of everyone. He would never pour water in her wine as if she were still a child. Never. Never. Never again for Vauban. For Maman. Everything was gone. Tears burned in her eyes, and the pain choked her. Grey held her to him so she was hidden.

Soulier said, "Child, there is no time for this. Set it aside."

She clung one minute to Grey's jacket. The rage had passed, leaving her hollow. It was as if her heart and mind had been scooped out of her altogether. She was nothing but a cold wind wrapped in a woman's skin.

She tried to push away from Grey and found herself still held—warmly, carefully, firmly. He did not let her go. He turned her within his arms so that she faced Soulier. It seemed she would have the comfort of his body whether she wished for it or not.

"I am composed," she said.

"Good. I must deal with Leblanc," Soulier said. "Give me the truth of this matter."

Truth. How strange that she could tell the simple truth in this company. There was no old man in his stone house in Normandy, depending upon her silence. Vauban was dead. Nothing could hurt him.

She said, "Vauban stole the Albion plans," and she watched the words stab to the heart of Soulier.

"That is impossible."

Behind her, Grey stiffened, deep in his muscles.

"He stole them to pass to the British. Not for the money. It was never for the money." She could not clear the lump from her throat. "It was . . . With gold as payment, even a small amount of gold, no one would suspect Vauban."

"No one would believe that of him." Soulier sank heavily into the chair. "He conceived a faultless operation. As always."

"He planned for months, alone, in secret." Her feelings were chaotic, even after so many months. "I think . . . I think Vauban went a little mad when his sons died in Egypt."

Soulier looked away, his lips tight. "Other men have lost sons."

"His sons died for nothing. Napoleon sailed home to hold parades and put sphinxes upon the feet of his tables. Émile and Philippe died in the fever and stink of Cairo, deserted by the man who led them there. They died for a Corsican's vanity, Vauban said."

How could Soulier not understand? He had been Vauban's friend. How could he look like that, shocked and condemning? "He was old and tired and sick. He lived his whole life in the service of France. He lost everything in the Terror—his home, his family, his wife."

"My child, I was there. I know."

"Only his boys were left. Then Napoleon threw their lives away on a grandiose whim to rule the East."

She shook herself free of Grey and began to pace the room. She could not stay still. The Frenchmen, Soulier's agents, followed her with their eyes, waiting for what she would say. Soulier's pain whipped at her with silent lashes.

She steadied her voice. "And now Napoleon planned another vast expedition. To England. That is why Vauban stole the plans. He said Napoleon had betrayed the Revolution."

Soulier passed his hand over his forehead. "Always, he was the dreamer among us. The idealist. But this . . ."

"There would be no more pointless battles overseas, Vauban said. No more French armies abandoned. He would prevent it."

Soulier lifted his eyes to her. "You were under his orders, Annique. If he told you to help him in this . . ."

Did he think Vauban would lay that upon her? "But no. He told me nothing. He brought me to Bruges to run the small errands, as always. To watch for the British. But Leblanc . . ."

Leblanc fought the men who held him, knowing what she would say next. Hatred washed over her in tides. She took shaking, hot breaths before she could speak.

"Leblanc's small worm in the Military Intelligence of England, Tillman, told Leblanc where the British would deliver the gold. The Englishmen were betrayed, first, by an English."

She turned to Grey. He remained expressionless, his eyes level and cold. It was to him she spoke. "Leblanc lay in wait. And killed. And took the gold. He has done endless murder for that gold."

When she said that, he nodded, just a fraction. Leblanc was dead from this moment. He might still walk and talk for an hour or a week, but he was dead. Soulier saw this. She did not think Leblanc yet realized.

"She lies. I swear, Soulier, this is lies." Leblanc writhed in fury and fear. Long scratches showed red on his face. "It was Vauban. Only Vauban. I know nothing of this."

She did not bother to look upon Leblanc. "I was with Vauban. Leblanc came to the inn with the blood of those murdered men still upon his clothing." She remembered the shock and the sickness. Vauban's incredulous anger. "Leblanc knew Vauban must have the plans. He demanded them, as the price of his silence."

"The bitch lies. She lies in her teeth. I was in Paris that day. I can bring a dozen men to swear this."

"He was there. He hid in the farmhouse of Paul Drouet that night, in Brésanne. No." She snapped, "Be silent, maggot. Your men, Plaçais and Vachelard, are dead by your secret order. The family Drouet burned in their beds. It has been unhealthy to know this thing about you, Leblanc. But one daughter escaped and lives. There is a witness."

The willingness of Yves and the other guards to keep violent hands upon Leblanc increased by the minute.

"You will not listen to this whore, this bitch in heat, who sweats and grunts under an English dog."

"You killed Maman when I was blinded and useless. And three Englishmen in Bruges. And two of your own men. And the family Drouet at their farm," she stared into

Leblanc's eyes, and her voice cracked, "even the children. The good God alone knows how many others. All for gold . . ." She could no longer speak.

Leblanc was a cornered rat, teeth bared. "You will regret this, Soulier. Fouché will crush you like an ant when I tell him this."

Soulier had become like ancient ice in the mountains, frigid and blue and glittering. "You are a greedy man, Jacques. Greedy enough that I believe this atrocity of you. It is the answer to some questions that have occurred to me this last year. And why else would you try to kill Annique?

"She lies," Leblanc hissed.

"You are stupid beyond belief to think you can attack in my own house someone I have given sanctuary. To do this to a woman Grey chooses to protect . . . Do you not realize, you idiot, that he has a dozen men outside? That this is his trap for you? That he has come for you tonight to hang you?"

Grey was at her back, and she could not see his expression. Leblanc did. He paled to the color of a fish belly. He did not like to look upon his own death, for all the death he had meted out to others.

Soulier threaded the thin sword cane into its concealing scabbard and secured it with a quick, vicious twist. "I will spare Grey his trouble, if he agrees. I will deliver you to Fouché, to make an example of. He will relieve his spleen by separating you from your head. You permit, Monsieur Grey?"

Grey's voice was quiet into her ear. "Annique, Leblanc is yours. Shall I hang him for you? Or you can kill him with your own hands, if that's what you need. Anything you want."

The thought of laying hands upon Leblanc to kill him made her sick. She shook her head quickly.

Grey said to Soulier, "Take him. Get him out of here. We need to talk. Alone."

Soulier waved impatiently. "Yves, put him . . . I do not know. I do not keep a cage for such rats in my house. Put him somewhere and watch him. The pantry. All of you go. Yes, all. Do not let him escape."

Leblanc was dragged from the room, leaving threats behind him like the trail of a snail, departing.

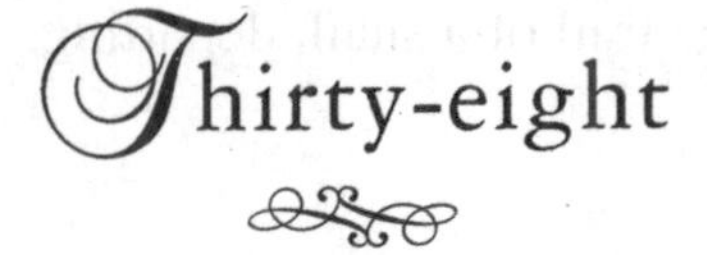

Thirty-eight

WITH LEBLANC GONE, THE ROOM WAS ODDLY quiet. She rested within Grey's arms, her cheek pressed against his sleeve. Truly, love plucked away all one's common sense. She was tempted to cling to him and feed off the strength of him and feel safe. She had not known such temptations existed until she met him.

When she pushed herself free, Grey let her go with one instant of hesitation that said he did not want to.

"Soulier must be told the truth of what I have done," she said, which was warning enough, for an astute man like Grey, that she was about to lie in a serious fashion.

This was the last throw of her game. This was what she had planned through her days at Meeks Street, lying by Grey's side, playing chess with Galba, teaching Hawker to juggle knives. If she lied well enough, she would end the threat of invasion, yet lay no advantage into the hands of the British.

Soulier sat, urbane and well-tailored, framed by the chair with its high tapestry back. He might have been a courtier of the old king, receiving an ambassador at Versailles.

She must make him look upon her, not Grey. Grey was unprepared and might make some small revelations upon his face. "I did not speak of the Albion plans in front of the others. I knew you would not wish me to."

"Then do not speak of them now." Soulier was testy with her.

"I must." She stood square in front of him. She had stood thus many times, reporting or receiving orders. "You have guessed most of it. The Albion plans are ashes. Vauban burned them in the fireplace of the inn that night, rather than give them to Leblanc."

"You have said enough."

"He gave them to me first, to memorize."

Soulier conveyed the need for discretion with an angry, emphatic shake of his head.

"The British know about my memory. I have spent days at Meeks Street copying out the plans, page by page." She made a picture of that in her mind, so vivid and exact it did not even feel like a lie. "They have them now."

It was done. France would not invade. England was safe. Now she must face what would come to her.

Soulier stared at his hands that rested, one upon the other, on the pommel of his cane. "You did this for Vauban."

"He asked it of me. In Bruges."

"Then he has condemned you to death." Soulier leaned back in his chair and closed his eyes. "Even I cannot save you."

The hairs on the back of her neck stood up. There is a difference between knowing one will die and hearing the sentence pronounced. "I have accepted the consequences of my actions. I delayed leaving for England for a long time, hoping Napoleon would turn aside from this invasion, and the plans would come to nothing, but it did not happen. I did not wish to die, you understand. And I was injured and made blind." Her mouth felt dry. "Which complicated matters. Leblanc has been a complexity, as well."

"Annique," Soulier said gently.

"Yes?"

"Be silent. I am thinking." He opened his eyes to frown at her. "And do not stand there like a loaf of bread. This room is disordered beyond belief by the men you brought here to fight over you. Do something useful." He closed his eyes again.

That was comforting. Perhaps Soulier would think of a way to save her from Fouché. It was not impossible.

Grey was saying nothing, for which she was grateful. He knew, better than anyone else, that the Albion plans were not in British hands. For the moment, he played her game.

She set the small table upright and put the silver tray upon it and knelt to gather shattered glass from the lamp chimney into the palm of her hand. Such mundane activities. Spying is a life of boring, ordinary tasks, performed while death scratches at the window. She had been seven when Soulier told her that.

Matters did not go so badly. Leblanc had not shot her, after all. The oil lamp that fell from this table had not set itself afire to burn her to death. She had told a convincing lie to Soulier, who was a master in detecting lies. Soulier had not yet been compelled to kill her. And she had, perhaps, prevented the invasion of England. Altogether, she had much to congratulate herself upon.

Soulier opened his eyes. "You did not give the Albion plans to the British Service."

Her stomach dropped like a stone. She had not been believed, after all. *Diable.* "Soulier, I have—"

"Do not chatter. It is Leblanc who just sold the plans to the British."

"Leblanc?"

"*Exact.* I am in a state of shock. Monsieur Grey is even

now informing me of Leblanc's guilt. He does this in a pique of revenge, for Leblanc's culpability in the matter of gold and murder at Bruges, which he has just discovered."

She did not glance at Grey, who was doubtless being impenetrable. "I see."

"You, my child, were never in Bruges. You were somewhere else entirely. Dijon perhaps."

"That is a dull town. I am delighted to have been there." She put broken crockery upon the silver tray. "It is convenient of Leblanc to be so guilty."

"Is it not? He will deny everything and tangle himself in a dozen lies and not be believed. Fouché delights in simplicities. We shall fasten one more crime upon this *salaud*, who has committed so many. He can only die once, unfortunately. And you, child, will not pay for Vauban's folly."

"It is not—"

"You have sufficient folly of your own to pay for," Soulier said sharply. "Which I must now deal with."

Grey's footfalls as he stepped forward had become the tread of a fighter, balanced and light. Tension, fierce and invisible, twisted in the air. "Then you deal with me."

"You saved her life tonight, Monsieur Grey, when my men failed me. I am in your debt. But she is safe now, with her own people. You must leave her to us."

Grey said, "This isn't negotiable."

"She is mine, monsieur. And I will not give her up." Soulier hesitated, then laid his cane aside, slanted against the arm of his chair. "But I am wise enough not to challenge you directly. Come. Sit. Let us discuss this like civilized men."

Grey picked an overturned gilt chair and set it upright so it confronted Soulier. He sat, and he pulled her to stand next to him, his arm around her. "Talk."

"*Eh bien.* We shall be blunt, as you English prefer." Soulier leaned toward him. "You have achieved the Albion plans. That must content you. As you care for my little one,

I ask you to leave her with me and go. Make your farewell as tender as you wish, but part from her quickly. It is the kindest way."

"I'm not letting you have her."

"Do you know so little of me? Do you fear I will do revenge upon her? We French take into account the human frailties. For a woman such as Annique, we will forgive a great many frailties."

"I don't give a damn what you forgive."

The silence lengthened. She heard the gilt clock on the mantelpiece very distinctly, ticking. She had not made plans that stretched beyond this room and facing Soulier. She had not expected Grey to come. Whatever happened, she would remember that Grey came for her.

Soulier sighed. "I had thought Annique's . . . unwisdom . . . was one-sided. She is young, and infatuated, and believes, just a little, in fairy tales. She does not understand that a relationship between the two of you is out of the question. You and I, Grey, we know this. If you take her with you in this selfish fashion, you will destroy her life. Quite literally. Fouché will see her dead within the month. Leave the Cub with me. I will arrange that no harm comes to her."

"She leaves here with me."

"Most touching." Soulier regarded Grey steadily. "You make me the villain in this play. But it is you who brought Annique to this disaster she faces. You have used her, Grey, without taking any thought for her at all."

"Listen, you son of a bitch—"

Soulier raised his hand. "Let me finish, please. Because you have seduced her away from France, Fouché has put a death order upon her. There is nowhere—not in the deserts of Arabia, not upon the face of the moon—that she can hide from such an order. I must clean up the debacle you have made of her life. I will bring her to Fouché and turn his wrath aside. I will prepare her to earn his forgiveness in the only way she can, if she is to live. This pretty love affair you have between you will make it horribly painful for her." His eyes glittered, black and opaque as onyx. "My Fox Cub is a woman of rare quality, beyond the price of jewels as an agent. Unique. You have come close to ruining her. I am angry at what you have done to her. Very angry."

"She's British Service."

"Silence! *Mon Dieu.* You shall not say that!" Soulier rose from his chair, enraged and shaking. "Not even in this room when we are alone. Not even to me. Do not whisper it. She is not recruited to you. All may be forgiven—except for an agent to turn. You make her death certain."

"She's mine. Her mother was ours."

Deep, unconditional love swept across her. Thus Grey paid for her freedom with that great secret from his store of secrets. He was like a rajah laying down the legendary ruby of his kingdom to ransom his woman.

Soulier stared. "Lucille?"

"She was British Service."

"*Nom d'un nom d'un nom.* No. I cannot believe." Soulier strode away with an abruptness that belied his years and crossed the room. "It cannot be."

"From the first day she arrived in France. I could show you reports twenty years old. She was always ours."

"*Ma belle* Lucille. That such a thing could be." He drew a curtain aside and faced into the night. It was a long minute before he spoke again. "Lucille . . . I knew she was the best France had. I did not realize she was the best England had instead." One could not see Soulier's face, only hear his voice. "She was . . . *lumineuse.* Nothing so ordinary as beauty. I was one of many who loved her."

"I'm told she was a remarkable woman."

"And she belonged to England. We shall be the laughingstock of Europe if this leaks out."

"It will. These things always do."

After a minute, Soulier let the curtain fall. He began to

chuckle. "Oh, Lucille, how you would laugh to see me *étonné* like this. *Mon Dieu*, but I shall indulge myself by telling this to Fouché, to his face. It will pay back many, many difficult moments I have had with him." He limped his way back to the tapestry chair, shaking his head. "My beautiful Lucille. You will tell me now that she was English . . . Yes, I see you will. It is enough to make a grown man weep to contemplate how many of our secrets have slipped to you over the years through those pretty fingers. What a very great deal of trouble I shall be put to, cleaning up this mess."

He lowered himself to the chair, muttering, "*Mon Dieu, mon Dieu*, what did that woman not know. I shall be busy for months." Soulier reached his hand out. "Annique, come to me."

He had been protector and teacher for so many years. She took his hand and looked down at him.

"Those secrets you gathered for me . . . The ones you carried back and forth for me in your pretty head. They are all in the hands of the British, are they not?"

She nodded.

"You were a double agent even when you were a child?"

To pretend she had lied to him all her life, that she had played a role to Vauban and to René and Françoise . . . There are some lies one cannot tell.

"I see. Not quite the British agent then. Lucille did not tell you."

"Annique was always ours," Grey said. "I have reports she wrote before she learned to spell."

"Doubtless you do, but I do not think my Cub sent them to you. No," Soulier said. "We shall let it pass. I am not hungry for her blood, God knows. I am still trying to think of a way to keep her."

She could only be silent. Soulier's ingenuity was formidable.

"Alas, Annique, we have not treated you well, have we?

Vauban makes you the ass for his load of madness, and Leblanc menaces you with knives and guns. I was dilatory and did not find you in time. You have fled to your mother's people instead of to me, and I have lost you forever. Leblanc should be killed several times over. I will attempt it. And Pierre, your father?"

"Ours," Grey said.

"*Morbleu*, but this must not become known. Pierre Lalumière is one of the martyrs of the Revolution. A man of passionate ideals. If he had not died young, perhaps there would have been less bloodshed in that time we all wish to forget." A spasm of dismay passed across his face. "Do not tell me, Grey, that he was British."

"I'm afraid so."

"I would not have believed it. A mind so enlightened. Next you will tell me Voltaire and Racine are the products of your Oxford University. No. Do not say it. I do not want to know. The world is a disillusioning place altogether." Soulier collected his cane and wrapped it in his hold and spoke low. "I will admit, just between these walls, that I am not sorry Vauban succeeded in his final folly. Napoleon has developed a taste for grandiose gambles, which should be discouraged. Our First Consul is not lucky upon the water. Oh, take her and go, Grey. She is your agent, and untouchable. She will doubtless drive you mad."

"I've given you Leblanc, neatly wrapped for disposal. We're even."

"On the contrary. I am, as you English say, your cat's paw. I am disgusted with this turn of events. I lose my splendid young agent of resource and cleverness and must now replace the section chief of central France, though he was an excrescence upon the boil of a pox and stupid to go along with it. The only compensation of this night is that I need not debauch *la petite*, which I did not look forward to in the least."

"Fouché's death order?"

Soulier made a sweeping motion, dismissing it. "You may consider it canceled. It was meant to stop the leak of secrets. It is far too late for that."

"Good." Grey was blunt. "Then I won't issue any of my own."

"We do not kill one another's agents, you and I." Soulier planted the cane and got to his feet, leaning upon it heavily. "Too much blood upon the chessboard of the Game, and we become no different from the military savages who litter the fields of Europe with the bodies of those poor young men. Annique, kiss me and depart. Our relationship has become so complicated even a Frenchman cannot untangle it. Take care we do not meet again, now that we are enemies."

"I shall be properly wary of you, Soulier." She kissed his cheek, as she had a thousand times. "I shall miss you."

"Go with the blessings of *le bon Dieu*. He is not fashionable in Paris these days but will doubtless reappear in his own good time." He sighed. "I think I shall declare it night once more and have a glass of wine before I go to bed."

Thirty-nine

The hackney coach that belonged to the British Service was waiting for them at the curb outside Soulier's charming town house.

"I do not know how to feel." She sat next to Grey. At this moment it did not matter much to her where they went. "It is strange not to have Leblanc attempting to kill me."

On the forward seat lay a pile of black wool cloth. When Grey unfolded it, it proved to be a long wool cloak, such as countrywomen wear. He wrapped it around her. She had not noticed she was shivering until then.

"I shake like a custard. It is spineless of me," she said. "I am still frightened, I think."

"I don't blame you. What a cold, calculating bastard that man is."

"I do not at all mind that Fouché should kill him. It is an excellent idea."

"I meant Soulier," Grey said dryly.

"Soulier? But he will face Fouché in Paris and tell lies to bargain my life back for me. He risks his career and perhaps his life. You must not blame him that he is not delicate with me. One is not delicate with one's agents."

"One does not pimp one's agents either. It's the first thing they teach you in spymaster school. No, don't argue. This is for you." He handed her a small, heavy sack that contained coins. She shook it open a bit and dipped her fingers in.

"There is a lot of money here," she said neutrally. She could not be sure of the value of British coins from just the feel, but there were many.

"I don't want you loose on the streets with no money in your pocket. I also have three pounds sixpence of yours in my desk drawer. I should get that back to you sometime."

"Oh, that. I stole it from Henri, if you will recall, so I do not know if it is rightfully mine or not. It is difficult to determine, with money."

"Isn't it?" He pounded twice on the roof of the coach with the flat of his hand. "Unless you have an objection, we'll get out here."

The coach stopped. "You are letting me go?"

"I am indeed." He jumped out without kicking down the step and reached back to lock huge hands around her waist and lift her to the ground.

It was a quiet, respectable neighborhood. The street was lined with prosperous houses, every door silent and dark in the hours before dawn. Even the cats slept. The breathing of the coach horses and the metallic click of their hooves made the only noise. If Grey were accompanied by many minions, they were not making themselves evident.

"You are letting me walk away with the Albion plans in my head." It was not the first time his behavior had bewildered her. "I do not object, you understand, but it seems inconsistent."

"The French are so sure we have them, it hardly matters whether we do or not. It should discourage them from showing up on the doorstep this spring." As soon as he latched the door, he thumped on the side panel, and the coach rolled away. She listened to its wheels on the cobbles while he settled the cloak upon her and tied it at the neck. "You've done what you came to England to do."

"Yes." She had not come to England to fall in love, but she had done so. She had made a botch of it.

"Kent is safe for a while. I can't grub through the plans and mine them for French secrets, so France is safe. Stalemate."

"Just so."

He did not seem to be angry with her. He brushed her hair from her forehead and set it behind her ear. "You've won."

She could not read his face in the dark. He was only shadows and gentle hands. But gentleness is not love.

She swallowed. "When I left you tonight, I did not want to go. I had no choice. There were many lives at stake."

"I know. What will you do, now that you're free, and nobody's trying to kill you?"

I will be utterly alone. "I have always thought I would become a cook, someday, if I lived to retire. I will go to Wales, perhaps. It seems to be a place where a woman with the name Jones can live without ridicule."

"I'd better let you get on with it. West," he said, pointing, "is that way."

She was most entirely free. Just as she had wanted. One must be careful what one wishes for.

There is nothing more to say to a lover when one has set his love aside and snuck secretly from his bed. And, in any case, the Head of the British Section cannot ally himself with an unreliable French spy. Perhaps Grey had lied to himself from time to time on the subject. As she had lied to herself.

So she turned and started walking west. She could smell the river on the left of her. The Thames.

She knew at once he was behind her. After twenty steps she was still not sure how she felt about it. "You are following me. Why are you doing this?"

"To protect you." Which was what he had said to her once before. "And because I want to."

She drew a long breath in and kept walking. "You are a difficult man to be in love with."

Even in the dim light, she knew he grinned.

Ahead of them was a park with sharp iron palings on its fence. She did not know which park. She did not know precisely where she was in London, as she had not been paying proper attention. "Are you planning to follow me all the way to Wales?"

"If I have to. We'll stop at Tydings on the way. Would you like to get married here in London or when we get to my parents' house?"

She bumped into him. Somehow he had put himself in front of her, blocking the path. He was warm and disconcerting to run into.

"You have not asked me to marry you." That was the most stupid thing of the several things she could have said.

"Marry me, Annique."

She wanted to step around him and walk away and be gone, but she could not make herself move. "It is not possible between us. I wish you had chosen to be wise. Then I would not have to."

He stroked her hair, like a warm wind. "Marry me."

It hurt, knowing she must say the many sensible things that must be said. "You will lose your position if you marry with a French spy, which I am, who cannot be trusted, which I cannot."

"Then I'll resign my bloody position. There's a letter in my desk drawer. I wrote it the day I brought you to Meeks Street. Doyle knows. He'll pull it out tomorrow when I don't come back."

"He will not find it, for you will go to your office immediately and tear it up."

"Would you like to go to India? I have a standing offer from one of the directors of the East India Company. We'd become tremendously rich, if that matters to you."

"I do not want to be rich. And I know you are already rich. Adrian told me. He thought I should know."

"Remind me to throttle Adrian. We can get married about five hours from now, at St. Odran's, if it suits you. That'll give me time to call everybody in. We'll invite Soulier . . . There. That's made you smile."

"You are entirely mad. You will doubtless stick straws in your hair and caper about the streets."

"Let's find some privacy for that." He considered the park. It was a big place. One could smell a great extent of greenery and perhaps a lake, somewhere within it. "You have a problem with these spikes and pointy things?"

The gates would be closed at this hour of night. "Hah. You make the joke. This little fence? But I am in skirts, though, and a large cloak, which is very warm and lovely, but awkward to climb with. So if you will . . . Yes. That is helpful." She stepped into his cupped hands and was over in a flash. Grey followed her a moment later.

He took her hand. The dark enclosed them. They might have been in the country, it was so quiet, with so many stars overhead. It came to her that she had never walked out under the night, hand in hand, with a lover. Or with the British Head of Section, for that matter.

They'd come to a flat, grassy hillock, deep in the park. He twitched her cloak off and furled it down to the ground before she could protest. "Hush. I'll keep you warm." Before she could speak, he spilled her downward, onto the ground, onto the soft wool, and sprawled beside her and put his arm around her and drew her to him. "Is this better?"

"This is foolishness."

"There hasn't been enough foolishness in your life. No. Stay close." He urged her with a whisper, a touch, till she lay beside him, body to body.

The stars spread out above her in patterns vast and mysterious.

"You'll like Tydings," he said. "It's old stone, the color of honey. There's meadow behind and a view of the hills that stretches on forever. We'll make love over every inch of it, at night, being sneaky about it."

How did he do this to her? "You entice me with dreams and entangle me with this sacrifice you make of yourself. It is like fighting shadows."

"Don't fight. When we're old, we'll stagger down the path to the river and collapse on the bench and watch our grandchildren play in the mud. We'll remember making love on that bench. And by the river. Maybe in the river, too, some hot night."

"I have never thought of being old."

"It's time you did. Be old with me." Dreams and impossibilities sheltered in his bones and muscles. When he held her like this, she could almost believe in them.

"I do not like it that you free me with one hand and entrap me with the other. It is not straightforward of you."

"I'm not a straightforward man."

"You cannot resign from the British Service, my Grey. Napoleon will not sail in the spring—I have done that much—but someday he will come. You cannot leave your post. You are one of the guardians of this land."

"So's Doyle. Let him sit in that stuffy office and be Head of Section for a while." His hands slid along her side, making themselves busy up and down her body. It had been only a few hours since she was in bed with him, and her body remembered.

"But you are Head. You hold those deadly men of your Service between your hands and protect them, and they trust you utterly. You are responsible for them." She was becoming limp and needy, clinging to him. "You do not listen. You are seducing me instead."

"Trying to."

She had not known that her eyelids would feel that way when someone had his lips upon them. Like silk. Light flowed where he licked with his tongue. "You make it quite impossible for me to think."

"Really?"

"You need not sound so pleased. It is a weakness on my part."

"That sounds promising. Are you going to marry me?"

"It is not that simple."

He leaned up on his elbow and looked down at her. His face was cast in moonlight, inches away, grave and intent. "But it is simple. Not easy, but simple. Even in Wales or India, you'll have to choose—France or England."

"Oh, I have chosen. I must fight against Napoleon, insofar as it lies within me. But marriage . . . It is a matter of loyalties, you understand. I cannot be English, even for you. I cannot tell you all I know. I have too many old friends—"

"Do you think I'd ask that of you?"

"You are a master of spies for the British. It is not unreasonable that you should—"

His fingers touched her lips. "I don't own my agents' souls. Adrian has a Frenchwoman I'm not supposed to know about. And Doyle's half French. His cousins are scattered all through the French secret service. You'd manage." He caressed her dress till it rose high up on her thigh.

"Sometimes the Rom lie with one another like this, on the ground with the sky above. I will marry you."

"Now?" His hands clenched, tight, upon her. "This morning? At St. Odran's?"

"Yes. All of those."

"Good." He let out a long, satisfied breath. Those clever hands drifted between her legs to entice and tempt and promise. "Are we going to Wales?"

Sensation flooded through her and swept away her last thoughts. "Not . . . immediately. We are going to make love, are we not? This is depraved to do in a park, I think."

"Isn't it?" As he'd promised, he kept her very warm indeed.

Don't miss the spellbinding third novel
in the *Spymaster* series

My Lord and Spymaster

A father wrongly accused of selling secrets to Napoleon.

His daughter kidnapped on the hunt for the traitor.

A valiant captain who swoops in to the rescue.

In a game of love and lies, will passion mask the treacherous truth?

'An undeniably powerful
new voice in historical romance'

All About Romance

Don't miss the intoxicating fourth novel
in the *Spymaster* series

The Black Hawk

An agent stalked mercilessly through the grey London streets.

An assassin who strikes shamelessly under the cover of rain.

Her only hope is the man she once loved and now hates.

Can passion overcome the past and defeat the hidden menace?

'Every word, every page, is a wonder'
All About Romance

headline
ETERNAL